THE I

Sara Hylton lives i
knows very well. S
when she is not writing. Her p
Caprice, *The Carradice Chain*, *The Crimson Falcon*, *The*
Talisman of Set, *The Whispering Glade*, *Glamara*,
Tomorrow's Rainbow, *My Sister Clare*, *Fragile Heritage*,
Summer of the Flamingoes and *The Chosen Ones*.

By The Same Author

Caprice
The Carradice Chain
The Crimson Falcon
The Talisman of Set
The Whispering Glade
Glamara
Tomorrow's Rainbow
My Sister Clare
Fragile Heritage
Summer of the Famingoes
The Chosen Ones

THE LAST REUNION

Sara Hylton

ARROW

First published in Arrow 1994

1 3 5 7 9 10 8 6 4 2

Copyright © Sara Hylton 1992

First published in the United Kingdom in 1992 by Century

This edition published by Arrow Books Limited in 1994
Random House, 20 Vauxhall Bridge Road, London SW1V 2SA

Random House Australia (Pty) Limited
20 Alfred Street, Milsons Point, Sydney,
New South Wales 2061, Australia

Random House New Zealand Limited
18 Poland Road, Glenfield
Auckland 10, New Zealand

Random House South Africa (Pty) Limited
PO Box 337, Bergvlei, South Africa

Random House UK Limited Reg. No. 954009

A CIP catalogue record for this book
is available from the British Library

ISBN 0 09 910741 4

Printed and bound in Germany by
Elsnerdruck, Berlin

For Simon Rhidian with love

PROLOGUE

Sunlight slanted across the lawns and a gentle mist lingered on the lakeland hills. It was late afternoon, a time of day that Amelia Garveston loved, a civilized time when a maid served her tea in her sitting room and there was quiet throughout the entire house.

She couldn't remember if Mark had said he would be home for dinner, but this didn't unduly concern her – the servants would know. She eyed with pleasure the delicate teapot filled with her special brew of China tea, the almost transparent cup and saucer, the heavily embossed silver tray – all of them gifts from her family on her marriage – then her eyes swept round the room like those of a child on its birthday morning, for Amelia never ceased to feel pride in the beauties and refinements she had brought to Garveston Hall.

Her head started to ache. The headaches were becoming more frequent now, as well as the sudden flashes of light she experienced whenever she stepped into a darkened room. The doctor called them 'early migraines' and had given her tablets, but she'd forgotten where she'd put them. If she mentioned them to Mark he merely said she was probably doing too much; she should give up the Bench and her committees, but she could never do that. Her charities were her lifeline.

Appreciatively she sipped her tea, carrying her cup and saucer to the window so that she could look out across the park. The gardens were coming to life. Daffodils were rampant under the trees and across the parkland, and the jasmine and forsythia shrubs were weighted down with blossom. She really must remember to bring some of it into the house tomorrow.

She wrinkled her brow in an effort to remember. There was something else she had decided to do but she couldn't recall what it was. It troubled her that she was so forgetful as she'd always been so meticulous about everything. Just recently she would put things away and forget where she'd put them, she constantly consulted Mark about matters she'd mentioned several times before, then miserably she was made aware of the sudden impatience in his face as he said irritably, 'You've already asked me that about half a dozen times, Amelia!' It would be awful if other people were noticing.

Her eyes swept round the room; it was her favourite room in the entire house. The water colours had all been chosen by her personally, unlike the pictures in the rest of the house which were priceless and which she had taken the trouble to have restored. The delicate chintz drapes and the soft colours in the Chinese carpet, the polished walnut furniture and beautiful porcelain had all been lovingly assembled by her, and now she believed they reflected her personality like no other room in the house.

She walked across to the mirror and looked into it, lifting up her hand to trace the tired smudges under her wide-spaced eyes. It was a lovely face that confronted her with its dark cloudy hair and delicate patrician features. Her lips curved wistfully in a half-smile as she smoothed her hands along her slender neck until they came to rest on the pearls that her father had given her on her wedding day.

She moved over to the alcove so that she could look at the framed photograph of the Lorivals girls taken nearly twenty years ago on the terrace in front of the imposing pile of the school. She allowed her finger to glide along the three rows of girls until she found those whom she sought. There was Maisie Jayson, pert and smiling with her red curls and freckles and beside her,

2

Lois Brampton. Amelia's finger moved quickly. She couldn't bear to think about Lois even now; memories of death should not be allowed to intrude into the peace of her special hour. Her finger moved on until it found Nancy Graham, smiling, lovely Nancy, and she frowned in a desperate effort to remember.

She'd been rather less than friendly with Nancy at their last meeting ten years before, when she'd hosted a reunion at Garveston Hall, one decade after their departure from Lorivals. Of course, Mark had once been in love with Nancy but that hadn't been the reason for her anger. Suddenly her mind cleared and she remembered Nancy's affair with Desmond, her sister Celia's husband. That had all ended a long time ago, and now Nancy was somewhere abroad, a journalist on Noel Templeton's team, surrounded by sudden danger. It was doubtful whether Nancy gave the past a single passing thought.

Amelia's eyes moved slowly along the back row until they came to rest on herself standing next to Barbara Smythe. She looked a gentle ethereal creature beside Barbara's vibrant beauty, and she recalled how she'd never felt truly comfortable with the other girl, who had been too sophisticated and streetwise even then. Suddenly she remembered what she had intended to do.

She went to her desk and took out several sheets of writing paper and some envelopes, then for a few moments sat staring down at them before opening her address book and starting to write.

The women she was writing to would have recognized that air of concentration, the slight frown on Amelia's smooth forehead, the pen, delicately poised, the hesitation before her brow cleared and the sudden relief at knowing what to write.

She was still writing when her husband entered her sitting room half an hour later.

'I'm just off,' he said with a smile. 'Obviously I won't be in for dinner. The meetings do tend to go on a bit and we usually have food sent up from the bar.'

'Meetings?' she queried absently.

'I did mention it at breakfast, Amelia,' he accused her. 'The hunt meeting.'

Her face cleared. 'Of course, Mark, I'm sorry. For the moment I'd forgotten.'

He approached her desk and stared down at the letter she was writing and quickly Amelia said, 'I know there's oceans of time but I wanted to make sure they'll be available in July. I'll send out formal invitations later.'

'Invitations for what?'

'Our second reunion.'

He stared down at her in amazement. There had been a time when he'd considered Amelia entirely predictable. He would know what she was thinking, where he could find her and what she would be doing, whenever he took the trouble, but now Amelia was unpredictable – a strange fey creature who could forget what they'd discussed at breakfast yet remember a reunion she'd discussed with her schoolfriends ten years before.

Irritably he said, 'You're surely not intending keeping this up every ten years. Isn't it a bit ridiculous?'

'I don't think so, Mark. There'll be a lot to talk about – Nancy's adventures, Barbara's travels, Maisie's children, our children.'

'All of which could be very boring. People change, Amelia. They grow apart, they don't want to be reminded of the past. I very much doubt if Nancy Graham will make the effort to come, and the Waltons will probably make some excuse or other.'

'Well, I've decided to invite them all for the weekend just like last time. If they don't want to come I'll realize it was a mistake.'

4

She folded the last letter and sealed the envelope, then with a little smile handed the three envelopes to Mark. 'Will you leave them with the rest of the post on the hall table, please.'

For a moment he stared down at them, then without another word he left her.

Amelia had set her heart on this reunion – whatever he said, he couldn't dissuade her. He placed the envelopes with the other mail on the silver salver in the hall, ready for one of the servants to take down to the village later on, but then with a small smile he turned back to retrieve one of them, sliding it into his pocket. With a bit of luck he'd be able to deliver this letter to the Waltons personally . . .

CHAPTER 1

For the third time that morning Maisie Standing looked in the mirror and her spirits dropped as a consequence. The clerical grey suit made her look fat and matronly. The cream silk blouse was schoolmarmish and the grey felt hat sat too tightly over her wiry red hair.

She hated hats. She'd hardly worn one since she left Lorivals – a panama in summer and a felt one in winter – and she had loathed those just as fiercely as she was hating this one. She found herself remembering that first morning at Lorivals when she had looked at her friends in their school uniform. Their panamas had sat comfortably on their hair, in Barbara's case dark silken locks that never seemed out of place, and Nancy's shoulder-length bob curling deliciously beneath the brim. Her own hair had been too wiry, and the hats had risen alarmingly until her mother insisted on stitching a piece of elastic from one side to the other, which left a mark under her chin and was anything but comfortable.

She looked round the kitchen anxiously. The table was set for tea and two notes were propped up against the teacups, one for her husband in case she should be late back, the other for Iris Gilbert who was coming to look after young Lucy. It was like her to be late. Maisie had stipulated one o'clock and it was now twenty minutes past. The girl was a scatterbrain; she'd probably met some boy or other in the lane and was chatting instead of hurrying to the farm.

Maisie was just checking her handbag for a clean handkerchief and a pen when the door opened and her husband Tom's head appeared round it, grinning cheerfully.

'Ready then?' he enquired brightly.

'As ready as I'll ever be,' she answered him, then fretfully, 'that girl hasn't arrived yet. I told her to be on time – I'll have to think about getting somebody else if she lets me down.'

'There's plenty of time, love. Let me have a look at you – do you look like a magistrate?'

She turned to face him and after a few minutes he threw back his head and laughed delightedly.

'What is it?' she snapped. 'What's wrong with me?'

'There's nothing wrong, love. You look great, but you certainly don't look like yourself.'

'Why not? What do you mean?'

'I reckon it's the hat. Who told you to wear one? I'm sure they don't all have them.'

'Mrs Smythe said I should wear one. I met her in Bob's shop the other morning and she said she always wore a hat, it was most essential.'

'Did she say it had to be that sort of hat?'

'She said it had to look businesslike.'

'Oh well, I reckon she knows – she's been on the Bench a few years now. The suit looks nice.'

'Don't you think it makes me look fat?'

'Well, you're not exactly a sylph are you, love? You've had three children and you like your food. The suit looks good and I'll bet it was expensive. Care to tell me how much it cost?'

'You don't usually ask what I pay for my clothes. I hadn't anything suitable and my mother said I must look the part otherwise there'd be some tongues waggin'.'

'Has your mother seen it?'

'Oh yes, and she approved. She asked how much I'd paid for it so I knocked half off and she still thought that was too much. She's no idea about prices. She never goes near the shops and she's wearin' clothes she bought twenty years ago.'

7

He laughed. 'You'll not be telling me the price you paid for it without knocking something off, then. I'll not ask you again. You're not scared are you, Maisie?'

She sat down weakly on the nearest chair and her eyes filled with tears. 'Oh yes, Tom, I am scared. I'm frightened to death. What did they want to ask me to be a JP for? I'm a farmer's wife – I don't know anything about the law in spite of the bit of trainin' they've given me and I'll only make a mess of things, I know I will.'

'They'll go easy on you for the first few months, love. You'll simply have to sit on the Bench and say nothin'. The chairman or chairwoman'll do all the talkin'. I have it on good authority that this is what 'appens, and the Magistrates' Clerk said as much when he came to see you.'

'But why did they ask *me*, Tom? There's dozens of people in Greymont who would have been better than me.'

'I don't see it like that. We've lived in these parts for a long time. Your father was a successful tradesman in the town and so are your brothers. I'm a farmer with a lot of land and we're respectable. Besides, you're a Lorivals girl, aren't you?'

'It seems that's a rope round my neck that refuses to go away.'

'You've allus said you weren't a credit to the school, that you should never have gone there, well I disagree. You're a nice woman, Maisie Standing. You're a good wife and mother and you've got a decent honest outlook on life. You're as good as any of those other women that sits on the bench, includin' Lady Garveston.'

Her eyes filled with tears again and she smiled at him tremulously. Then, gathering up her gloves and handbag she said briskly, 'Where is that girl? She'll get a piece of my mind when she does show up.'

At that moment they heard the sound of footsteps running lightly across the cobbled yard and Tom said

8

with a smile, 'She's here now and don't be upsetting yourself by chiding the girl, you've plenty of time.'

Iris Gilbert was a small pretty girl with a mass of golden curls and rosy cheeks, made even rosier by her exertions.

The words came tumbling out fast. 'I'm sorry I'm late, Mrs Standin'. Our Kevin 'adn't come 'ome from school and I 'ad to go and look for 'im. Mi mother's not well, she's bin in bed all mornin' and our Kev was playin' on the fell when 'e should 'ave bin 'ome eatin' his dinner.'

Before Maisie could utter a word her husband said quickly, 'That's all right love, you're 'ere now. Lucy's a good child and I don't think she'll give you any trouble.'

'Nora Grimshaw's looking after her in the parlour,' Maisie put in quickly. 'She's anxious to be off so perhaps you'd better get in there. I've left milk and cakes out for you and when our Alice gets home from school see that she behaves herself and doesn't interrupt Peter when he's doin' his homework.'

The girl stared at her solemnly. 'Ey, Mrs Standin', she won't be takin' any notice of me.'

'Tell her what I say, Iris. She's to behave herself until I get back. I'm hopin' not to be late. I must go, Tom, I promised to call in at our Bob's for a few minutes on the way into town.'

He grinned. 'Showin' them your finery, then? I don't reckon Mary'll be burstin' with enthusiasm.'

'Our Bob asked me to call. I'm not interested in what his wife thinks.'

He followed her through the door and out to where her red Mini stood in the middle of the farm-yard. After opening the door for her he bent down and embraced her quickly. 'Good luck, love, and don't worry about anything. You look lovely and a real credit to Lorivals.'

'Oh, Lorivals,' she grumbled quietly before starting the engine and driving slowly out into the lane.

She was glad it was fine; she hadn't wanted to arrive at the court wearing a raincoat over her new suit and Tom had made a good job of cleaning the car the day before. She liked September. They'd had a good harvest and it had been a good summer. The earth smelt warm and moist, good homely autumn smells of golden bracken and woodsmoke, and all along the lane the hedgerows and trees were turning from green to red and gold.

She felt irritable, hardly the right sort of feeling to be harbouring on her first day as a JP. There was so much to do at the farm. Fruits to be bottled and chutneys to be made. She'd spent all the previous day baking bread and cakes, pies and puddings, and her three children needed looking after. It was true Peter and Alice were at school but Lucy was only two, little more than a baby.

There were times when she thought they hadn't been too wise in having another baby when Alice was seven, but Lucy was a happy contented child who gave hardly any trouble. Sometimes when Maisie looked at her smiling face and shock of red curls she couldn't help wishing that Lucy had been a boy. There was the farm to think about and Peter wasn't the least bit interested in it.

He had to be cajoled and persuaded in every small job he was asked to do and she knew it troubled Tom even if he said nothing. Tom was a good farmer, it was his life, whereas Peter always had his head in some book or other and his school reports were so very good.

Of course they were proud of him but it didn't solve the problem of what would become of the farm when Tom felt he was getting too old to run it. Lately she'd tried to discuss it with him but he'd only smiled, saying, 'That's years away, love. Maybe Peter'll discover he has

10

a liking for it, after all. If not, maybe one of the girls'll marry a lad who leans towards farming.'

'Not Alice,' she'd put in quickly.

'Let's just wait and see, love. She's a problem now but she'll grow up, and there's Lucy. It'll work out, it isn't something we should be worryin' our heads about now.'

Alice got bad school reports. She was like a piece of quicksilver, vain and mercurial, inattentive in her lessons and rebellious when asked to help in the house. She had to be bullied into seeing her grandparents, and Maisie's mother complained bitterly about the cheek she received and the girl's often mutinous face.

She shouldn't be thinking about Alice and her tantrums, not now when she particularly wanted to arrive at the court serene and untroubled. She was driving along the leafy roads of suburban Greymont, where tall Georgian stone houses with long gardens gave the area a prosperous look even though younger people preferred the other side of the town where builders were busy erecting new blocks of red-brick houses and bungalows.

This was Maisie's side of town. She had spent her childhood on the corner opposite the park and the area had changed little. She remembered the glow of joy she had felt on leaving the park gates as a girl and seeing in the distance the light from her father's shop on the corner. How she had run and skipped along that road, snatching an apple from the fruit set out in front of the shop in spite of her mother's disapproving glance.

Her father had begun the changes. Now one shop had become a miniature market with the name *Jayson* written in large iron letters above the frontage. Gone were the mops and buckets of the former ironmongers, and old Mr Williams' sweetshop was now a small supermarket run by Maisie's youngest brother.

A huge glass canopy covered the front of the green-grocers and modern plate-glass windows had replaced the old ones with their leaded lights. Her sister-in-law Mary had seen to these renovations – she didn't want her customers getting wet while they queued for fruit and fish – but Maisie reflected grimly that those customers were not nearly as numerous as they had been in her parents' time. Renovations had to be paid for and people were not averse to walking a little further to save twopences and threepences. Mary never learned and Bob was too soft with her, too afraid of her sulks and angry silences.

She left the Mini round the side of the shop and walked the short distance to the entrance. Two women were being served by Mary at the fruit counter but she didn't look up as Maisie passed behind them on her way into the living room at the back of the shop. She could hear Bob humming to himself in the kitchen beyond the living room but she didn't immediately go through. Instead she stood looking around her. How different it was from her mother's day. Gone was the black-leaded fireplace with its roaring fire and the kettle bubbling on the hob. It had long since been replaced by a tiled fireplace but no cosy fire burned there. Instead, clean newspaper was bunched in the empty grate and in front of it stood a potted palm in a terracotta plant-holder.

Mary didn't believe in fires being lit before the beginning of October. If it was cold then she condescended to allow the one-bar electric fire to be switched on, but Maisie was missing the shabby warmth of her old home. Gone, too, were the two comfortable fireside chairs with the cushions and chair-back covers her mother had made, along with the large whitewood table at which they had eaten their meals, done their homework and jigsaw puzzles, and over which they had teased each other and quarrelled. In its place stood a polished oak table and matching chairs next to an oak sideboard with a fruit bowl and cut-glass vase – Mary's only concessions to homeliness.

Now Bob came into the room and seeing his sister his face lit up in a welcoming smile.

'Hello, love!' he said quietly. 'I didn't hear you come in. How long 'ave you been 'ere?'

'Just this minute. I heard you in the kitchen, I guessed you wouldn't be long.'

'Mary's in the shop.'

'Yes I know, she was busy serving.'

'I'll tell her you're 'ere, she'll be wantin' to see you in your new finery.'

'No, please Bob. Don't interrupt her if she's busy. There isn't much time and I don't want to be late on my first day.'

'She'll not keep you a minute, Maisie. I'd like her to see you lookin' so proper and dignified.'

His sister was wishing she'd been firmer when a few minutes later Mary stood in the doorway eyeing her from top to bottom.

'I haven't seen you wearin' a hat since your Lucy's christening,' she stated. 'I take it you've had to buy one specially.'

'Yes. Mrs Smythe said I should wear one.'

'I should think you've copied the style she wears. They look all right on Mrs Smythe but big hats don't suit you, Maisie. That's the outfit I saw in Jeannette's window, isn't it? *I* couldn't afford her prices.'

'I can't really afford them, either. This is destined to last a lifetime.'

'What was wrong with that dress and jacket you had for your mother's Golden Weddin'?'

'Nothing, except that it was pale blue, hardly suitable for a morning in court.'

'No, I suppose not. I wonder who put your name forward to be a Magistrate.'

13

'Several people, I think. I wish they hadn't, I haven't the time.'

'I don't suppose it was Mrs Smythe. She hinted in the shop that you hadn't had much experience of life, havin' spent it all on the farm so to speak. Of course you went to Lorivals – that stood you in good stead, and perhaps Lady Garveston said the right words in the right ears.'

Mary always had to bring Lorivals into everything. She bitterly resented the money Mr Jayson had spent on Maisie's education when he should have used it for the business. It wasn't enough that he had set his sons up in three shops which he had been able to buy; if there'd been less for Maisie there'd have been more for Bob. The retort was quick on Maisie's lips but she bit her tongue. One day she would have to say it, but not now when she wanted to keep calm and unruffled. There would be dozens of times when Mary would provoke her, and she could retaliate.

'Are you callin' in to see the other two?' Mary asked sharply.

'No, there isn't time. I'll call on them the next time I'm down here.'

'Did Bob tell you I had to have words with Eric? Closed the shop they did, all last Saturday, simply because it was her birthday and he wanted to take her out for the day. There was I trying to tell his customers some ridiculous story about there bein' sickness in the family and them having been called away. If they found their Sunday joint elsewhere you can bet your life they'll get it from there in future, either there or at the market.'

'Perhaps he won't do it again.'

'He'll do whatever she wants him to do. He should have married a girl with a bit of interest in the business, not some flibbertigibbet who spends half the week at the hairdresser's and gets herself up like a sixteen-year-old.'

'I must go, Mary. Time's getting on.'

14

'I see your Alice has been in trouble again at the school.'

'Trouble! What sort of trouble?'

'Well, our Joyce's girl is in the same class. Miss Kirby kept her in after school two nights for chatting during lessons and not getting on with her work. Didn't you know? She'd have been late home, I'm sure.'

'I was busy – I thought she'd just been playing on the fell.'

'I expect that's what she told you. Really, Maisie, you'll 'ave to put your foot down with young Alice. Either that or expect trouble later on.'

'I must go,' Maisie muttered, making good her escape. She was angry with Mary, with Alice and with herself for having been unwise enough to pay them a visit on this day of all days.

When she rounded the corner to reach her car she found her younger brother Eric standing beside it grinning widely.

'Well,' he demanded cheerfully, 'have you been hearing about my closing the shop and any other piece of bad news she could dig up?'

'I reckon you can please yourself. It's your shop, but I'll tell you this, mi mother wouldn't have done it.'

'Mi mother would have opened Christmas Day if she'd been sure of any customers. It was Gloria's birthday – I promised I'd take her into Kendal for the day to look for a present.'

Maisie opened the door of her car but, hearing voices, Gloria came out to stand next to her husband, eyeing Maisie with a bright smile.

'You've got a new suit on,' she proclaimed airily. 'It's a bit dark – I prefer you in your blue one, it makes you look younger.'

'This is more suitable for the court. Eric said it was your birthday last Saturday, Gloria. I didn't know –

15

I'll get you a present next time I go into town.'

'It doesn't matter, I didn't expect anything from you. Your mum and dad are comin' to tea. I've just made a cake, I hope nothing's wrong with it.'

'Why should it be?'

'It's the first I've made. I followed the recipe exactly.'

She was such a pretty girl, Maisie thought, slim as a reed and delicate-looking with great baby-blue eyes and hair that could have been pretty if she hadn't bleached it to death. Her bare legs were tanned under the too-short skirt and she was wearing beige sandals on her feet and a blouse with a plunging neckline that would earn Mrs Jayson's instant disapproval. Seeing Maisie looking at it doubtfully, she said, 'Eric says it's a bit low, but it's new and I wanted to wear it today. I suppose your mother won't like it.'

Maisie was saved from answering by the sight of a long sleek red car nosing its way into the space next to hers. They turned to stare at the slim, fashionably dressed woman easing herself out of the driving seat and Maisie realized that she knew her.

They were new people in the area but already John Forsythe was a force to be reckoned with. He was Sales Director for a large firm of industrial chemists on the other side of Greymont, and his wife Deirdre had suddenly blossomed on to various committees necessary to the life of the town.

He was constantly abroad on business but she was a leading light in the local operatic and dramatic society, and they had both joined the Golf Club, where already he was Vice-Captain. She served on the agricultural committee although Maisie wasn't sure what qualifications she had brought to the role, unless it was the fact that the Forsythes lived in a large modern house on the outskirts of the town which boasted a very fine garden.

Money had been no object when the largest nursery in Greymont planned their garden, and in no time at all they were entertaining everybody in Greymont whom they considered worth knowing.

On their first meeting Maisie had found herself staring at Deirdre; she reminded her so very much of Barbara Smythe – in looks, personality and lifestyle.

Deirdre Forsythe had the same tall slender figure and short, fashionably styled dark hair. She wore her clothes with élan and they were always the right clothes, tweeds for the country and elegant suits for the town, glamorous cocktail dresses and ethereal ballgowns, although she looked just as elegant in a simple cotton skirt and tailored shirt. She couldn't have been more like Barbara if they'd been sisters, and Maisie resented her just as she'd always resented Barbara.

Now Deirdre favoured Maisie with a bright smile and stalked off along the pavement watched by the others until she entered the grocer's shop run by Jimmy Jayson.

Eric and Gloria looked at each other and giggled so that Maisie asked sharply, 'How long has she been shopping here?'

Eric grinned. 'A month or two now. She usually comes round when it's quiet.'

'Why are you smiling? What's so funny about her shopping here?' Maisie demanded.

'She doesn't come for groceries, love. It's our Jimmy she comes to see. They talk for hours across the counter, and sometimes not across the counter,' Eric said with a broad smile. 'I reckon she's bored.'

'Don't be stupid,' Maisie retorted. 'She's got everything she wants. She's not likely to be interested in our Jimmy, and if he says she is he's more of a fool than I take him for. I suppose all his other customers are sniggering about it behind his back.'

17

When Eric and Gloria dissolved into laughter Maisie got angrily into her car and drove away. Jimmy was a bachelor but he was also a fool. He was good-looking and knew it, moreover he wasn't averse to bragging about his so-called conquests and his ability to 'love 'em and leave 'em' as he put it. Deirdre Forsythe was a different kettle of fish – she was the sort of woman who could eat Jimmy Jayson alive.

Bored and spoilt she would pander to his conceit, his gullibility, for her own amusement but in the end women like her knew which side their bread was buttered. She would dine out on her grocer's infatuation, laugh with her friends at their coffee mornings, perhaps even tease her husband about her latest conquest and he would be amused by it, see it for what it was worth.

By the time Maisie reached the court she was whole-heartedly regretting the visit to her brothers. It was not for her to worry about Bob's waspish wife or Eric's feckless one, and it was certainly not her business if Jimmy wanted to make a fool of himself over the likes of Deirdre Forsythe. All the same why had she witnessed her family's stupidity today, just when she wanted to keep her mind clear and her senses alert?

CHAPTER 2

Maisie drove into the car park behind the courthouse and stared with dismay at the rows of parked cars, then she proceeded to drive along the aisles looking for a space. She was grateful when a young policeman came to her assistance with a cheerful grin, saying, 'You've left it a bit late, ma'am, if you don't mind me saying so. There's probation meetings and goodness knows what on today besides the court. There's a space over in that corner that might just about take a Mini.'

Fortunately there was just enough room to open the door and get out of the car. It was now five minutes to two and Maisie almost ran across the yard and into the courthouse. A police sergeant consulted his watch with a frown and she hurried upstairs and into the Magistrates' Room.

She was instantly aware of a crowd of faces looking at her and she tugged at her hat to make sure it was properly anchored. One or two of the faces smiled but she saw with a sinking heart that there was only one other woman present and it was somebody she didn't know.

The Magistrates' Clerk bore down on her with a toothy smile, extending his hand and saying briskly, 'I was beginning to think something had happened to prevent you coming, Mrs Standing, but I felt sure you would have let me know. If ever you find you can't attend, please inform me in good time so that I can find a replacement quickly.'

'Yes, of course. I'm sorry but I was detained and the traffic was heavy. It isn't quite two, is it?'

'No, not quite. We are giving you a smooth passage as it's your first attendance – all traffic offences, but most of them are cut and dried. Your Chairman is Mr Greenacre. You will sit on one side of him and Mr Rouse will sit on the other. All you have to do is listen. Mr Greenacre will do any speaking that is necessary. When you adjourn you will discuss matters together and you will be asked for your opinion but, like I said, most of these cases will go undefended and the one that is defended will cause you little trouble.'

By half-past three it was all over and Maisie couldn't believe that she was actually sitting in the Magistrates' Room drinking tea and chatting about bottling fruit with one of the court ushers.

Only one case was defended and this was a 'No Due Care' case: if the defendant had lost his licence his job would have been in jeopardy. His solicitor was eloquent and earned every penny of his fee, and the rest of the cases were mere formalities.

Maisie found Mr Greenacre condescending and a trifle pompous. Mr Rouse had sat on only one case before as he too was new. She thought him helpful and blessed with a sense of humour.

'You looked like a startled rabbit when you arrived,' he said, grinning at her.

'I felt like one, too. I did so want to be early, I don't know what possessed me to call and see my brothers today.'

'Oh, well, there's no harm done. It's not the most interesting court but they tend to let the newcomers loose on it. Old Greenacre sits on most of 'em – he's got the time, and his occupation is listed as "Gentleman".'

'What does that mean, exactly?'

'He doesn't work, he's loaded, and magisterial work is his hobby as well as his employment.'

'Is he always on the motoring offences?'

'No, but he always sits in with newcomers. They like to think he's a pattern we should follow.'

She watched the other Magistrates drift in from a different courtroom and the woman she had noticed

20

earlier came over to sit with her, extending her hand and saying, 'I'm Elsie Waddington, Mrs Standing. I'm the headmistress at Lorivals, which happens to be your old school, I'm told.'

'Why, yes. I heard Miss Clarkson had retired.'

'Yes. She's living in Suffolk with her brother. They have a very nice bungalow on the coast – I've visited her several times.'

'I do hope she'll be happy there, she was such a nice person.'

'Yes, indeed. How have you enjoyed your first afternoon in court?'

'I didn't think it would be quite like this. It was boring. Everything was cut and dried – there was just the one defended case and he got away with it.'

Miss Waddington laughed. 'You expected to be faced with desperate criminals to say the least, then?'

Maisie blushed. 'Well, I really didn't know what to expect, but one reads such awful things in the papers. I thought I'd have something to tell my husband when I got home.'

'Have patience,' Miss Waddington advised her. 'You won't get away with motoring offences: you've yet to face the criminal court, the children's court and the matrimonial court. Rome wasn't built in a day.'

'It's not that, Miss Waddington. I'm a farmer's wife and I've left a thousand and one things undone. I've a son and daughter at school and a little girl who's just two, and all afternoon I've been thinking I'd have been more usefully employed at home.'

So their talk went on to making jam and bottling fruit until Miss Waddington consulted her watch and said, 'Well, I must get back to the school. We have a meeting tonight and there are new girls to talk to. I'm sure you haven't forgotten all that went on at the beginning of term.'

21

'Gracious no, I'll never forget. I remember feeling just as out of place there as I do here.'

'We're all very proud of you, my dear. It isn't often we have four notables in the same year at school.'

'Notables!'

'Why, yes. You're a Magistrate and your husband a well-known landowner, then there's Lady Garveston, and Nancy Graham – it's marvellous what she's accomplished – and I hear from Mrs Smythe that her daughter is a very accomplished hostess married to a highly successful man. We can only hope that every intake produces four such success stories.'

She smiled in the friendliest fashion and Maisie found herself blushing furiously and feeling acutely embarrassed.

As she drove along the road bordering the park Maisie saw that children were already pouring out of her old primary school, and at the sight of three girls arm in arm she couldn't help remembering her two childhood friends. She hadn't seen Barbara Smythe for over two years, not since that weekend reunion at Lady Garveston's when they'd met over dinner on the Sunday evening. Maisie had talked too much that evening, about the farm and about the children. She'd been miserably aware of Barbara's face across the table, of her fixed smile and assumed air of interest. Martin, her husband, had been holding forth about his boats and his car, their holidays in the Bahamas and their house-parties.

She'd cried on the way home, sobbing quietly against Tom's shoulder, and he'd been so kind, laughing at her fears, telling her that people like the Waltons didn't matter. The Standings had more than the Waltons would ever have – they had their children and the land, things that were worth more than a thousand house-parties or holidays abroad.

She'd come to believe it long before she went to bed that night. She had more than any of them, more even than Amelia Garveston with her beautiful ancestral home inherited by her fickle resentful husband Mark, and more than Nancy Graham who didn't have a husband, only memories of unhappy love affairs. Amelia had proposed a second reunion in another ten years' time, but Maisie for one hoped it would never happen: she'd have less than ever in common with any of them.

Her thoughts were brought sharply back to the present on seeing her father's ancient Morris parked outside the Jayson shops. That was all the driving he permitted himself these days, from home to the shops and back again, and impulsively Maisie pulled in beside him. There was plenty of time; she'd thought the court would last much longer, so they wouldn't be expecting her back at the farm just yet. It would be nice to catch her parents at Eric's. Her mother would relish seeing her neat and spruce in her magisterial garb.

As soon as she entered the room behind the butcher's shop, Maisie sensed that the atmosphere was anything but pleasant. Her parents sat at the table opposite Eric and Gloria, and in the centre reposed the cake, sunken and burnt; tears flowed down Gloria's face unchecked and two bright spots of colour burned in Eric's cheeks.

'Stop your crying,' he admonished her sharply. 'The cake'll eat all right, won't it, Mam?'

Maisie met her mother's eyes and Mrs Jayson said bravely, 'Ey lass, there's nothin' to get so upset about. Many's the one I spoilt in mi early married life. I reckon our Maisie did too, didn't you, love?'

Maisie rose to the occasion with a bright smile saying, 'And not only cakes, Mother. There were custards where the crusts rose to the top and tarts where the pastry wasn't cooked properly.'

Gloria remained unconsoled and matters were not improved by the arrival of Mary, who took one look at the cake and said sharply, 'That's not fit to eat. I'll bring you one of mine. Which do you prefer, fruit cake or date and walnut?'

Sobbing wildly, Gloria left the table and ran into the kitchen and Mrs Jayson said, 'Ye shouldn't have said that, Mary. She's hurt enough as it is.'

'What have I said?' Mary demanded. 'I've only offered to bring another cake in. I can't do right for doing wrong these days! I won't bother with the cake if that's how you feel.'

She departed in a huff and Mrs Jayson sighed. 'Now the pair of them are upset. See, I'll cut into the cake, it'll not be so bad inside.'

If anything the inside was worse – a soggy sticky mess, and Eric said sharply, 'Leave it, Mam, I'll throw it in the bin. We've got biscuits and our Jimmy'll 'ave a cake or two on the shelves. I'll go and get one.'

'I'll go,' Maisie said quickly. 'Get rid of the cake and try to persuade Gloria to come back to the table. I'll join you for a cup of tea in a minute.'

Jimmy was serving a customer when she entered his shop so she passed the time looking round the shelves for something suitable. After a few minutes he joined her with a wide grin on his good-looking face.

'I thought you made all the cakes up at the farm,' he commented, eyeing the boxes in her hands.

'So I do. These are for Gloria – mi mum and dad are having tea with them.'

'What happened to the cake she was makin', then? She came in here for the flour and other ingredients.'

'It didn't turn out too well.'

He threw back his head and laughed. 'I'm not surprised. I'm amazed that girl can boil water.'

'She'll learn.'

'I doubt it. He should have married a plain good wife and played around with somebody like Gloria.'

'Well, at least he had the sense to leave married women alone,' she snapped.

24

'What's that supposed to mean?'

'Deirdre Forsythe, that's what. Letting her come in here, stand chatting to you, then sayin' she fancies you. Of course she doesn't fancy you – she's amusin' herself.'

'And you're an authority on it, I suppose.'

'I know her sort. If her husband cut up rough about you she'd drop you like a hot brick. One of these days your other customers are going to start tittle-tattling about you. Is that what you want?'

'What I do in mi own shop is nobody's business except mine, and there's no call for you to be actin' the big sister part. I'm quite capable of runnin' mi own life, Maisie Standin'. Now do you want these cakes or did you just come in 'ere to give mi a lecture?'

Maisie left the shop wishing wholeheartedly that she'd gone straight home. If she told Tom he'd think she was foolish for worrying about her family but there'd never been a time when she hadn't worried about them.

Gloria was back at the table by now, dabbing at her eyes while Mrs Jayson looked on, her face set in lines of disapproval. Her father looked uncomfortable; he hated what he called women's tantrums and tears, and he was probably wishing he was back in his garden tying up his dahlias.

Maisie accepted the cup of tea and offered round the cakes and it wasn't long before her mother said, 'I hear ye closed the shop on Saturday, Eric.'

'I suppose Mary told ye?' he answered testily.

'She mentioned it, but I knew already – Mrs Lord told me. She came for her meat as usual and found ye closed. It's not a good idea to shut up on a Saturday, you get a half-day during the week.'

'It was Gloria's birthday. I'd promised to take her into Kendal.'

'What was wrong with your half-day?'

'Leave it, Mother,' Mr Jayson said quietly. 'What they do is none of our business.'

25

For several minutes there was silence until Mrs Jayson suddenly remembered that this was Maisie's first day in court. 'Ey, I'd forgotten about it with all this to-do with the cake. You look very nice, love,' she said quickly. 'I thought you paid too much for that suit but the hat's nice. It's a sensible one, not like that silly blue thing you had for the christening and our Golden Weddin'.'

Maisie didn't argue but inwardly made up her mind that her mother could have the hat if she discovered not all the women Magistrates wore them.

She was glad when she could reasonably make an excuse to leave, for by this time her father and Eric were talking about business and her mother and Gloria were looking at the dress Eric had bought her in Kendal.

'When are you goin' to be able to wear that round here?' Mrs Jayson demanded.

'It's for our holidays,' Gloria explained. 'We're goin' to Spain at the end of October.'

Oh no, Maisie thought desperately. Her mother's eyes had opened wide in shocked surprise. She rose to her feet and hastily collected her bag and gloves.

'I must go, Mother,' she said. 'The children will be ready for their tea.'

Mrs Jayson ignored her and Maisie stood hesitantly at the door listening to Gloria prattling on about two weeks in Malaga, the hotel, the flight, the clothes she would need. Finally in rare exasperation Mrs Jayson said, 'What's goin' to happen to the shop? You can't just close it for two weeks – it's unheard of!'

Gloria paused in her flow of exuberance, and turning to Eric her mother-in-law said relentlessly, 'What's all this about closin' the shop, our Eric? I've never heard of such a thing.'

'We're entitled to a holiday, Mother,' Eric answered her.

26

'I thought you had two weeks in August. Why didn't you go away then?'

'Everybody goes then,' Gloria said petulantly. 'Besides, it's too hot for Spain in August.'

'Do you hear that, Father?' Mrs Jayson said sharply. 'They're talkin' about closing the shop for two weeks in October. Talk some sense into them.'

Maisie escaped without any of them noticing. She had no intention of listening to an argument which was likely to go on well into the evening. She realized that she had a headache and was glad to take off her hat and fling it on to the back seat, but her thoughts were angry as she drove upwards across the fell towards the farm. Nor was she at all appeased to meet Iris Gilbert sauntering airily down the lane.

Bringing the car to a stop she lowered the window and called out, 'I told you to wait until I got home, Iris. Where are you going?'

'I'm goin' 'ome, Mrs Standin'. Mr Standin' said I could.'

'You mean my husband's arrived home?'

'Yes, and it's after five o'clock so 'e said I'd better get off 'ome. I told your Alice what ye said but it didn't stop 'er quarrellin' with Peter when 'e got 'ome.'

The girl gave her this information with some relish, and biting her lip in annoyance Maisie said, 'Get off home then, Iris. Did Mr Standing give you your money or shall I pay you?'

'He gave it to mi and said I should ask you when you'd be needin' me again.'

'I'll let you know, Iris. I hope you'll find your mother much better.'

The girl grinned at her cheerfully, then turning on her heel started to run as fast as her legs would carry her along the lane.

It was going to be one of those nights. She'd have something to say to young Alice and it was unlike Tom

27

to get in so early from his work on the farm. Perhaps he wouldn't be in a good humour and she desperately wanted somebody to talk to about the afternoon's events.

By the time she parked the car in the farmyard her frustrations had mounted. She was already convincing herself that nothing in her life had ever run smoothly. If her friend Nancy Graham had allowed herself to fall in love with Bob Jayson instead of wanting something bigger and better he wouldn't now be married to Mary Gibson, and what was so wonderful anyway in Nancy spending her life in one trouble spot after another, South America and China, now the Middle East where she was likely to be shot at every time she stirred out.

Then there was Amelia. Maisie had no doubt Amelia had endorsed her elevation to the Bench. It was all right for *Amelia*. Lady Amelia, living at Garveston Hall. There they were, just her and Mark in that great place waited on by an army of servants. Her children were boarded out at Lorivals – they did not come home to meals and everlasting squabbling over the table – and what did Barbara Walton née Smythe know about being a farmer's wife and bringing up a family? If her mother was to be believed, she did nothing all day except go to the hairdresser's, play golf or disappear for weeks at a time to some exotic place abroad. Maisie sniffed loudly.

Tom stood at the stove stirring something in a pan but he turned round when he heard the door open and gave her a warm smile.

'You've survived it then?' he asked cheerfully.

'Yes. I met Iris in the lane and she said you were home.'

'I left two of the men to finish off. I thought I'd have your tea ready.'

'Has Lucy been good?'

'Of course. Peter's doing his homework and Alice is in her room. They were quarrelling as usual and when

I was a bit sharp with her she threw one of her famous tantrums and ran upstairs. I'll let you sort her out.'

'We're going to have to do something about Alice. She wasn't playing on the fell last week, she was kept in for chattering. I won't have her lying to me, Tom.'

'It was only a white lie, love. Didn't you ever fib to your parents about your escapades on the way home from school?'

'I never lied to mi mother. I daren't, besides I don't think I ever dawdled on the way home. I knew there was work to be done.'

'Don't tell me you and those two cronies of yours didn't play in the park instead of going straight home.'

'No, we never did. For one thing, Barbara Smythe never got her clothes dirty and Nancy used to go to her grandfather's surgery to help out.' As Maisie spoke she went into the lobby to take off her outdoor clothing but she was remembering that rush from their junior school through the park, the autumn leaves crunching under her feet, the glow from her father's shop shining a welcome through the early evening gloom.

She stared at herself in the hall mirror. Was she so very different from that girl who had skipped through the park, her school satchel slung carelessly over her shoulders, her red curls flying in the wind. She'd been small and wiry then with a pert face dusted with freckles; now she was plump and matronly. Tom was forever reassuring her that she was a comely woman and that he liked her better with a bit of flesh on her bones, but she longed to be like Amelia.

Amelia could look wonderful, cool and distinguished, in those insipid colours she favoured. She could walk like a queen in brogues and tweeds, not like a country bumpkin. And Amelia would never wear those flowered skirts that made Maisie look like a sack of potatoes tied round the middle.

Maisie hung her coat on a hanger and fastened the buttons. The suit was nice even if it did make her feel like a schoolmarm, but she wasn't so sure about the hat.

Peter sat at the living-room table with his books spread out in front of him, a pensive frown on his face. He lifted his head and smiled at her and immediately her heart warmed to him. She was so proud of him. He was clever – one day he'd be somebody, she told herself confidently, and he was good-looking into the bargain. Then her expression changed as she thought about Alice. It was time she gave that young lady a piece of her mind.

She found Alice lying on her stomach staring at a girls' magazine; she did not bother to turn round when the door opened. Maisie stood beside the bed wanting badly to shake the child, her voice rising shrilly with temper.

'What's this I hear about your quarrelling with Peter and then flying upstairs when your father scolded you? I won't have it, Alice. You're becoming a real problem. Besides, you lied to me about playing out on the fell last week.'

The girl sat up, her face mutinous, her bottom lip thrust out in childish defiance.

'Well?' Maisie demanded. 'What have you to say for yourself?'

'I suppose it was sneaky Aunt Mary who told you. She got it from stupid Mona Gibson.'

'It doesn't matter who told me, and watch your tongue! I won't have you lying to me, Alice. I don't know what we're going to do with you. Your school reports are always bad and you haven't a hope of getting to the grammar school.'

'I don't want to be a swot like our Peter.'

'I'd be interested to know just what you do want. Don't you want a decent job when you leave school?'

30

'That's ages away. Besides, you didn't 'ave a decent job in spite of goin' to that posh school where they're all snobs.'

'At least they were willing to take me. They wouldn't look twice at you unless you decided to mend your ways.'

'I wouldn't want to go there anyway. I'll probably do what you did – get married and 'ave a baby.'

Her eyes were dancing with malicious humour and unthinkingly Maisie slapped her face. Immediately the girl's eyes filled with tears and she ran sobbing from the room. Maisie followed slowly. She hadn't meant to slap her daughter, but there were times when Alice exasperated her out of all telling, and today had been filled with frustrations.

Tom was standing at the bottom of the stairs when she started to walk down. His eyes were concerned, even a little condemning.

Maisie passed him without a word; she didn't intend explaining her actions to Tom. Tom spoiled Alice, undermining her authority, and the only times they ever quarrelled was when, somehow or other, Alice was at the bottom of it.

'Where is she?' she enquired, seeing that her daughter was not in the kitchen.

'Crying in the living room,' Tom said gently. 'There was no call to hit her, Maisie.'

'I won't have her lying to me, Tom, and I won't have her speaking to me the way she just did. It doesn't help when you always take her part.'

'I don't, love. I just want a bit of peace and quiet when I come home in the evenin'.'

'Do you think I don't, then? My day hasn't actually been all plain sailin'.'

He looked at her doubtfully as she settled Lucy at the kitchen table. 'I'll get them in for their tea then and let's try not to 'ave any arguments over the table,' he said evenly.

31

Peter came and took his place, his face flushed. Maisie knew how much he detested the shouting matches that went on between her and his sister. Tom came next, his arm around his daughter's shoulders, her face streaked with tears, never once looking in her mother's direction.

Maisie served the meal in silence, watching while Alice moved her food about her plate, wanting to scream, 'Either eat it or leave it alone!' Tom engaged Peter in conversation about the school's football team and by the end of the meal some normality had been reached, enough at least to allow Alice to consume two helpings of apple tart.

After they had eaten Peter went back to his homework while Alice asked if she could accompany her father on his visit to the shippen. Maisie was glad they'd left her to clear away alone. Normally she was reluctant to let Alice escape helping her with the dishes, but today was not an ordinary day; she'd be glad when the children were in bed and she could tell Tom what had transpired to put her in a bad mood.

CHAPTER 3

It was the time of day Maisie liked best. The two girls were in bed, and Tom sat at the table going over his accounts before taking his last look round the farmyard. Of late they'd been plagued by marauding foxes but tonight there'd been no noisy barking from the dogs and the evening inspection should be only a formality.

Maisie sat in a deep armchair with her mending. The television was switched on but she had only been half watching; she wanted desperately to talk to Tom before he started to get interested in the football match that was due to start later. However, seeing his concentration and the frown between his eyes, so much like Peter's, she realized she would have to wait.

Immediately the nine o'clock news was over he looked up with a smile saying, 'I'll look in on Peter when I've done my rounds. He's probably finished his homework by now and will come down to watch the match with me. I'll make us a cup of tea when I get in.'

'No, Tom, you see to the farm, I'll make the tea. Don't be too long.'

A gardening programme had just started on the television and hearing the words 'Garveston Hall, the home of Sir Mark and Lady Garveston', Maisie's interest quickened and she laid aside her mending.

The cameras were showing views of the Hall — its warm Pennine stone towers and turrets, enough of them to fire any child's imagination. They moved down the steps towards the river, revealing enchanting vignettes of the Italian garden and rose garden, the rockeries that tumbled above the weir and the giant oaks and beeches Maisie had last glimpsed from the terrace on that memorable Sunday of their reunion.

Amelia appeared on the screen, elegant in beige cashmere and tweeds, pointing out her favourite shrubs. Her dark cloudy hair framed a serene lovely face and her voice, low and slightly breathless, had hardly changed since that first morning at Lorivals when she had waited for Maisie on the stairs. Then there was Sir Mark on horseback, his handsome face smiling down at his wife, his fair hair glinting in the sunlight, and with a rare cynicism Maisie tried to remember the number of times she had seen them together.

She didn't look round when the door opened, and then Peter was sitting on the floor near her chair, a cup of cocoa in his hands.

'It's Garveston Hall, love,' she explained. 'I remember it looked just like that when I went there for dinner with your father.'

'Have you just been the once, Mother?'

'Yes. It was something we decided to do the day we left school, to hold a reunion in ten years' time.'

'Will you be going again?'

'I don't suppose so. Amelia did say something about having another reunion ten years on, but I shan't want to go.'

'Why ever not?'

'Well, we never see Barbara, and Nancy Graham's miles away.'

'I sort of remember her. She came to see us now and again.'

'Well yes, we were always best friends.'

'I thought she was pretty.'

'Yes, I suppose she was.'

'The chaps at school didn't believe me when I said Nancy Graham was a friend of my mother's. They thought I was fibbing.'

34

'Well you can tell them you weren't, and if I get the chance I'll let one or two of their mothers know.'

Peter laughed. 'It doesn't matter. I'm going to bed now, Mum. I can't be bothered to watch the match. I told Dad goodnight before he went out.'

'Goodnight, darling.' She wanted to put her arms around him and hug him, but such demonstrations of affection embarrassed him; he was growing up too quickly.

A little later Tom came in. 'Is everything all right out there?' she asked. It was a question she had asked almost every evening of their married life and his answer was always the same.

'Everything's fine, Maisie. Now tell me about your day. Something put you in a bad mood – was it the court?'

'No. The court was just boring – I thought of all the things I could have been doing here. They didn't need me.'

'What did you expect on your first day, love – a nice juicy murder, gang warfare perhaps?'

'They were all motoring offences, radar speeding in the main and the cases were already cut and dried. Everybody was very nice to me, but I just don't want another afternoon doing something anybody else could have done just as well.'

'Well, you're on the rota now whether you like it or not, love, and you'll have to get used to it. That wasn't what upset you, though, was it?'

'No.'

'What then?'

'My family upset me. Every time I see them, if it isn't one of them it's another. I wish we didn't live so close.'

'What was it this time?'

'I'll never get on with Mary, then mi mum and dad came to tea at Eric's and Gloria'd made a cake that sank in the middle. She was in tears, mi mother did her best to pacify her then Mary came in and offered to let them have one of hers.'

Tom threw back his head and laughed until Maisie snapped angrily, 'I didn't think it was funny, and you wouldn't have thought so either if you'd been there.'

'You've surely not let that upset you all afternoon!'

'I was more upset about our Jimmy. He's so stupid, he thinks every woman fancies him and now that Deirdre Forsythe's shopping there and spending hours chatting to him across the counter. In no time at all he'll be the talk of the town and he hasn't the sense to see it.'

'Deirdre Forsythe?' Tom asked in a puzzled fashion.

'Yes, you know, the new people from the other side of Greymont. Her husband's on the committee for the show, and she's a lot like Barbara Smythe.'

His face cleared. 'Ah, that's who she reminded me of. She's cool and sure of herself, a bit of a fashion-plate.'

'She's only amusing herself. Our Jimmy'd never be her sort in a thousand years.'

'Well, love, it's none of your business. If he wants to make a fool of himself over a woman like that there's nothing you can do about it, but it's my bet it's a harmless flirtation with a bored spoilt woman. She'll know which side her bread's buttered so I doubt if it'll get out of hand.'

'But the gossip,' Maisie protested.

'If they're not talking about your Jimmy they'll be talking about somebody else.'

'Mi father and mother are livin' in that tiny bunga-low in a village mi mother never liked so that their money could go on those shops for the boys, so you'd at least think they'd do their best to keep their noses clean. Now there's our Eric talking about shutting the shop for a fortnight in October so he and that Gloria

36

can go to Spain. He'll be lucky if he finds his customers waitin' for him when he gets back.'

'It's their business, love.'

'Couldn't you talk to Jimmy at least?'

'No, get your Bob to talk to him. It's got nothing to do with me and he'd be quick to tell me so.'

'You know Bob won't do anything. He won't say boo to a goose unless Mary tells him to. I get so cross, Tom. It didn't need to be like this.'

'I don't see how it could have been any different. They're three grown men who've made their own decisions. Nobody made your Bob marry Mary or Eric marry Gloria, and as for Jimmy, hasn't he always been a show-off?'

Maisie picked up her mending and started to sew furiously. Of course Tom wouldn't see things her way. Men were always so logical, viewing everything in black and white and never looking for the shades in between. She wished now she'd never told him about the family, and even as she wished it Tom was anxious to change the subject.

'Did you watch the programme on Garveston Hall, love? I forgot to tell you it was on.'

'It only showed you the gardens, it never took you into the house.'

'Well of course not, it's a gardening programme. Was Lady Amelia there?'

'Yes, wearing that tweed skirt she's had for years. She's worn it for goodness knows how many agricultural shows but as usual she looked so right and elegant. Sir Mark was there on horseback just as if they were the most devoted couple, and yet they're never together at anything here.'

'I've reminded him several times about those two fields but he agrees something should be done and then conveniently forgets it.'

'Why is that, do you think?'

37

'He lets the hunt run across them and they pay for the privilege. I think I'd get more joy if I mentioned it to Lady Amelia.'

'She'd probably spend a lot of money on them and he'd be resentful – I think that's the trouble between those two.'

He smiled. Maisie could be remarkably astute sometimes: he wished she was more astute about her family.

'When are you next in court?' he asked her.

'Next Monday afternoon. Oh, I wish I'd had the good sense to say I couldn't possibly be a Magistrate. You could have helped, Tom!'

'I thought it would be good for you, give you some much-needed confidence.'

Driving into town several weeks later, Maisie had reason to remember that conversation. Her confidence *had* improved. Now she could face an afternoon sitting on the Bench with complacency, and yet it was a feeling that could be shattered by a few words spoken carelessly by somebody like Barbara Smythe's mother.

They met on the steps of the court and immediately Mrs Smythe looked disapprovingly at Maisie's bare head, irrespective of the fact that her hair had been shampooed and styled only that morning.

'You decided against wearing a hat then,' she stated, and Maisie wished she didn't feel the need to apologise.

'I never suited hats, Mrs Smythe. Since I left school I've tried to go without, except for special occasions.'

'You don't think attendance at court is a special occasion?'

'I did, until I saw that not all the JPs wore them.'

'I think you'll find that the more senior Magistrates do. Miss Lester and I always wear a hat, and so does Lady Garveston.'

Maisie felt obliged to remark that Miss Lester wore a hat whether she was at court or not; she'd never seen her without one.

Mrs Smythe made no comment to this but as they walked along the corridors together she remarked, 'Did you know that John Forsythe's been approached to sit on the Bench? The Forsythes haven't been in the area long but they're already making their presence felt.'

'No, I didn't know.'

'Hasn't your brother mentioned it?'

'My brother?'

'Yes, your Jimmy. That Mrs Forsythe shops with him and spends a good deal of time chatting over the counter. I had to demand to be served the other morning. Goodness knows what they find to talk about every day.'

'My brother's never mentioned her to me.'

'People talk, you know. I should drop a few words on the quiet if I were you, Maisie. Deirdre Forsythe is a very bored and often lonely young woman.'

'It's none of my business, Mrs Smythe. If my brother wishes to talk to his customers it's got nothing to do with me.'

'Well, of course not, but when people start talking I think you should make it your business, Maisie.'

She stalked through the door in front of Maisie and immediately was lost among the crowd. It was the busiest day of the week with three courts sitting, and as she accepted a cup of tea gratefully Maisie saw across the room that Mrs Smythe and Miss Lester were in earnest conversation.

Her friend of the first day approached her with a conspiratorial smile saying, 'I see you've had the courage to leave it at home. It's so much more comfortable without one, isn't it?'

'I've given it to mi mother. She admired it, and she likes hats.'

Miss Waddington smiled. 'Miss Lester's been called in to take the place of Lady Garveston. Apparently she couldn't make it this morning.'

'I see.'

'She had to go to meet her sister from the train. Lady Atherton is spending quite a lot of time here since her handicapped daughter died.'

'I didn't know she'd died!'

'Oh yes, over twelve months ago. It was a blessing, for the girl would never have been normal. There was no hope that she would recover.'

'No, I suppose not.'

'Amelia told me they'd all been devastated. It often happens that a child like that can leave a family absolutely crushed after her death. I suppose they gave her so much love and attention that now they all feel strangely bereft.'

'Yes, I can understand that. I'm so lucky to have three normal children even if the middle one does sometimes make me wonder.'

Miss Waddington laughed. 'Perhaps a taste of Lorivals might be good for her.'

'I'm sure it would, but we haven't the money to spend on school fees. Our son Peter is clever, so we think it's more important for him to go to university. Anyway, Alice wouldn't thank us for sending her to Lorivals.'

'Alice is a rebel, I take it?'

'Oh yes,' Maisie replied feelingly. 'Sometimes I wonder what we're going to do with her. She's involved in every quarrel there is in our house.'

'Don't worry, she'll grow out of it. Rebellion is often a part of growing up. Here we are, which court are you in?'

'Number Three Court.'

'That's the break-in at the paper mill. It'll probably go on for a while.'

For the first time since she became a Magistrate, Maisie found herself on the same Bench as Miss Susan

Lester and was very conscious of her clericalgrey-clad figure presiding over the courtroom, her dark hair pulled back into its customary bun and topped with a grey velour hat which added to her severity.

She favoured Maisie with a swift smile before shuffling her papers and as they sat back to listen to the evidence Maisie stared at the two boys standing dejectedly in the dock. They were thin lanky teenagers, the taller one with a short crewcut, the small one with shoulder-length hair. Both had narrow pinched faces although the older boy showed an air of defiance unlike the younger one, who seemed on the verge of tears.

Maisie felt a swift rush of sympathy for the boys' parents sitting side by side in the body of the courtroom – poor ordinary people, the two women sobbing quietly, the men staring at their sons in anguished disbelief before they looked away, embarrassed and bewildered.

What would she do if it was one of her children, she thought to herself desperately. It would never be Peter – he was too responsible – but Alice, Alice worried her . . .

The two boys were accused of breaking into the offices of the paper mill and stealing petty cash and two computers valued at two thousand pounds. Maisie couldn't imagine why the boys should want to steal computers until she heard that they'd sold them in a public house that same night for a hundred pounds each to a man who paid them cash. The man had not been traced and at the end of the day the case was adjourned awaiting further evidence, but leaving the courtroom with Miss Lester Maisie said ruefully, 'What do you suppose will happen to them eventually?'

'Oh the younger one will probably be put on probation, and the older boy receive a minimum prison sentence. They're both naive and stupid, neither of them are blessed with too much intelligence.'

'It's a terrible responsibility having children,' Maisie commented ruefully.

'Yes. Some parents could do more to control their children, some of them are helpless. How is your Peter coming along at school?'

Maisie's eyes brightened. 'We're getting very good reports. He's always well up in the class and we hope he'll get to university.'

'He's not going into farming then?'

'I doubt it. He's no interest in the farm. Tom's a bit disappointed about that.'

Miss Lester nodded. 'And the two girls?'

'Alice is a bit of a problem, she likes too much of her own way, but Lucy's a good child, very much like Peter. Have you heard from Nancy recently, the last I heard was a letter at Christmas?'

'She's back in the Middle East as you've probably noticed from the newspaper. It doesn't suit me that she's gallivanting all over the globe from one trouble spot to the next but it was her choice. I daresay her father would have been proud of her.'

'I wonder if she'll ever settle down?'

'I have my doubts. She's out there with four men, she could be having an affair with any one of them for all I know. Still it's nothing to do with me and she'd be the first to tell me so.'

'Perhaps she'll surprise us all one day,' Maisie said hopefully.

'Perhaps. I must go, I don't want to get into conversation with Nellie Smythe. All I hear is Barbara's new house and her husband's ever increasing status. He's now on the board of several public companies.'

'I didn't know that.'

'You will, my dear, unless you make yourself as scarce as I intend to do. My car's in for servicing today so I don't want to miss the next bus.'

'I'll take you home, Miss Lester, it isn't much out of my way.'

'Well, that's very kind of you, Maisie, it is getting late and the bus could be a bit crowded.'

That would mean she would have to drive past her brothers' shops. For several weeks she'd studiously avoided driving into town that way which meant that she hadn't had to look for Deirdre Forsythe's car parked round the corner, seeing the odd customer in Eric's shop and Mary's tart expression amongst the fruit and vegetables laid out on the pavement.

She knew from local gossip that Eric had lost customers after closing for two weeks in October, and Bob's prices were soaring to accommodate Mary's new marble fish counter and tiled floor.

She drove past the shops without looking at them and Miss Lester remarked idly, 'Your sister-in-law's made a great many alterations to the shop but most of us liked it the way it was.'

'Yes I know.'

'And their prices were more competitive.'

'Yes. My mother tried telling her.'

'I should think that's one young woman who's not prepared to take advice from anybody.'

'No. Mary likes her own way.'

Maisie would have been surprised if she could have known the thoughts passing through the mind of her companion. Susan Lester was thinking that Maisie Jayson had more commonsense in her little finger than the other three had altogether, and this was the girl she'd once tried to prevent her niece being friendly with.

She looked at the plump pretty woman sitting beside her with her eyes fixed firmly on the road ahead. She should be wearing a hat, she didn't approve of Magistrates appearing like office girls in the park, but the suit was nice, and the crisp white blouse set off her red hair and pink complexion.

There was something very wholesome about the girl, like the acres of well-tended farmland and the cosiness

43

of the stone-built farmhouse. Something as honest and enduring as the forest of Bowland stretching above them, and who wanted complications, life was too short for them.

'Will you be calling in to see one of your brothers on the way back?' she asked innocently.

'I haven't the time today. We don't see much of one another, I've a lot of work on the farm.'

'Yes, of course you have.'

Miss Lester's reply was placatory and Maisie was tempted to ask, 'Do you still shop with mi brothers, Miss Lester?'

'Well I have the car now and if I'm on duty I do some of my shopping in the town. Sarah goes for the things we run out of, but Eric was closed for two whole weeks in October and Sarah did so much grumbling we tend to buy our meat at Rogers now.'

'It was a stupid thing to do.'

'Couldn't your brother Bob have covered for them?'

'He could, but Mary wouldn't let him.'

'I see. He does rather let her have all her own way doesn't he?'

Maisie stayed silent and Miss Lester stole a quick look at her face to find it strangely remote and frowning.

'Well here we are,' she said cheerfully. 'Would you like to come in for a cup of tea, Sarah will have the kettle on I'm sure.'

Maisie consulted her watch. It was late and she knew she should be getting home; on the other hand she had to talk to somebody and if Miss Lester had never exactly approved of her, she could always be relied upon to give sound advice.

Making up her mind quickly she said, 'Thanks, Miss Lester, just for a cup of tea then, but I mustn't stay late.'

While Miss Lester was in the kitchen instructing Sarah she took a look round the drawing room, which Miss Lester insisted on calling it. It was a lofty well-proportioned room overlooking the front garden, but she was struck by its severity, a severity Nancy and she had often giggled at. Ponderous mahogany furniture and dark oil paintings. Thick Wilton carpets and a marble fireplace topped by a black marble mantelpiece on which rested two bronze gladiators and a massive Chinese vase.

She found herself comparing it with her mother's living room behind the shop with its black-leaded grate and white-topped table. She guessed Susan Lester had never replaced a single stick of her father's furniture, it wouldn't surprise her if somewhere in the house there wasn't his old pipe and slippers.

The door opened and Sarah came in pushing a trolley containing a silver tea service, delicate china cups and saucers and a massive fruit loaf. Miss Lester followed having taken off her jacket and Maisie saw with some amusement that she was wearing a pale cream blouse similar to her own.

Sarah beamed at her good-naturedly. 'I 'ope the children and Tom are all well,' she said as she cut the cake. 'Nice bonny children they are too.'

'Thank you, Sarah.'

She accepted the tea and a piece of the cake, placing them on a small table Miss Lester had drawn up beside her chair.

'This is a lovely room,' she said. 'It's nice being able to look over the garden.'

'Yes, we quite like it, don't we, Sarah?'

'It's right enough, but it's a lot of work. I reckon it's too big.'

'I wasn't getting rid of Father's furniture to buy inferior modern stuff,' Miss Lester retorted, 'besides I like big lofty rooms, I've always been used to them. I've got help three days a week in the shape of Mrs Townley and you've all those modern conveniences in the kitchen.'

45

Behind her back Sarah grinned at Maisie wickedly before saying, 'I could get round this house while Mrs Townley's thinking about it,' then before Miss Lester could think of a suitable reply she was out of the door closing it firmly behind her. Miss Lester sighed, and Maisie said with a laugh, 'I used to hear about Sarah from Nancy, she'll not get any better with age.'

'She's a good soul really and she looks after me very well, just like she looked after Father. I suppose we're just two old maids who see too much of one another. How are your parents, Maisie?'

'Very well. Mi mother has a bit of arthritis but apart from that she's fine and mi father never complains. I think mi mother misses the shop.'

'I've often wondered why she never went down to help. She'd have been very good for Mary. Your mother thought the customer was always right, now the boot is on the other foot.'

'I know they've lost customers through her sharp tongue, and I know it's worried mi mum and dad.'

'Your father spent a lot of money on those three shops, it's a pity if the boys let them go down.'

'Surely they won't.'

'Well the answer's in their own hands. Bob should keep his wife in order and Eric should think about his customers instead of the wants of that young wife of his.'

'Well at least Jimmy seems to be coping well,' Maisie added hopefully.

Miss Lester gave her an odd look before saying, 'I believe John Forsythe's joining us on the Bench.'

'Is he, I didn't know. In any case I don't really know them very well.'

'He's away a lot on business and if he joins us on the Bench that wife of his will see even less of him. Bored silly young women often get into mischief, unfortunately they sometimes include other people.'

She looked pointedly at Maisie and she in turn could feel the rich red colour flooding her cheeks and Miss Lester said, 'So you know about it do you, Maisie?'

'I don't drive past any more. Is she still visitin' the shop as much as ever?'

'Well, talk never loses anything. They were seen having lunch together one day last week, some country pub out on the fells where neither of them expected to be seen. One of these days your mother and father are going to hear about it and her husband too if they're not careful. Can't you slip him the hint, Maisie?'

'No, I tried and he wouldn't have it. It's worrying me, Miss Lester, I've asked Tom to talk to him but he says it should come from Bob.'

'I agree. Bob's his brother, but I can't see any advice coming from that quarter.'

Silently Maisie agreed with her, then changing the subject Miss Lester said, 'Amelia's sister is staying with her for several weeks, so she may not be able to take her seat on the Bench every time she's on the rota, more for the rest of us I suppose.'

'Yes. I was sorry to hear about her niece.'

'It was a blessing, my dear, there was no hope of the girl ever being any different. I wouldn't be a bit surprised if her illness hasn't had a disastrous effect on her parents' marriage.'

'Amelia was very fond of her niece.'

'Mmmm. It was a sort of bondage, my dear, for all of them.'

It was evident that nothing more was going to be said about the Jayson shops so Maisie finished her second cup of tea and said she must leave. Miss Lester accompanied her to the front door and it was there on the hall table that she confronted a large photograph of Nancy. Maisie picked it up and together they stood staring at it.

Candid blue eyes stared back at them out of a wistful oval face framed by hair the colour of silvered corn. It was the face of a cool English beauty, poised yet strangely ethereal, but it was a face far removed from the laughing girl Maisie had always thought of as her very best friend.

That girl had laughed with a joyous freedom, long legs loping across the fell, her blonde hair flying in the wind, eyes sparkling in the sunlight, unshadowed by any hint of sorrow. The face of the woman in the picture was different, there were things behind that elusive smiling face that neither of them would ever know.

'She's so lovely,' Maisie said softly, 'I never realised how lovely she was, it was always Amelia and Barbara.'

'Nancy's far prettier than either of them, she's simply not quite so obvious.'

'I never thought Amelia was obvious,' Maisie argued.

'Not in the way you mean perhaps. Amelia could never be hurt like Nancy, there's something like steel behind that cool patrician composure. Nancy's is a façade fate has compelled her to adopt.'

Maisie stared at her for a few moments before putting the photograph back on to the table. She didn't think Nancy would have any idea how keenly her aunt had analysed their characters and as if she guessed something of her thoughts Miss Lester said, 'I've become quite a student of human nature, my dear, one has to be you know, otherwise how would we ever have the nerve to sit in judgement on others?'

CHAPTER 4

It was almost dark when Maisie drove back past her
brothers' shops. Nearly six o'clock, she should have
been home an hour ago. She was determined not to
look but she couldn't help herself.

There was a light on in Jimmy's grocer's shop and she
could see him standing at the counter but she couldn't
see who he was talking to. The blinds were already down
at Eric's window and the shop was in darkness. When
she reached the corner she could see Bob and his wife
taking in the fruit and what was left of the vegetables and
she felt guilty that she passed without stopping, but neither
of them looked up from their work.

She quite purposely averted her eyes from the side
entrance in case Deirdre Forsythe's car was parked
there, and then in a sudden burst of freedom she was
driving up the road towards the fell. She had almost
reached the lane leading up to the farm when she saw
two figures trudging along it and recognized them as
farmhands leaving for home. She lowered her window
and called out, 'Goodnight! Is Tom home?'

They came to the window of the car and Sam Glover,
the older of the two, said, ' 'E went off early, Maisie.
That Mrs Edge came round, somethin' to do wi' young
Alice.'

'Alice! Why, what's she been up to now?'

'I can't tell ye, Maisie, but she was in a rare old
state, standin' in the yard and yellin' at the top of 'er
voice. Tom's taken 'er into the kitchen . . .'

Without waiting to hear another word Maisie put her
foot firmly on the accelerator and drove swiftly towards
the farm. Lights streamed out of the kitchen window,

illuminating the yard. Not bothering to lock the car, Maisie left it and ran across the cobbles towards the house. She flung open the door and took in the picture at a glance.

Mrs Edge sat on one of the kitchen chairs. She was a tall gaunt woman with a felt hat pulled down firmly on her greying hair and her raincoat reaching the top of her black wellington boots. Facing her stood Tom, red of face and stern, while Alice stood dejected and tearful on the rug. The three of them looked up at the suddenness of her entrance, and then Alice burst out crying afresh. Tom said gently, 'Come and sit down, love. It's all a storm in a teacup.'

'It is *not* a storm in a teacup,' Mrs Edge said tartly. 'I found your girl stealin' mi apples last week, Mrs Standing, and this mornin' there they were the two of 'em, brazen as brass in the middle of mi kitchen cuttin' into mi gingerbread. Broken the kitchen winder they had, they must have watched me go out. All I got was a mouthful o' cheek when I chastised 'em, the young hussies.'

Maisie looked at Tom in dismay, then at Alice standing rubbing her eyes, the picture of dejection. Turning to face Mrs Edge she said, 'Alice has no need to steal your apples, Mrs Edge. We have plenty of our own, and the pantry's full of gingerbread and other cakes. Are you seriously trying to tell me that they broke into your house?'

'That's what I'm sayin', and that's not all. Twice this month I've had to chase 'er out of mi barn where she's bin with that Smithson lad and 'im nigh on sixteen.'

'Who was the other girl?'

'Mary Pearson, that's who, but it was your girl who was the ringleader. It was her that gave most o' the cheek.'

'Have you been to see Mrs Pearson?'

'No, but I'm goin' after I've left 'ere. I came 'ere first because ye could do wi' supervisin' that lass o' yours instead o' sittin' in judgement on others. Ye've allus thought too much o' yerself, that posh school ye went to and now yer a Magistrate. Well, I should look to your own afore ye start tellin' other folks 'ow to bring up their children.'

Maisie recoiled from the vindictiveness in her face. She'd never realized how much envy and bitterness her years at Lorivals had engendered in those less fortunate women she'd known as children, but before she could reply Tom said stiffly, 'I'm not havin' you sitting in my house talkin' to my wife like that. Alice has done wrong and I'm willing to pay for the apples and the cake. Whatever damage she's done to your property I'm willing to pay for that, too, but you can be sure we're quite capable of chastising her. She'll not be troubling you again, Mrs Edge. Now I'll be askin' you to leave. I don't want to see you around 'ere again.'

'Don't worry, I shan't be. Just think yourselves lucky I 'aven't gone to the police. You'll be 'avin' trouble with that one, right little madam she is. If Mrs Pearson has any sense she'll be keepin' their Mary away from 'er.'

'I thought you said both children were to blame,' Tom said quietly.

'So I did, but she was the ringleader, never fear.'

Tom strode over to the door and held it open wide, then after a shrug of her shoulders and a contemptuous look at Alice the woman stamped out of the room.

Alice looked at her father fearfully, and then the inner door opened to admit Peter staring helplessly from one to the other.

'What was all the shouting about?' he asked anxiously.

'It's got nothing to do with you, get back to your homework,' his father answered.

'But I'm hungry, it's long past teatime.'

'There's something your mother and me 'ave to sort out first. It won't take long before tea's ready.'

51

Peter turned away, closing the door softly behind him.

Maisie sat down weakly at the table and Alice cowered away as her father strode towards her.

'I'm not goin' to hit you,' he said coldly. 'I simply want the truth. Whatever possessed you to break into that woman's house and steal things we have plenty of here?'

The tears started afresh and in some exasperation Maisie snapped, 'Stop snivelling, Alice, and answer your father! By the time that woman's done it'll be all round the town, so now stop your cryin' and tell us why you did it.'

'It was only a bit of fun, Mum, honestly. She's a horrible woman, she's allus shouting at us. We've only to cross the stile and she's out of the door yellin' at us.'

'Did you apologise to her?'

'Nay, the girl couldn't get a word in edgewise. Neither could I for that matter,' Tom said wryly.

'Ye'll get washed and go straight to bed,' Maisie decided. 'I'll bring some tea up to you later but I don't want to see you down here again tonight. You've caused enough disruption for one day.'

Tea was a silent meal with Peter looking uncomfortably from one parent to the other and Tom picking at his food in a deep study. In some exasperation Maisie jumped up from the table saying, 'I'm not hungry either. I'll take some food up to Alice and see what she's got to say for herself.'

Watched by the others she filled a plate with roast beef and Yorkshire pudding, mashed potatoes and vegetables, finishing with a large chunk of apple pie. Tom said gently, 'She'll not starve if she eats that lot. Still, it's my guess she'll be too upset to eat.'

'We'll have to see, won't we? I somehow don't think our Alice is as sorry as she makes out she is.'

Alice sat on her bed, her head burrowed into her pillow, her sobs audible from outside the room. Maisie

52

put the tray down on the side table and said sharply, 'Stop your crying, Alice, and eat your meal before it gets cold.'

'Don't want anythin', her daughter muttered.

'Just as you like, but if you don't eat this there'll be nothing else until breakfast.'

The girl struggled into a sitting position and eyed her mother balefully.

'What's got into you?' Maisie demanded. 'Stealing apples and gingerbread when you know we've plenty of our own – and to break into her kitchen like a common thief! I'm hearin' tales no worse than that at the courthouse – and what was all that about the Smithson boy, you and him in her barn?'

'We only went into her house for a bit of fun.'

'Stealing isn't fun, it's breaking and entry. Think yourself lucky she didn't call the police in. Now, what about that boy? What were you doing in the barn?'

Sulkily Alice answered, 'We weren't doin' anything wrong.'

'Were you smoking?' Maisie watched the rich red colour flood her daughter's face and she breathed a sigh of relief.

'He was,' Alice muttered. 'He gave me one but it tasted horrible. Honestly, Mother, that's all we were doin'.'

'Well, you can be sure that by morning it'll be all over Greymont. Your Aunt Mary'll be gloating and I'll have Mrs Pearson saying she doesn't want you to be friendly with her daughter any more. What am I going to say to people?'

'You don't care about me, you're only worried about what they'll think about you, a Lorivals girl and a JP.'

Maisie could quite cheerfully have slapped that small spiteful face, but then the tears started afresh and she said helplessly, 'I don't know what we're going to do with you, Alice. We've done our best for you. Why aren't you more like Peter? He never gives us any trouble.'

'It's always Peter, Peter, Peter. *He* never does anythin' wrong!'

'He works hard, he's got ambition, but what sort of ambition have you got? What sort of job are you going to get when you're old enough to go out to work – and what sort of man'll want to marry a girl who steals from other people? Now eat your meal and stop sniffling. Your father and I are going to have a serious talk about you.'

With that Maisie went to the window and drew the curtains sharply, shutting out the night. She would have been surprised to see the small secretive smile on her daughter's face only minutes after she'd closed her bedroom door, and the glee with which she picked up her tray and started to eat.

Peter was back in the living room finishing his homework and Tom was stacking the dishes into the sink when she returned to the kitchen. He gave her a questioning glance but she ignored it, saying, 'I'll do the dishes, Tom. You stoke up the fire before you take a look round. We're going to have to have a proper talk about Alice. Something's got to be done.'

'They'll forget to gossip about her when somethin' else comes along,' he said gently.

'Can you see our Bob's wife forgetting to talk about it? Mary and those sisters of hers'll revel in it. Then there's mi mam and dad – they're too old to have somethin' like this to worry about.'

Tom said nothing as he applied himself to stoking up the fire and for what seemed an eternity silence reigned in the kitchen apart from the dishes clattering in the sink and the loud ticking of the clock on the wall.

Maisie heard him going out on his last rounds of the day and after putting the dishes away she covered the

54

white-topped table with its red chenille cloth, restored the vase of flowers to the centre of the table and sat waiting for him to return, her work basket beside her.

There was a jagged tear in Alice's plaid skirt. Climbing fences, Maisie had no doubt, or trees, and there were two buttons off her blouse. She was surely old enough to sew buttons on for herself. Maisie looked ruefully at the tapestry cushion cover she had started and longed to finish. Somehow or other there were always too many things to mend instead of working on the cushion, and it was such a pretty design of birds and flowers.

She couldn't settle. She walked through the living room, where Peter's head was bent studiously over his books. She went first of all to Lucy's room, where her daughter's teddy bear slept serenely in the narrow, empty bed. Maisie was relieved that her youngest child was staying overnight with a neighbour and had missed the unpleasant scenes at home. When Maisie went to Alice's room to retrieve the tray, she noted with grim satisfaction that the plates had been wiped clean.

'Are you awake, Alice?' she whispered, but there was no response from the still form on the bed and Maisie turned away. Quite evidently her daughter didn't have a guilty conscience about her morning's work. She'd eaten a good meal and was sleeping innocently in her bed and Tom would shy away from anything he thought of as trouble.

He wasn't normally out so long and she hoped nothing was wrong. Foxes were a nuisance and there had been intruders at Lower Meadow Farm. She began to worry, for what match would Tom be for a gang of hooligans from the town? She put the kettle on and stood at the kitchen window waiting for it to boil, more than relieved when she saw him walking across the yard, his face staring at the cobbles, not bothering to look up until he reached the door, then seeing her at the window he smiled and raised his hand.

He had hardly got settled in front of the fire when Maisie said firmly, 'We've got to talk about Alice, Tom. It isn't something we can brush under the carpet.'

'It's a child's trick, love. Didn't you ever pinch the odd flower out of somebody else's garden?'

'I did not! Mi mother'd have killed me. We've gone wrong somewhere, love, but the thing is, what are we going to do now? She'll not do well at school and I shudder to think what's facing her when she leaves.'

'That's a long time off, Maisie.'

'I know that but she doesn't take any notice of anything I tell her. She needs firmer discipline but I don't know what the answer is.'

Tom remained silent, stirring the tea she had placed in front of him, his face thoughtful, and she felt if he didn't say something soon she'd scream. Unable to accept his silence any longer she snapped, 'You've always left the children to me, Tom. It was all right with Peter, but it isn't all right with Alice, don't you see that?'

'I can see you've made up your mind something's got to be done.'

'Yes, but what?'

'We could send her to Lorivals, providin' they'd take her.'

She stared at her husband aghast. 'Lorivals! You must be mad! We haven't got that sort of money and even if we had, she'd never want to go. She's always throwin' out snide remarks because mi father paid for me to go there. She calls the girls there snobs and she'd never want to board out. You're not serious, are you?'

'I'm very serious. We've a bit of money put by. I can allow the hunt to ride across the bottom fields and I can let one of the meadows for a showground – heaven knows, they've bin after one for years. It'll all bring in extra money so you needn't worry yourself about the fees.'

'What will the family say? You can imagine dear Mary's reaction for a start.'

'It's got nothin' to do with her, nor with the rest of them for that matter. Now, they might take her after Christmas. You could always ask that woman you've become friendly with at the court – isn't she the headmistress?'

'Yes. I suppose I could mention it to Miss Waddington.'

'That's settled, then. Alice goes to Lorivals whether she likes it or not.'

'We should be spending this money on Peter. He deserves it more than she does.'

'He's clever enough to get by on his own, and if he doesn't there's always the farm.'

'He's no interest in the farm.'

'It's possible to find an interest in somethin' when it's your bread and butter, love.'

Maisie cleared the teacups off the table and started to rinse them, her face thoughtful, unsure, and seeing it Tom decided to change the subject.

'I'll be having a word with Sir Mark soon about that land of his over at Ellwood. It's time he made his mind up about it.'

'You won't be able to afford it, Tom.'

'No, I don't want it but I might be able to persuade him to work it himself, then with a bit of luck he might pay me for managing it.'

'He already has an estate manager.'

'Who knows precious little about farmin'.'

'It just seems to me that we're havin' to alter our entire way of life to suit our Alice. All you can talk about is changin' this and that and assumin' it'll all fall into place. Suppose it doesn't and we're left with a rope round our necks – Alice at Lorivals and not enough money to pay her fees.'

'You talk as if we're paupers, love.'

'I know we're not, but most of it's tied up in the farm and the farm's for all of us, not just Alice.'

57

'Leave it be, Maisie. Alice goes to Lorivals and let me worry about the farm.'

She broached the subject to Miss Waddington when they met in the courthouse the following week and immediately the headmistress sensed her distress. A wise woman, she was accustomed to parents betraying their worries regarding their daughters but she left it to Maisie to confide in her without any prompting.

Out came the story of the stolen apples and gingerbread and a little shame-facedly Maisie added, 'I'm so busy on the farm that perhaps I haven't watched over her like I should have done.'

Sympathetically Miss Waddington said, 'Girls are complex creatures. Many of them go through a period of rebellion, with the need to draw attention to themselves. I think it will do Alice good to join us at Lorivals.'

'She's going to cost us a great deal of money and we have two other children. The farm was badly run down when Tom's father handed it over. He had a lot of debts Tom didn't know about at the time but they've been paid off thanks to our hard work and we're just beginning to see daylight. We need to spend money on the farmhouse but if Alice is going to go to Lorivals that'll have to wait a while.'

'Well, we don't usually take girls after the start of the academic year in September but I'm prepared to fit her in after the New Year. I'm sure she'll soon settle down.'

Maisie was considerably less sure but Tom told her she was worrying needlessly and Alice accepted her news with sulky silence.

CHAPTER 5

Alice stood in the kitchen wearing her new gabardine coat and grey felt hat; her face was mutinous, her eyes stormy, and Maisie looked her over anxiously to check that her daughter's red hair was tied back decorously by its black ribbon and that her shoes were polished to perfection.

'We'd better get off, then,' she said, 'before the snow starts. The forecast wasn't good.'

Tom picked up Alice's case and put an arm round her shoulders. 'You look very nice, love. You'll be the prettiest girl at that posh school of yours.' Alice merely shrugged herself free and Maisie gave him a warning look.

Tom decided against giving his daughter a farewell embrace, and stood in the yard waving them off. They drove in silence, and all the time Maisie was conscious of the girl's set face beside her, but at least there had been no tantrums that morning.

The sky was threatening, and dark clouds tumbled across the Pennines. For much of the journey she drove behind a lorry throwing salt and grit on the road and she could feel her tyres crunching through the stuff.

At last the tall wrought-iron gates of Lorivals stood before them, and the long drive up to the school. Maisie felt like a girl again; on that first day of term she had come along this same path with her father in his ancient Morris. Then, the terraces and steps had been crowded with girls but this morning there was no sign of life except the solitary figure of a gardener brushing leaves from the steps.

Nothing in the great entrance hall had changed. Brigadier Sir Algernon Lorival's portrait still occupied the place of honour at the head of the first flight of stairs, and there was an all-too-familiar smell of floor polish.

Right on time, Miss Waddington came running lightly down the stairs and greeted Maisie with a smile. She eyed Alice with a degree of sympathy and said, 'Welcome to Lorivals, Alice! I know you'll be happy here.'

Alice made no reply and her mother said anxiously, 'She's a little tearful this morning, Miss Waddington. It's natural, I suppose. I know I felt exactly the same.'

'Of course, she's bound to miss you but I'm sure she'll soon make friends and adapt to new ways. Do you have time for a cup of tea?'

'No, I must get back. It looks like snow and I've so much to do at home.'

'Then Alice will see you off and I'll wait for her in the common room, which is just along there.'

Alice walked with her mother to the car and Maisie embraced her with tears in her eyes, feeling her daughter's withdrawal, hurt by the cool remote smile on the pretty closed-in face.

She held Alice's thin childish body against her for several minutes, then anxiously she said, 'I do hope you'll be happy, darling. It's meant to be for your own good. We'll be thinking about you and praying for you. It'll soon be half-term and you can come home and spend it at the farm.'

Alice didn't speak. Instead she watched her mother's sad face crumple into tears and then Maisie was in the car driving through a mist towards the gates. For several minutes Alice watched her, then she turned and walked back to the school. Maisie would have been astonished if she could have seen the bright confident smile on her daughter's face and the way she ran lightly up the steps.

Inside the front door she allowed her gaze to fall again on the carved curving staircase and the rich panelling, on the leaded window panes and softly gleaming floor, then she walked briskly across and let herself into the common room.

She made herself smile tremulously at Miss Waddington, who was standing looking through the window, and the headmistress smiled in return. She wasn't quite sure what to make of this girl who one minute had been confidently striding across the terrace yet who now managed to look so pathetic. She decided to keep her reservations to herself until she'd had a degree of time to observe Alice Standing. Maybe she had been putting on a brave front for her mother's benefit, maybe she really was a lost sad young girl making the best of a new environment, but the teacher wasn't sure. Alice had not quite had time to wipe that self-satisfied smirk off her face before it changed to one of sad acceptance.

'You'll be sharing with three other girls, Alice. I suggested to your mother that she brought you immediately after lunch as I thought it might seem a little over-facing to throw you in with pupils who have known each other since the end of last September. Term began yesterday and they are in class at the moment so I suggest you go up to the dormitory, get unpacked and come down for three-thirty when the girls change classrooms. You'll be able to meet them and have tea, then you can go into class with them.'

'Thank you, Miss Waddington.' Alice picked up her case and followed her out of the room.

'I'll have your trunk sent up to you later,' Miss Waddington said. 'I take it that case contains all you will need for tonight?'

'Yes. My mother packed for me, she said it would be like this.'

Miss Waddington smiled. 'I do hope you get along well with your room-mates; I believe your mother kept in touch with hers.'

Alice smiled but remained silent. What was keeping in touch? Her mother received a Christmas card from Sir Mark and Lady Garveston, Mr and Mrs Martin Walton and Nancy Graham every year, and occasionally she received a letter from Nancy and talked about it for days on end. If that was all keeping in touch meant, Alice would make her own friends at Lorivals – and they wouldn't necessarily be the girls with whom she roomed.

The bedroom was small and overlooked the vegetable plot at the side of the school. Alice supposed that the rich girls with handles to their names had the better rooms at the front of the house. Like Maisie had told her, it contained four narrow beds covered by pretty floral bedspreads, four chairs and four single wardrobes. Her lip curled with disdain at the sight of a teddy bear on one bed and a fluffy tiger on another.

She hadn't brought any of her childhood toys. From today onwards she was going to be a new Alice; she'd be a match for any girl here, never the tame little mouse her mother had been, afraid because she thought everybody was better than she was.

She unpacked her nightdress and the dressing gown her mother had made for her, and by the time she'd put the contents of her case inside the empty wardrobe a middle-aged man appeared carrying her trunk.

'If you'll unpack, miss, I'll take yer trunk down to the cellar out of yer way,' he said with a smile. 'We don't often get girls comin' in at this time o' year.'

Alice smiled politely as she unlocked her trunk and he said, 'I'll be back in fifteen minutes, miss.'

Inside the trunk were skirts and blouses, all labelled by Maisie, cotton underwear and sports gear which had cost her father a bonny penny, and packed at the bottom was a tuckbox filled with biscuits and sweets, Maisie's home-made fruit loaf and a selection of small cakes. Alice took out an almond slice and bit into it

with her sharp white teeth; she decided that here was
the start of her popularity. She doubted if any of the
other girls would have a mother who could bake like
hers.

Promptly at three-thirty she heard the bell and made
her way down to the small hall where the girls took
tea. She could hear the sound of many voices, laughter
and crockery and she entered the room unobserved
because everybody seemed to be sitting around in
groups chattering like magpies.

For a moment she hesitated at the door then, pluck-
ing up courage, she approached the long table where
two women in white overalls were dispensing tea and
scones.

One of them looked up and grinned. 'Well, what's it
to be love – tea and scones, or tea and fruit loaf?'

'Tea and scones, please.'

'Well, come along then. Mind you don't spill the tea
– I've put too much milk in it.'

Alice took the cup of tea and the plate with two
scones on it, then turned and observed the room.
Nobody had noticed her but just then Miss Waddington
came through the door, and Alice thought she'd never
been more glad to see anybody in her entire life.

'Come with me, my dear,' the headmistress said
cheerfully. 'Your room-mates are sitting near the window, I'll introduce you.'

Girls were staring at her now as she followed Miss
Waddington towards the little group by the window.
They looked up expectantly and Miss Waddington announced, 'This is Alice Standing, girls. She's been
placed in Room Sixteen so do make friends and see
that she settles in well.'

With a brief smile all round she left Alice to take her
place at the table with the others, who moved closer
together to make room for her.

'I'm Joanne Proctor,' said a plump girl with a pretty,

63

well-scrubbed face and a smear of strawberry jam on her chin. 'You're in my dorm and Miss Eaves has put me in charge because I'm the eldest. This is Margaret Sharp and this is Monica Darwin.'

The girls eyed her warily and if they took stock of Alice she certainly took stock of them.

Margaret Sharp was small and pale. Her fine mousy hair was drawn back from her face and held in place by a large tortoiseshell slide. She wore spectacles through which she eyed Alice solemnly before extending a thin pale hand.

Monica Darwin was considerably taller and lanky in build. She had dark frizzy hair which she had endeavoured to tame with innumerable kirby grips and Alice was already thinking that none of her room-mates was remarkable either for beauty or style.

'Why didn't you come in September like all the others?' Joanne demanded.

'It wasn't convenient. I got permission to come after Christmas.'

'What part of the country do you come from?' Joanne then asked.

'From this part. Just a few miles from here, as a matter of fact.'

'So you'll know the Garveston twins, then?'

Ignoring that particular question Alice said confidently, 'My mother roomed with Lady Garveston when she was here. There were five of them altogether.'

'Then your mother'll know Nancy Graham. She roomed with Amelia Garveston too.'

'Of course, she's my mother's best friend. They were friends even before they came here.'

'You mean she actually visits?'

'Not a lot these days, as she's always abroad, but she writes and Mother writes back to her all the time. I remember seeing her when I was little, but Mother never talks about their other room-mate Lois Brampton

64

– there's some big mystery about her. As for Barbara Walton, the fifth one, she lives in Cheltenham.'

'What sort of mystery?' Margaret breathed with wide curious eyes.

'Like I said, she doesn't talk about it. Lady Garveston's a JP like my mother and she's always around at the local shows.'

'The shows?' the girls echoed in unison.

'Why yes. The agricultural shows. My father owns most of the land around here so naturally we have to attend the shows. It gets awfully boring but it's expected of us.'

Alice was warming to her subject and Joanne said sharply, 'Pippa Garveston's over there, but her sister's still at home with a chill.'

'Oh dear.'

'We're all in the same form. Pippa's much cleverer than her sister and she's nicer. We all think Berenice is stuck-up.'

'Are you clever?' Margaret demanded suddenly.

'Not clever enough for my mother, that's why she's had me sent here.'

'I got an A in chemistry and maths and Joanne's good at history. Monica's in the hockey team.'

'Do you play any games?' Joanna asked.

'Not any of the games you play.'

'What do you mean by that?'

'Well, I don't play hockey or tennis but I suppose I can always learn.'

'I'll be able to tell if you'll be any good,' Monica said importantly.

Alice was saved from further interrogation by the school bell and Joanne whispered, 'We're going into the art class now. I suppose you'll be coming with us?'

'I suppose so.'

They got up from the table and started to walk towards the door. As she neared the area occupied by

Pippa Garveston and her friends their eyes met, and Alice smiled. In a carrying voice she said, 'I'm Alice Standing. My mother was here with your mother and she said I should introduce myself to you.'

Pippa smiled and extended a slim brown hand. Alice was immediately struck by the girl's resemblance to Amelia. She had the same creamy skin and soft shining hair, the same patrician grace. In a low voice Pippa said, 'How do you do, Alice. I hope you will be happy here.'

Unabashed Alice shrugged her shoulders and said, 'I can get used to anything.'

If Pippa was surprised by the brashness of her response she didn't show it but waited for Alice to pass in front of her then joined her own friends in their walk to the Art Room.

Pippa wasn't at all sure that she and the newcomer would become friends despite their mothers' bond. There was something vaguely aggressive in Alice's bearing, something hostile, and Pippa hoped she would quickly make some friends and not expect too much from her.

Fundamentally kind, she was ashamed of her recoil from the new girl. After all, Amelia and Maisie had roomed together at Lorivals. However, even as she pondered this, Pippa was becoming increasingly aware of Alice's voice, stridently louder and more confident than the voices of the room-mates she had only just met.

CHAPTER 6

Maisie had long since decided that there was nothing worse than lying sleepless in bed listening to the clock striking downstairs, the rustling of branches against the window and her husband's steady breathing on the pillow beside her.

She eased herself gently out of bed and shrugged her arms into the sleeves of her dressing gown, then tiptoed across the room and carefully opened the door. Moonlight came through the landing window and with a finger to her mouth she quickly silenced the two dogs that padded across to meet her in the kitchen.

Tom had always spoiled Alice, and yet he could sleep like a baby while she lay awake staring up at the ceiling, worried out of her mind. Maisie was remembering her first night at Lorivals, the heartache and tears, the homesickness and desolation, and Alice had been so antagonistic about going there. She imagined her daughter lying in her narrow bed, her pillow wet with tears, trying desperately to stifle her sobs.

Maisie walked across to the window and pulled back the curtains. Frost shimmered on the rooftops, and somewhere in the night an owl hooted mournfully, followed by the insistent barking of a fox. The dogs moved to the door, growling in their throats, and she silenced them with a sharp word before putting the kettle on top of the Aga to boil.

She made herself a cup of coffee and took it with her into the living room then, after stirring the dying embers in the grate, she sat in one of the deep armchairs to drink it.

She didn't hear the door open and when Tom gently touched her hair she looked up, startled.

'Oh Tom, I'm sorry I disturbed you,' she said plaintively. 'I was so careful not to make a noise.'

'What are you doing here? The room's cold – why aren't you asleep?'

'I keep thinking about Alice. She'll be crying herself to sleep up at Lorivals, I just know she will, like I did.'

'She's a lot tougher than ever you were, Maisie, and it's time you realized it.'

'Well, of course she isn't. I was ten when I went to Lorivals, which is young to be torn away from home and family. Alice will be desolate.'

'Look, love, there's dozens of girls at that school who've had to get used to leavin' home – our Alice isn't the only one. She'll soon make friends and settle down. I don't think it's worth spendin' all the night worryin' about her and catchin' your death of cold into the bargain. Come back to bed, it'll all look a lot better in the mornin'.'

'I'll come up in a few minutes, Tom. I just want to sit here for a while and finish my coffee. You go, you've to be up early.'

With a shake of his head he left her and Maisie sat back in her chair sipping her coffee.

The morning paper lay unopened on the table and she reached out and turned it over to read the headlines. Nancy Graham's face stared out at her from some town in Central Africa where dust hung heavily on the air from buildings recently bombarded by gunfire. The people standing around her looked dejected and desolate.

Bob had always thought a lot of Nancy, gently teasing her, calling her his 'Nancy of the laughing face', but there was no laughter in it now. Nancy's hair was tied back from her face and the black and white photograph had failed to capture the gold in it. She was wearing

68

casual trousers and a cotton shirt with the sleeves rolled high above slender elbows but Maisie was remembering her eyes – wide-spaced candid eyes as startlingly blue as the tarn on a summer's day.

It was all so far away and long ago, those walks through the park on their way home from junior school. Laughter had come easily then, but there had been squabbles too, mostly with Barbara who strode off across the grass, her back rigid with indignation, her dark hair restrained by its ribbons swinging around her slender shoulders and her long legs beating a steady tattoo as she went towards the gate. Maisie recalled how proudly Barbara had allowed Martin Walton to take her satchel and carry it with his own, and how she and Nancy had giggled in their wake.

Maisie had always supposed those days would go on forever, growing up in Greymont, marrying local boys. They would be guests at each other's weddings, godmothers to each other's children, even grow old together – but Lorivals had changed all that. With Lorivals had come Amelia Urquart and Lois Brampton.

Nothing had gone as she'd imagined it would. Barbara hardly ever came back to Greymont in spite of the fact that her parents remained here. Lois had tragically taken her own life in that house she shared with Nancy and two other girls in London, and if Nancy knew why she had done it she had remained maddeningly silent.

Maisie picked up her empty cup and placed it on the tray before carrying it into the kitchen. Thomas, the largest of the house cats, sat on the rug staring at her with large unblinking eyes, which then fastened themselves on a spot just over her shoulder. She shuddered delicately, wishing he wouldn't do that. Her mother had always maintained that animals saw things humans didn't, and one of the dogs had a nasty habit of wagging his tail and leaping up as if he was greeting someone when there was nobody there. Tonight of all nights Maisie didn't want to be bothered by abnormalities.

The bedroom felt cold but for a few minutes she stood at the window staring out across the frozen fields glistening under a midnight-blue sky studded with stars. Suddenly she was filled with a deep sense of pride. As far as she could see this was Tom's land, on which he'd worked since his father had handed it over soon after their wedding. It was good land, and the better for Tom's hard work. There'd been bad times and good times but she'd never had reason to doubt that loving him and wanting to spend the rest of her life with him had been the right choice. Tom was the rock on which she'd built her life; what did it matter that Amelia, safe in her role as mistress of Garveston Hall, could flash her that cool remote smile and then forget about her. Tom was worth a hundred Mark Garvestons, boasting about his beautiful home and vast acres paid for and maintained by Amelia's money.

Nor did she hanker for the sort of life Barbara had, with a man obsessed by fast cars and boats and foreign travel with the so-called jet set. If anything happened to Tom she at least would have her children, but who and what would Barbara have? Maisie refused even to think about Nancy, moving from one war-torn area to another. A woman's life was never meant to be like that; men went to war, didn't they, and the women stayed at home to welcome them back. Wasn't that the normal way of things?

She crept between the sheets, grateful for the smooth feel of them and the warmth of Tom's body beside her and the sound of his steady breathing. She prayed silently for God's mercy on all those she loved, and especially Alice.

Across the lonely silver fells Lorivals stood in isolated splendour, surrounded by its forest and circled by the river under its shallow coating of frost. The windows were all in darkness, except for one at the side on the second floor, and Maisie would have been astounded if she could have seen inside that room.

Alice sat with her room-mates on her bed and between them stood her well-stocked tuckbox into which they were dipping with muted squeals of delight. Shortbread and currant slices, jammy doughnuts and apple tarts disappeared with greedy enjoyment, and all the time Alice regaled them with stories of her life at home – stories she embroidered to suit her audience.

'Why exactly was it you didn't come here last September?' persisted Joanne, after swallowing her last portion of doughnut.

Alice launched herself readily into a romanticised version of the stolen apples from a woman she described as the village witch. The three other girls hung on to her words with wide eyes and bated breath.

Joanne was the toughest and most practical of the three, and until that day she'd been the ringleader, so she wasn't entirely in agreement with this new girl coming along with her high-falutin' stories and cocky ways, but at least she was generous with the goodies her mother had packed for her.

The other two were firing questions about the witch and, nothing loath, Alice was describing witches dancing out on the fells, broomsticks and black cats – indeed all the things she had read about witchcraft in Lancashire from a book she'd acquired in the public library and which she and Mary Pearson had read with breathless anticipation sheltering from the rain one afternoon in the barn.

'That's ridiculous,' Joanne said firmly. 'There are no such things as witches. They belong to the Dark Ages – nobody would be allowed to be a witch now.'

'That's just where you're wrong,' Alice said defiantly. 'There were witches up at Pendle and they were all hanged in Lancaster Prison. And don't think they all died out, as they had relatives who spread themselves all over the country and Mrs Edge is one of them. She has black beady eyes that can make you feel awful and she would put a curse on you as soon as look at you.'

'Why didn't she put a curse on you, then?' Monica asked sharply.

'She did. I didn't want to come to Lorivals. I wanted to go anywhere but here, yet here I am so that just goes to prove things, doesn't it?'

'I think I feel sick,' Margaret Sharp said plaintively and Joanne snapped, 'It serves you right, you ate all the apple pie. Have a glass of water and go to bed.'

Alice folded tissue paper over what was left in the box, then with a satisfied smile she said, 'There'll be enough for tomorrow, but I can always ask my mother to send more. She bakes every week.'

'We're not allowed to have tuckboxes every week,' Joanne demurred.

'That's all right. Yours have to come by post or when your parents visit, but I can always meet Mum on the fell somewhere.'

She put the tuckbox back in her wardrobe and kicking off her slippers snuggled into bed while Joanne went to put out the light. Perhaps Lorivals wouldn't be so bad after all. Margaret and Monica were already her friends and she could handle Joanne. A self-satisfied smile spread over Alice's face; she felt at least ten years older than any of them. She hadn't thought it would be so easy.

CHAPTER 7

Jimmy Jayson straightened his tie, removed an invisible speck from the sleeve of his new sportscoat and surveyed himself in the mirror with complete satisfaction.

He was a pretty good-looking chap, he assured himself. Tall, with not an ounce of superfluous fat – which came from keeping fit at the gymnasium twice a week – and shining mahogany-coloured hair in direct contrast to the startling blue of his eyes.

Getting all dressed up to walk on the fell hadn't been his idea of the best way of spending his half-day. Before the advent of Deirdre Forsythe into his life he'd have spent it in Lancaster or Kendal in the winter and Morecambe in the summer. He liked the summer best when girls from all over the country were on holiday and looking for a good time. He'd made his choice from girls giggling in bars, strolling on the promenade or hanging about the pleasure ground. He had money in his pocket, a nice car and most of them had been over the moon about being invited out by such a presentable guy. Fortunately, he'd always emerged from these encounters heart-whole and eager for more.

He'd never met anybody quite like Deirdre before. She had such style, she could look like a queen in a pair of old slacks and a cotton shirt with her dark hair blowing in the wind and those long slender legs that seemed to go on forever. She'd come into the shop very late one day, asking for French mustard of all things. Luckily he'd had some, and she'd said airily, 'How nice to find a shop that stocks this variety. I was just passing, I only tried on the off-chance. I'll be sure to shop here again.'

She'd favoured him with a brief remote smile and he'd gone to stand at the window to watch her climb into a low-slung sports car. That had been the start of it. She began to come into the shop once a week, then twice, then almost every day, then she'd go missing for a couple of weeks and return smiling and friendly, and like a welcoming puppy he'd be anxious to clear his shop of its customers so that they could chat.

Jimmy had been careful not to ask too many questions. He didn't want Deirdre to think he cared or even that he'd missed her, but he learned a great deal from those conversations. He knew that she was married and that her husband was often away from home; he knew that she was bored in spite of her coffee mornings and bridge parties, the Tennis Club and the Golf Club and he guessed that she was looking for something more exciting than chatting to a gaggle of women over the teacups.

He had intended closing the shop for a week last summer and she'd found him one day poring over road maps, planning his holiday. She'd enthused about the empty roads of Scotland and Northumberland, asking idly, 'Are you intending to go off on your own?'

'I haven't decided. I suppose I could pick up a pal from somewhere.'

He'd watched her long painted fingernail tracing a quiet road in the Highlands of Scotland. Casually she described a small hotel she knew in the region of Loch Maree and he listened to her voice extolling its beauty and its remoteness.

He wanted to ask her to go there with him but if she refused he'd feel a fool, so instead he put the maps away and started to talk about other things. It was Deirdre who asked casually, 'How long do you intend to be away?'

'I'm not closing the shop for more than a week. Mi father never closed it for longer.'

74

'I'll be so fed during August,' Deirdre said plaintively. John will be in America for about three weeks and it would be so nice to get away — if only for a few days.'

'Do you want to come with me, then?'

'I could meet you in Scotland and spend a few days with you. I have to be careful, though, Jimmy. I can't just set off in the car with you. It will need a great deal of thought.'

Now, looking back on those few days in Scotland he could only think of them as pure magic. Deirdre had arrived late on the Monday afternoon. They had sat at separate tables in the dining room and exchanged the usual impersonal smiles of holiday guests. After dinner she'd ignored him. She'd sat in a corner of the lounge with her head buried in a book, while he hovered uncertainly at the bar in a position where he could see her. Eventually she was joined by an elderly woman and her daughter. They'd chatted for what seemed hours, until with a little smile Deirdre had excused herself by saying she'd had a long drive and was a little tired, then she'd passed Jimmy on her way to her room with the briefest of smiles.

Peevishly he'd ordered another drink. If that was how she wanted to play it, it was all right with him! For the rest of the evening he'd drunk with anybody who came to the bar and it was very much later when he climbed the stairs to his room.

He was angry. He didn't like Scotland, damp cold place that it was with the mist hanging low on the hills and across the loch — even his room felt chilly. It was Deirdre's fault that he was here; he could have been some place where there was laughter and music instead of these stiff-necked guests who were only interested in walking and fishing. If Deirdre intended keeping this up he was going home next day.

The water in the bathroom was barely warm and angrily Jimmy thought if he'd known her room number he'd have made it his business to tell her enough was enough. Shivering, he dried himself. Even the water here was hard – it was pretty well impossible to get a lather! And so it was in this sulky frame of mind that he returned to his bedroom and found Deirdre sitting on the edge of his bed with a half-smile on her face.

At the sight of his striped pyjamas buttoned cosily to the neck she'd dissolved into laughter and he'd stared at her puzzled until she held out her hands and drew him towards her. 'You look so angry,' she said softly, 'like a little boy deprived of his sweets.'

'How did you know where to find me?' he asked grumpily.

'I looked in the register.'

'I'm surprised you bothered, as you've ignored me since you arrived.'

'I thought we agreed that this was to be a chance meeting, that neither of us knew the other. Surely you didn't expect me to greet you like an old friend!'

'A friend, yes. I didn't expect you to sit at your own table across the room and spend all evening chatting to old Mrs Worthing. And I didn't like the way you smiled at me – I felt like something the cat had brought in. What a waste of an evening.'

'I'm here now, Jimmy,' she said softly, 'and I promise tomorrow we'll become better acquainted. We'll talk and we'll go walking together.'

'Walking!'

'I don't want our fellow guests to think I'm some sort of predator on the look-out for a man to latch on to.'

Her voice was cajoling and sensuous, her hands as light as a butterfly against his skin as she disrobed him. Her body was a wild tempestuous thing in his embrace, but deep down she was an icicle; the real Deirdre remained strangely out of reach.

For the rest of their stay they kept to separate tables but walked together as though they had met casually along the road that edged the lake. Fellow guests smiled at them indulgently – two solitary people who for a few days felt capable of enjoying each other's company. When Deirdre drove home alone on the Friday morning Jimmy stood with the others waving her off, and the rest of the day found him prowling across the bracken on his own, angry and lonely.

He wouldn't admit even to himself that Maisie had been right – he *was* out of his depth with Deirdre Forsythe. There'd been girls before, snatched fumbling moments in the back of his car or under the pier on the soft sand, moments that had meant nothing to any of them, but this affair with Deirdre was different – *she* was different – and he feared that he meant as little to her as all those giggling young girls had meant to him.

He wasn't quite the fool his sister took him to be.

Now, after making sure that the shop door was locked and the shutters in place, he let himself out at the back where his new car was parked. His eyes lit up at the sight of the long sleek body. It was the sort of car that boys drooled over and girls looked at dreamily. He didn't like to think of the big hole it had made in his bank balance; it was sufficient that Deirdre leaned back against the soft leather upholstery with evident enjoyment. His mistress and the car were made for each other.

He drove up the winding lanes towards the fells and as he drove through the pale spring sunlight Jimmy's spirits brightened. The fells were beautiful at this time of year. A pair of curlews circled lazily in the sky above the tarn and there was peace in the harsh waving grass and new young bracken. Below him he could see the tall chimneys of Garveston Hall and smoke curling into the pale blue sky.

The lane petered out as it climbed the hill and he ran the car into a small clearing where he could already see Deirdre sitting in her car looking down pensively on the Hall. As he crossed the grass to meet her the spaniel sitting beside her started to bark and he wondered irritably why she always had to bring her dratted dog. A cover-up, he supposed, but he'd never been overfond of dogs.

'Thinking what it's like to live in a place like that?' he said, when she didn't turn her head to greet him.

'I was wondering what they did for servants. They must need them, and it's taken me weeks even to get a daily.'

'I shouldn't think they have any trouble. I've counted at least three gardeners working down there and I doubt that Her Ladyship does any housework.'

'Do they own all the land around these parts?'

'They own a great deal, but I reckon my brother-in-law owns the rest.'

'Your brother-in-law!'

'Yes, Tom Standing.'

'Is Maisie Standing your sister?'

'She is.'

'I didn't know that.'

'There's no reason why you should. I take it you know her, then.'

'Not well. John introduced us at a Magistrates' dinner she's small and plump with very pretty red hair.'

'That's our Maisie.'

'Why didn't you tell me?'

'Why should I? I don't see much of her and there's been no need to tell you anything about the family. Does it make any difference that she's my sister?'

Deirdre didn't answer him, but opened her car door and slid out of the seat. She was wearing slacks and a warm sweater with a silk scarf knotted round her neck, and Jimmy fell into step by her side, reflecting that Deirdre could look elegant in sackcloth and ashes.

The spaniel scampered ahead of them, almost tripping over his long curly ears, his head darting this way and that in search of anything that moved. Jimmy sensed constraint in the air but then Deirdre surprised him by asking, 'Wasn't your sister at school with Lady Garveston?'

'Yes, they were in the same dormitory, five of them.'

'So they're very good friends?'

'I wouldn't say that. I expect she had a say in getting our Maisie elected to the Bench, but they don't visit if that's what you mean. I think Maisie was asked up to the Hall once several years ago, but the Garvestons do sit on one or two committees connected with agriculture.' That was the moment when Jimmy suddenly realized they were not alone on the fell. A girl had been sitting on a crag and on seeing them she jumped to her feet, waving her school scarf in her hand. At first Jimmy didn't recognize her, then muttering under his breath he said, 'Damn, it's young Alice.'

'Who?' Deirdre demanded.

'My niece, Maisie's eldest girl. What's she doin' up here on her own? She should be in school.'

The girl was coming forward to meet them, a smile on her pretty face, her eyes immediately assessing her uncle's companion. Jimmy said sharply, 'What are you doin' up here, young Alice? Shouldn't you be in school?'

'I've had a virus,' she explained brightly. 'Matron said as it was a fine day I could go for a nice long walk and get some fresh air. Mother doesn't know, because Matron said there was nothin' to worry about.'

She looked from one to the other of them and Jimmy said hesitantly, 'This is Mrs Forsythe. We met on the fell where she was walking with her dog.'

'I thought you always went into town on your half-day?' Alice said innocently.

'Well, today I felt like a walk.'

The spaniel had returned to them and Alice bent to pat him. Jimmy said, 'So how's Lorivals, then? I've not seen your mother for some time so I've been unable to ask her.'

'It's all right.'

'Made friends, have you?'

'Some.'

Their conversation was spasmodic but all the time he could feel his niece's eyes shifting from him to Deirdre and back again, and to his annoyance Deirdre said coolly, 'Well, you go ahead and chat to your niece, Mr Jayson. I'll be getting back. Come, Jonty.'

She favoured them both with a brief smile and set off in the direction she'd come with the spaniel darting on ahead.

'She's pretty,' Alice commented.

'Yes, I suppose she is.'

'You can catch her up if you hurry,' she said precociously. She grinned at him, and Jimmy suddenly realized that for all her tender years this niece of his was very wide awake.

'I suppose you'll be telling your mother you've seen me up here, then Aunt Mary'll be informed and all those sisters of hers. Are you going to be responsible for all that, young Alice?'

'Not if you don't want them to know.'

He took out his wallet and extracted a five-pound note. 'I suppose there'll be somethin' to spend this on?' he said, handing it to her.

She nodded, and he watched her tuck it into the pocket of her coat, then with a bright smile she said, 'I'll walk with you to the stile, Uncle Jimmy, then I'd better get back. Matron said I could stay out for a couple of hours, that's all.'

'Shouldn't you be going straight back?'

'I can walk along the road to the gates, it's better than across the fell.'

They set off side by side. There was no sign of Deirdre and he wondered if she'd already reached her car and driven off or if she would wait for him. At the stile Alice said brightly, 'I'll be goin' now, Uncle Jimmy. I reckon she'll be waitin' for you.'

With a gay wave of her hand she set off up the lane while he turned in search of Deirdre. He found her sitting on a bank half a mile on, and as soon as he looked into her eyes he felt that something had changed. He said anxiously, 'That was rotten luck, love, but Alice won't say anything. We're good pals, me and Alice.'

'I suppose you gave her some money.'

'Well, naturally, I'm the girl's uncle! I always see that she's got a bit of pocket money whenever I see her.'

'But not hush money.'

'What does that mean?'

'I don't think we should be seen together after this, at least not for a while, and I shan't be coming into the shop quite so much.'

'That's ridiculous, Deirdre. Alice is only a child, and she's not going to say anything. It was your suggestion that we came up here on the fell, remember. We'd have been a lot better taking a drive somewhere.'

'I've too much to lose, Jimmy.'

'You don't seem to have given that much thought before.'

'I know, it was stupid of me and very reckless. When I saw that young girl looking at me today I realized what it would be like if ever John found out. Suppose she tells her mother she's seen us together, particularly when I'm likely to be meeting Mrs Standing at some function or other.'

'Maisie's not my keeper.'

'I know, but I don't want to have any guilty feelings when I meet her. I don't want her thinking I'm a bad wife and feeling sorry for John.'

'Be honest, Deirdre. You're ambitious to be seen with the right people. You want to hobnob with the

Garvestons and such-like, and you're afraid Maisie might put a spoke in your wheel.'

'I'm not thinking on those lines at all. I simply think I've behaved very foolishly, so foolishly that my entire future might have been threatened.'

'So this is the end of it?'

'I'm awfully fond of you, Jimmy. I'm not going to stop shopping with you but I am going to cool it a little. I don't think I should call in quite so often or spend half-days in your company. Please see it my way, Jimmy, I have far more to lose than you have.'

He didn't answer. Instead, he stood on one side waiting for her to get into her car, then he watched her drive away. Rage consumed him, rage because Maisie'd been right, rage with Alice for being out on the fell when she should have been in school, and rage with himself for being such an arrogant fool. Then he went to stand near his car, kicking one of the tyres savagely as if this act alone compensated for hurt pride and shattered illusions. He got into the driver's seat and slowly eased the long body of the car into the lane. He drove swiftly down the hillside but had the presence of mind to slow down when he spied a police car parked at the bottom of the slope. Suddenly his anger left him, and a sort of grim amusement took its place. There was still time for him to drive into Lancaster for a meal. He knew one or two girls there – perhaps one of them would be pleased to see him . . .

Alice swung briskly along the road feeling happy and at peace with the world. Her hands curled around the note in her pocket and a small secretive smile hovered round her mouth. The virus had lasted roughly a day and after that she'd felt fine even though she had spun out the debility for Matron's benefit.

Lorivals was all right. She'd been invited to spend Easter at the home of Monica Darwin in Essex although she'd yet to ask her parents if she could go, and Joanne had hinted that they might spend the summer holidays with her parents in their villa in Brittany. She'd made the hockey team after the games mistress had discovered she was a hard hitter and a good runner, and she'd done well in the pool, grateful that her father had insisted that she and Peter had learned to swim at a very early age.

Alice was so filled with her own importance that she failed to see Sir Mark Garveston bearing down on her on his big bay horse and she had to leap into the bushes quickly while his horse shied nervously and almost threw him. He favoured her with an angry frown before asking curtly, 'Are you all right?'

She nodded her head and he said sharply, 'Surely you saw me coming! You shouldn't have been walking in the middle of the road.'

'I'm sorry,' Alice stammered in a whisper.

'Be on your way then,' he said haughtily, then pacifying his nervous horse he cantered down the lane leaving her staring after him. For several minutes she stood at the edge of the road while she regained her breath and her composure, then instead of continuing her journey she climbed the stile, and maintaining a safe distance, made her way to where a circle of crags stood high on the fell. Here she sat on the grass with a rock against her back and watched Sir Mark dismount from his horse and go to stand near the old Pilgrims' Cross looking in the direction of the town.

Neither Sir Mark nor Alice had long to wait. A woman was climbing up the hillside, raising her hand to wave when she saw him near the Cross and Alice knew immediately that this was not Lady Garveston. She couldn't remember having seen her before. She was tall, slender and elegant in a slim tweed skirt and soft leather jacket, her short dark hair blew freely in the wind and she walked with long graceful strides until she reached his side, then he held out his arms and she walked naturally into them.

It seemed to Alice that their embrace lasted forever but at last he released her, then taking her hand in one of his and the reins of his horse in the other he led them both up the hill and over the crest.

Alice sprang to her feet hardly able to contain her excitement. Now she knew something that would wipe the superior smile off Berenice Garveston's snooty face. She didn't like either of the Garveston twins, but she disliked Berenice the most. Pippa did manage to smile when they met in the corridor, but her sister stayed aloof. They might have come from different ends of the earth rather than the same area, and their mothers might have been complete strangers instead of old schoolfriends. Sooner or later Alice would make them pay for ignoring her: the weapon was here in her hands.

Maisie brushed Lucy's fine corn-silk hair until it shone. Satisfied, she tied it back with a crisp blue ribbon the colour of her party dress and with a little push she said, 'Go look in the mirror, love. You look so pretty.'

Lucy complied happily, turning round so that she could see the back of her dress in the long cheval mirror, then Maisie held out her hand saying, 'We'd better get going, love, or we'll be the last to arrive.'

As they walked down the stairs she went on, 'I'll be calling for you about five o'clock. Mrs Abbot said it would all be over by then. Have you got your present for Jenny?'

Lucy ran across to the settle and picked up a gaily wrapped parcel. They were letting themselves out of the front door when Maisie heard the telephone shrilling urgently in the hall. For a few seconds she hesitated, then with a sigh of annoyance she said, 'You go along to the car, love. I'll see who this is.'

She was surprised to hear Miss Waddington's voice at the other end of the telephone, and her first thought was to ask if there was anything the matter with Alice.

'No, she's perfectly all right, Mrs Standing. I don't want you to worry but I wonder if you could find the time to call in at the school to see me within the next few days.'

'Can't you tell me what's wrong?'

'It isn't something I wish to discuss on the telephone. Now, what time will suit you next week?'

Miss Waddington had asked her not to worry but she couldn't help it. At the court the headmistress called her Maisie, and the mere fact that she had addressed her as Mrs Standing now seemed decidedly sinister.

They'd been so sure that Alice had settled down well. She'd made new friends and in the one compulsory letter she wrote home every week she was enthusiastic about the hockey team, and had requested a tennis racket for her birthday.

For two long days Maisie agonied about the reason for that call. She didn't want to worry Tom as it was his busiest time of the year – hers too, for that matter – and on top of it all Lucy had caught a bad cold at Jenny Abbot's birthday party and had a fever. It worried Maisie to see Tom arriving home so tired he fell asleep night after night in his chair as soon as the meal was over, or at the table nodding over his account books. There was no way she was going to ask Tom to go with her to Lorivals, and all the time she drove alone along the quiet country lanes to the school Maisie thought she would be driving back with Alice sitting tearful and miserable in the front seat beside her.

Miss Waddington received her graciously. Maisie sat opposite the large mahogany desk in the beautiful airy room feeling just as vulnerable as she'd once felt facing Miss Clarkson. They talked pleasantries until, unable to stand it any longer, Maisie said sharply, 'Please, Miss

Waddington, I'd like to know why you've sent for me. What is it our Alice has been doing this time?'

For a few seconds the other woman seemed disconcerted by her directness, then she said gently, 'Please don't be upset, it isn't really so terrible.'

'She hasn't been stealing, has she?' Maisie interrupted her anxiously.

'Well, of course not, nothing like that. In some ways this has been more difficult to deal with but I must tell you that her vindictiveness has caused another of my pupils a great deal of misery.'

'I don't understand,' Maisie muttered in dismay.

'Let me tell you as briefly as I can. Apparently Alice was out on the fell one day. She was alone, she'd had a virus and Matron suggested she spend a couple of days in the sick bay. It was nothing serious so we didn't worry you with it and when Alice recovered Matron allowed her out to get some fresh air. While she was on the fell she saw Sir Mark Garveston meeting a lady out near the Pilgrims' Cross and she was unwise enough to inform his daughters of this.'

'But why would she do that?' Maisie cried.

'The more I see of young girls the harder it is to understand them, or their motives. Fortunately I don't have too much trouble, but now and again one or another of them defeats me by their behaviour.'

'But that was a terrible thing to do. I can't understand why she did it.'

'I rather think Alice arrived at Lorivals with the idea that the Garveston twins would be her instant friends since you were here with their mother, and when this didn't happen, she was determined to punish them in some way. You must understand, my dear, that Amelia's daughters had already been here for several years when Alice arrived, and they'd already formed friendships. Alice doesn't lack for friends, she gets along very well with her room-mates and she's popular on the playing field. Pippa Garveston is a sensitive girl, and although she is a twin she is not as robust or self-assured as her sister. She adores her father – consequently, she was the one who suffered most from Alice's disclosure.'

'Have you spoken to Alice?'

'Naturally. I don't like interfering in the quarrels of the girls, but in this case I had to be very severe with your daughter. I made her apologise and told her if she ever did anything like it again she would have to leave. I gather the girls sent her to Coventry for a day so that must have had some effect. I had quite a time comforting Pippa. The poor girl was devastated – I think even Alice was frightened when she saw the state she was in.'

'What do you want me to do?' Maisie asked fearfully.

'Talk to her, here in my office. I have to go down to the Music Room and shall be away about half an hour; that should give you time to make her see how much you deplore what she has done.'

'I do hope Amelia doesn't know anything about this. Will the girls have told their parents, do you think?'

'I should imagine their parents are the last people they would tell, and I'm confident I managed to convince them that the incident wasn't worth a second thought. Don't be too hard on Alice, now. She's already paid the penalty for her indiscretion.'

Five minutes later Alice sidled into the room with a wary expression which became more penitent by the minute as Maisie demanded an explanation for her behaviour.

'I didn't want to upset Pippa, honestly, Mother. It just slipped out somehow, but that sister of hers is so uppish she treats me as if I wasn't there.'

'You had no right to tell them you'd seen their father with a woman on the fell. She could just have been an old family friend.'

'She wasn't a friend.'

'How do you know?'

'He had his arms round her and they were kissing.'

'Men do kiss family friends. Your father kisses his cousins whenever they meet. He kisses all the family at Christmas.'

'Not like that, he doesn't. Besides, it wasn't Christmas.'

'You're very lucky Miss Waddington didn't expel you. My only hope is that Amelia doesn't get to hear of this. She'd be so distressed and I'd hate her to think you were responsible.'

'Miss Waddington told the others they must not discuss it at home. She said I was just being spiteful because they'd ignored me and they should forget what I'd said.'

'And have they?'

'I don't know. Pippa speaks to me, Berenice doesn't.'

'You have other friends, don't you?'

'Yes of course. I don't need the Garveston twins, anyway.'

'You bother me, Alice. I thought you'd be different when you came to Lorivals and settled down, but now I'm not so sure. You're costing us a mint of money and it's money we could do with. I'm wondering if the results are worth the effort and expense.'

Alice's eyes opened wide with anxiety. 'Oh Mother, I will be good, honestly! I like it here, I like my friends and I'm in the hockey team now. Please don't even think about taking me away.'

'I'll have to talk to your father about it.'

The tears filled her daughter's eyes and rolled unchecked down her cheeks. 'Please don't let him take me away. I promised Miss Waddington I'd never do or say anything spiteful again and I won't. Nobody spoke to me for a whole day – I shouldn't be made to suffer anything else.'

Maisie already knew she would say nothing to Tom but thought it would do Alice no harm to fret for a few days. She had the strangest feeling that her daughter wasn't all that sorry for what she'd done, only that she'd been found out. Of course she didn't want to leave Lorivals. She had lost most of her friends at home, even Mrs Pearson's daughter since the episode with the stolen gingerbread. Threatening to take her away was the only weapon Maisie had to make Alice behave.

At that moment Miss Waddington came back to her study and meeting Maisie's eyes she said quietly, 'Get back to class now, Alice. I'm sure your mother has been very firm with you, and we both hope you have learned your lesson.'

Alice was glad to go and Miss Waddington said, 'I don't think we'll hear any more about it, Maisie. I should be very surprised indeed if Alice ever behaved so maliciously again and I don't think Amelia will get to hear of it. Perhaps for a while Pippa will feel some measure of restraint against her father but it will pass. We all have illusions, and many of them are destroyed on our journey through life. In Pippa's case I'm sure she will convince herself that her father is all she believes him to be.'

Once home, Maisie started the evening meal but she couldn't forget her daughter's mutinous eyes and the straight set line of her mouth. What had she ever done to deserve Alice? She'd been a good mother, always putting Tom and the children first, seeing that they were well-fed and clothed. Why was Alice so different from either Peter or Lucy?

She put a casserole in the oven and prepared the vegetables but she did it all automatically; when she started to weigh out the ingredients for a sponge pudding she looked across at the kitchen clock and saw that propped against it was an air-mail envelope which Tom must have left for her.

Wiping her hands on her apron she went across to it, holding it in her hands for several seconds before she took up a knife and slit it open. She forgot about Alice. It was months since she'd received a letter from Nancy Graham and, pulling out a chair, she sat down at the kitchen table to read it.

CHAPTER 8

For three long years Nancy Graham had known little beyond the evil that men do to each other; she lived amidst plunder, rape and fire, the desire for conquest, the urge for conflict and the desolation of defeat.

Growing up in the postwar peace of north Lancashire she'd often heard her father and grandfather discussing war; now she only knew peace as a flimsy tenuous thing, clinging with frail fingers to the crumbling fabric of civilisation.

In her travels from South America to Korea, Africa and the Middle East, it sometimes seemed to Nancy that there was no peace, nor any hope of it. They'd lived from day to day, four Englishmen and one woman, perilously close to death and pestilence in order to shake the complacency at home by their reports to the English press.

Once, cocooned in her infatuation for Noel Templeton, Nancy would only have seen the glamour and ignored the squalor, but now in the heat of the bush or the silence of the desert she could only dream about the joys of civilisation. Cotton skirts and jeans were no substitute for beautiful clothes, music was confined to Alec Fielding's rapidly deteriorating tapes of the classical music he loved, and weariness took the place of those nights of love she had believed she would experience with Noel.

Noel had promised that she would learn, and she certainly did. She learned to write about war as lucidly as Noel, to avoid the bullets of snipers from the rooftops and to crawl through rubble while her throat ached and burned with the dust. She learned to hide her grief

at babies swollen with the effects of famine, and at the
women carrying their dead children at their breast,
their eyes hopeless, their lives over. She learned not to
be nauseated by the sight of soldiers raping the women
they had thrown on the floor, unfeelingly, bestially, and
with this new knowledge came an understanding of
Noel's dedication so that her love for him became a
torment, an unwavering prayer that one day he would
recognize it and return it.

She liked her colleagues. The two cameramen Ph'l
and Clive were her own age, they had great skill and
they were fun to be with while Alec was her confidant,
a shy sensitive man who talked nostalgically about
books and music and occasionally about his wife Rosalind, who had died of leukaemia two years after their
marriage.

He showed Nancy photographs of his wife, a pretty
fair-haired girl smiling shyly in the garden of their
Hampshire home.

Alec took risks that annoyed Noel because there were
times when his actions put the rest of them in danger.
After such episodes Noel lectured them on the need for
care if they were all to survive. Privately he said to
Nancy, 'Alec knows he shouldn't do it, but since his
wife died he's constantly been reckless. It's almost as
though he doesn't care what happens to him. That's
all right for him, but it doesn't help the rest of us.'

Nancy didn't answer. She understood Alec: if anything happened to Noel she wouldn't care about her
own fate. As if he could read her thoughts Noel said
quietly, 'Life has to go on, Nancy. I knew Rosalind,
and she wouldn't want Alec to feel the way he does.
If anything happened to me I'd want the rest of you
to go on as you were. That's what this job is about.'

This was Nancy's first trip to Israel, and she enjoyed
her excursions with Alec or Noel into the arid countryside surrounding Jerusalem. She liked it best in the early

evening when the droves of tourists had left and she could walk in the quiet of the Garden of Gethsemane. At such times she felt closest to Noel; she would see his eyes grow tender and knew that the love they had kindled together in Hong Kong was still there, even if it was now shadowed by the anxieties of the present.

Alec knew how she felt about Noel from the very first morning of their meeting at Heathrow Airport, and there and then he had doubted the wisdom of her presence in their team. Noel didn't like to get involved, it suited him to keep his private life on an even keel, but there was this girl with her beauty and her warmth and Noel hadn't been able to help himself. For the first time he'd allowed his heart to rule his head and Alec asked himself which one of them would suffer most before it ended.

He liked Nancy and they'd become great friends. He admired her courage and her honesty. There were times when he surprised a rare and elusive sadness behind her straight blue gaze but she rarely talked about herself. She talked instead about her late father and his work on the local paper in Greymont, and the arguments he had had with her grandfather every Sunday after lunch. She spoke about her mother, who had moved to live in Canada and her formidable Aunt Susan.

Occasionally Nancy would mention her years at Lorivals, that most upper-crust of girls' schools, and the four companions with whom she had shared her schooldays. Alec got her to describe her work on the local paper but he learned little about the period she had spent in London before leaving for Hong Kong where she had met Noel. He was not one to probe. There were times when he sensed a deep loneliness in her, and he felt like saying to Noel, 'The girl's in love with you! For heaven's sake take her in your arms and tell her how much she means to you. Committing yourself for the first time ever can only enrich your life – it doesn't have to destroy it.' He never spoke to Noel, of course, who would only have regarded his interference as uncalled-for.

Noel had many friends in the area, both Arab and Jew. He listened to their arguments and made up his own mind, but he reported faithfully and impartially to the paper. Nancy thought it strange that he should have friends in both camps and when she questioned him he merely smiled and said, 'One day I'll take you to meet them and then perhaps you'll understand.'

'Do they each know about the others?' she asked curiously.

'Of course, why shouldn't they? I'm an Englishman, I'm not taking sides. I only report what I see.'

'And what you feel in your heart,' she added.

'That too, but none of us are here to pontificate on how these people should resolve their differences or run their country. With any luck, one day something good and just will emerge out of all this miserable conflict.'

Nancy had her doubts. She watched the Israeli soldiers armed to the teeth and strutting through the streets of Jerusalem, and the throngs of Arab youths intent on stoning them to death. At such times great fear clutched at her, for she knew that Noel never counted the cost, never balked at danger. She was learning to live with this but every new crisis was as terrible to her as the first had been.

Noel sat with his host Abraham Schoefer on the balcony of his house on the outskirts of Jerusalem watching the great red ball of the sun disappearing over the rim of the western horizon, leaving behind it all the tragic glow of rose and crimson, colour that threw into sharp relief the conglomeration of buildings before them.

'This is the time I like best,' Abraham said softly. 'It brings a lull into the turmoil of the day and a new wonder into the eyes of all who behold it. At this time I feel closest to God.'

From the city below came the cries of the imams standing high on the balconies of their minarets calling the faithful to prayer, and Noel said softly, 'This at least you have in common.'

'Except that they call us the infidels and tell us there is no God but Allah.'

'Very much the same sentiments as expressed by other religions,' Noel muttered dryly.

Abraham laughed. 'Religion, my friend, is the altar on which all our sins are committed. You in England only have to look across the Irish Sea to realize that truth.'

'I agree. If we all had the same religion I wonder what we would find to quarrel about. There would be something, I feel sure.'

'You're probably right. How long are you in Jerusalem for this time?'

'Until something else blows up, then when the public are sufficiently sated we go on to another part of the world where mayhem or revolution is a little bloodier perhaps.'

'Is Alec with you? Do bring him for dinner one evening.'

'There are five of us. I have a woman journalist with me this time.'

Abraham raised his eyebrows. 'I've never known you bring a woman out with you before. She must be rather special.'

'She's going to be good. It's a girl I knew in the Far East, she's only worked on a local paper but she's got what it takes.'

'In the Far East?'

'Yes, in Hong Kong. Her name is Nancy Graham. Actually my father knew her father years ago when they were both young reporters.'

'I'd like to meet her. Perhaps you'll bring her along one evening.'

'Of course. It will make a nice change for her to eat in a civilised house without listening to footsteps running down the alley beside the hotel and gunfire in the distance.'

'Is that what you're experiencing?'

'Yes. A man was stabbed last night in the road in front of the hotel. We heard his assassin running along the alley but apparently he was swallowed up in the maze of streets in the Arab quarter. The man died.'

'Who was he, do you know?'

'Just a man mistaken for a Jew; actually he was Turkish.'

Abraham shook his head dismally. 'These assassins,' he muttered darkly. 'They are too young, too ill-informed and too bloodthirsty with no power of reasoning. We came back to the Promised Land for a little peace, but all we have had is continuous war.'

When Noel didn't reply he said with a wry smile, 'You never thought there would be peace, did you, Noel? You made that very plain.'

'How could there be, when so many Arabs had to leave their homes to make room for you? You had the Promised Land once before, why did so many of you leave it to wander the face of the earth?'

Abraham laughed. 'We've had this argument before, my friend, and found no good answers. We are a clever people, we Jews, and the rest of the world needs us as history has proved.'

Noel was saved from answering by the arrival on the balcony of his host's second wife, Leah Schoefer. Abraham's first wife had been shot down on the streets of Jerusalem six years before and he had subsequently married Leah, the daughter of his American friend, Isaac. Leah was gentle and adoring. She had always admired this scholarly kind friend of her father's and she had determined from the day they married to be a good wife and mother to his infant son suddenly left without a mother. Now three years after their marriage she still adored him, and Abraham counted his blessings every time he looked at her soft brown eyes and beautiful gentle face. She greeted Noel warmly by kissing his cheek and asking if it was his intention to eat dinner with them.

'Not tonight, Leah, as I have to get back, but tomorrow if it's convenient?'

'But of course.'

'And please bring Nancy and Alec,' Abraham said with a sly smile. 'The two cameramen too if they're available.'

Noel laughed. 'I doubt they will be. They have their own means of finding enjoyment around the city.'

'Nancy?' Leah asked gently.

'A new colleague, the first woman in my team,' Noel answered.

'Ask no questions, Leah,' Abraham advised. 'Tomorrow evening we'll make our own minds up, so ignore anything Noel might say.'

When Noel informed Nancy and Alec of the invitation the first thought that entered Nancy's head was what to wear. When she said as much both men laughed and Noel said, 'I'm sure you brought something from home.'

'No I didn't. You said to bring only the basics and that's what I did. I thought it would be all dust, work and more dust.'

'You'll think of something, Nancy,' Noel said airily, and that night she went through her skimpy wardrobe in despair. The following day she bought a dress she'd been nostalgically drooling over for days, wishing there might be an occasion on which she could wear it and look beautiful for Noel. It was cornflower-blue wild silk, simple but exquisitely cut, and exactly matched the colour of her eyes.

She smuggled it up to her room without anybody seeing, but that night as she walked down the stairs to meet the others she was instantly aware of their stares of appreciation.

'Gosh,' Phil said with youthful candour. 'You look stunning, Nancy. You don't look like yourself.'

'I do look like myself,' she retorted. 'It's that other me you normally see who doesn't look like herself.'

'I like that Nancy best,' Clive said. 'I can relate to her, not this femme fatale you've suddenly become.'

'Well tonight I'm going to be me, the real me, not that apology for a boy whom one old man addressed as Sonny because I was wearing trousers and my battered old cap.'

They laughed in high glee at her resentment and Noel chuckled, 'What did you say to him?'

'I said, "I'm a girl", and he said "Sorry Sonny", and sidled off.'

They laughed again and Alec said gently, 'Well, nobody could take you for a boy tonight, Nancy. You look very beautiful.'

She wished it was Noel saying she looked beautiful but he remained silent; it was only later when he held the door of the car open for her that her eyes met his and she blushed joyfully at the admiration in them.

Dinner was a light-hearted meal with Abraham entertaining them royally. He was a good conversationalist, witty and intelligent, and she enjoyed greatly the repartee that passed between him and Noel. After the meal and while the men lingered over their brandy she went with Leah to the nursery where the little boy Benjamin sat up in bed reading. He greeted her shyly, his dark brown eyes with their long curling lashes curious. She reminded him of a fairytale princess. He'd never believed in women with golden hair and eyes the colour of the summer sea, but here was this lovely lady smiling down at him with gentle warmth.

'What are you reading, Benjamin?' she asked.

He held out the book and taking it into her hands she turned it so that she could read the title – *My First Nursery Rhymes* – and her eyes shone with delight.

'I read this book when I was about your age too,' she said smiling, and turning to Leah, 'I hadn't thought he would be reading something like this.'

'Oh yes,' Leah answered. 'He reads many books. Benjamin is a normal child living in a normal home, however abnormal the world outside might be. Losing his mother was a terrible thing and at first he couldn't accept me – it was understandable. Now Benjamin and I are good together. I would like to think that it will continue to be so.'

'But of course it will, why do you doubt it?'

'I doubt a great many things. Abraham's parents and my grandparents all died in concentration camps. My own parents escaped the holocaust and were lucky enough to be taken to America by relatives. I was born in freedom and lived in freedom until we came here. It was their dream to come here, my dream to stay here in peace.'

They looked back at the boy immersed in his book and Leah said gently, 'Don't read too long, darling. The story will keep for another day.'

There was no talk of strife as they sat under the dark blue sky ablaze with stars, no thoughts that outside in that busy teeming city death lurked round every corner and deep and dividing hatred and resentment burned between two peoples.

They talked about music and books, food and wine, and only once did Abraham let the mask slip and that was when Noel said, 'Nancy would like to see more of the country. I wish it was possible to drive freely about the roads but of course at the moment it isn't.'

'No, that is a pity. I would like you to see how we have made the desert bloom, my dear. Now orange groves stretch for miles where once there were only unending dunes, where mangy camels wandered and pariah dogs scavenged for food in the gutters.'

Nancy did not miss the warning look that Leah gave him, and in the next moment he said brightly, 'No, my wife is right, I promised that tonight I would speak only of good things. Now fill up your glasses and tell me what you think of this wine. It comes from the best grapes grown near the site of old Tiberias.'

Later, as they were leaving, Abraham took Nancy's hand and said, 'Noel did not tell me you were beautiful. There are a great many things he did not tell me.'

Noel came to stand beside them and Abraham said softly, 'I was telling Nancy that she was beautiful and that a great many things had been left unsaid when you told me about her.'

Noel smiled easily. 'I like to make up my own mind about people and I leave it to my friends to do likewise.'

'You must come again, my dear, as often as you like. It will be good for Leah.'

'Well?' Noel asked her on their way home. 'Did you like my friends?'

'Very much. Don't you find it difficult to have both Jewish friends and Arab friends?' she asked him again.

'It is good to listen to both points of view.'

'And make up your own mind as to who is wrong and who is right?'

'I wish it was quite as simple as that. Abraham asks himself in all honesty why his race has been so persecuted throughout the ages, ever since that Egyptian Pharaoh unleashed his anger against them three thousand years ago and the Israelites led by Moses walked out of Egypt in search of their Promised Land. My friend Ali Ben Makobi believes he has the answer.'

'And do you believe in this answer?'

100

'He has a point; the Israelis have a point – I believe it will take the Almighty to solve this one, Nancy. By the way, I have to go into Haifa early tomorrow. I'd like you to come with me, Alec.'

'Certainly. Anything unusual?'

'I'm not sure. I'll tell you about it when we get back.'

Nancy left them poring over some papers Noel produced from his briefcase, and after murmuring goodnight she walked up to her room. She took off her dress and hung it in the wardrobe and anger brought scalding tears into her eyes. If Noel loved her, he'd be with her instead of sitting out there on the terrace with Alec. War and unrest was all they knew, all that interested them.

In the next moment she was calling herself a fool for being unreasonable. This was Noel's job, her job too for that matter. Love was a secondary thing, it was not what they were here for. Love to a man was a thing apart, it had always been so, while a woman lived on her emotions, tended to make love her first priority. It was a story as old as Time so there was little hope that she and Noel could change it.

If the men went to Haifa in the morning she would be alone for most of the day. The prospect didn't daunt her in the least: she could buy lunch from one of the street stalls and wander round the city, but how she wished she could saunter into an ordinary café and ask for a cup of coffee without being ogled by an army of men.

The café lounges within the hotels were entirely without character, but men only was the norm in those coffee houses in the city where the all-male clientèle sat in groups arguing or at small tables playing backgammon. There were so many things she missed, ordinary everyday things, but the others had been anxious to instruct her in where she could or could not go.

Most of all she hated the commercialism. Rivalries between Christian denominations reduced what should have been the greatest Christian shrine in the world to the level of farce, as all over Jerusalem rival churches vied with one another in order to push their individual claims on being the real one.

When she said as much to Alec he responded, 'Stay away from the tourist traps, then, Nancy. Even without them Jerusalem is still an interesting city. Concentrate instead on the remains of Roman, Herodion and Masada. Think about the Crusades and perhaps one day we can take you to see the medieval cities at Acre and the Negev Desert.'

'When will Noel ever have the time?'

'Oh he will, believe me.'

Noel had surprised her one morning as she set off alone on her sightseeing saunter by saying, 'Don't mind too much about the commercialism, Nancy, what does it matter that the scenes have changed, if the faith has lived on in people's hearts?'

It was at times like that when she loved him most, when the sensitivity shone through and she could look into his dark eyes and think, this is a good man, a kind honest man who is well worth loving.

CHAPTER 9

Nancy set off immediately after breakfast the next day
and walked quickly in the direction of the old city. She
knew that it was divided into four parts and on this
hot sunlit morning she headed for the Moslem quarter,
shrugging off the hustlers who soon tired of trying to
interest her in a guided tour.

She fought her way through the street markets which
sold everything from food to electrical goods, clothing
to furnishings, and eventually reached the Via Dolorosa
which she crossed, heading into the Moslem quarter.
Mosques fascinated her with their domes and minarets,
the patterns of their exquisite mosaics, and she watched
fascinated as a stream of men waited to enter the
mosque, a procession where no woman intruded, and
she marvelled at a religion which excluded women and
reduced them to the status of chattels.

Noel had told her that he would take her to meet
his Arab friend who was married to a Syrian, a woman
who had been educated in the West and who despised
utterly the Arabs' subjugation of their women. Now
men stared at this fair-skinned golden-haired woman
walking confidently along the streets of their part of
the city. They leered at her with dark almond eyes but
she deliberately looked straight ahead, glad of the fly
switch which she carried and used to hide her face
from their stares.

She had not gone far when she realized it had been
a mistake to come. She had no place in this teeming
Arab street where the men sat outside their shops
smoking hookahs, or squatted on their haunches in the
road gambling so that she had to step over them.

She knew it would have pleased them if she'd suddenly turned tail and run but she forced herself to saunter back towards the gate, while beside her suddenly trotted two Arab youths, little more than children, slyly making improper suggestions which only a few months ago would have brought the hot blood to her face but which now she could loftily ignore as being beneath her notice.

Jerusalem is a city of gates and Nancy was glad to reach the Damascus Gate and the city beyond. She had had enough of the old city for one morning; it was almost noon and the heat was overpowering. Tourists crowded the streets as they waited to view the religious sites and she was glad to turn into the foyer of the nearest hotel and sit on the terrace with a cool drink.

From here she could view the street where a conglomeration of races mingled, but it was not a peaceful scene. It was noisy with the marching feet of a body of Israeli soldiers, the chattering of tourists, the cries of the Moslem priests calling the faithful to prayer and Nancy marvelled anew that this land which in her innocence she had once thought of as a haven of peace in a turbulent world could be the exact opposite of all she had believed in.

Dimly from the distance she heard shouts and then footsteps running in the alleyway beside the hotel. Those sitting on the terrace leapt to their feet and ran to the balcony rail where they could look down the street. From the alleyway a man emerged clutching his breast, and she could see the bright red blood gushing through his fingers over the hilt of a knife. He staggered into the centre of the street before falling to the ground. The sound of rushing feet became louder and seconds later two Arab youths ran out into the street followed by a group of Israeli soldiers carrying guns.

The youths ignored the shouts of warning but carried on in their headlong flight, then a soldier raised his gun and fired whereupon one of them dropped to the ground while the other ran on unheeding. The soldiers gave chase.

Those people sitting on the hotel terrace headed for the doorway as all hell broke loose on the street. Arabs appeared as if from nowhere and more soldiers were racing down the hill. Nancy took to her heels and ran, keeping close to the wall, remembering that Noel had told her always to carry a large scarf or handkerchief to help combat the smoke bombs that would be thrown. She had almost reached the junction in the road when she heard her name being called urgently from a car which was endeavouring to move along the crowded street. Looking up, she saw that Leah was motioning her to get in the front seat. Keeping her head down and holding her handkerchief close to her face she ran to the slowly moving car and managed to crawl inside.

'Are you alone?' Leah asked sharply.

'Yes, the others are in Haifa.'

'Abraham warned me not to come into the city today. He said there would be trouble.'

'How did he know?'

Leah shrugged her shoulders. 'The men have their meetings, they know when trouble is brewing. What happened down there?'

After Nancy had told her she said quietly, 'The man is probably a merchant, no doubt somebody they have been watching for some time. Did they kill him?'

'I don't know. He was surrounded by a crowd of people but there was a knife in his chest and he was bleeding terribly.'

'When we get through the crowd I will take you to our home. You must stay with us for the rest of the day.'

'Thank you, you're very kind. I'll write my notes up for the paper there. Noel might think this is an incident they need to know about.'

'My dear, there are a hundred and one incidents like this happening every day in Jerusalem and all over Israel.'

'I know that, but it could be the start of something much bigger.'

Leah nodded. 'Perhaps. We shall have to wait and see.' She edged the car forward and slowly the crowd parted so that she could drive through. On the outskirts of the city the streets were peaceful again and when at last they drove up to Leah's villa it seemed like another world, one of gracious houses and peaceful gardens where waterfalls tinkling into shady pools were the only sounds that disturbed the quiet afternoon.

Abraham's expression was stern as Nancy related the morning's events. Faced with her concern he said quietly, 'This may be an isolated incident or it could be the beginning of something much worse. The next few days will tell us.'

'Have you any idea who the man was?'

'It could have been one of a dozen men. It could have been me, had I been visiting the city this morning.'

'But why you, Abraham?'

'I am a Jew, I am rich and I am here. That is the only reason they need.' Fear shone in Leah's eyes and Abraham smiled at her, saying gently, 'It is better that you should know, Leah. I thought there might be trouble in the city today so I asked you not to go in but I didn't want to worry you unduly. I tried to telephone Noel this morning but he had gone to Haifa. Why has he gone there, Nancy?'

'I don't know, but there must be some reason.'

'When is he returning?'

'I'm not sure, but I hope by this evening.'

'Ask him to telephone me or, better still, perhaps you would like to dine with us again tomorrow evening?'

'Thank you, I'll ask him to let you know if he gets back from Haifa today.'

106

All afternoon she sat with Leah in the garden while Benjamin rode round the paths on his tricycle. Watching him fondly Leah said, 'It is sad for a child to be brought up in a war-torn land. In three weeks there will be Christian celebrations down there in the old city – had you realized that it will be Christmas Day, Nancy?'

Nancy stared at her in dismay. Of course she hadn't realized it and her face grew suddenly sad as her heart filled with memories. At home in England Christmas trees would be appearing in windows, singers would be carolling out Christ's message in town hall squares and children would be taken in their thousands to see a multitude of Santa Clauses in every department store.

Leah smiled, aware of her thoughts, and Nancy asked impulsively, 'Do you ever regret coming here? Do you ever think how much more peaceful your life would have been if you'd stayed in America?'

'I was happy in America but even there I was not able to live my own life. I met an Arab boy called Nagev at university and we fell in love. We never thought about the things that divided us, only the things that united us, but when my family found out they stopped me seeing him. To me, a seventeen-year-old student with independent leanings, nurtured in the freedom I'd taken for granted over so many years, I couldn't comprehend their cruelty in keeping us apart. It seemed illogical when all my friends had a different kind of freedom.

'It was the same for his family. They were horrified, and when I returned to university after the summer holidays they had taken him away. We never saw each other again.'

'And how soon afterwards did you marry Abraham?'

'I was twenty-four by then. I'd known him many years as a friend of my father, and I also knew Miriam, his wife. I liked them both, then when she died I grew

107

very fond of their child. Abraham had visited Israel and had this dream to come back here. He had a vision of a new and glorious Israel in which he had the talent to contribute a great deal. He is a lawyer by profession and he wanted Benjamin to grow up here. I used to sit and listen to the talk between my father and him and gradually I began to want to come here too. It became my dream, a new start, a new land, and my parents were pleased when Abraham asked their permission to marry me.

'We have had some good times – don't think it has all been bad, Nancy. I love my home, I love Israel and we have done so much to make it a better land, but I also know the many wrongs we have done to the displaced Palestinians. If I met Nagev tomorrow there would probably be hatred in his eyes instead of love.'

A car was climbing the hillside and Leah ran to the edge of the terrace when it came in through the gates and swept up the drive.

'We have visitors, Nancy. Now perhaps we shall hear what happened in the city.'

She called to Benjamin and together they walked back to the house. Nancy was surprised to find Noel sitting with Abraham and when their eyes met he smiled.

'I can't leave you for five minutes without your getting into trouble,' he said humorously.

When she stared at him curiously Leah admitted, 'I telephoned the hotel with a message, Nancy. I thought if Noel returned from Haifa he would expect to find you there.'

'I'm beginning to take sudden death in my stride,' Nancy said dryly.

'Do you know who the victim was?' Leah asked urgently.

'Rabbi Lehmann. They stabbed him as he was leaving his house to go to the synagogue. One of the youths

108

responsible was shot dead, while the other has been swallowed up in the city.'

'But that is terrible,' Leah cried. 'Rabbi Lehmann was a good man – he was not concerned with politics. How could they do this!'

Abraham said softly, 'This atrocity will be one of many and in turn we shall retaliate. A great many innocent people will die, most of them needlessly. The terrorism has not been invented that will force us out of what we believe is ours. The killing will go on.'

As they rose to leave Abraham said, 'When shall we see you again, Noel?'

'I'm not sure. We shall be back, of that I have no doubt, but the day after tomorrow we're leaving for Ethiopia.'

'More trouble?' Abraham asked.

'Unrest, famine – the usual story.'

Nancy was quiet on their way back to the hotel. The events of the day were still very much on her mind and she sensed a foreboding atmosphere in the city streets despite the crowds – their talk and laughter seemed somehow forced.

Looking at her pensive face and her hands, clenched together on her lap, Noel said lightly, 'You're not sufficiently blasé, Nancy. Sudden death still has the power to trouble you.'

'Why, doesn't it still trouble you?'

'I suppose it does but I've learned to put it behind me as you must. All this is still very new to you.'

'Will it make you happy when I'm blasé and uncaring?'

He smiled. 'Happy no, reassured yes.'

'You'd prefer me to be hard and uncaring?'

'As a reporter, yes. It's all to do with self-preservation.'

'And as a woman?'

'I shouldn't be doing this to you, should I, Nancy? Perhaps I should have left you in that nice north-

109

country town writing about garden parties and amateur operatics, nice safe things, things that wouldn't change you as this life certainly will.'

'You think it's going to make me like you – believing that I'm an island and that everything and everybody is outside it?'

He didn't answer, and stealing a look at his calm serious profile she remained silent.

They found Alec in the hotel lounge. He waved to them when they entered and looked at Nancy. 'All right, love?'

'Yes, thank you, Alec.'

Alec isn't an island, she thought savagely. Alec hadn't let the brutalities he'd witnessed change him from the kind tolerant man he'd always been, so why should Noel be any different? She listened to them discussing the day's events, and after a while Alec said, 'I suppose Noel's told you we're moving out?'

'Yes, the day after tomorrow.'

'Will you be sorry to leave Israel?'

'No, I'll be glad. What the Arabs did today was horrible, killing an innocent old man. How can there ever be any hope that this will be a united land one day?'

'Neither side wants a united land, that's for sure,' Alec shrugged.

'Well, you've spoken with Abraham and Leah, and tomorrow I propose to drive out to Jericho. I want you to meet my Arab friend and his wife Hadassah. You've heard one side of the story, perhaps now you should hear the other,' Noel said evenly.

All Nancy cared about at that moment was that she would be spending the next day with Noel and her spirits revived.

110

CHAPTER 10

Maisie laid the pages down on the kitchen table with a bemused expression. Nancy's letters were always filled with news of a world of which she had no conception. Her old friend also wrote about men Maisie had never met, but she was astute enough to read between the lines. Nancy was in love with Noel Templeton, however much she tried to disguise it. She wrote about him as if he was God. He was the hero of all her adventures and there seemed to be no end to them. She wrote about death and destruction as an everyday experience and Maisie had difficulty in reconciling the land of her early scripture lessons with the troubled country in which Nancy was living.

Nancy Graham was her dearest friend but Maisie didn't understand her. She couldn't see how any woman could forsake the gentle joys of a normal life and replace them with such a turbulent scenario. However, when she said as much to Tom he simply commented, 'It takes all sorts, love. She obviously enjoys what she's doing.'

She decided to read Nancy's letter again later when she didn't have so much on her mind. At the moment it was obsessed with Alice, Alice who blithely broke into somebody's kitchen to steal their gingerbread and who saw nothing wrong in telling Amelia's daughters that she'd seen their father kissing a woman out there on the fell.

She knew girls could be spiteful to each other – she herself had often been horrid to Barbara Smythe, who'd been horrid to her in return – but she never managed to get through to Alice.

She looked up as Peter entered the kitchen, his fresh young face rosy after his walk across the fields, and she responded to his bright smile by asking, 'Are you hungry, love? I must get on with my pudding. Will you just take a look at Lucy for me. She was fast asleep when I looked in earlier on.' Lucy was unwell with a viral infection.

Dutifully he obeyed her while she went about her chores, returning a few minutes later to report that his little sister was still sleeping. Seeing the letter with its foreign stamp on the table he asked, 'Can I read it, Mum?' and even before she agreed he was sitting down eagerly scanning Nancy's closely written pages.

His eyes were alight with enthusiasm and Maisie said feelingly, 'Don't tell me you would like that sort of life, love.'

'It's better than farming,' he answered her. 'It must be wonderful to travel and be a part of what's going on out there in the world. I wouldn't mind it. How did she get to be a journalist?'

'Her father was one, so it was probably in her blood.'

'Well, my father's a farmer but farming isn't in my blood.'

'No, love. I rather wish it was, and so does your father.'

He stared at her thoughtfully, then after a few seconds he said, 'You're always telling me to work hard, Mother, but I don't need to swot over my books to become a farmer like Dad.'

She had the grace to look uncomfortable. It was true she was glad that Peter was clever. She gloried in his ability. None of her brothers had been good at school and she'd been no great asset to Lorivals, but at the same time she sensed Tom's disappointment that he was working all hours to ensure the success of a family business in which his son had little interest.

The boy rightly read the expression on his mother's face, and with a little smile he said gently, 'Maybe our Alice'll marry a boy who's interested in farming.'

'I very much doubt it,' Maisie snapped sharply. 'Alice'll have other notions when she leaves Lorivals, Peter. Still, our Lucy might be different.'

'Oh, she will be,' he agreed. 'She's different now.'

'What do you mean by that?'

With all a young boy's candour he said innocently, 'She's nicer than Alice.'

For a moment Maisie was inclined to take him into her confidence, then thinking better of it she simply said, 'Will you lay the table for me, love. Dinner won't be long.'

She left Peter laying the table while she took a tray up to Lucy's room. She sat on the edge of her bed, pleased to see that she looked a little better. As she smoothed the fair hair from her forehead Lucy opened her eyes and smiled.

'Better, darling?' Maisie asked, and Lucy nodded. 'I've brought you some broth. Here, I'll help you to sit up then I'll stay with you until you've drunk it.'

Lucy was never any trouble; she had a sunny disposition and she obeyed her instructions without argument. Maisie's eyes clouded: Alice would be home for Easter soon, then would follow the squabbles with Peter, the sulks when Maisie asked her to help in the house, the baiting of Lucy and the sly jibes at her father's countrified accent.

Lucy finished her broth and Maisie said gently, 'You're so much better, love, perhaps I'll let you get up for a while tomorrow. Shall I put out the light now?'

'Leave the lamp, Mum,' Lucy said with a smile.

'We're going to have our meal now. Your daddy'll be up to see you later.'

She served the evening meal and sat down at the kitchen table with Peter to eat it. Tom would still be

113

busy with the milking and the thousand and one jobs he had to do before he could call it a day. If Peter'd been interested he would have been out there with his father, but he had already got his schoolbooks open on the end of the table and there was no use her worrying about it.

By the time Tom came in Peter was in the living room finishing off his homework, the table was cleared and there was only Tom's meal to serve. He looked tired as he went up to the bathroom to wash, but Maisie heard him go into Lucy's room and the sound of their laughter.

'Had a good day, love?' he asked her as she served him.

'Nothing unusual,' she lied. 'Lucy's looking better, isn't she?'

'Yes, I reckon she'll soon be up and running about.'

'What's your day been like?'

'I ran into Greymont this mornin'. I had to go to the bank and I called to see Bob.'

'How are they then?'

'They're all right. Mary said they hadn't seen you for a long time – I should call in the next time you're in town, love.'

Nancy set her lips firmly. 'I'd call more often if Mary'd stop picking on us. If it isn't me then it's our Alice.'

'But you're very fond of Bob.'

'Yes, I know. He should shut her up but he never does.'

'I ran into Councillor Smythe in the bank. He said his wife was thinking of going to see their Barbara for a few days. Apparently they've moved again – to a bigger house outside Cheltenham. Perhaps Martin's goin' in for bein' the country squire.'

'That wouldn't surprise me, and she'll be entertainin' and showin' off, no doubt. She was allus good at that.'

Tom chuckled. 'You're jealous, love.'

'I'm not in the least bit jealous. I don't want anythin' Barbara Walton's got and that includes her husband.'

'He was always a clever lad, a bit pompous perhaps. I hope our Peter doesn't get like that.'

Maisie stared at him aghast. 'What a thing to say. Peter's nothin' like Martin Walton!'

'It's only that he's more interested in books than anythin' else.'

'That's because he's clever. You should be glad he's bright instead of sayin' he's like Martin Walton.'

Tom pushed his plate to one side. 'Time will tell, Maisie. Now – is there any pudding?'

CHAPTER 11

Barbara Walton slammed down the boot of her car and after reassuring herself that it was locked turned to get into her Mercedes coupé.

She was frowning irritably as she unlocked the car and the frown intensified as she heard her name being called from the door of the clubhouse. She turned to see two women bearing down on her with evident speed. Cursing softly under her breath she looked up to greet them with a hesitant smile.

'Aren't you coming to the meeting, Barbara?' the taller of the two called out. 'I thought you'd ordered lunch with the rest of us!'

'No, I'm sorry,' Barbara said calmly. 'I have to get back. Martin's going away on business this afternoon and we have workmen in the house. I know I said I'd stay but now it isn't possible.'

'Do you want us to make an apology for you?' Mona Kirkham persisted.

'No, I told them this morning I wouldn't be able to attend the meeting or the luncheon.'

Why was it Mona always reminded her of the games mistress at Lorivals? It was probably her toothy smile and hearty manner. Mona invariably did all the talking while her sister Alma acted the part of a very faithful Greek chorus. At the moment Alma stood back eyeing Barbara's new car enviously until Mona said, 'Don't tell me you've got workmen in your new house. Why, it hasn't been up five minutes!'

'We've been in the house over twelve months, Mona, and I've never liked the kitchen. We're having a new one put in.'

Two pairs of eyes went round and Alma breathed, 'But your kitchen was lovely, Barbara. So was the last house you lived in – why ever did you move?'

'It was Martin's idea, not mine. He likes the country, he thought we should look around for something out of town and it is very lovely where we are.'

'Oh, we agree,' Mona was quick to reply, 'it's just that we don't see you as often as we did before you moved. You've not been playing in many of the competitions and I can't remember the last meeting you came to.'

'I know, it's been really remiss of me but there's been so much to do since we moved and we have been away quite a lot. I've played a wretched game this morning. I really shouldn't have come but Betty couldn't get anybody else to play with her at such short notice.'

'We make it a rule not to let anything interfere with our golf or our committees,' Mona said importantly.

'But then you don't have a husband going here and there at unexpected intervals,' Barbara said sweetly. 'Still you're right, of course. I really should think very seriously about resigning from the committee. I'm just not doing my fair share.'

'Oh, I didn't mean that,' Mona put in quickly. 'We love having you, Barbara, and Martin's so very generous and so are you. What would we do without your prizes? They're always so perfect.'

'I think you'd find we'd continue to give prizes even if we can't give our time.'

'No, really, Barbara, you mustn't think of it. Somebody would always be prepared to stand in for you.'

'Well, it's something I shall have to think about. Do enjoy your lunch,' she said, and with another smile entered her car and reversed into the drive.

'Do you think she was serious about resigning from the committee?' Alma asked on their way back to the clubhouse.

'She could be. They're into a new crowd, racing people. They gave parties during racing week and not many people from the Golf Club got asked.'

'The Swensons went.'

'Only because he's on the Board of Westons and so is Martin Walton.'

'Eileen Swenson said there were quite a few titled people invited; one of them was staying at the Waltons' for the whole week – somebody from the north where Barbara and Martin come from.'

'They couldn't get into the Golf Club quick enough when they first came here, now they've other fish to fry. Did Eileen Swenson say what their new house was like?'

'She's never stopped talking about it. A positive showplace, she said. It must have cost them a fortune and now a new kitchen. Don't you think it's ostentatious?'

'Oh yes I do, very ostentatious.'

Barbara's frustration was still with her as she drove along the leafy lanes to her home. She was well aware she'd be the topic of conversation at the luncheon she was missing: they'd be discussing her husband, her house and her game, and Mona would lose no opportunity of telling them she'd hinted at resigning from the committee.

Martin wouldn't like her to resign. He liked her being a committee woman – if she sat on a different one every day of the week it would please him but she'd become bored by the same old wrangling, the chivvying for position and the milling over old and new scandals.

She brought her car to a standstill on the hill overlooking her new house which nestled on the lower slopes of a wooded hillside surrounded by formally laid-out gardens. It was a long low house built on terraces, with french windows opening out on to a large patio, with the sun shining on the tall windows of the large conservatory.

118

Martin's long sleek Jaguar stood on the drive in front of the door and at the side of the house a large lorry was parked, presumably belonging to the men working on the new kitchen.

She finished her journey, noting that the boot of Martin's car was open and it was already crammed with dark leather luggage and a set of golf clubs. She smiled to herself. He always maintained he was too busy to do anything but attend meetings and work in the evenings, so when he got time to play golf she couldn't imagine – but she had no doubt he found time.

She let herself into the house and crossed the hall in the direction of the knocking noise. A workman touched his cap respectfully, saying, 'The units are mostly in place, Mrs Walton. They look very nice but it were a right pity to take the others out.'

'I think these make the kitchen look a lot larger,' Barbara said firmly.

'Oh, aye they do that, missus, but the others made it look a lot warmer. Still, there's no accountin' for taste, is there? I take it the boss is havin' these back?' he said, indicating the dark oak units they had removed.

'Yes, he has a customer for them.'

She was glad when the man left a few hours later. She didn't want Martin to hear his criticism and the limed oak units to her mind were far more in keeping with the rest of the house, giving a mauvish-grey appearance that toned with the marble floor with its odd tiles in deep purple.

She was standing in the middle of her new kitchen looking round appreciatively when her husband came to stand in the doorway, his attitude entirely critical.

'Are you satisfied now?' he asked tersely. 'I couldn't see what was wrong with the others. It's cost a small fortune to have them changed.'

'It was you who wanted an ultra-modern house well

119

out of town. I was perfectly happy with the other one,' she replied.

'You complained that it was too small to do much entertaining. You were happy enough to show this off to your racing friends.'

'My racing friends! They were largely your business colleagues, Martin. Mark Garveston was the only outsider.'

'Are we expected to repeat the experiment every March?'

'Not if you object, and don't mind gaining a reputation for stinginess. Personally I enjoyed every moment of it and so did our guests.'

'Of course! It was less expensive than a five-star hotel and it meant they had more money to wager on the track.'

'How crotchety you are today. There's a whole week of what you enjoy most before you and you're like a bear with a sore head. I should be the one who's annoyed at being left at home.'

He frowned, then changing the subject swiftly he said, 'How did you go on at the club this morning?'

'I played very badly and I didn't go to the meeting.'

'Why ever not?'

'Because I wanted to come home before you left. I also wanted to see how the workmen were getting on with the kitchen. I'm seriously thinking I ought to resign from the committee now that we're living further away.'

'There's surely no need for that. We're only six miles from the club, and that's nothing in a car.'

'I'm losing interest in the club. Listening to the same old gossip, all the rehashing over forgotten scandals as well as the new ones.'

'We've never been the subject of scandal so why should it affect you?'

'It doesn't, I'm simply bored by it all. Besides, I promised Lucy Belbin I'd go with her to the riding stables.'

'I've always heard one should start to ride as a youngster. Haven't you left it a bit late?'

'No, I haven't. I'm hardly in my dotage. Mark went riding every morning when he was here and neither of us was able to go with him simply because we'd never ridden. I intend to do something about that and I think you should too.'

'I have enough interests. I like my golf and I like my boats. You've lost interest in sailing as well it seems – at least you never show any enthusiasm for it.'

'I see you're taking your clubs to the conference.'

'I doubt there'll be time to play but one never knows.'

They moved back through the hall and out to the waiting car. Barbara watched as her husband checked that everything was in the boot before slamming it shut, then he walked back to her, kissing her briefly before climbing into his car.

Tall and slim and elegant, he looked every inch a prosperous businessman and he was glad to be leaving. Martin enjoyed the importance of mixing with prosperous men, the camaraderie around the bars and on the links where successful men vied with each other over their business deals, their cars and their boats. He was peevish about the kitchen; either that or something else had annoyed him, but he'd get over it.

Never for one moment did Barbara trouble herself that there might be other women or one woman in particular in Martin's life. He was proud of her. He liked her style, her beauty and elegance. He had never been a charmer but he was a good talker where his career was concerned, a good debater in the boardroom, a great communicator in the advancement of his business interests. However, where women were concerned he was singularly uninterested – an indifference which Barbara believed extended to herself. If she was there to entertain his friends, grace his home, participate in those increasingly rare moments of passion they shared then he was satisfied.

She had always had the ability to be completely honest with herself. She had a small circle of women friends who accepted her independence and the fact that she was not one to mill over her marriage with any one of them. She had never felt the need for a bevy of friends; even as a schoolgirl there had only been Nancy Graham whom she'd ever really thought of as a friend. Maisie Jayson she'd tolerated and later at Lorivals she'd jumped on Amelia's bandwagon and suffered Lois Brampton.

She'd kept in touch with none of them, even when she agreed with Amelia that they should all meet ten years after leaving Lorivals. She'd never expected such a reunion to materialise, and was consequently astonished when Amelia remembered. The gathering at Garveston Hall had been better than she'd anticipated, too.

Maisie and her husband had bored everybody by their talk of the farm and their young children, Nancy had been singularly detached and between Nancy and Amelia there had been a certain animosity, probably due to the fact that once Amelia's husband had fancied Nancy. What fools women were to bother about men's little indiscretions. When the chips were down the wife usually won.

As she went back into the house she heard the telephone shrilling noisily and she hurried to answer it, anticipation in her step and a certain impatience when the voice at the other end of the line was not the one she had hoped to hear.

'How are you, Mother?' she enquired solicitously.

'I'm not very well,' Mrs Smythe complained. 'I've been having more of my headaches and the doctor says I badly need a change.'

'Can't you persuade Father to take you on holiday somewhere? You haven't been away since the spring and the weather's quite lovely just now.'

'You know what your father's like. He's all tied up with the Council meetings and he hates hotel life, having to dress up for dinner and eat when he doesn't want to.'

'Why don't you get a cottage somewhere for a few weeks? You could live exactly like you do at home and it would be a change of scenery.'

'And I'd be doing all the cooking just like I do at home! It would be no change at all for me, Barbara.'

She knew what was coming, and the frown on her face deepened.

'I thought I might come and spend a few days with you,' her mother said plaintively. 'I've never seen your new house and I love Cheltenham. We could go round the shops and take tea in that lovely little café we found. I'm sure Martin wouldn't mind.'

'No, Mother, Martin wouldn't mind. In any case, he's away for five or six days at a conference. When were you thinking of coming?'

'I could come tomorrow morning if that's convenient. Can you meet my train?'

'Yes of course, the one that gets in around noon?'

'Yes, your father'll take me to the station. You're sure I'm not inconveniencing you in any way? I'll leave before Martin gets home.'

'You needn't do that, Mother, you know Martin doesn't mind how long you stay with us. He's seldom in anyway.'

'I'll see you in the morning, then. I've so much to tell you. Goodbye, dear.'

What could her mother possibly tell her that would be news? She'd go on at great length about the Jayson brothers and Maisie. She'd talk about Amelia as if they were bosom chums which Barbara knew they weren't and she couldn't tell her anything about Nancy, as Barbara knew all about her activities from the daily newspaper.

The workmen were back now, clattering in the kitchen while one of them whistled cheerfully, and she asked herself savagely why she hadn't made her new kitchen the excuse not to have her mother just now. Oh well, better get it over with. At least she wasn't likely to be visiting again in the foreseeable future.

Martin had left the dressing room in something of a mess. The wardrobe doors were open and a selection of ties were strewn across a chair seat. After she'd tidied up she decided on a tour of the house in order to reassure herself that her mother would be impressed by its glossy perfection.

She would give Mrs Smythe the lavender room at the corner. Barbara scanned its pale mauve-grey carpet and lavender curtains and bedcovers. Beyond, the lavender bathroom was equipped with soft lavender and purple towels, lavender toiletries and bowls of lavender pot-pourri, and she imagined how her mother would bore all her acquaintances at home with talk of the luxury she'd enjoyed during her stay in Cheltenham.

Barbara smiled as she thought about her poor father having to listen to it all. He would be trying to read his paper or watch television, then unable to stand it any longer he'd disappear into the greenhouse or take the dog out and her mother would accuse him of being unsociable and uninterested in the life of his only daughter and son-in-law.

She couldn't remember how long it was since her father had visited them. For one thing he didn't get along with Martin, they had absolutely nothing in common, not even golf because her father was an inferior player and Martin always beat him. He thought Martin was a show-off, and Martin thought her father was a bore with his obsession with the local Council.

Her mother he tolerated, because she so obviously thought he was wonderful and that her only child had been more than fortunate to capture such a prize. Barbara had no illusions about her husband or her mother, while her father she loved – even if it was love at a distance most of the time.

She went downstairs and into the kitchen. There would be no opportunity to cook anything for herself while the workmen were there.

The foreman grinned at her cheerfully. 'We'll 'ave it fully installed before five, Mrs Walton. I 'ope you're not wantin' to use the kitchen afore then.'

'No. I have to go out this afternoon but I'll be back before five. What sort of a work-top are you putting on the breakfast bar?'

'There it is, Mrs Walton, same as the floor. The boss said it'll look better than the unit work-tops. It's 'ardly a bar, more of a table in the middle o' the room.'

'Of course. I think it will look very well.'

'I still thinks them other units looked warmer.'

She smiled briefly and left them to get on with their work and as she closed the front door behind her the workman remarked to his companions, 'Money to burn, they must 'ave. Sacrilege it were to take them units out. I wouldn't like these i' my kitchen, too fancy they are, too modern.'

'Well it's a modern 'ouse, isn't it,' one of them replied. 'Would you like this sort of place?'

'No. Like livin' in a goldfish bowl it is. Take your shoes off and we'll 'ave a look upstairs while she's out.'

They crept from room to room, their eyes widening as they went, and when they returned to the kitchen the foreman said, 'The boss said I should look round if I got the chance. My missus'd like to see it, but I reckon she wouldn't much care for it.'

'My missus would,' another man said. 'She'd think we'd won the pools if I bought her somethin' like this.'

'Maybe they 'ave.'

'Nay,' the foreman said. 'He's a businessman, you've only to look at 'is car, and there's a boat in the other garage waitin' to go to the coast that's as big as mi 'ouse. No pools win ever bought all this.'

'She's a great-lookin' bird,' the youngest workman commented appreciatively.

'She is that, but 'e's a dry stick. I reckon if I 'ad a wife like that I'd not be leavin' 'er at 'ome as often as 'e does.'

'She looks as if she could take care of 'erself. I reckon it's 'im who has to watch 'er, not the other way around.'

The laughter was general before they picked up their tools and got on with their work.

As for Barbara, she decided to pop in to the White Swan for a sandwich before calling for her friend. The inn was crowded with lunchtime locals, men thronging round the bar or sitting at small tables eating their lunch, so she selected a table tucked away in a dark corner, well aware that she was being eyed up by the customers at the bar, but then she was used to that.

She ordered a chicken sandwich and a lager, feeling confident that she looked well turned out in her beige trousers and tweed hacking jacket, a brightly coloured silk scarf tying back her shoulder-length dark hair.

Barbara was accustomed to men staring at her and it didn't bother her. She never encouraged them, for if life with Martin wasn't exactly a world-shattering experience she knew which side her bread was buttered; to jeopardise that life it would have to be something very special. Mark Garveston was something special, but he would never be more than an affair. Mark would no more think of leaving Amelia than she would think of leaving Martin.

It was comforting to know that she could accept it as such. She had great affection for Martin, she had no desire to hurt or humiliate him. Twelve years of

126

marriage, of watching him grow from a small-town solicitor into the successful businessman he had become could not lightly be set aside. She was proud of his accomplishments, nor would she ever be the one to cut the solid earth from under his feet. They had a good, well-adjusted marriage even if the romance had largely gone out of it.

The arrangement with Mark suited them both and Amelia had asked for it. Barbara's mind went back to that weekend she and Martin had spent at Garveston Hall. She'd known then that Mark admired her; the invitation had been there in his eyes that night when they'd stayed downstairs to dance after the others had gone to their rooms. On that occasion she'd treated his advances lightly; she hadn't been ready for anything else.

When the weekend was over she and Martin had left. Her husband had offered a half-hearted invitation for Mark to stay with them for the race week in Cheltenham, and Mark had equally half-heartedly accepted. She had thought that had been the end of it, but fate had ordained things differently.

Mark reminded them later of their invitation and he had been a popular and uncomplicated guest. She knew he still desired her but he had made no advances and it was five months before she met him again.

She had received a tearful petulant letter from her mother to say that Mr Smythe had gout and would be unable to take her to the Mayor's Ball. Barbara responded sympathetically then forgot about it until her father telephoned Martin at his office to say that the least Barbara could do was visit them and accompany her mother to the Ball.

The entire episode had annoyed her even though she had no recourse but to agree. Mark and Amelia were fellow guests, and she'd hoped Amelia might have included her mother and herself in their crowd; not so however. Amelia had greeted her graciously, kissing her cheek and pressing her hand, but the Smythes had been left to sit alone at their table until a friend of her father's had invited them to join his party.

She'd been furious, and later when Mark invited her to dance with him she'd refused on the grounds that she and her mother were just leaving.

'You're angry,' he'd said, looking down at her with the hint of a smile at the corner of his mouth.

'Yes – I'm angry with Amelia. How dare she entertain me in her home like a dear friend and practically ignore me the next time we meet!' she'd stormed.

'I doubt if she meant to ignore you, Barbara,' Mark said.

'Well, it looked that way to me. I have to go now, goodnight.'

'Please don't go like that. We're still friends, aren't we?'

She'd looked up into his good-looking anxious face and her own had relented a little. 'I suppose so. It doesn't matter anyway, as we're not destined to see very much of each other.'

'I'd like very much to think otherwise.'

'I don't see how.'

'How long are you here for?'

'I'm driving home on Saturday.'

'We can't part bad friends. I ride every afternoon on the fell – do you ever go walking?'

'I walk round the shops and across the golf course.'

He smiled. 'Please make the effort. You should, it's beautiful up there.'

'I know what it's like up there, I had a surfeit of the fell when I was at Lorivals.'

'Meet me at the Pilgrims' Cross, Barbara. We need to talk.'

'I don't see why.'

'I'm asking you very humbly to come. I'm sorry you're annoyed with Amelia, she'd be devastated if she thought she'd hurt you in any way.'

128

That had been the start of it. Angry with Amelia, annoyed with her mother for insisting that she came, Barbara had been ready for consolation. It was possible Amelia didn't like her mother. Barbara knew that Mrs Smythe wasn't too popular in Greymont, as people considered her stand-offish and pushy. She was tolerated because Councillor Smythe was a well-liked figure but none of that should have counted with Amelia.

She'd gone on to the fell to meet Mark. He'd stood next to his horse up there near the Cross with the sunlight glinting on his fair hair, a smile of welcome playing on his mouth and in spite of herself she'd gone naturally into his arms, her vanity restored, her pride intact.

They conducted their affair discreetly even though there were times when Barbara would have dearly liked to remove that serene gracious smile from Lady Amelia's face and tell her that her husband had been her lover for two years.

Drat her mother. It would have been a golden opportunity to telephone Mark and hope they could spend the next few days together; now instead there would be her mother peeking and prying into everything, telling her things she didn't want to hear, talking about Mark's wife as if she was something to wonder at, gushingly grateful that they sat on the same Bench, spoke to each other on the friendliest of terms, lived on the same planet even, so that now and again her mother could telephone her to say that Amelia had enquired only that morning if Barbara and her husband were well.

CHAPTER 12

Amelia had thoroughly enjoyed herself: it was the type of day she'd looked forward to all summer, the local agricultural show where she was to present the prizes.

She'd practised years ago in the solitude of her nursery, bowing and smiling in front of the long mirror, handing packages to her dolls, murmuring a few gracious words, promising herself that one day she'd be involved in the same sort of functions as her mother was.

She had been a lonely child, very much an afterthought in her parents' lives, with two brothers and a sister much older than herself and no longer living in the family home. It was true she had her pony and her dogs, the doting love of both her parents, but what she lacked in companionship she more than made up for in dreams and longings.

She'd loved summer shows as a child, when she'd watched her mother smiling pleasantly, murmuring the few words of encouragement, or gentle regret that once again her black labrador had taken the Best of Show Gun Dog Award, and Lord Urquart's new rose had been singled out for special consideration.

It didn't matter that old Mr Andrews the gamekeeper with his golden labrador Bess had taken second place once again, or that Mr Charlesworth's rose was deemed inferior to her father's; the other competitors went away with smiles on their faces, well pleased with her ladyship's praise and their second-place rosettes carried proudly in their hands.

Her mother had trained her well. 'You must make them feel that one of these days they're going to beat you, Amelia. They won't, but the challenge will be there and they'll be proud to come second-best when you make them feel you've only just won.'

As she grew older she'd often thought it wasn't really fair for her parents to win every time; it surely wouldn't have done any harm if just once old Bess could beat Rory at his own game, and that her father's rose would peak at the wrong time, but it never happened.

Today Amelia had opened the show with a speech of welcome and thanks to all those who had contributed to the displays. The September day was warm and sunny and she'd looked cool and elegant in her beige skirt and soft leather jacket under which she wore a deeper beige silk blouse. Her mother had always worn a hat, usually a battered felt one in the autumn and a cream straw one in the summer, but then Mummy had never been a clothes horse. She looked her best in country tweeds, her favourite brogues and sturdy Harris tweed skirts.

Amelia's soft brown hair framed her face, her only adornment her pearl stud earrings and the rings on her long slim fingers. To those in her audience there seemed to be a timelessness about her; it didn't matter what she wore – somehow or other it always seemed right.

She moved from tent to tent, untiring and charming. Always saying the right thing, admiring the flowers and vegetables, just as enthusiastic with the birds and the rabbits, and then she'd gone on to sample the cakes and pastries, home-made jams and chutneys with evident pleasure, asking for recipes with equal alacrity from the losers as well as the winners.

She sat in the stands with the local dignitaries to watch the show-jumping and the dog parade, and charmingly she asked the Chief Constable to present the dog prizes because her spaniel Barnum had taken first prize.

The day had gone well, just as it always did, and later when Mark put in an appearance to present the

131

prizes in the large ring she slipped quietly into the background to drink a welcome cup of tea.

Maisie served her in the Women's Institute canteen. She was somewhat flushed in her large floral apron, with her red hair tied back from a rosy perspiring face, and Amelia said sweetly, 'You've been working so hard, Maisie, that I don't suppose you've had much chance to see anything of the show.'

Maisie smiled. 'I'm not interested in the horses or the dogs. Our dogs are strictly functional and they don't have pedigrees – neither do our horses, for that matter. Still, I thought the flowers were lovely and I took a second prize for my shortbread.'

'How nice! If you will let me have the recipe I'll get Cook to make some. The girls love shortbread.'

'Tom didn't get a prize with his bull, but he told me it's only a young animal – he'll do better next year.'

'Of course. There's always next year, that's why I enjoy these shows so much.'

She finished her tea and moved out of the tent. It had been a good day; she'd go to the dog enclosure now to pick up Barnum then she'd see if she could catch Mark before she left. He would have resented spending all day at the show, but no doubt by this time he'd have completed the judging and prize-giving and would be feeling mellow at the bar with some of the men.

She heard his laughter from outside the tent. No doubt he'd be regaling them with some of his more ribald hunting stories and she realized she hadn't been far wrong when a discreet silence greeted her arrival.

Mark grinned at her over his glass. 'Are you off home now, my dear? I gather it's been a good day.'

'Yes, one of the best, I think.'

The men hastened to agree with her and one of them said, 'I'll collect your dog, milady, then perhaps you'll be joinin' us for a drink?'

132

'Thank you no, but I'd be very grateful if you could collect Barnum.' After he'd gone she said to Mark, 'Who won the show- jumping?'

'Young Alison Steadwell on a horse called Gypsy. She rides well – they could go on to better things, I think.'

'I wish Pippa could have competed. She rides well too and she's very keen.'

'I doubt if her horse could have matched Gypsy's performance,' Mark said coolly.

'Perhaps we should buy her another and bring the show forward a week or so next year. It was a pity the school term started before this, otherwise the girls could have come.'

Mark smiled. 'You mean you're not content with your dog coming first, you'd like one of the girls to come first too?'

She looked at him sadly. 'Oh Mark, don't tell me you wouldn't be pleased.'

'Pleased yes, uncomfortable definitely. Doesn't it ever strike you, my dear, that other parents breed exceptional children? Alison Steadwell's father was my father's groom for years. The kid's grown up with horses, she's schooled them and cared for them since she was a small child, so don't begrudge her this little triumph.'

'I don't.'

'But you'd look out for a better horse. You could afford it, Steadwell couldn't.'

'I thought you said Gypsy could match anything.'

'Anything in our stables at present, not a horse you were prepared to spend a fortune on.'

'Oh well, we'll see before the next show. Why do you always try to thwart me, Mark?'

His smile was tantalizing, filled with sly mockery. 'Because I know, my dear, that when you set your heart on anything by hook or by crook you achieve it. It

133

rankles that you achieve it on your own, without my help or my money.'

They looked at each other steadily for several seconds, then with a cool shrug of her shoulders she said, 'I'm going home now. I suppose you'll be in for dinner?'

'I'm not sure. It will depend how soon I can get away from here. I might join the chaps at the bar for a sandwich and help to clear away.'

She turned and left him.

His eyes followed her tall slender figure as she made her way out of the tent, graciously smiling at those she encountered on her way, occasionally stopping to exchange the odd word, then she was lost in the crowd.

There were days, weeks even, when he felt he could relate to Amelia. There was no denying that she was a brilliant asset to his home and his life: the perfect wife, the loving mother, the gracious chatelaine of a house she'd transformed from the shabby ruin of his father's time into a place people travelled miles to see.

Three times a week in the summer months strangers from all over the country wandered through the gardens and across the parkland of Garveston Hall. An army of villagers served afternoon tea and morning coffee in the restored barns, and Amelia often moved among them with cool assurance, accepting their reverence like a queen, but none of them really knew the real Amelia, because Mark himself had never discovered her.

She'd given him two daughters, but even in their moments of rare passion he'd never really possessed her; she'd remained an enigma. At first he'd thought it was because she should have been his elder brother's wife if that fatal plane accident hadn't ended Phillip's life, but after a time he realized it had nothing to do with that. It was simply the way she was, cocooned in her reserve, bolstered by her pride.

Mark was an earthy man. He needed, demanded even, both warmth and passion from the women in his life. He'd always known he must make a good marriage; he had no money of his own, and his father had squandered whatever assets he had on horses and dodgy investments when Mark and his brother were still children. Phillip's engagement to Amelia, the youngest daughter of an earl, was welcomed joyfully by his parents, but then Phillip had been killed in that tragic air crash and the onus fell on Mark to find a suitable bride.

Amelia was beautiful. She was not unwilling to marry Mark since her father had already begun to transform Garveston Hall into the sort of home his daughter wanted, and when Mark considered some of the women who had been trotted out for his inspection, marriage to Amelia was a very desirable prospect. Up to a point it had worked. She made few demands on him so long as he created no scandal and was there when he was needed. She on the other hand fulfilled her part of the bargain to perfection so that on the surface they were an ideal couple.

After Amelia left the showground she decided to drive the long way home beside the river. She often drove this way when she was alone and the day was so beautiful. The leaves were only just turning and the river mirrored the blue sky until it rippled into silver shafts of light before it dropped over the weir.

She drove slowly, and when she reached the narrow bridge beyond the weir she brought the car to a standstill. For a few moments she sat looking at the view, then calling to the spaniel, she left the car and started to climb the hill. From the summit she could look down on the turrets and chimneys of Garveston Hall and a smile of pure delight lit up her face.

She'd sat on this hill with Phillip Garveston as a schoolgirl. They'd known each other for a great many years and Amelia had been invited to afternoon tea when Lady Garveston heard she was a pupil at Lorivals which was close by.

After tea Phillip had shown her the gardens and the park and they'd finally sat on the hillside looking down on the river. Amelia had been a guest in other stately homes far more lavish and better preserved than Garveston, but she was enchanted with the house, its situation, even to the walls of the ruined abbey at the edge of the forest. The house seemed at one with the lonely Pennine hills, the rolling fells and the long silver line of the sea she could see in the distance, and her mind was even then obsessed with the way she could change it, if it had belonged to her.

She was finding Phillip Garveston both kind and interesting. She liked his good-looking thoughtful young face and the way a lock of dark hair fell on to his forehead. She liked his voice and the youthful desperate pride in it when he talked about his home and what he would do to it, if only he had the money.

'Perhaps if you were to marry a girl with money it would solve all your problems,' Amelia had volunteered, and Phillip had smiled gently before replying, 'I doubt if any girl with money would want to squander it on restoring this place.'

'I don't see why not,' Amelia said stoutly. 'One day she'd be Lady Garveston and this could be so very beautiful.'

Her words had pleased him, and they'd walked back to the house hand in hand, a fact that hadn't gone unnoticed by his parents watching them from the window of the drawing room.

She'd seen Phillip constantly over the next few years. Her father had allowed him to visit her at Drummond and proclaimed that he was indeed a nice boy with good manners and a sensible outlook on life. He did not, however, think him a suitable contender for his youngest daughter's hand in marriage. She could do better than Phillip Garveston.

Amelia had overheard her parents talking together

136

in the drawing room one evening when she'd deliberately sneaked downstairs to listen. Phillip had returned home only that afternoon and she felt pretty certain he would be the topic for discussion.

Her father had said the daughter of an earl could do better than marry the elder son of an impoverished baronet whose entire life had been given up to the pursuit of beautiful women, uncertain horses and gambling at casinos on the continent. The fact that Phillip's mother was the daughter of an earl was a matter for commiseration rather than an example for Amelia to follow.

She heard her mother pointing out that Amelia had set her heart on Garveston Hall, that she loved the house and had great ideas for its restoration, whereupon her father had snorted in some disgust, 'And where's the money coming from? Not from Garveston, I'll be bound. I'm the one she'll look to and what's so special about Garveston Hall? Amelia wants to look around a bit more – the country's groaning with stately piles.'

She'd cried herself to sleep that night, but in the months that followed she'd shown her father that it had to be Phillip Garveston or nobody. She wasn't interested in the silly season, where it was likely she'd have found a young man more to her parents' liking. She was a beautiful girl and she had great charm, even if she wasn't very intellectual. Lorivals had educated her to be a suitable mate for the best in the land, and yet those years at school had blinded Amelia against anything beyond Garveston Hall.

Her father capitulated and began to spend money on the Hall's restoration. Phillip's father sat back and watched the proceedings while his wife, whose health was rapidly failing, felt she could die in peace knowing that Phillip would be safely married to the right sort of girl. His brother Mark inwardly seethed that he was made to feel very much the second and inferior son, and that the Hall he loved, even if it was crumbling and shabby, was being put to rights by people he hardly knew.

So it was that on this fine September afternoon, Amelia's thoughts were on the past rather than the present. Whenever she came up here she was reminded of those long walks with Phillip and the plans they had made, plans that came to nothing when his plane crashed on a lonely hillside.

She'd come up here on the day they'd told her of his death and the tears had rolled down her cheeks so that she'd viewed the landscape through a haze of tears and pain. It would never belong to her now. Some other woman, Mark's wife, would be riding her horse across the parkland, strolling in the gardens, standing on the terrace looking out towards the distant mountains. That beautiful house which was slowly coming to life would deteriorate in Mark's hands, because he was too much like his father, too careless with money and too easy with women. Since his friendship with Nancy Graham had ended there'd been too many females in his life, and none of them suitable to become the mistress of Garveston Hall.

She'd mourned her fiancé but more, much more, she'd mourned the loss of the Hall. Her parents had sent her to stay with her sister Celia in Cornwall but that hadn't helped. Celia was far too preoccupied with Dorinda to pay much attention to Amelia, and Dorinda was a tragedy with her vacant stare and slobbering mouth. Amelia felt that her life was over until the afternoon she'd visited Garveston with her father several months after Phillip's death. She had left the adults to their discussion while she climbed to her favourite spot above the river.

It was there that Mark found her and he had been very kind. He didn't resemble Phillip: if anything, he

138

was better looking, he didn't have his brother's sensitivity or his practical mind, but one day he would be Sir Mark Garveston, Baronet, and Garveston Hall would be his home.

Never reluctant to talk about himself, Mark had confessed that he had no interest in marrying any of the women in his life. He'd been very fond of Nancy Graham at one time but that wouldn't have worked either, as for one thing her father didn't like him and for another her family didn't have the right sort of background, nor sufficient money.

They came together with no illusions about each other. Her parents saw their match as a solution rather than a blessing, and Mark's father was gratified that he didn't have to think about repaying any of the money her father had spent on his home. Their marriage was a quiet affair because of the circumstances and here she was, thirteen years later, driving home through the parkland with the sun setting in a blaze of glory behind the turrets of Garveston Hall.

Amelia was complacent about her marriage to Mark. She led a busy life as a JP and chairwoman of a great many committees. She enjoyed her status in the community and she and Mark were seen together when it was necessary. She regretted that both her children were girls as she had no wish to have another child, and for his part Mark didn't seem to care either way. The future would take care of itself; for the present she was content.

Mark had only the pittance his father had left him, so he contributed nothing to the upkeep of the Hall, and he had his horses and his cars. If they were successful he spent lavishly; if they let him down he became peevish and resentful but continued to live well on his wife's money. Amelia asked no questions, just as long as he kept his indiscretions far enough distant from Greymont and her life.

CHAPTER 13

As Barbara sat back in the cosy warmth of the Café Goya in Cheltenham's exclusive High Street she watched her mother push the last crumb of her scone into her mouth and sit back with a long, contented sigh.

'There's another if you'd like it, Mother,' Barbara teased her.

'No, dear, that one is yours. I couldn't possibly eat another.'

Her mother had already consumed three of the small scones bulging with clotted cream and strawberry jam, and even as she declined the other her eyes lingered on it greedily.

'I'm not having it. I only ever have the one, I find them very rich.'

'You don't need to worry about your figure, dear. Your father thinks you're too thin. We both think you should eat more,' her mother said, before she took the last remaining scone. 'We can't possibly leave just one. Oh dear, I shan't want anything later if I eat this.'

'We'll have something around eight, you'll be ready for it then.'

'I do so love shopping in Cheltenham and having you to myself. It's not the same when Martin's at home.'

'Why ever not? He doesn't mind what we do.'

'I always have the feeling that he'd rather be at his club or entertaining his friends, not your old mother.'

'Actually we don't entertain as much since we moved. You'll really like the house, Mother.'

'I'm sure I shall. I liked the other one and it was nearer to town. If you were busy I could always get the bus from there.'

Ignoring that remark Barbara rose to her feet. 'I think we should get off home before the evening traffic builds up. I'll help you carry your parcels.'

'I shouldn't really have bought another handbag, but I've had that old black one for years and that brown one your father bought me the last time I was here doesn't hold enough.'

Her mother had made several purchases – two new nightgowns and a pair of shoes with heels that were far too high for her and which she said would only be worn on special occasions.

Barbara was convinced she could have purchased identical items in Greymont but her mother liked to explain that they had been bought in Cheltenham when she was visiting her daughter.

She didn't like the low-slung coupé; she preferred a more sedate car and complained that she hadn't the same room in it, and it was far too low. 'I do think your father's Ford is more comfortable, dear. Why, there's no room at all on the back seat of this car and the boot is very small.' Barbara merely smiled but undeterred her mother went on, 'I suppose if you go any distance you travel in Martin's car?'

'Yes, Mother. This is my car and adequate for my needs. Usually there's just me in it. If necessary I can always borrow Martin's for the day.'

'It's very pretty country,' her mother remarked. 'Is that why you moved?'

'That amongst other things.' Barbara brought the car to a stop on the hillside and Mrs Smythe's eyes opened wide at the view of the large house with the sun glinting on its array of windows.

'It's awfully big,' she commented.

'Yes, it's larger than the other. Don't you think the gardens are lovely?'

'Well yes, although I suppose you have to employ a

141

gardener. Martin didn't look after the garden at your old house, did he?'

'We have a local man who comes every morning.'

'More expense, I suppose.'

'Martin wouldn't have engaged him if he couldn't afford him, Mother.'

'No, I suppose not.'

She watched the speculation in her mother's eyes as they moved from room to room, and her delight at the décor of the bedroom which Barbara said was to be hers during her stay.

'Well,' Barbara said. 'Do you like it?'

'It's beautiful, dear, absolutely perfect! I doubt if your father'd like it, though.'

Barbara laughed. 'Why ever not?'

'Well, you know what he's like. He prefers old things – old houses and churches, antique furniture, traditional things – he'd think this house cold and far too modern.'

'Oh, Daddy's an old fusspot. He never comes to see us and yet when you tell him about this he'll have a great deal to say. Martin and I love it here. I doubt if we'll ever move again.'

'I should think not indeed. I must tell Lady Amelia about it when I see her next. She'll be very interested.'

Mrs Smythe persisted in calling Amelia by her title in spite of the fact that she had roomed with her daughter at school. It was a kind of antiquated subservience and Barbara felt irrationally annoyed by it.

'What would you like to do tomorrow?' she enquired later after her mother had brought her up to date with Greymont gossip and had given her the usual inquisition.

'Well, I thought we were going into Cheltenham again. Mind you, Tewkesbury's nice and it's ages since you took me to Gloucester. What do you think?'

'Anything you like, Mother but I can't make any plans for the day after tomorrow. I've fixed up to go riding with a friend.'

'Riding?'

'Yes. There's a riding school just outside the village. I've been meeting my friend Lucy there two or three times a week and I must say I'm enjoying it.'

'We wanted you to learn to ride when you were quite young but you said you weren't interested in horses. I always understood it was something you had to do from being a youngster.'

'I don't think it matters if you enjoy it. Let's go to Tewkesbury tomorrow – we'll have our lunch at that new place on the way in. Martin's been there with some business associates and he said it was very good.'

'I hope it's a nice day. I brought my new suit and my mink ties, as I never get the chance to wear them at home; your father says I look too dressed up in them.'

Barbara smiled. 'I'll make us some coffee. I don't suppose you want to sit up late on your first night away.'

The telephone rang while she was in the kitchen and she thought it was probably Lucy Belbin checking up on their date. She was disconcerted to hear Mark Garveston's voice, low and faintly amused, asking, 'Where have you been? I've been trying to get hold of you all day.'

'My mother's here, we've been in Cheltenham.'

'How long is she staying?'

'Five or six days, I think. Martin's away on business.'

'I know.'

'How do you know?'

'I rang him last week to see if I might stay with you for a few days, but when he said he'd be away I didn't pursue the idea. One has to observe the proprieties, don't you think?'

'So where are you staying?'

'That new place in Tewkesbury. It's very good – if you didn't have your mother you could have joined me for a few days.'

She laughed. 'Actually we were thinking of having lunch there tomorrow, now we'll have to choose somewhere else. What are you doing in these parts anyway?'

'I'm looking at a horse for Pippa as she's outgrown her pony. I thought you might help me make up my mind.'

'I know practically nothing about horses.'

'I understood you'd taken up riding.'

'Oh Mark, I'm a learner! How could you possibly have thought I'd be able to influence you one way or another?'

'Does this mean that we are not going to meet, not even when I'm so near to you?'

'I don't see how.'

'But I'm sure you'll think of something, darling. I'll telephone you in the morning – perhaps you'll know by then if you can shelve your mother for a day. Do try, Barbara. I'm anxious to see you.' She heard his chuckle of amusement before she replaced the receiver.

Her mother's voice came plaintively from the doorway. 'Where are you, Barbara? I thought you were going to make coffee. Can I help?'

'No thanks. There was a telephone call. You go and sit down and I'll bring the coffee in, in a minute.'

She wondered how much Mrs Smythe had heard and how she could conveniently leave her to her own devices for one day. It was just like Mark to think it would be easy.

Her mother's face was petulant as Barbara poured the coffee and set her cup in front of her and her voice was equally plaintive as she said, 'Don't think I don't agree this is a beautiful house, love, but I feel like a prisoner in it.'

'What exactly do you mean by that?'

144

'Well, when you were in the other house if you didn't want to take me with you I could always get on a bus. I knew all the bus stops and I never minded taking a trip out by myself, but there aren't any buses around here.'

'There is one from the end of the lane on the hour.'

'What use is that? And I don't suppose they run very late.'

'What's brought all this on?'

'Well, it was this date you have to go riding. I'm only here for five or six days but you don't intend to put this woman off until next week. I expect that was somebody else on the telephone inviting you out.'

'As a matter of fact it was, someone asking me to play golf.'

'What did you say?'

'I told them I had you staying with me and I'd ask if you minded.'

'Well, I do mind – that's two days out of five. What shall I do in this place while you're out of the house and me not knowing when you'll be back?'

'Mother, I didn't know you even wanted to come here until yesterday. You gave me no notice and you never even asked if I had other plans. I'm sorry, but I do have commitments I can't possibly put off.'

'In that case I'll go home tomorrow. I don't want to stay where I'm not wanted.'

'There's no need for that – I'm only asking for a little time to myself!'

'You can have all the time you want. Maisie Standing never misses a week without going to see her mother, and she's got her hands full at the farm with three children to cope with.'

'Mrs Jayson does live within walking distance, Mother.'

'I'm very upset, Barbara. I thought you'd be glad to have me, to go to the shops together and talk about old times. Your father'll be very cross, I just know he will.'

'Look, there's really no need to go home tomorrow, you're just being silly.'

'I'm going to telephone your father to meet the train. I suppose it's not too much to ask if you'll take me to the station.'

'Of course – if you insist on going.'

'I do. I'll ring him from the kitchen.'

Mrs Smythe got up from her chair and stalked into the kitchen leaving Barbara all on edge. She didn't really want to offend her mother; she had made up her mind she would only be able to see Mark for a short time but now she alternated between joy that it might now be longer, and a certain regret that her mother would be leaving in a temper and her father wouldn't be pleased.

When Mrs Smythe returned she said peevishly, 'Well, that's that. Your father has had to cancel a meeting to be able to meet the train. He wasn't pleased.'

'I'm sorry, Mother, it's all so unnecessary.'

'Well, I don't think so. I might as well go upstairs and pack. If you want me to visit again perhaps you'll invite me when it's convenient.' She made a grimace as she finished her coffee which was now stone cold, then bidding Barbara a frigid goodnight she stalked out of the room.

After she'd washed the coffee cups Barbara telephoned Lucy Belbin, who answered the telephone accompanied by the usual sounds of barking dogs in the background.

'Lucy, I'm so sorry but I don't think I can keep our appointment to ride on Wednesday. Something's cropped up. Will you be very inconvenienced?'

'Actually, no. Samson's gone lame this afternoon, goodness knows how, but I'm having to get the vet out to him in the morning – and you know that Betsy pulled a tendon, so that means I'm two horses short. I'll have to take the group out in relays. I'm rather glad to be let off Wednesday.'

'Well, that's a relief, but I'm sorry about Samson.'

'I suppose it's your mother.'

'Well, no. She's going home tomorrow.'

'Really? I thought she was staying a few days.'

'She was, but she doesn't like being so far out of town, and I can't be with her every hour of the day. I'm going into Tewkesbury to meet a friend whom I haven't seen for quite a long time.'

'I can see you're having your problems. Give me a ring when you get home.'

She hadn't believed it would all be so easy. She felt guilty about her mother but Mrs Smythe would get over it, it wasn't the first skirmish they'd had. However, her guilty feelings encouraged her to telephone her father.

His first words reassured her. 'I suppose you two have been squabbling again. Not gettin' all her own way, is she?'

'She doesn't like being so far out of town, and really, Dad, her visit was right out of the blue. She's expecting me to drop everything and then getting offended when I can't.'

'Take no notice, love, she'll get over it. I told her you'd probably made arrangements but she'd have none of it. I'll meet her off the train and I'll probably have to listen to a tirade against you for the next few days. Your ears'll be burnin', love.'

CHAPTER 14

Martin Walton enjoyed conferences. He liked being with men who had made it in the world of big business, who could talk intelligently on all manner of subjects, who knew how to eat well and were knowledgeable about good wines – men, in fact, who were similar to himself.

He enjoyed the camaraderie at the bar and round the dining table as well as in the boardroom, and when the conference was over he relished the discussion of what they had achieved, the interests that united them and the interests that divided them, and he also enjoyed the traditional golf match after their last meeting.

However, this was one conference he had not enjoyed. For one thing, they had a cuckoo in the nest – somebody he had never met before and to whom he had taken an instant dislike. Sam Barber never tired of reminding his colleagues that he was a self-made man who had come up the hard way from the shop floor to the boardroom without any attempt to change his personality.

His accent was broad, he wore the wrong clothes and smoked a foul-smelling pipe. He boasted about his big house and his powerful car to men who didn't flaunt their achievements or their possessions, and he called his wife the 'little woman' which infuriated Martin, since from the photographs he persisted in showing everybody, Mrs Barber appeared to be a lady of considerable proportions.

He wasn't a golfer yet he insisted on accompanying the others round the course, and because his room was next to Martin's he invariably invited himself in on the way down to dinner. This afforded him the opportunity to scan Martin's wardrobe, the gold monogrammed cuff-links and the gold wristwatch Barbara had presented him with on his last birthday.

'I don't suppose you came up the hard way,' he said to Martin as he eyed the younger man's impeccable dinner jacket. 'I didn't bring one of those, the little woman said it wouldn't be necessary.'

'Is this the first conference you've been to?' Martin asked curiously.

'Oh, I've been to one or two local ones. They don't dress up and the work gets done just the same.' He was wearing a light grey lounge suit and Martin couldn't help noticing the frayed cuffs and the stain on one lapel. Seeing him looking at them Sam said, 'I had to pack in a hurry. The little woman was away at her mother's so I just grabbed the first things I could find. Do you get to many of these affairs?'

'Quite a few over the year.'

'Doesn't your wife object – I take it you're married?'

'Yes. No, of course my wife doesn't object. Barbara's always been aware of my commitments.'

'Well, my wife wouldn't thank you to be involved in anythin' like this. We went to one once, some years back. She didn't enjoy any of it, trips out for the wives when their men were working, nights round the cocktail bar talkin' business. It wasn't Nellie's scene.'

'There are a number of functions we take our wives to, but Barbara would be bored at something like this.'

'What's she like then, your missus?'

Martin flinched, but even so he extracted a photograph out of his breast pocket and handed it over, saying, 'This was taken last year on the Isle of Wight. We were there to do some sailing.'

Sam looked at the photograph and whistled. 'Mmm, classy dame. Not frightened of her getting into mischief while you're away so much?'

149

'Of course not.'

'What does she find to do while you're away then? Do you have kids?'

'No. Barbara's a golfer, she's also taken up riding and she enjoys gardening among other things.'

Sam handed the photograph back saying, 'If I had a wife like that I'd not be the one for too many conferences.' Martin didn't respond, and after a few minutes Sam added, 'My Nellie's as plain as a pikestaff, but she does have good legs and a pleasant personality. There's nothing toffee-nosed about my Nellie.'

They walked down to the dining room together and Martin was relieved to find that they were not the first down.

During the first couple of days of the conference Sam had been an outsider, but he was quite unsnubbable. Now they were amused by him. They thought him a bit of a lad, the sort of chap who had revitalized their free time. Indeed, Martin had been amazed at the positive response of most of them to his brash good humour.

It was the last night and Sam said over drinks at the bar, 'I reckon we ought to paint the town red tonight.' Smiles and glances were exchanged, and seeing that he had an audience Sam went on, 'I came down here last Friday and because I was on my own I spent it in the public rooms. Right eye-opener it were, too. Here we are in an atmosphere that Queen Victoria might have found old-fashioned and out there suddenly there's life.'

'What do you mean – life?' Alan Jeffries said curiously.

'Girls havin' a night out away from their husbands, other girls from the shops and factories and offices lookin' for a bit of fun. There was nothin' on the agenda to say we shouldn't sample the local dishes as well as the goods we're payin' for.'

Nobody took him up on the invitation, but they were amused by him. Unabashed, Sam determined that the

150

night was young; with a few drinks inside them he could make them change their minds. Even that stuffed shirt Walton mightn't be so bad if he could be persuaded to let his hair down a little. That smashing wife of his wasn't spending her time at the sewing circle, he felt sure. How on earth had Walton ever managed to pull a bird like that?

Sam determined to keep up the pressure; they wouldn't take much persuading to make their last night one to remember.

Over dinner they discussed the golf match in the morning, the likely venue for their next meeting, and then Sam got to work on his near neighbours. By the time the meal was over and they had downed several bottles of expensive red wine they were more in the mood to listen to him.

'This is the last night for us chaps who are not golfers,' he encouraged them. 'What's wrong with a bit of fun with the local talent?'

Martin hoped his particular cronies would not listen to him, but as the rallying went on Sam began to receive some support. Martin interrupted sternly, 'You're surely not really thinking of going out on the town? Don't we usually play a rubber or two of bridge?'

They dithered, but Sam's persuasions were more potent than his own. 'Come on, Martin,' Sam urged. 'It's our last night – don't be a spoilsport.'

Justin Forbes looked at Martin across the table. If anybody disliked the idea Martin had expected it to be Justin, but with an expressive shrug of his shoulders he signified that they were outnumbered and if they didn't want to appear unsociable and priggish they would have to fall in with the general consensus.

The public rooms of the hotel were spacious and more elaborate than the more restrained good taste of the residents' lounge. Sam led his group to an alcove near the bar from where they could view the room in general and then he summoned a waiter saying, 'This round's on me, boys. The place is a bit quiet yet, but it'll liven up.'

Martin sat next to Justin and began a conversation about the conference but after a few minutes Justin said, 'We didn't bargain on Sam, Martin. I suppose he means well, he's just not the sort of chap we're used to.'

'I could have done without this,' Martin admitted.

'Yes, well, around ten we can start to make our excuses – an early night, golf in the morning. How's Barbara? It must be over a year since I've seen her.'

'She's fine. You must come for dinner one evening with your wife, we'd both be pleased to see you.'

'We'd like that, and I expect Joan'd like to see your new house. Happy there?'

'Oh yes, very happy.'

Then girls started to arrive in groups of four and six, and they sat in giggling groups drinking their glasses of lager and vodka. Four of them sat in the next alcove and it was impossible not to hear their conversation, which was of boys and gossip about their work in shops and offices, boys and the cinema, boys and their summer holidays. Sam chuckled and putting his head round the corner he said, 'We can hear all your secrets, girls, so be very careful.'

The laughter was general, and after a few minutes another group at another table began casting sly glances in their direction, and lips and eyes were smiling in open invitation.

This was what they had come for. It started out as an evening with the girls, but they were looking for something more than this, some man to buy their drinks, to invite them to a local dance or for a stroll along the waterfront if he was young and handsome.

Before Martin knew what was happening two groups of girls were sitting at their table and Sam was saying

152

genially, 'Come on, we can't have you two men sitting together. That's right, love, you go in between Martin and Justin. Now, what are we all having to drink?'

Martin was aware of two brown eyes assessing him curiously, eyes made up with too much pink shadow and mauve mascara, and chestnut hair teased into a tortuous shape which nature had never intended. He could smell the girl's perfume, lightly floral, probably inexpensive he thought, and she was pretty and when she smiled her teeth were white and even behind the glossy cyclamen lipstick, again too heavily applied.

He smiled back, and immediately the girl cast her eyes down and he realized that in spite of her brash appearance she was very shy.

'Do you live in Southampton?' he asked gently.

'I came in by bus. We live nearer to Langstone if you know where that is.'

'Langstone Harbour?'

'Yes.'

'I know it well, I have a yacht down there.'

The girl's eyes grew round with admiration and Martin felt uncomfortable. He hadn't wanted to impress her, he had simply stated a fact but with naive innocence she was asking, 'Have you really got a boat? There's some beauties in the harbour there. Mi sister and me goes every Sunday mornin' just to look at them.'

Sam laughed. 'Don't hide your light under a bushel, Martin. It's not one boat he's got, love, it's two.'

By this time Martin was racking his brains as to how he could change the subject, but the girl said breathlessly, 'Have you really got two at Langstone? Oh, I would like to see them.'

'I only have one at Langstone, the other's at home in the garage.'

'In the garage?'

'Why yes, I haven't decided where I'm going to sail her yet.'

153

'Don't you live round here, then?'

'No, I live near Cheltenham.'

'That's in the Midlands, isn't it?'

'Yes. Have you ever been there?'

'No. You'd think I wouldn't want to go to the coast for my holidays but we always do. Brighton or Weymouth.'

He smiled, then the drinks arrived and the men passed them round good-humouredly.

Martin Walton was not really a snob. He was the only son of doting but undemonstrative parents. They were proud of his accomplishments and the good life had come easy to him because he had a sound brain and had been fortunate enough always to be in the right place at the right time.

His father had served on Greymont Council with Mr Smythe and the two families had thrown them together more or less since childhood. He'd grown up with the idea that one day he and Barbara would marry, and she'd been ready and waiting. He'd always been proud of her. She was beautiful, she knew how to dress and how to entertain his guests, and he'd always believed they had a nice life and the perfect marriage.

There were times when Barbara worried him, however, and he couldn't exactly put his finger on the time when things had begun to change. She'd been as proud of his achievements as his parents had, but these days whatever he did wasn't enough. Take the house, for instance. He'd engaged the best interior decorator outside London and what had she done when the man had finished? Simply ripped out the kitchen units and found fault with the dining room. The trouble with Barbara was that she was spoilt, and he'd been the one who'd spoiled her.

Now she was talking about resigning from the Golf Club, dropping people they'd been glad to cultivate when they first arrived in Cheltenham, and what did she intend to put in their place? – the racing crowd.

It was true that everybody had enjoyed themselves during the race week but they weren't really his crowd. He knew nothing about horses, and if Barbara went hacking from here until next race week she'd be no wiser when she came up against experts.

He would have a serious talk with Barbara when he got home. Obviously they couldn't cut themselves off from the people at the Golf Club and he'd have to be firmer with her about the house or she'd be replacing the carpets next.

He suddenly became aware that the girl next to him was speaking and apologizing for his lack of attention he said, 'I'm sorry. My mind was wandering.'

'I know, you were miles away. Are you leaving here in the morning?'

'No, Sunday morning. We usually finish up with a golf match.'

'Your friend there, he's all for having a run along the coast.'

Martin gave Sam his undivided attention; he was well launched into persuading the others to get into their cars first thing in the morning, and take the girls for a drive along the coast. Catching Martin's eye he added, 'We can take a look at old Martin's boat on the way. How does that appeal to you chaps?'

By this time they were all exceedingly mellow and the girls were quick to add their voices to Sam's.

'Why don't we?' the girl beside him said. 'It's goin' to be a lovely day and you can always play golf at home. I'd love to see your boat.'

He looked across at Justin but his colleague's eyes were all for the pretty redhead looking up at him provocatively from under her false eyelashes, and Martin became convinced that there would be no golf in the morning. Instead, there'd be a convoy of them driving down to Langstone.

The girl's name was Sandra and her enthusiasm for his Jaguar matched her passion for his boat. Before lunch six of them were on board and in a stiff morning breeze they were heading out into the Channel. Later on when he had had time to think, Martin never quite knew how they had got that far, but he was laughing as he hadn't laughed for a very long time, and a girl was looking up at him with the sort of desperate longing he'd never thought to see in a woman's eyes again.

There was nothing exciting about Sandra Stubbs. She was pretty, and laughter came readily to her lips. She worked as a shop assistant in Southampton's largest department store and she was the youngest of five children. Her father worked on the docks and her mother served school meals. Anybody less ordinary it would have been hard to find, but she had a simple and trusting enthusiasm that Martin found strangely touching. She was having the time of her life, loving every minute of it, and he warmed to the task of making the day one she would remember for a long time to come – without any thought that it would go further than just one day . . .

CHAPTER 15

Mark Garveston eyed his brother-in-law across the breakfast table with a frown of speculation on his face. They'd never really hit it off, they hadn't anything in common. Mark was a countryman, Desmond was a Townie, or so Mark told himself, simply because Desmond was a diplomat and had spent most of his adult life in one capital city after another.

Desmond Atherton was engrossed with *The Times* crossword, he would have been singularly surprised if he had known of the thoughts in Mark's mind.

Desmond was a stuffed shirt, or so Mark thought. He'd received a knighthood for his work at the Foreign Office and he'd never discussed it or his work there. Celia, his wife and Amelia's sister, lived in Cornwall and spent very little time in London; Mark speculated wildly on the sort of life he led in London when his wife was not in residence. That there were a host of women he doubted, Desmond was a dry old stick, hardly likely to do anything that might create scandal, and like Mark himself he must know which side his bread was buttered; on the other hand he couldn't be expected to live like a monk.

Celia'd been more concerned with that poor idiot child of theirs, and even now that she was dead she had to be mourned over as though her death was a tragedy never to be forgotten.

Desmond never spoke of her, Celia wept about her and Amelia wept with her. This exasperated Mark beyond endurance and he made himself most unpopular by talking about it. Celia had been staying with them for two weeks. Desmond had come up for the weekend. He wondered how long it would be before they saw each other again.

He took another piece of toast and slowly buttered it, then he left the table to replenish his coffee cup asking, 'More coffee Desmond?'

'Yes thank you,' was the terse reply.

'What time are you off then?'

'After lunch I expect.'

'Celia staying in London for a time then?'

Patiently Desmond laid his newspaper on the table. 'I'm not sure, we haven't discussed it.'

Mark returned to the table to take up Desmond's cup. 'Rum sort of arrangement you have I must say,' he mumbled. 'There's no call for her to be in Cornwall on her own now Dorinda's gone, can't you insist she stays in London?'

Desmond permitted himself a half-smile. 'It's a long time since I insisted about anything to Celia. In Cornwall she still feels close to Dorinda, she feels London is impersonal, uncaring.'

'It doesn't matter that you have to be there?'

'Apparently not.'

'I'm not very sure I understand Amelia, must run in the family. Finished the crossword then?'

'Yes, it wasn't very difficult today.'

'I don't suppose there's any good news in the paper?'

'There's the usual trouble in the Middle East and Africa.' He picked up the paper and handed it across the table.

There was a picture on the front page of two men and a woman standing beside a burnt-out tank in the Lebanon and Mark smiled. 'She gets in the news these days. To think I knew Nancy Graham when she worked with her father on the local rag. She was a nice girl, I thought a lot about Nancy.'

When Desmond remained silent Mark said, 'Her father didn't approve of me, he made that very plain.

I always thought she'd marry a local boy and settle down in the town, it just shows how wrong you can be about people.'

'Wasn't she at school with Amelia?'

'Yes. I took her to the end of term dance, Phillip was taking Amelia and Amelia asked if I'd escort Nancy. She was a pretty little thing, blonde hair and the biggest cornflower-blue eyes. I like to think she fell for me at that dance, I certainly fell for her even when I knew it couldn't last.'

'Why couldn't it last?'

'Need you ask? Nice girl, no money and an absence of blue blood.'

'Were you surprised when she went off with Templeton?'

'Dumbfounded, after all I never thought Nancy was in his league. I'd never have thought she'd have jumped into his sort of life from the local rag.'

'Perhaps she met him in London or in the Far East.'

'Mmmm, that's a thought. I must say she was mighty cagey about her life in the Far East that weekend she was here. Do you know Templeton?'

'Yes, I've been in his company several times.'

'What sort of a chap is he?'

'Dedicated, adventurous, likeable.'

'Good-looking?'

'Obviously.'

'Unmarried?'

'I believe so.'

Mark grinned. 'In which case he's got it made.'

Desmond rose from his chair saying abruptly, 'I'll see if Celia's made her mind up about whether she intends to stay in London or not.'

He reached the door just as Amelia was about to enter it, they wished each other good morning and Amelia said, 'Celia's almost finished breakfast, she's looking so much better now, Desmond.'

'You know we're leaving later today,' Desmond said.

'I wish she could have stayed on a little longer, there's nothing to rush back for.'

Desmond merely smiled and made his way across the hall.

Amelia helped herself to fruit juice and coffee and Mark said testily, 'For heaven's sake don't ask them to stay on longer, Celia's constantly in tears and Desmond's wrapped up in reserve.'

'They've both suffered a great tragedy, Mark, can't you understand that?'

'The tragedy was that the girl lived to be twelve, it was a blessing when she died.'

'They don't see it like that and neither do I. Dorinda was adorable, we all loved her.'

'Pity isn't love, Amelia. I pitied her, I didn't love her and neither did our two daughters.'

'But of course they did, they wept inconsolably when she died.'

'Because they thought it was expected of them, and they wept out of pity. Let us be realistic, Amelia, Dorinda didn't know them, she didn't know anybody; she sensed her mother was there, she didn't know Desmond or her brother, she didn't know you, only that you were the being who cared for her when mother wasn't around. Those dogs of yours have more perception.'

'I don't want to talk about it.'

'That suits me fine, but we do talk about it, don't we, Amelia? We talk about Dorinda loving Cornwall, she'd have loved anywhere else just as much, she didn't know where she was or who she was with. We talk about that summer at your father's when she was well and running through the gardens, we never talked about the years that came after when she was a veritable cabbage.'

'I said I didn't want to talk about it, not with you at any rate, Mark. You're unkind about Dorinda, you don't try to understand. Desmond doesn't talk about her because it hurts too much, Celia and I talk about her because we loved her and it helps to keep her memory alive.'

'But you talk about her as if she was a normal child, that's what I can't understand. Instead of being grateful that she's gone you want to recreate her all the time. I don't like you doing it when the girls are at home.'

'Pippa and Berenice understand, Mark.'

'No, Amelia, they only pretend they understand. Dorinda was imperfect and you can't bear to think that anything imperfect happened to your family. Everything has to be perfect, come first, conquer against all comers. I'd understand you better, Amelia, if just once you realised there are flaws even in the Urquart circle.'

He got up from the table and flounced out through the open french window and Amelia's eyes followed him doubtfully.

Mark would never understand about Dorinda in a thousand years. Philip would have understood, but then Philip was sensitive and notably kind. Mark prided himself that he didn't suffer fools gladly, he was often impatient and arrogant, but she'd learned to tolerate his idiosyncrasies because she'd had what she wanted from her marriage, the house and her two children.

He'd settle down once Celia and Desmond had left. He had absolutely nothing in common with Desmond and he and Celia had never professed to care very much for each other.

Desmond knocked on his wife's bedroom door and received a quiet invitation to enter.

She sat back against her pillows reading her mail, her breakfast tray thrust aside, and after looking up with a cool smile she allowed him to gently kiss her cheek.

He could smell the delicate floral perfume she'd worn as long as he'd known her, warm with a hint of freesia.

Unemotionally he told himself that she was still a very beautiful woman. Soft dark hair framed an oval porcelain face and he could see the long silken lashes against her gently curving cheek. There was a timeless quality about her beauty, it was like Amelia's, cocooned in the genteel perfection of ageless class, but he would have preferred there to have been more warmth. It was a beauty devoid of sparkle, a stranger to laughter.

He went to stand near her bed so that he could look down at her, and when she raised her eyes to meet his he said gently, 'I'd like to get away immediately after lunch, Celia, does that suit you?'

'Oh yes, I think so. This is a lovely house isn't it, Desmond, perhaps Amelia was right to want it after all.'

When he didn't reply she went on, 'We all thought she was throwing herself away on Mark, there were so many men she could have married, but it was this house she wanted, even more than the man. Do you think they're happy?'

'I would imagine so.'

'We'll never know for sure, Amelia's always lived in her own private world, she was often lonely as a child.'

'Will you want any help with your packing?'

'Amelia's maid will help me. I might stay in London for a couple of days, perhaps Mother'll come up for the odd day so that we can lunch together.'

'Have you asked her?'

'No, I'll telephone her when we get to London.'

'Have you decided when you're returning to Cornwall, I take it you are going back there?'

'Darling, you know I am. That flat of yours isn't home, it's your bachelor pad. I'm only really happy in Cornwall, I just wish Dorinda was there to share it with me.'

He turned away abruptly so that she couldn't see his face, impatient, suddenly withdrawn.

'I suppose I should get up,' she said, 'it was ages before I slept. Darling Dorinda, I thought about her all night and how much she loved this place.'

The angry retort died on his lips. What was the use? If he'd said to Celia that to Dorinda one place was like another he'd have had to watch the hurt in her eyes followed by the tears. How was it possible to believe that a child who was both blind and dumb, with a brain permanently damaged by meningitis at the age of two, could ever again feel love or delight? Celia deluded herself but he couldn't, and God help him he didn't know how to handle her delusion.

'I'll see you downstairs then,' he said with a smile.

'Yes of course. Is that *The Times*, you have with you Desmond? I'll just take a look at it before I get up.'

He passed the paper over and left the room as she settled down to read it.

Her eyes were hostile as she stared at the photograph on the front page. There'd been a great many photographs of Nancy Graham recently, photographs that reminded her that while she was caring for Dorinda her husband was conducting an affair with Nancy Graham in London.

Her friend Mrs Ethrington-Grant had warned her about what was going on and Desmond had made little attempt to deny it. Her mother had warned her she was courting disaster by staying in Cornwall with Dorinda and leaving Desmond to his own devices in London but she'd always been so sure of him.

Desmond hated scandal. He'd always been supercilious about other people's scandals, he was hardly likely to be involved in one himself, besides he would never jeopardize his marriage. She'd said as much to her friend, but the woman had merely smiled cynically and suggested she ask Desmond straight out.

She'd never forget his face the night she taxed him with it. Cold, remote, calling Mrs Ethrington-Grant a poisonous woman, but he'd been more anxious to protect the girl than reassure his wife. In the end he'd admitted that he and Nancy Graham had been having an affair for several months, she knew that he was married, she knew he had no intentions of ending his marriage, neither of them had any wish to create a public scandal.

She'd stormed and raved at him until coldly he'd said that when a man was pushed into loneliness and desolation it was perhaps inevitable that he sought consolation. Then she'd agreed to accompany him to Russia and the next she'd heard about Nancy Graham was that she was in Hong Kong working for some Chinese importers.

That the Ethrington-Grants lived in Hong Kong provided her with an ongoing insight into the life of Nancy Graham. It was in Hong Kong that she'd met Noel Templeton and she'd obviously played her cards well enough to be included on his team in the Middle East. Men were such fools when it came to a pretty face but Celia wasn't altogether sure that the girl was pretty, not pretty like Amelia at any rate. Of course she was always photographed wearing shirts and slacks, she might conceivably look very different in fashionable clothes.

She'd tried to get Desmond to talk about her but he'd refused adamantly, saying that it was all over a long time ago and they should try to forget about it.

She'd asked Amelia what she was like and all Amelia'd said was that she'd liked her at school but had seen little of her since they left. Amelia could be cagey, she drifted through life with her head in the clouds pretending things didn't exist, ignoring Mark's too loud friends, and his doubtful extravagances. If there were other women she would ignore those too; in fact the more she saw of her sister the less she understood her.

She stared down at the paper and into Noel Tem-

164

pleton's face with its clear-eyed courage, and the smile Mrs Ethrington-Grant had described as fascinating. He was probably having an affair with Nancy Graham, her friend had been convinced of it, Nancy Graham was that kind of girl.

Impatiently she flung the paper to the end of the bed, then she swung her legs on to the floor and pushed her feet into the satin mules waiting for them. From the window she could see Mark walking round the house towards the stables with the sun glinting on his blond hair. He walked quickly, completely immersed in his own thoughts, and she reflected impatiently that he had little in common with her husband. They never rode together or conversed about matters of interest to them both. Very occasionally they played the odd round of golf, but she was well aware that Martin thought Desmond was a dry old stick and Desmond believed Mark to be a playboy of monumental insensitivity.

She found Amelia in the conservatory with one of the gardeners discussing the orchids. Amelia looked up with her gentle smile and the gardener touched his cap respectfully.

'Good mornin', mi lady,' he muttered, and Amelia said, 'Are you looking for Desmond, dear? I thought I saw him out on the terrace.'

'I was looking for you. We're leaving immediately after lunch, have you finished in here?'

Amelia turned to the gardener saying, 'They're doing very nicely, I really think we've hit on the right treatment this time.'

After they'd left the conservatory Celia said, 'You love all this don't you, Amelia? It would bore me.'

'What do you find to do all day in Cornwall then, what sort of interests do you have these days?'

'I do a lot of walking, it wasn't possible when Dorinda was there, and I think I might take up sailing again.

Desmond doesn't seem interested but the boat's there in the yard at Falmouth, it seems such a waste if neither of us uses it.'

'You're looking much better, Mummy said you were more like yourself.'

'Oh Mummy! She never sees beyond her nose, she's so engrossed with country pursuits and she's never once mentioned Dorinda since she died.'

'Perhaps she thinks you'll get over her better if she isn't talked about quite so much.'

'But I have to talk about her, Amelia, you don't think that surely?'

'I talk about her with you, but Mummy's always been self-contained, you know that, even more so since Daddy died. She seems quite happy in the small Dower House.'

'I suppose so. I see your friend Nancy Graham's photograph is in *The Times* again.'

Amelia didn't answer and Celia continued, 'Do you suppose she'll ever come back to Greymont?'

'I don't know. Her aunt doesn't know.'

'I was very concerned when you had her here to stay, Amelia, particularly when you knew she and Desmond had had an affair.'

'I invited all the girls I roomed with at Lorivals, all except Lois that is.'

'Mrs Ethrington-Grant tells me she very quickly forgot Desmond when she went out to Hong Kong and met Noel Templeton.'

'Why do you listen to all her gossip, Celia?'

'I don't, only to the gossip that concerns me.'

'You knew it was all over between Desmond and Nancy, she went to Hong Kong knowing there could never be anything permanent between them. Why shouldn't she meet other men, particularly men who are free?'

Mrs Ethrington-Grant says he'll never marry her, he's too wedded to his job and there have been a great many other girls before Nancy – no doubt there'll be a great many more when she's passed into oblivion.'

'Perhaps, I don't know Noel Templeton.'

'But you know her.'

'Yes.'

'Did you honestly like her?'

'At school, yes I did. I took her to stay with me at Drummond and I went to stay with her at her parents' house. They were nice people, her father was a journalist, her grandfather was a doctor, they made me very welcome. They made a much greater effort to entertain me than my parents made to entertain Nancy.'

'What do you mean by that?'

'Celia, you know what Mummy and Daddy were like. Too immersed in their own little world to care very much about what went on outside it. Sometimes Mark accuses me of being like them and in some way I suppose I am.'

'There's no call for Mark to be passing disparaging remarks about our parents, it's thanks to them that this house looks the way it does.'

'That doesn't make him grateful, it makes him resentful.'

'It shouldn't, he's had every opportunity to make money, I suppose what he makes he spends.'

Amelia didn't answer, instead she went to stand at the window where she could see Desmond sauntering along the path that skirted the park. He walked with his head down, his hands behind his back, his step measured, obviously deep in thought.

Celia said irritably, 'Nothing will ever be the same again between Desmond and me. He's a political animal, his entire life is centred around the Foreign Office or some embassy abroad, and I don't want to live abroad again, I've done my share.'

'You mean you'd refuse to go?'

'He knows how I feel about it.'

'But would you refuse to go?'

'If I could possibly get out of it then I would.'

'And yet you can blame him so utterly for what happened with Nancy.'

'Yes I can. There was I with my daughter in Cornwall. I couldn't leave her, we couldn't live in London, she knew the way things were.'

'I'm not even thinking about Nancy now, Celia. Dorinda is dead and you and Desmond are still living apart. You are saying you wouldn't go with him if he was sent abroad. Would you honestly blame him if he found some woman to take your place.'

'I can't think what's come over you, Amelia, we always used to stand up for one another, now family loyalty doesn't seem to matter to you any more.'

'Believe me it does, Celia, I just want you to think about the consequences now that you haven't Dorinda to produce as an excuse.'

'Dorinda was never an excuse, she was a reality.'

'She's not a reality now, Celia,' Amelia persisted, and sharply Celia snapped, 'Mark Garveston's changed you, Amelia, either Mark or those girls you met at Lorival. Let's face it, none of them were exactly your sort, no doubt they had the usual middle-class way of thinking which you've quite obviously adopted.'

Gently Amelia held out her hand and touched her sister's. 'We shouldn't be quarrelling, Celia,' she said quietly, 'I've always admired you, wanted to be like you, I still do, but you have to meet me halfway, you have to try to understand. I'm trying to make you see that if you care about your marriage you've got to make an effort to keep Desmond. I take it you're still in love with him?'

Celia remained silent, her eyes following Desmond as he walked towards the house. Then, when Amelia thought she was not going to answer her she said, 'I loved him terribly when we married. He was so clever, everybody said he'd go far and he was ambitious. I loved living abroad with him in those days, we were asked everywhere, we mingled with interesting exciting people and even after Edward came we got on with our lives just as we had before. It was Dorinda that changed everything, Dorinda and her illness.'

'Desmond wasn't responsible for that, he suffered too, and now he's alone and you're alone, you have to think about where you go from here.'

'You sound so smug, Amelia, and you can't afford to be smug. You married Mark not Philip, and you may think you're serene and inviolable in your fairytale palace but Mark's reputation where women are concerned hasn't been entirely blameless.'

Amelia looked at her sister steadily and recognised Celia's need to repay hurt with hurt. 'I'm not going to ask you what you know about Mark, Celia, it would delight you to tell me and in the morning you would hate yourself for it. I don't want to know. Perhaps I'm a less than perfect wife, maybe he needs some woman to bolster up the pride I seem to have taken away.'

'Then you're a fool, Amelia, to let him get away with it.'

'When Mark comes to tell me he's fallen in love with someone else and wants his freedom then I'll think about it, until then I have my children to think about. They love their father and I believe he loves them. He had little choice in his marriage, we were thrown together like two peas in a pod and told to get on with it, if we fell in love so much the better, if we didn't nobody would be surprised.'

Celia stared at her, then without another word she turned and walked out of the room.

CHAPTER 16

Amelia had taken great delight in restoring the dining room at Garveston Hall. She had been horrified on her first visit to find that the family either ate in the morning room or in the vast kitchen, whilst the dining room remained in shuttered oblivion.

Since the first day she came to it as a bride, the dining room was always used, even if it did mean that she sat at one end of the long walnut table and Mark at the other when they dined alone.

Mark grumbled. 'The servants need roller skates, and the food gets lukewarm while they wander from one end of this damn great table to the other.'

So Amelia installed a heated hatch from the kitchen below up to the dining room and he ceased to grumble about tepid meals. She loved the shining expanse of the table set with silver and glassware, and invariably in the centre, her own creation of flowers from the conservatory.

Mark's mother had been a semi-invalid for years before her death and had no interest in food. Her sons were absent for months at their respective schools and her husband tended more often than not to eat out. Amelia had made it her business to search for a good cook and now the meals were excellent and Mark had to agree that she'd worked wonders.

She watched him eyeing the leg of roast lamb with appreciative eyes before Johnson started to carve it, then help himself to the array of vegetables. He was in a good mood. He'd had an excellent day at the point-to-point, which he'd attended no doubt in the company of the friends he'd had since youth.

Amelia was well aware that Mark's crowd considered her stuffy and snobbish, while she in turn was unimpressed by their raucous good-humour and their brash assumption that if they had money, they didn't need breeding.

Most of them were on their second marriage, in some cases their third; often their parents had made money in dubious ways and when they had sufficient of it they proceeded to buy up old farms in the area, renovate and enlarge them and acquire horses and stables to go with them. Their offspring were the bane of the neighbourhood, with their fast cars and rowdy parties.

These were the newly rich, and the fact that his wife looked down her aristocratic nose at them was a source of increasing annoyance to Mark, who couldn't have cared less.

They were at the dessert stage when he said, 'What time did they get off, then?'

'Around three. Desmond wanted to get off much earlier but Celia lingered on. It will be dark long before they reach London.'

'One of these days he's going to cut and run, always providing he's got it in him to do so.'

'What do you mean?'

'I'm surprised there hasn't been some woman before now, heaven knows she's given him every opportunity.' When Amelia remained silent, Mark grinned at her wickedly. 'You're not saying anything, my dear. That usually means you have no argument against it.'

'Desmond's a very responsible man, as well as a senior public figure. He'd hate a scandal. They've lived their own separate lives so long now they're probably used to it.'

'He's a man isn't he? He might seem like a stuffed shirt, but he's no monk.'

'Perhaps Celia will finally make up her mind to live in London now.'

'Huh – pigs might fly.'

'What is that supposed to mean?'

'She'll never live in London, not as things are at the moment anyway. If he finds another woman then she might consider it on the understanding that nobody takes anything from Celia Urquart, not for any other reason.'

'You don't appear to think very much of the Urquarts.'

'I admire their tenacity, their subtle way of getting what they want.'

'Are you trying to pick a quarrel with me, Mark?'

'Gracious no, it's one I wouldn't win and I'm on a winning streak today.'

A servant appeared with their coffee and they remained silent while he poured it. Amelia indicated that he should leave the coffee pot behind and when they were alone again she said evenly, 'You're always in an argumentative mood when you've been out with your friends. I know they don't like me, but I don't much like them.'

'You know it's funny that you don't like them. Nancy Graham didn't like them, either – was it that toffee-nosed school you both went to that made you dislike lesser folk?'

She knew he was trying to provoke her. Whenever he mentioned Nancy Graham she could feel the throbbing anxiety in her throat. Nancy and Mark, Nancy and Desmond – her husband and then her brother-in-law – how much had either of them meant to her? And yet at the back of Amelia's mind was the Nancy she'd known and liked, the happy open girl with her frank blue eyes and serene lovely face.

Mark was watching his wife with a grim amusement. He knew that any mention of Nancy still had the power to ripple the placid waters of Amelia's life, not because she was jealous of that early innocent first love, but for some other, mysterious reason. One of these days he might reach behind that composure of hers and make her reveal why Nancy Graham's name still rattled her, why on that reunion several years ago they'd been something less than friends.

It was true that Nancy hadn't liked the Hooray Henry men and the dizzy unintellectual girls. He'd told himself that she was jealous of them just as he liked to think Amelia was jealous, but in his heart he knew it wasn't true. Both Nancy and Amelia had expected more than he had to give. His choice of friends reflected his inadequacies and even now the memory of Nancy's father's caustic questions had the power to make him angry. The fact that he was Mark Garveston had cut no ice with Mr Graham; Nancy hadn't seen it then but she'd come to see it later.

He was so engrossed with his thoughts that he had to ask Amelia to repeat her question.

'Have you thought any more about another horse for Pippa?'

'So, you were really serious about wanting her to win at the next show. Suppose the committee are not prepared to change the date?'

'There'll be other shows. Besides, she'd have to get used to the horse before she could expect to win, but she rides so well, Mark – she deserves her chance.'

'I'll look in on those stables in Tewkesbury. I could give them a ring in the morning to say I'm going down.'

Her face lit up with pleasure, and Mark couldn't help thinking how easily everything was falling into place. Tewkesbury and Barbara. Amelia happy because he was selecting a horse for Pippa. Martin at one of his interminable conferences . . .

He had no illusions about Barbara Walton. She was beautiful, selfish and not a little greedy, but none of this had the effect of putting him off her, rather it drew him to her because he recognized her failings as very much his own. Barbara was intelligent but she was fun to be with and as he watched his wife serenely drinking her coffee he wondered if her cool façade would crumble if he told her that another of her schoolfriends was the woman with whom he was hoping to spend the next few days.

Instead he said evenly, 'I see that Nancy's picture was in *The Times* this morning.'

'Yes, I saw it. What an exciting life she is having.'

He smiled. Nancy had been youth and joy, Amelia was calm serenity, but Barbara was something else, something to look forward to with excitement and anticipation. Mark never looked too long into the future, it would surely come whether you wanted it or not. In the meantime, there must surely be a lot of mileage left in his affair with Barbara.

CHAPTER 17

The road to Jericho on a golden glowing morning filled Nancy with breathless delight as it plunged through a stark dramatic landscape. On either side of the serpentine route rose dramatic white limestone hills which in early December briefly burst into glorious colour.

Noel pointed out to her the scars of goat tracks and the nomadic settlements of Palestinian Bedouins. He was a mine of information on the places they passed through and it was obvious he had learned his geography and history well. Driving through the tiny village of Bethany he told her that it was here that Lazarus was resurrected from the dead and it was here also that Jesus' feet were anointed with precious ointment at the house of Simon the Leper.

All the schoolgirl scripture lessons were coming vividly alive for Nancy on that morning as Noel indicated the Tomb of Lazarus and the house of his sisters, Martha and Mary. He smiled as he showed her the block where, according to the Crusaders, Jesus had mounted his donkey on that last fateful journey into Jerusalem. It was also on this road that the Good Samaritan had stopped to show compassion to an injured traveller. By the end of the morning Nancy's head was spinning with monasteries and mosques, churches and holy places until Noel brought the car to a stop at a fork in the road.

Below them stretched the Jordan Valley and the Dead Sea, and Noel pointed to where Jericho, the City of Palms, sweltered under the heat of the morning sun. Beyond the valley the desert hills of Moab shone purple in the distance and taking the right fork away from the city very soon Noel was showing her a large white villa surrounded by palm groves which was to be the end of their journey.

His friend Ali Ben Makobi received them in his garden, indicating that they should sit round the pool where the gentle sound of tinkling waterfalls and the scent of oleanders created a haven of peace. It was hard to imagine that beyond this haven lay a land torn by strife and unrest but she did not have long to think about it. Ali's wife Hadassah came out of the house accompanied by a young man and introductions were performed.

Hadassah Ben Makobi was a tall beautiful woman in her mid-forties; she had dark liquid brown eyes and although there was grey in her hair, once it had been a glorious mahogany. The young man beside her was also tall, and although his dark eyes were velvety brown Nancy sensed hostility in them as he bowed over her hand.

Noel greeted him coolly. They did not shake hands, and she could not be unaware of the tension that suddenly descended on what had been a companionable group. Conversation became stilted in spite of Hadassah's attempts to talk normally with Nancy, and Noel was unusually silent.

Girgis Boutrous was annoyed to find that his uncle was entertaining English guests and particularly when one of them was that accursed journalist Templeton. And the girl – who was she? English journalists, he believed, were prejudiced. They showed the Arabs up in a bad light. He had had this argument with his uncle many times over the years and Ali had always been anxious to point out that Noel Templeton was a reporter of the very highest integrity and would not be biased in anything he wrote. Girgis didn't believe it. He had little time for infidels, be they Christian or Jewish.

The talk around the table gave him time to look at

the girl. She was beautiful, with honey-coloured hair and eyes like a mountain stream. She resembled his aunt in that she talked too much; she was obviously too emancipated. The women in his family, his mother and sisters, knew when to keep silent. They did not enter into men's talk, but were content to chat about their clothes, their jewelry and their children.

His eyes met Nancy's and she smiled politely. His heart started to do odd things within his breast. He wanted her, she was a goddess of beauty, and furiously he asked himself what was she to Templeton – little more than a dancing girl, obviously, or she would be wearing his ring.

He met his aunt's eyes. She was watching him curiously, and knew well the thoughts that were in his head. It was a pity, Hadassah thought, that he had felt the need to visit the family this morning when the newcomers were here.

Hadassah suggested gently that perhaps Nancy would like to take a tour of the garden and Nancy agreed quickly. She was strangely embarrassed by the sullen regard of the young Palestinian and Hadassah said softly as soon as they were out of earshot, 'Girgis is unused to speaking to young women on an equal footing, particularly young Englishwomen. His sisters are completely unworldly, it's doubtful if they have a serious thought in their heads.'

'He seems a very serious young man,' Nancy agreed.

'I am sorry he is here today. He is obsessed with the troubles but Ali will try to keep the conversation light. Perhaps he will take the hint and leave.'

'Does he work actively for the Palestinian cause?'

'Yes, he is very involved with the Intifada, and not the most peaceable aspect of it.'

'I see.'

'If we were to speak of the troubles in the city last night Girgis would allow his prejudice to show. His

177

conversation would be an embarrassment to us and to you. Noel knows Girgis well, and they have no liking for each other.'

'Noel doesn't take sides, so why should Girgis think that he does?'

'Girgis doesn't think straight about the things he believes in. The garden is beautiful, isn't it, Nancy? It isn't easy making a garden out of the desert. I admire the Israelis for the success they have had in that quarter.'

'You don't hate them, Hadassah?'

'I don't hate them, the people. I hate their politics, their ruthlessness in taking from us without asking, although history too is to blame. I hate the Israeli army marching in the streets and I hate it that they are now openly calling for the mass deportation of Palestinians who have been here for centuries.'

'Noel says we report on superficialities. The underlying problems go so much deeper.'

'He is right. Ah, here comes Girgis who has grown tired of men's talk. I am going to see about our meal, Nancy. Talk to him, try to draw him out but do not let him make you angry.'

When his aunt moved away he made as if to follow her, but Nancy said gently, 'The garden is beautiful, isn't it, Girgis? Are you interested in gardening?' She realized instantly that she'd said the wrong thing.

'There are more urgent matters here in my country than gardening,' he said coldly. 'My aunt made the garden, it is women's work.'

'It would be a sad world if everybody lost interest in gardens and we only thought about killing one another,' she retorted quickly.

'You think we should allow the Israelis to take everything without retaliation, then?' he demanded, and she was acutely aware of his dark eyes burning into hers with fanatical anger.

'I think perhaps you hate too much,' she replied softly.

'And why should I not hate them, these strangers who came from all over the world to spread themselves over the land, worming themselves in where they were not wanted, bringing with them their equally fatal adaptability and their cleverness, as well as their thrice-damned aura of superiority. A man can forgive all else except this last. The Jews – let them be cursed. This last insult is one that can only be wiped out with blood!'

Seeing her face suddenly frightened by his vehemence he said more rationally, 'Why did they come here? Why here?'

'They believe God promised them this land many centuries ago when Moses led them out of their bondage in Egypt.'

'And what of our holy writings? Isn't it from this land that the Prophet Mohammed ascended into Heaven? And your scriptures, too. It was here in Palestine that Christ was born, here where the Jews crucified Him. Your hatred should be as deep as ours.'

'Girgis, last night in Jerusalem an old man was killed, a good rabbi. Surely you can't believe that the death of that one old man will bring the liberation of your country one step nearer? It is wrong-headed and mis-guided to believe it.'

'I don't believe it, but it is one less Jew to be reckoned with.'

She stared at him sadly, then turning away she said despairingly, 'While men think as you do there is no hope for a world at peace.'

When they left the villa in the late afternoon their host walked with them to their car. He offered excuses for the day, which he considered had been spoiled by his nephew's presence.

'One of these days he will come to a sad end because the authorities know how deeply involved he is in much of the terrorist activity within Israel. I have tried talking to him but he doesn't listen. He considers me weak and ineffectual. He thinks I, too, should take up arms against the Israelis. He doesn't believe in diplomacy. My wife and I have been interrogated by the police because of Girgis' activities, and it was not pleasant I can tell you.'

When Noel didn't speak he said gently, 'When shall we see you in Jericho again, my friend?'

'I'm not sure. Stick a pin in a map and you'll find unrest; it could be weeks or even years before we return.'

'Not years, Noel. Months – I'll give it months.'

'Then you know something I don't know, Ali.'

Ali merely smiled enigmatically and touching his heart, his lips and his head in the graceful Arab salute he bade them farewell.

Noel was unusually quiet on the way back and Nancy knew his thoughts were elsewhere. They had almost reached the city gates when he turned to her with a smile saying, 'I'm sorry you met my friends when Girgis Boutrous was visiting them.'

'You don't like him, do you?'

'His kind do more harm to their cause than they realize. Young hotheads. Girgis lost sight of his original dream a long time ago, now he's only interested in killing – the old, the young, it doesn't matter as long as the victim is Jewish. I wonder if Alec's around. I wanted to have a chat with him about our plans for tomorrow.'

'Why are they taking us away from Israel just now?' she asked him curiously. 'And why to Ethiopia?'

'There's trouble there – uprisings and famine. A change of scene keeps us on our toes, they think, and perhaps it does. I'm accustomed to moving around.'

They found Alec sitting with the two cameramen in a corner of the hotel lounge and Nancy quickly made an excuse to leave them together.

She spent the rest of the evening writing letters, to Aunt Susan and Maisie and in her imagination she could see Aunt Susan clucking impatiently to herself, thinking what a fool her niece was to prefer the uncertainty of her present life to the peace of working on the *Greymont Gazette* with its preoccupation with local events. She pictured Maisie sitting at her kitchen table, surrounded by bottled fruit and bowls filled with pudding mixture, her fingers crusted with flour, frowning at the letter in her hands and no doubt sharing Aunt Susan's misgivings.

It was almost midnight when she started to pack her clothes for the flight to Ethiopia the following morning. She had nearly finished when there was a light tap on her bedroom door and Noel came in. For a moment he looked down at her case before his arms reached out for her, then when she looked up into his face she was surprised to find it strained and unhappy.

'Is something wrong, Noel?' she asked anxiously.

'It's my father, Nancy. There was a message waiting for me when we got back from Jericho to say he's had a stroke. He's in Lancaster Infirmary. Obviously I will have to go home, he has nobody else.'

'Oh Noel, I am so sorry! Is it very serious?'

'I'm afraid so. I've been given extended leave and I've managed to book a flight home tomorrow. I'm afraid you'll be going to Africa without me but I'll get back as soon as I can. It's your big chance, love. Show them you don't really need me.'

'They know it wouldn't be true.'

'The lads'll look after you. You know what I've always taught you, so don't take any undue risks. It's better to be a survivor than a heroine.'

There had been so many times when he hadn't needed her, fed by his excitement, the heady intoxication of danger, but this was different. This was a situation when he needed her warmth and her com-

181

passion, this was a time when there was nothing and nobody else.

Selflessly she gave him the comfort of her love, generous in her giving. There were those times when he had taken her in passion and in joy, but this time he took her to fill the anguish in his heart and later when he lay sleeping in her arms she told herself that if in the end they went their separate ways he might remember her generosity and recognize it as love.

CHAPTER 18

Barbara thought about the telephone conversation she had had with her father as she drove along the country lanes towards Tewkesbury. Whenever she saw her father, which regrettably hadn't been all that often since she'd left the north of England, he went on at great length about Maisie's children, particularly their boy Peter.

Barbara had never been the sort of woman to drool over babies. She'd seen women in shops and restaurants making ridiculous clucking noises over any nearby infant lying in its pram. And Martin wasn't interested in babies, either. They were both of them only children: they'd had no siblings to contend with and that had suited them both. Martin wasn't good with children; they embarrassed him because he was incapable of coming down to their level. In any case, they'd had a good life without the clamour of children, the school fees, birthday parties and everything else that came with them.

Mark Garveston was proud of his twin daughters, but from a distance. When they were at home they were mostly with Amelia, and Mark saw nothing unnatural in that. When Barbara'd been a child, both her parents had always been there – she'd never had a nanny – and listening to Mark's description of the procession of nannies to which he and his brother had been subjected, she felt pity rather than envy for him.

Barbara had to admit that Amelia was conscientious about everything that belonged to her – her children, her parents, and she'd been a positive gem over her sister's sad daughter right up to the day Dorinda had died.

Barbara drove through the tall wrought-iron gates and along the winding drive towards the large hotel in the distance. Built in warm Cotswold stone, it had once been the home of a baronet who, when down on his luck, had been only too anxious to sell to the syndicate capable of transforming it into a large and expensive hotel. Something like that could have happened to Garveston Hall, she mused thoughtfully, if Amelia hadn't come along with her will and her money.

There were a great many cars in the car park but she had no difficulty in parking, then after putting up the hood and locking the car she picked up her hand-bag and sauntered to the entrance. On the way she looked round to see if she could recognize Mark's car but by this time he'd probably changed it; cars were his hobby, the flashier and faster the better.

She entered the vast foyer and looked round with casual interest. Her feet sank into the deep pile of the crimson carpet and she duly admired the great bowls of flowers, thinking they must have cost a fortune.

A young man in morning dress approached her with a smile. 'Can I help you, madam?'

'I'm not sure,' she replied with a smile. 'I am expecting to meet a friend here, so I'll just look around for a few minutes.'

'Of course, madam. If you need any help don't be afraid to ask.'

At that moment Mark came through the tall glass doors and ran lightly down the centre steps into the hall, a smile lighting up his face, his hands outstretched while the young man who had spoken to her beat a tactful retreat.

'Good morning, Barbara, how nice to see you! Are you alone?'

'You know damned well I'm alone,' she hissed.

'Oh well, never mind, come along and have some coffee, we can talk later.'

He shepherded her into the coffee lounge and she remarked acidly, 'Who exactly am I supposed to be – a friend of Lady Garveston or the wife of a friend of yours?'

'I don't suppose anybody's remotely interested, but we both know the score, don't we, darling?'

It wasn't like Barbara to feel suddenly tongue-tied but she did. Mark was so self-assured, charming and casual that if anybody in that hotel foyer saw them together they would think it was merely a chance meeting between two old friends who hadn't seen each other for some time.

'I thought we'd have lunch at a little inn I know near the stables. The food is excellent.'

She allowed him to guide her out of the foyer and across the car park.

'I thought we would be lunching here,' she said somewhat resentfully.

'Actually no, I checked out this morning. We'll find somewhere quieter – the place is full in the evenings, it's not really my cup of tea.'

'You mean there may be too many people who might know us.'

'That too, and you don't want to be recognized any more than I do.'

Even when she agreed with him she resented him. Her face became sulky, and squeezing her arm Mark said lightly, 'Come on, darling, you should be enjoying yourself. I know you don't want to hurt old Martin any more than I want to hurt Amelia. We enjoy each other's company, I've been missing you like the very devil. Where is your car?'

'There under the trees.'

'Very nice, too. New, isn't it?'

'I've had it about six months.'

'I've no doubt it was a present from Martin, just like mine was a present from Amelia. The stables are about ten miles away, I suggest you follow me.'

185

She strode away from him seething with resentment and yet she knew that this was how it had to be played. They'd set the rules together, and they'd agreed that if either one of them found them impossible to obey that would be the parting of the ways. Women weren't good at obeying rules; they wanted the best of both worlds, they were too emotional.

At that moment Barbara would have liked to step into her car and drive away, anywhere just so long as she didn't have to see him again, but something more primitive than logic made her follow Mark's long black sports car down the country lane as slavishly as some harem woman might have followed her lord and master.

She followed him eventually into the stableyard where he was greeted by two men in riding breeches, then Mark strolled over to her car bringing them with him.

He introduced her as Mrs Walton, an old friend who had just taken up riding. 'I'm here to introduce her to reputable horseflesh. Buying a decent horse is as dodgy as choosing a second-hand car,' he added with a wry grin.

Lucy Belbin would have known what they were all talking about, but Barbara could only portray an assumed interest. She duly admired the horse they had come to look at and she listened for a while while they discussed the price, then she wandered away to look at the horses with their heads hanging over their stable doors. One horse in particular eyed her with interest and she went forward to pat his head. Immediately one of the men was beside her asking, 'Are you thinking of buying a horse for yourself, Mrs Walton?'

'I've only just taken up riding. I'm a complete beginner.'

'You'll do better on your own horse – you'll get to know him and he'll get to know you. Have you got the room to stable one?'

186

'We haven't got stables although I suppose we've room to build them. I doubt if my husband would take to the idea, though.'

'He doesn't ride, then?'

'No.'

'What are his interests?'

'Business first, cars and boats in that order.'

'What's good for the goose is good for the gander. He likes his boats, you like your horses.'

'I doubt if he'd see it that way.'

'I'm sure you'd know how to make him see it your way.'

By this time Mark and the other man had joined them, and Mark said with a broad smile on his face, 'Be careful' Barbara, these fellows are capable of selling you a Bactrian camel.'

'Do you like this horse?' the new man asked.

She nodded. 'He's very friendly – is he docile?'

'Docile no, predictable yes. There is a difference. He's got a fair turn of speed and he's a thoroughbred. I could bring him round for you to try if you like.'

'Like I said, I'm a beginner and we don't have stables.'

'That needn't be a problem. We could stable him here until you can fix something up locally. You might be a beginner but you have an eye for a good horse.'

Her eyes met Mark's looking at her quizzically, and with a smile he said, 'Didn't I tell you they'd try to sell you a horse? They're not content with having extracted the top price out of me for that one. Are you tempted?'

'I would have to discuss it with Martin.'

'You can manage Martin.'

'I know. I just don't like to be rushed.'

'We have one or two other clients interested in Jupiter, Mrs Walton. You'd need to make up your mind pretty soon.'

187

'Isn't that what estate agents and car salesmen usually say?'

The man laughed. 'I suppose it is, but it also happens to be true.' Turning to Mark he said, 'Your wife was interested in Jupiter last year when she was here. I honestly thought we'd be hearing from her.'

'She mentioned him to me. She'll be down here again when she visits her mother, perhaps she'll take him this time.'

They started to stroll away and in that split second Barbara made up her mind.

'My husband gets home next Sunday afternoon, so we can talk about it then. Can I let you know about the horse?'

Mark stared at her with a wry smile on his face, and the elder of the two men said, 'I'll hold him until you let me know, Mrs Walton, then if you're still interested we can discuss the price and other matters with your husband and yourself. Do you live in the area?'

'I live nearer to Cheltenham than Tewkesbury.'

'What are you riding at the moment?'

'One of Lucy Belbin's horses. Do you know of her?'

'Yes, of course. Some of her mounts aren't bad, but she's got nothing in this class. I hope you decide to have him, Mrs Walton.'

As they walked back to their cars Mark said, 'You're serious about this horse aren't you, Barbara?'

'I could be.'

'I wonder what exactly made you interested?'

'It was probably that man talking about Martin's interests, his cars and his boats.'

Mark smiled, but she knew he didn't believe a word of it. No, it was talk of Amelia wanting the horse that had suddenly made her keen to have him, and even when she despised herself for being so childish, she couldn't help it.

'Lunch, I think,' Mark said cheerfully. 'The inn's about five miles further on, you'll be delighted with it.'

Once again she followed him in her car, and when she saw the inn nestling in the curve of a hill her heart quickened with thoughts of how they would spend the next few days.

The inn was old with dark oak rafters and huge fireplaces piled high with logs waiting to be lit in the evening. There was a lot of shining brass and copper, and thick Persian carpets on the floor.

Mark smiled his appreciation. 'This is what I like,' he said enthusiastically. 'Not that new place with all its glass and chromium-plating. I haven't asked you, is this meeting just for today or can we spend the next few days together?'

'My mother went home, so I can stay until the weekend.'

'Well done, that suits me fine.'

Again she was aware of the resentment she had felt earlier. That she had inconvenienced her mother never even occurred to him and somewhat savagely she thought it must be hell to be married to Mark. He was selfish and egotistical – but maybe that was part of his charm.

She watched as he left the room to talk to the manageress. He was no better looking than Martin, but he had a debonair easy grace about him that Martin had never acquired. Martin Walton had worked hard for his place on the board of several companies, while Mark had had them handed to him on a platter without the need to contribute either his time or his acumen. He had his finger in a great many pies – horses and cars, boats and agriculture – but they had come about as a result of his title and the fact that he had married the daughter of an earl. Nor had Barbara any illusions about his feelings for her. When the time came for them to part he would simply walk out of her life with few regrets and grateful thanks for·what had been.

He came back to her with a smile on his face. 'We're in luck, love. They're not taking guests at the inn because the rooms upstairs are being decorated, but there's a flat over the garages – a sitting room, two bedrooms and a bathroom, and we can have that for a couple of days.'

'Did you tell her we were married?'

'She didn't ask, but she assumes we are, I'm sure. This afternoon we'll drive out to look at an old church on the edge of the forest. It's a place I used to go to with my father; he was pally in those days with the vicar, they were at school together.'

How like Mark. He didn't ask if she would enjoy seeing this old church, he merely assumed that his company was sufficient incentive.

The flat above the garage had a certain olde worlde charm. The carpets were faded into soft muted colours as were the delicate chintzes on the chairs and at the windows, but there was a large stone fireplace laid with logs, and there were plenty of lamps with rosy shades which would give the room a cosy warmth when they were lit.

They ate in the oak-panelled dining room on succulent Welsh lamb and fresh vegetables, and the landlady produced a bottle of excellent Chablis.

Addressing Barbara she said, 'I hopes you find the flat satisfactory, ma'am. The fire's laid so Joe'll put a match to it at dusk. I'll send one o' the girls up to draw the curtains and turn on the lamps.'

'Thank you, everything is very nice. We'll be back for our evening meal.'

The landlady smiled before she bustled out of the room and Mark said with some feeling, 'Isn't there an old saying about what a dangerous web we weave when first we practise to deceive?'

But Barbara wasn't listening to him. She had gone out into the yard to open the boot of her car. When Mark joined her she said briskly, 'I think you should take the luggage in now. Who knows how many eyes are watching this manoeuvre; some in my car, some in yours – they'll wonder what we're about!'

'I doubt they'll care. It's not busy at this time of the year, so they'll be only too glad they've let the rooms.'

He looked down at the beautiful petulant face of his companion and thought idly that there was a lot to be said for life with Amelia. His father had once told him that wives made fewer demands than mistresses, whose insecurity made them peevish.

Taking the cream leather suitcase from her he said lightly, 'You needn't be afraid of seeing any of your Cheltenham crowd round here, it's too far off the beaten track.'

'I wasn't thinking of them at all. I was simply wondering how we're going to spend our time.'

'We can pretend we're newly married in our own little love nest. Some women would be delighted at the prospect,' he answered, his eyes lit with devilish amusement as slamming down the lid of the boot she said crossly, 'I suppose all the others would have been touchingly grateful simply to be alone with you.'

He laughed, then seeing the real anger in her eyes he said soberly, 'Honestly, Barbara, there haven't been all that many, and mostly they've been one-night stands. I didn't intend that my affair with you should be much more than that, but now when I'm away from you I can't get you out of my mind.'

For a long moment they stared at each other, then with a brief smile he picked up their suitcases and walked back to the inn. Barbara's eyes followed him and she found her heart was racing madly in her breast. What a devil he was, she thought angrily, he could twist her heart and make her believe she really meant some-

191

thing to him, when she knew his feeling for her was as transient as a summer storm.

All those years ago before he married Amelia and when Nancy Graham had been the woman in his life, she'd thought her friend was a fool to expect anything permanent from Mark Garveston. She'd been smug in those days, cushioned from the usual young girls' traumas by doting parents who had spoiled her, and the fact that she wanted Martin Walton and he wanted her.

Right from those early days at the primary school across the park, Martin had been the anchor on which Barbara had fastened her life; she'd never imagined that one day their marriage would settle into mediocrity, even boredom. She was honest enough to see her affair with Mark as a thing of today, with no strings and no comebacks, but such clear-eyed vision was now destroying the heady intoxication of their union. Passion and logic were very strange bedfellows, Barbara thought as she waited for Mark in the front seat of his car.

Mark lay back against the pillows watching Barbara move about the room through half-closed eyes. He contemplated her beauty as analytically as he would have judged the beauty and grace of a thoroughbred horse. Her body was no more attractive than Amelia's, but Amelia had never walked about their room naked, and after the girls were born she had indicated her intention of having her own bedroom.

Barbara sat at the dressing table where he could see her long slender back and the gentle curve of her hips. She was brushing her dark hair with long sweeping strokes, strokes that lifted her breasts and smooth upper arms, and the eroticism of her movements aroused in him a desperate urgency to possess her once more.

Breathlessly he called her name so that she rose from the stool and came to stand near him, then he reached out for her and dragged her into his arms. For two long days they'd talked about looking at churches and stayed in to make love. They'd made plans to do this and that but their plans had been forgotten as quickly as they'd made them; nothing had been important beyond the joy they found in each other's bodies and once again, their passion spent, he looked down at her beautiful exotic face.

It was hard to imagine that her ordinary north-country parents had produced something as enchanting as Barbara. Her beauty had a strangely Eastern quality with its dark slanting brows and eyes as green as jade. Her mouth was full and voluptuous, her high cheek-bones and wide brow from which the blue-black hair sprang in dark rippling waves would have done credit to some raven-haired harem beauty but he knew that the Barbara pulsating in his arms would become another Barbara once reclothed in the anonymity of her expensive fashionable clothing.

He found himself thinking about Martin Walton, austere, correct, lounge-suited Martin with his precise pronunciation and analytical mind geared to the board-room table and the minions who bolstered up his career and his pride. No wonder Barbara became a wild thing in his arms: never in a thousand years would Martin Walton satisfy his wife.

By mutual consent they had decided to part company after breakfast on Saturday morning, with Mark driving north to Lancashire and Barbara driving home to Cheltenham. It was Mark's decision to visit a local nursery that altered their arrangements.

He explained that Amelia was fond of exotic plants for the hot-houses, and the nursery in question had a reputation for producing the best. Barbara decided she too would buy plants for her conservatory and they would part company after they had made their choice.

They were paying for their purchases when Barbara was hailed across the room by a voice she instantly recognized as one of the Kirkham sisters. She groaned inwardly.

'Hello, Barbara, fancy meeting you here,' Mona gushed. 'We always come here for our plants, they do so well. What is that you've been buying?'

Barbara smiled. 'A present for Martin, orchids. I hope they do well in the greenhouse as he's developed a passion for them. The palm is for the conservatory.'

At that moment Mark came over carrying a particularly showy bromeliad and not realising that she was with people she knew he said, 'I hope Amelia likes this one, I'm hopeless with plants.'

Quickly Barbara said, 'Mark, may I introduce Mona and Alma Kirkham, both members of our Golf Club.'

Mark struggled to place his plant on the counter before extending a hand to each of the women in turn while Barbara said, 'Sir Mark Garveston.'

He favoured them with a smile, and with the devastating charm for which he was well-known he said, 'Didn't I meet you when I was staying with Barbara and Martin in March?'

'Oh no,' Mona said with a giggle. 'We're not racing people. We only hope racing isn't going to keep Martin and Barbara away from the Golf Club.'

'I'm sure it won't,' Mark said gallantly, and immediately Alma said, 'Isn't Martin with you, Barbara?'

'Martin doesn't get home from his conference until tomorrow.'

'How silly of me, I'd quite forgotten he was away. Did you like Barbara's new house, Sir Mark?' Alma gushed.

'Very much, who wouldn't!'

'We've yet to see it, haven't we, Alma?' Mona said ruefully. 'Everybody's talking about it, though. You don't live in these parts, Sir Mark?'

'No, I live in north Lancashire, quite near to Barbara's home town. We've known each other a great many years.'

'How nice, and to meet each other here of all places.'

'Yes, it's a rum old world.'

'I expect you'll want to be getting off, Mark,' Barbara said. 'Do give my love to Amelia. Perhaps we'll see you both for race week this year.' Turning to the sisters she said easily, 'Sir Mark's wife and I were at school together,' then with a smile that embraced them all she turned and strode off towards her car.

After a murmured goodbye Mark followed and the two women watched as he helped Barbara to place her plants in the back of her car, then he took her hand for a few moments before walking to his car.

Barbara was furious – with the Kirkham sisters, with Mark, with circumstances. It wasn't exactly the perfect ending to their time together. He allowed her to drive through the gates before him, waving a nonchalant hand and affording her the benefit of his smile, and Barbara put her foot down hard on the accelerator. If Mark expected her to wait for him along the road he was going to be disappointed, and driving behind her Mark grinned. He knew exactly what her thoughts would be but he had no intention of overtaking her. Intrigue a woman and it kept her on her toes, kept her interested. She had one predictable chap in her life – he most certainly wasn't going to be another.

CHAPTER 19

Nancy had been in Ethiopia six weeks, a time of famine, exhaustion and scorching heat. Alec called it a hell of dust and flies, where the distant horizon shimmered as though on fire and where the stench of death and disease was everywhere. It was like a physical pain in her heart to see the hopelessness in the eyes of farmers standing white-robed and dismayed in their long furrowed fields, lifting up dried handfuls of dust and allowing it to fall in hard crumbs on to the land. The fields should have been thick with maize by now but there had been no rain to make the desert green and now there was no food to feed Ethiopia's starving people.

They had had no word from Noel and when Nancy began to doubt that he would ever rejoin them Alec said easily, 'Obviously it's his father's illness that keeps him in England.'

She'd grown accustomed to sudden death, to the horrors of war and to what passed for heroism in aid of a cause, even though many who fought had long since lost sight of what their cause was about. What she could not accept was famine – and the sight of starving children.

They stared at her with unseeing eyes, great caverns in skulls over which the skin was stretched tight. She watched them hobbling on legs no thicker than sticks, caricatures, stumbling and rocking as if they were controlled by strings until one after the other they were seen no more.

It was a scenario of despair: a procession of people who moved like sleepwalkers through a desolate landscape. A deep, impenetrable hatred filled Nancy's entire being for the soldiers who strutted through the villages, prodding the women, using their rifles like axes to beat down the old and cripple the children. Men without pity, made brave by the weapons they carried, men who were less than animals.

Her contempt for them shone in her eyes and if they recognized it they merely grinned insolently. Alec was quick to say, 'Don't let them see how much you despise them, Nancy. Learn to treat them with indifference.'

'Alec, how can I?'

'You are expecting pity from men who have never known any themselves. These men were born to barbarism, they will die in it.'

Alec had no easy answers for her and she soon had something else to think about besides the dying children.

Late one afternoon Clive was carried into the compound with blood streaming from a wound in his shoulder. She helped the doctor cut away the blood-sodden clothing and watched helplessly while the wound was cleaned and stitched, then she sat beside his bed while his voice moaned on in his delirium throughout the night.

In the morning Phil took her place so that she could get some rest and Alec told her that the doctor's main fear was that the knife which had inflicted the wound was contaminated. If Clive survived the first twelve hours there was a chance that he had escaped infection, and the next day would see him completely out of danger.

Nancy's spirits lifted when she found the young cameraman propped up against his pillows, pale and with dark circles under his closed eyes, with Phil watching him anxiously from his chair beside the bed. Phil smiled at the unspoken question in her eyes.

'He recovered consciousness last night, Nancy, but he didn't speak, just smiled and went back to sleep. We're hoping he'll be able to tell us what happened this morning.'

'Have you had breakfast?' Nancy asked practically.

'No.'

197

'Do please go and eat something, I'll stay here now. Were you with him?'

'No. We went off on our own that afternoon.'

'Have you spoken with the doctor?'

'Yes. The fever has gone, he thinks he's going to be all right. Septicaemia would have been evident by now.'

'Then do please go and have some breakfast. I won't leave him for a moment.'

Just then a young Irish nurse came into the room and seeing Nancy she said quickly, 'My, but he's a better colour this mornin'. Sure and the doctor thought he was a goner. You'll be surprised how quickly he recovers now.'

Clive's recovery was slow, however, and Alec, who was in charge in Noel's absence, contacted the paper with a view to sending him home if a replacement could be found.

Clive objected, but only half-heartedly, and at the beginning of February he returned to London where there were the proper facilities to attend to the wound in his shoulder that was responding very slowly to the treatment available in Ethiopia.

His replacement arrived three days later – a young, brashly eager cameraman called Harry Colman. It didn't take him long to chat Nancy up and antagonise the others and Alec remarked dourly that Noel would soon sort him out when he returned.

It was over dinner on his second night with them that Harry said, 'When do you suppose Templeton expects to be back?'

'When his father's out of danger, I imagine,' Alec replied shortly.

'I've seen him round and about, they're keeping him pretty busy. He wasn't much concerned about his father the last time I saw him.'

Alec didn't speak. Nancy looked up sharply but Phil asked, 'What's that supposed to mean?'

'He was dining out with a cracking girl. Long red hair and legs to match. They looked very much at ease with each other.'

Nancy clenched her hands under the table until they hurt and across the table her eyes met Alec's. She surprised a sympathy in them that brought the hot tears into her eyes so that she jumped up quickly and made a muttered excuse to leave them. She ran unheedingly along the street outside their modest hotel oblivious to the stares of passers-by, curious that the English girl who always seemed so composed should be running for dear life, her eyes luminous with tears.

The straggling street petered out, and now she was hurrying along a rough track that led through scrubland on to a plateau with the backdrop of purple mountains. She felt a fool. Her heart was hammering uncontrollably in her breast, and she started with a cry when she felt a hand slip reassuringly round her shoulders.

It was Alec, who turned her to face him. 'Gracious me, girl, you're surely not making more of Noel's dinner date than there is! He's known a great many girls in his time, girls to dine with, take to the theatre, perhaps even to make love to but none of them have meant anything or he'd have done something about it.'

Nancy didn't speak. Of course he'd have done something about it, only Noel wasn't the marrying sort – he'd made that very clear over the years. At this moment she felt utterly desolate. She was one of a stream, a bit of light relief from the sterner things of life, a girl to be forgotten as soon as she was out of sight.

Alec watched the changing expressions on her face and he went on gently, 'Come on, love, you've heard a bit of gossip that wasn't even worth repeating. In no time at all Noel will be back to what is important in his life, and don't forget he thought you were important enough to share it with him.'

'Do you call this sharing, Alec? I don't. It's something that could end tomorrow. I just happened to be a journalist, while that girl in London represents the glamour I can never give him dressed like this, looking like this.'

'He's known Libby for years. She's a nice girl but he's never been in love with her.'

'How do you know it's Libby?'

'By the red hair and long legs. She's a girl he can telephone when he's at a loose end, a friend who can make him smile when there isn't very much to smile about. Don't let's go back yet or that lad Colman will put two and two together and make five. At the end of the scrubland there's a patch of marsh that's a birds' paradise. You'll see birds you never dreamed existed, but not through a haze of tears you won't. Come on, dry your eyes; they should only cry over things that are important, never over nonsense.'

Three days later in the early light of a rosy dawn, Nancy heard Noel's voice in the corridor outside her room. Leaping out of bed and throwing on a light robe she opened the door and looked along to where he was letting himself into his room while Alec looked on sleepily.

Their eyes met and he smiled, a smile that made her heart race, bringing the warm colour into her face.

Every instinct in her body made her want to run to him, to feel his arms around her, his eyes smiling into hers, but she hung back. The smile died on her lips and by then he had unlocked his door and Alec was helping him to push his luggage into the room.

She heard the low hum of their voices, then Alec was leaving the room, closing the door behind him. Their eyes met and he smiled gently. 'He's dead beat, Nancy. I've told him to get to bed so no doubt it'll be later today when we get to know his news.'

She nodded and returned to her room.

It was indeed much later when they met over drinks in the dingy hotel lounge. It was sundown, and Noel sat looking out along the street, made suddenly enchanting by the colours of rose and crimson in the sky. He put his arm easily round her shoulders saying softly, 'It is amazing, isn't it, Nancy? Out there is nothing but squalor and disease, and yet in this glorious evening light it looks sublime enough for the Kingdom of Heaven.'

He held her close for a brief moment so that his chin rested on her hair and she could feel the gentle beating of his heart, then he released her.

'What about your father, Noel?' she asked quietly.

She saw the sudden look of pain in his eyes, the haunting gravity in his face before he said quietly, 'My father died last week. That is why I stayed away so long.'

'Oh Noel, I'm so very sorry.'

'I thought he was going to get over it. He was so cheerful when his speech came back; he was busy making plans for the summer, altering the layout of the garden and he was bothered about his cat.'

'Matilda?'

'Well, no. Matilda went to the happy hunting grounds last year – she was sixteen years old. This was a new kitten the vicar had given him, a ginger kitten. The vicar's cat was his mother.'

'What will happen to the kitten now?'

'Dad kept going on and on about the house, what I would do with it if he died. Would I want to sell it, I'd probably never live in it. It became an obsession with him, then he went on about how much Matilda had loved the garden, how the new kitten loved it and what would happen to Domino if I sold the house. I knew in his innermost heart he didn't want me to sell it. "One day you'll get fed up with travelling the world," he said, "then you'll want to put down roots. What better place is there than in this house on the edge of the fells."'

'I remember that house,' Nancy said quietly. 'It's a lovely old building, and the virginia creeper clings so lovingly to that warm Pennine stone.'

He nodded. 'There were times when I couldn't understand Dad. He was so interested in my job, so very proud that I'd done well in it, always wishing he'd been able to do as well, and yet at the same time he wanted me around living a normal life with a wife and kids. He desperately wanted me to hold on to that house.'

'And have you decided what you will do?'

'I went to take a good look at it just before he died. I could understand why he loved it and yet it seemed foolish to hang on to it afterwards. When am I ever going to get the chance to live in it?'

'What will you do, then?'

'I've ended up doing nothing at all. The vicar is looking after Domino, he'll play in the garden and no doubt he'll look for Dad. I decided against all my better judgement to wait. Time alters many things – I've learned that over the years.'

When she was silent he said, 'If you were in my shoes, what would you do with it?'

'I'm not sure. Most of your friends are in London. One day you may marry but your wife might not care for the north of England. You have a problem on your hands, Noel.'

She moved away from him and went over to the table to sort among the mail lying there. He watched her through narrowed eyes, her sudden aloofness disconcerting him, and then on a light note he said cheerfully, 'I ran into Desmond Atherton in London. He was dining with some friends in one of my favourite restaurants.'

'I hope he's well,' she responded steadily.

'He seemed prosperous enough.'

'Did you get to talk to him?'

'For a few moments. He was with two other chaps and I was with Libby. She's not into politicians, she finds them infinitely boring.'

It took Nancy's entire concentration to go on looking through the mail and she was aware that Noel was standing beside her looking down at her with maddening amusement in his dark eyes.

'I was with Libby the first evening I saw you,' he said lightly.

She took time to slit open a long envelope before responding to his banter. 'I remember – red hair and long legs, a very pretty girl.'

'You're not curious about her?'

'Should I be?'

'I'd be curious about some man you were spending an evening with.'

She stared at him. 'What do you want me to do, Noel, cry like a baby because you spent some time in London with an old flame? You're a free agent to do as you like.'

'I know that, Nancy. I'm glad you're not possessive. I can't do with possessive women, I suppose that's why Libby and I have been friends all these years. I can go without seeing her for ages, then we can pick up the threads as if it was yesterday.'

'How nice that must be for you, Noel. London can be such a lonely place. She's worth hanging on to, your Libby.'

'Except, my dear, that she isn't my Libby. Like me she's a very free spirit indeed.'

He was tantalizing her, playing with her like a cat plays with a mouse, and she was glad of the anger that she was feeling, otherwise she might have wept those treacherous tears that would have irritated him so that later she despised herself.

She puzzled him. He was aware that behind those candid blue eyes she was curious. She wanted to ask questions but he couldn't make up his mind whether her questions would concern his friendship with Libby or Desmond Atherton.

They were both relieved when Alec and the two cameramen came into the room and immediately Harry

203

said, 'I didn't think you'd be back so soon, Noel. You didn't mention it when I saw you in London.'

'There was no need to mention it; in any case I wasn't sure.'

'Smashing girl you were with, who was she?'

'Just an old friend.'

'I wish I had old friends like that.'

'You will have if you live long enough. Remind me to explain to you the rudiments of survival.'

'What are they?'

'In a crisis you're on your own. You don't put your life in jeopardy needlessly – nobody expects it of you – and you don't put the rest of us in jeopardy by a thoughtless act. That is why you're on your own in a crisis.'

'Isn't that a bit unchivalrous? Suppose it's Nancy who is in danger?'

'Nancy knows the score,' Noel replied curtly.

Nancy looked at Noel with sudden anger. She doubted if he would have behaved in quite that cavalier fashion with the delectable Libby, but his face betrayed nothing. It was the face of a man who was sure of himself, confident in what he was doing with no room for sentimentality.

She loved him but had to admit that he had never lied to her. Right from that first evening when he had smiled down into her eyes on the balcony overlooking Victoria Harbour in far-off Hong Kong, he had never been less than honest about his job in which there was no room for permanency in love. From the first moment she joined his team he had spelled out for her the rules she must obey, rules which had disregarded those more tender moments which obviously meant little to him – moments that were set well apart from this dangerous travesty of life which mattered more.

Like a besotted bewildered child she had believed it had been his feelings which had prompted him to include her in his team; now she believed it had been nothing of the kind. Now she believed that he had simply thought he owed her something for making her love him, and this had been the prize he had offered – to be the girl on Noel Templeton's team. It was a prize for which many women would have given a great deal. She should be grateful.

Turning her back on the rest of them she ran lightly down the steps that led to the street and set off briskly, her eyes blinded with tears.

Noel looked after her with a puzzled frown on his face. Women were the very devil and something had obviously got into Nancy. Looking up he found Alec watching him, lazily leaning back in his chair, his pipe between his teeth.

Noel grinned. 'Come on then,' he said lightly. 'What is it?'

'You're an unfeeling bastard sometimes, Noel. Nancy's not one of the boys and she never will be.'

The two cameramen were sitting some distance apart arguing about something they evidently disagreed on, and Noel allowed his eyes to follow Nancy's retreating figure before he turned to Alec saying, 'Perhaps it was a mistake to bring her. Perhaps she expects too much.'

'No more than any woman in love with a man.'

'Exactly. That's why I've been a fool to bring her, it should have been anybody but her.'

'Does it have to be like that? For once in your life can't you allow your heart to rule your head?'

'I'm not too sure that it is my heart.'

'No, you're just too stubborn to admit it.'

For several minutes Noel sat staring down the street and Alec kept quiet, watching his deeply serious face with its frown of concentration. He recognized that Noel was more troubled than he would admit. Eventually he rose to his feet, pausing besides Alec's chair as he made for the door.

'I'm going to take a shower, this dust clings to everything. I'll see you at dinner.' Alec didn't answer, and after a moment Noel laid his hand lightly on his shoulder. 'What do you suppose Nancy will do if I send her home?' he asked.

'Do! She'll do nothing, but it'll probably break her heart. Besides, what excuse will you give? She's good at what she does – who would you replace her with?'

'There are dozens waiting to take her place. I probably wouldn't replace her, anyway.'

'Like I said, what excuse will you give?'

'That we're running into danger, that I'd worry about her and I can't afford to worry about any of you, that I want her to be safe.'

'They're excuses she wouldn't believe. You'd have to do better than that, Noel.'

'Then I'll have to start thinking about it, won't I, Alec?'

'You're surely not serious about sending her home.'

'I've been thinking about it for several weeks now, in fact all the time I was up there in the Pennine country sorting out Dad's things. Nancy doesn't belong here, she belongs there where the silence is so beautiful you can almost hear it. She has an affinity with those dark Pennine hills and those moorland tarns, the same sort of affinity my father had with them. She is not like us, Alec. We belong here where there's dust and danger, trauma and turmoil.'

'It's a life I would have been glad to give up if my wife had lived.'

'But she didn't, did she, Alec – so you were never asked to make a choice. Looking at things now and looking at them then are very different. I wonder if you'd have said all that if Rosalind had lived.'

Alec didn't answer. Noel was right, time altered many things. Dimly he heard the closing of the door and realized that Noel had left him.

CHAPTER 20

Barbara had been prepared for a long discourse on what had transpired during the conference, but for the first time Martin had little to say about it. Now they were facing each other across the dinner table while she watched him playing with the stem of his wineglass, his thoughts obviously occupied elsewhere.

He'd arrived home just before four, and although she'd greeted him on the drive with her usual perfunctory kiss he'd gone immediately up to the bedroom to unpack and take a shower.

They'd made desultory conversation over dinner. He'd admired the orchids and said the kitchen looked very nice; he'd leafed automatically through the pile of mail she'd placed near his plate, and in some exasperation she finally said, 'You're very quiet, Martin. You're normally so full of the conference – wasn't it a success?'

He roused himself to reply normally. 'Oh yes it was, a great success. We're thinking of holding the next one there too.'

'You weren't enthusiastic about Southampton before. What's changed your mind?'

'The hotel accommodation was excellent and so were the facilities for the conference. It's a new place, of course, and they can only improve.'

'Did you play any golf?'

'No. As usual there wasn't any time.'

'Was Justin Forbes there?'

'Yes, he's hoping to bring Joan round one night for dinner. I said we'd be in touch.'

'I like Justin but Joan's got absolutely no conversation unless it's about their children.'

'That's pretty normal with people who have children. I like Joan, she's always very nice.'

'Oh well, I suppose we must have them, I'll let you make the arrangements.'

Again there was silence, and suddenly aware that she was looking at him thoughtfully he roused himself to ask, 'What have you been doing with yourself? How's the riding?'

'I haven't been this week. My mother asked if she could come for a few days but it didn't work out.'

'You mean she didn't come?'

'Oh, she came, but when I told her I had one or two appointments already fixed she took umbrage and decided to go home. I'll have to extend the olive branch before I'm forgiven.'

'What did she think about the house?'

'She thought it was nice, but too remote. She said if we'd been in the old house she could have used the buses to get out and about. I think we should go up to spend a few days with them soon, Martin. We could carry on from there and see your parents in the Lake District.'

'I'm not sure when I can get away again.'

'You did say you'd take the boat up to Ullswater or Derwentwater. Surely you haven't changed your mind?'

'I'm thinking of taking it to Langstone instead. I'd get more use out of it down there.'

'But you already have the yacht down there. It seems pointless to have both of them at Langstone and besides, it's ostentatious.'

'I don't see why. It's just a different kind of sailing, that's all.'

'I told Mark Garveston you'd probably be taking the boat up to the Lakes.'

'When? When did you tell Mark Garveston?'

'Yesterday. He called on his way back from the nurseries near Tewkesbury. I met him there when I went for the plants.'

'Well, I really hadn't decided, Barbara. Did you tell him I was away?'

'Of course. The Kirkham girls were at the nursery – I introduced them to Mark.'

'That reminds me, have you decided what you're going to do about the Club?'

'I haven't thought about it. If you don't want me to resign then I won't.'

For a few minutes he remained silent, surprised that Barbara was being particularly cooperative.

'We were very glad of the Golf Club and the friends we made there,' he said finally. 'Yes, I would like you to remain on the committee, Barbara.'

Barbara poured the coffee and sat back to enjoy it. Martin was unusually thoughtful. Obviously the conference had not been all it should have been because normally he'd be chatting about who was there, the wheeling and dealing that went on, somebody's new car . . . but on this occasion he was being remarkably reticent.

They drank their coffee in silence and idly he helped himself to another cup. She had been lucky enough to find two daily women who lived in the village because Martin objected to having a live-in housekeeper or help. 'They're often more trouble than they're worth,' he'd said firmly, 'and it's not as though we have children to see to.'

Her 'treasures' were now gossiping in the kitchen, waiting to do the washing up. They would fill their baskets with whatever was left, and there was plenty, before trotting off down the road to the village. Barbara learned most of the local gossip from Gertrude and Milly and she had little doubt that the villagers would all be familiar with her house and aspects of her life, when her husband was away on business and when he was home, and it amused her to think that they would not have been quite so well informed if she'd employed

209

a housekeeper or an au pair. It had given her a certain vindictive pleasure to remark on this fact to Martin.

As she loaded the dinner things on to the trolley he said, 'What do you say about driving down to the Golf Club tonight? It's ages since I've been and you can tell them you've changed your mind about resigning.'

'I thought you wouldn't want to go out tonight. Usually conferences tire you out.'

'Not this one, it was very smooth going.'

They were on their way home when he mentioned Mark. 'Wasn't it rather a long way for Garveston to go to buy plants?' he surprised her by asking.

'He didn't go there merely to buy plants. Apparently he went to find a horse for Pippa from some people near Tewkesbury. He also suggested I'd be a better rider if I had a horse of my own.'

'Where on earth would we stable a horse?'

'We could convert the garage when the boat goes.'

'Then you could tire of it just like you've tired of golf.'

'I haven't tired of golf, you're the one who never has the time – I've just tired of going there on my own! I kept the address of the stables – we could drive up there one day and have a look around.'

'They could sell you any old thing. You need to be a good judge of horseflesh.'

'Mark told me I could mention his name to them and they wouldn't cheat me – he's too good a customer.'

'I still think it's a bad idea.'

'Why is it so right for you to have two boats and so silly for me to want a horse? I think keeping them both in Langstone Harbour is stupid but you'll no doubt have your own way. Now I want my own way about a horse.'

Martin allowed his eyes to leave the road for a split second, taking in her beautiful resolute face. She sat beside him aloof and elegant and he thought about

210

Sandra Stubbs perched on the edge of the same seat, her eyes flashing with excitement, revelling in the speed of his car, and the sheer exuberance of her gratitude after their morning sail, the good lunch they'd eaten and the ride home. That's all it had been, but he was suddenly exasperated by the guilty feeling that washed over him. He'd entertained a young girl for a few hours, surely that was no worse than his wife entertaining Mark Garveston, and somewhat peevishly he said, 'Do you suppose Garveston was fishing for another invitation?'

'Why should he? No doubt he'd be welcome at a great many places.'

'I don't mind him coming, although it'll probably be another few years before we're invited back to Garveston Hall.'

'If ever,' she finished shortly.

Almost imperceptibly, the life they lived together began to change after that day, and try as she might Barbara couldn't pin down the cause.

Martin never asked her to accompany him to any of his conferences and invariably these were held in Southampton. He went off happily enough and the following spring he left pulling the motor launch behind his car; it was destined for Langstone Harbour.

Work began on the spare garage to convert it into a stable for Jupiter, Barbara's chestnut horse which had hitherto been stabled at the local riding school; she was becoming more and more proficient.

She loved riding: she loved the speed of her horse on the short green turf of spring and the wind in her hair, but she was careful not to suggest resigning from the Golf Club again. She played a game with Betty Bernstein every Thursday and occasionally joined in if there was a competition, and Martin seemed well content with this arrangement.

They entertained Justin and Joan Forbes to dinner as promised, and while the men sat with their whisky Barbara showed Joan over the house.

Joan was plainly envious. 'I wish we could get out of our old place, but it belonged to Justin's parents and they'd be horrified if we left it.'

'Can't you please yourself where you live?' Barbara asked curiously.

'Not really. They were so proud of the house and let us have it for a song. I've dropped a few hints that it is old-fashioned and needs a lot of work but his mother simply smiles and refuses to take me seriously.'

'How does Justin feel about it?'

'Quite honestly I don't think he wants to move. Not even this house will push him into it!'

They laughed, then Joan said, 'What do you think about the conferences in Southampton? Apparently we're not to be invited yet again.'

'I'm not really sorry about that but Martin hasn't mentioned it.'

'Justin says wives are out for the time being. It wasn't so bad when they were going off to different venues where there was more for us to do, but it's not like that where they are now. I'm not really sorry either, I suppose, as we were often bored.'

'I was always bored! We had to listen to it every evening, all that hashing over what had gone on during the day, and there were times when I felt I could scream.'

'I know. All the same, I did enjoy London and Harrogate. I'm a shopaholic – I suppose that comes from spending so much time buried in the country.'

'I daresay you're right.'

'What do you find to do when Martin's away? I know you ride and play golf, but you must miss him terribly.'

'Well, of course. I catch up with all the things I can't do when he's at home.' She'd spoken nothing but the truth.

Mark had a list of Martin's conference dates. There were times when it was impossible for them to meet, but mostly they managed to see each other for two or three days and Barbara had little or no conscience about it.

She loved Martin, her marriage was in no danger and neither was Mark's. She honestly believed that she could have her cake and eat it, and the longer the situation continued the more complacent she grew.

The shock when it came was therefore more devastating than it would have been to a more perceptive woman.

CHAPTER 21

Mark sat on the terrace watching his wife and daughters with a frown of annoyance on his face. He'd been looking forward to watching Pippa tackle the course he'd designed for her in the park but immediately after lunch she'd rushed out with Berenice followed by Amelia without a second glance in his direction.

At breakfast he'd asked her to walk round the course with him but she'd said stonily that she preferred to walk there herself, then when he'd put a teasing arm round her shoulders she pulled sharply away, a cold angry frown on her face.

Girls were the very devil, especially at that age, but he'd thought Pippa was different. She had always been Daddy's girl, sweet and adoring with not an ounce of complication in her make-up — unlike the other one, who had smiled maddeningly at her sister's behaviour.

Now they were all out there on horseback watching Pippa tackle the jumps — which Berenice had no intention of trying — while Amelia called her encouragement and Pippa performed competently.

Grimly he thought to himself, she's good, but she's not as good as young Alison Steadwell. Pippa was riding like an automaton; there was no verve in her jumping, not like Alison whose face was alive with joy whenever her horse cleared a fence, and Alison's horse hadn't cost anything like the money he'd paid for Tondelao. She'd cost a bloody fortune.

He'd looked forward to this afternoon with Pippa; now for no reason at all it was spoiled. Thoroughly disgruntled, he strode across the terrace and up to where his car stood in front of the house. He would

214

drive up to the Standing farm to have a talk with Tom
about the bottom meadow. He was reluctant to let
Standing acquire it, as that family had quite enough
land already – nearly as much as the Garvestons – but
Amelia was always on at him to get it sorted out.

He was aware that his wife and daughters watched
him drive through the park but he made no acknow-
ledgement of them; it was petulant, but he felt like that.

A small fair-haired girl answered the door at the
Standing farm, smiling at him shyly. Mark was good
with little girls. He grinned at her amiably. 'Is your
father around, my dear?' he asked gently.

She shook her head. 'No, he's at work.'

At that moment the door opened wider and Maisie was
there, self-conscious as she always was in his presence.

'Hello, Maisie,' he said genially. 'Your daughter tells
me Tom's out on the farm somewhere. I would like to
have a word with him about the bottom meadow.'

'I'll send Lucy to fetch him,' Maisie said. 'She knows
where to find him.'

'Is it going to be a lot of trouble?'

'Why, no. Will you come into the house until he
arrives?'

He was ushered into the parlour where a dark-haired
boy sat at the table surrounded by schoolbooks. His
mother said hastily, 'You can work on the kitchen table,
Peter. Sir Mark's come to see your father.'

The boy hurriedly gathered his books together and
escaped into the kitchen, while his mother said, 'Will
you have a cup of tea, Sir Mark, or would you prefer
a lager?'

'Lager, I think, Maisie, and please call me Mark.
We've known each other a long time.'

She blushed. She was a pretty woman, a bit too
buxom for his liking, but comely nevertheless. He'd
never thought Maisie Standing looked like a Lorivals
girl, she'd always been a farmer's lass as far as he was

215

concerned. Now he looked round the parlour appreciatively. It was a nice, lived-in room, homely, a bit like Maisie herself.

'I hear you've got a very clever son,' he said by way of conversation.

She smiled, well pleased. 'We have very good reports from his teachers and he wants to go to university.'

'Not into farming, then?'

'No,' she said ruefully.

'How does Tom feel about that?'

'He's accepted it. At first he was a bit put out, but if Peter's clever enough to go to university we can't stand in his way.'

'Is it three children you have?'

'Yes, but the other two are girls.'

'Mine are both girls, so when I shuffle off this mortal coil it'll be my Cousin Austin who takes over Garveston Hall.'

'Oh dear, and all that money Amelia's spent on it! As well as you, too, of course,' she added hastily.

'You've lived in these parts long enough to know what it was like in my father's time, and you've seen what it's like now, Maisie.'

She was blushing furiously, appalled at her insensitivity, and Mark was trying to be kind about it. They didn't pull their punches, these north-country people, they said what came into their heads and thought about it afterwards. He'd experienced it with Nancy's father, but at least Maisie had shown some contrition; Nancy's father had meant every word.

At that moment the door opened and another girl came into the room. She was a teenager with a pretty freckled face and her mother's colouring. She looked at him in surprise and Maisie said, 'This is my daughter, Alice, on holiday from Lorivals. Say good afternoon to Sir Mark, Alice.'

Alice murmured a greeting and lowered her head.

216

There was something about her that seemed familiar but he couldn't think what. In any case she showed no desire to linger and escaped quickly through the door into the kitchen. Her mother said, 'She's not usually so shy – she's usually the forthcomin' one.'

'They're all very different aren't they? Sometimes I feel I don't know my daughters at all. One minute they're all over me, the next they don't want to know. Is that what they call growing up?'

Maisie smiled then excused herself while she went for his lager.

He settled down to drink it in one of the deep comfortable chairs while Maisie sat opposite. Mark did most of the talking. He realized that she felt uncomfortable in his presence, but as they chatted she began to relax and he admired the way the dimples appeared when she smiled and the soft northern burr in her voice which no amount of Lorivals schooling had managed to erase.

They talked about the land and farming in general and just once they spoke of Amelia, when Maisie enquired if she was quite well.

'You meet at the court, don't you?' Mark asked.

'Very seldom. Amelia's not on my rota but of course we are sometimes there on the same day.'

'And your other old room-mates,' he asked curiously. 'Do you ever hear from them?'

'It's months since I heard from Nancy, but then she's all over the place, but I did see Barbara in the town one day when she was visiting her mother.'

He nodded and in the next moment Maisie said, 'This sounds like Tom. I'll leave you two to it.'

Tom came in smiling genially, his good-humoured weather-beaten face shining with exertion, and Mark said, 'It's easy to see you've been working hard. I promise not to keep you long, I just wanted a word or two about the bottom meadow.'

217

'Aye well, it's time we had a talk about that,' Tom said. 'Bring us a lager, love, and another for Mark if he'd like one.'

They talked most of the afternoon yet, as usual, reached no firm resolution. Tom had the impression that Mark had come for something to do rather than with any real desire to finalise details about the meadow. All the same, it was late afternoon when Mark drove down the lane towards the road. As he drove along he suddenly remembered where he had seen the girl, Alice Standing, before. She was the schoolgirl he had almost run down with his horse on the path near Lorivals.

He could see her now, that pesky kid sauntering down the centre of the lane so that his horse shied to avoid her. It had riled him then to think that a Lorivals girl was wandering across the fell just when he'd arranged to meet Barbara. Suppose she had spied on his meeting and then gone back to the school and informed his daughters that she'd seen him with a woman on the fell . . . that would account for Pippa's withdrawal. I've got to put things right between Pippa and me, he thought soberly, and the sooner the better.

The opportunity came that night after dinner. The twins sat silent and moody while he and Amelia chatted spasmodically. After the coffee had been served and the servants had retired Mark remarked casually, 'I've been to the Standing farm this afternoon to talk about the bottom meadow. We haven't exactly reached any decision yet but things are under way.'

'All you ever do is talk about it, Mark.'

'Well, it does require some thought. I don't want to do anything in a hurry. I had a chat with your friend Maisie, nice woman.'

'Yes.'

'Very different from your friend Barbara. Always shy with me she is, calls me Sir Mark and holds out her

218

hand as if she's afraid I might suddenly grab her. When I saw Barbara Walton up on the fell one day recently, she held up her face for me to kiss her – as different as chalk from cheese.'

Amelia smiled but offered no comment, and after a few moments Berenice said, 'What is she like, this Barbara?'

'Dark, slim, very attractive. Your mother knows her better than me.' Mark didn't labour the point. He believed he'd said just enough, nor did he miss the look that passed between his two daughters. He knew now that it *was* that nosy Standing brat who had upset the applecart.

Later that evening Pippa sat on the side of his chair with her arm round his shoulders and he breathed a deep sigh of relief. What a good thing that he'd gone up to the farm that afternoon and met young Alice. The angels were still on his side . . . he and Pippa went on to talk about the next day when she promised to show him her prowess on Tondelao over the jumps.

Mark was well pleased. He'd spent a marvellous few days with Barbara and had come home expecting Pippa's gratitude when she returned from school to find the new horse waiting for her. He'd solved the problem of her withdrawal and now it felt good to spend an evening in the bosom of his family.

He looked across the room to where Amelia sat leafing through her diary, with Berenice curled up at her feet. Life was very good to him. He had Amelia and Garveston, and his wife was the easiest person in the world to be with; she gave him so much freedom and asked few questions.

He'd spend tomorrow in the park with the girls. Berenice pretended to be bored with horses, but she'd change her mind as she grew older. She didn't like her twin to beat her at anything – there was a lot of himself in Berenice.

Amelia's eyes swept over the room from her seat at the centre of the top table. Beside her Mark was trying to warm to his conversation with the new Mayor's wife and she knew he was wishing he was a million miles away.

He had come to support her and because it was expected of him. It was the occasion of the magisterial dinner and in just a few minutes' time they would be subjected to a string of speeches from members of the judiciary who were the honoured guests.

A faint smile hovered on Amelia's lips. She had little doubt that Mark would sit back in his chair with his eyes closed so that from time to time she would be required to nudge him awake. As if to confirm her thoughts, the first speaker was announced and was on his feet, and Mark immediately muttered, 'God, I hope he doesn't go on forever.'

'Try to keep awake,' she hissed.

'That will be extremely difficult, my dear,' he replied, settling back in his seat.

The speech continued at some length, and looking across the room Amelia could see Maisie Standing next to her husband. Their faces were blank, and again the smile hovered on Amelia's lips. Maisie was a fairly new Magistrate, so the speech would be entirely over her head, and no doubt Tom's thoughts were centred on all that he could have been doing at the farm if he'd been left to get on with it.

There were one or two unfamiliar faces – new people to Greymont from the large modern houses at the edge of the town. A very pretty woman in a quite lovely expensive gown smiled at her and Amelia recollected that she'd been introduced to her on several occasions, when she'd thought how pretty she was and how like Barbara. She'd also found the woman pushy and something of a social climber. Amelia was very good at keeping people like her at arm's length.

The applause at the end of the first speech was gratifying and then that speaker was followed by another. It was well over an hour later before she was able to circulate amongst those present and Mark muttered feelingly, 'Thank God that's over. How soon can we decently hope to make an excuse to get away?'

'Not for some time. Oh, do try to make an effort, Mark. This is the only function I ever expect you to attend and people are looking at us.'

'Most of 'em are no doubt thinking the same thing as I'm thinking.'

Amelia wasn't listening to him, shaking hands instead with a tall slender woman who seemed vaguely familiar. 'This is Miss Susan Lester, Mark, Nancy Graham's aunt,' she said, and he felt his hand taken in a grip as firm as his own.

'Have you heard from Nancy recently?' he asked her.

'She's in Ethiopia now. Twelve months ago it was South America, then Israel. It's difficult to keep track of her movements.'

'It's strange to think she's in that sort of life at all,' Mark commented.

'Do give her my love when you write to her, won't you, Miss Lester,' Amelia said graciously, and both Mark and Susan Lester nourished the same thought – why didn't Amelia write to Nancy herself?

Mark's eyes swept across the room and encountered those of Deirdre Forsythe, and she smiled. He'd been introduced to her at the agricultural show but her name escaped him for the moment.

'Who's the woman in that crowd near the door, the one in the green dress?' he asked his wife.

'Mrs Forsythe. Her husband has just joined us on the Bench.'

'She reminds me of your friend Barbara.'

'Yes, they're not unalike. She's the sort of woman who would be flattered by your attention.' He looked at her sharply, but her tone was bland and she smiled airily as she moved away.

They went their separate ways, Mark genial, Amelia gracious, and across the room Deirdre's eyes followed his unhurried progress until he reached her side.

She introduced her husband, a nice enough chap who was not averse to talking about himself, his job and his wife's participation in the life of the community. When Mark remarked on the speed of his elevation on to the Bench he was quick to explain that he'd been a Magistrate before, in the town they'd removed from, and went on to intimate that they were inviting a group of friends to their home for drinks at the end of the month and would be more than delighted if Sir Mark and Lady Amelia would join them.

'I never know what my wife's got planned these days,' Mark said diplomatically. 'It really is most kind of you but obviously until I've spoken with Lady Garveston I can't accept.'

'Oh, but we shall most certainly put it into writing,' Deirdre said quickly. 'We would both love to have you join us.'

Mark smiled, feeling intrigued. She really *did* remind him of Barbara, for she had the same colouring, the same tanned skin and sultry red mouth, but she was younger than his mistress and obviously still on the make. Give the Forsythes a few years and they'd be like the Waltons, but as yet she was very anxious to please whereas Barbara expected to be pleased. For the first time that evening he was enjoying himself.

Mark smiled as he moved on. Drinks at the Forsythes' house with Amelia was one thing, a discreet lunch with Deirdre at some quiet country inn, another. After all, Barbara was a long way away in Cheltenham and she played him up by not always being readily available when he wanted her.

From across the room Amelia read the signs well. Mark was intrigued by the newcomer but at least the bored expression was now not so evident; she no longer need worry that people were noticing.

She moved among several groups, enquiring after the health of the old and the achievements of the young, and then she came to Maisie sipping a glass of sherry while Tom stood beside her looking self-conscious in his new dinner jacket.

'How nice you look, Maisie,' Amelia said with her gentle remote smile, and Maisie's face flushed with pleasure. She was wearing a dress she'd worn on several other occasions – a deep azure-blue silk jersey dress that made her appear slimmer and which had cost her a great deal of money. So much money that she'd made up her mind it needed to be worn again and again for whatever function they needed to attend.

'Is your daughter happy at Lorivals?' Amelia enquired.

'I expect so, but she doesn't say much.'

'I'm sure she is. My girls love it there, they're never reluctant to go back after the holidays are over.'

Maisie gave a small bleak smile. Alice gave her no indication that she was happy about anything. She sulked in her room, mooned about the house, quarrelled with her brother and sister and generally Maisie was the happy one when the holidays were over.

Amelia didn't labour the point, and after a few minutes she moved away and was joined by Mark.

'Surely we've done our duty now,' he protested softly. 'Other people are making their excuses.'

She nodded. 'I'll get my wrap if you'll bring the car round.'

They spoke little on the way home; a thin frost covered the road and driving needed all his attention. He dropped her at the front door before going to put the car away, and Amelia was pleased to see that a tray had been left out for them containing a Thermos jug of coffee.

Mark grinned when she handed him a cup. 'I must say this is a far cry from Dad's servants. Whenever I came in late the house was cold and if there was any milk there was never any coffee.'

She smiled. 'It's not often I have your appreciation, Mark. Normally it's your resentment that shows through.'

'I know. I'm an ungrateful wretch, Amelia. That you put up with me at all is incredible, but you do know that there's no woman on earth I'd change you for.'

Amelia smiled. She knew he had stated nothing but the truth, but it was not a truth that elated her. Some men stayed with women because they loved them, couldn't envisage a life without them, but there were others who stayed because the disruption of their lives would be insupportable. Mark wanted to have his cake and eat it. She was here, his wife, a part of Garveston as solid as the walls and the roof, as enduring as the fells surrounding the house, but it was not out of love that he stayed with her, it was because of Garveston.

The incredible thing was that it didn't matter. As long as he continued to be discreet and created no scandal, she had Garveston and her children, and it was by Mark's grace that she had them.

She watched him appreciatively sipping his coffee to which he'd added a fair tot of brandy, and in a rare fit of mischief she said, 'You were very taken with Mrs Forsythe, Mark.'

He stared at her in some surprise, but deliberately kept his voice light as he answered her. 'Pretty women always bowl me over, you know that, love. That husband of hers is a bit full of himself.'

'He's rather nice, actually – she's the social climber.'

'Why do you say that?'

224

'From the way she mingles only with people who may help her to rise socially; she seems to have little time for the others. She obviously pushes her husband into things. If it wasn't for his wife I doubt he'd take the trouble.'

'It's not like you to be quite so caustic, Amelia.'

'Perhaps not. She does remind me of Barbara, though. Barbara was always anxious to cultivate any girl she considered worthy of her attentions. She never had much time for Maisie Standing and that is why I always made myself be particularly nice to Maisie.'

He stared at his wife uncomfortably. It wasn't like her to talk about people's shortcomings; she usually left that to others, merely smiling her cool aloof smile so that people were left wondering whether she agreed with them or not.

Why was Amelia suddenly mentioning Barbara? She couldn't possibly have any idea what was going on. Her face remained serene. There was a half-smile on her lips but no animosity, and pulling himself together sharply Mark said, 'The Forsythes have invited us to drinks one evening. They're putting it in writing, do you want to go?'

'Do you?'

'Well, no. If we attend that one it's going to be a snowball. We'll be hard put to it to refuse the others.'

'I agree. I'll make some excuse, Mark, leave it to me.' She rose to her feet and, letting her hand rest for a brief moment on his shoulder, she said, 'Goodnight, and thank you for your support at the dinner. I know how much those things bore you.'

After she had left the room he poured himself another coffee and added more brandy to it, then sat back in his chair staring into the embers of the fire. Amelia could be relied upon to decline the Forsythes' invitation with every appearance of regret, sufficient to appease them without their feeling snubbed. She would put herself out to be charming to John Forsythe whenever they met at the court, and if he bumped into Deirdre again he'd make a fuss of her. Women enjoyed that, particularly women like Deirdre.

Idly he wondered what sort of a conference Martin Walton had had, and whether Barbara was already bored to tears by his account of it. Lifting his cup with a smile he said softly, 'Here's to the next time, my dear.'

CHAPTER 22

Maisie sat with Tom in the headmaster's study at Peter's school discussing their son's future.

It was a careers evening at the end of June and Maisie's face was flushed with pride from the headmaster's unstinting praise of Peter's dedication in the classroom and his general popularity with the other boys and members of staff.

Mr Prothero expected him to do well in his fifth-year public exams, which he had just finished taking, and he informed them that when Peter returned to school after the summer holidays he would be made a prefect, and possibly Head Boy one day. After he had taken his A-levels, university beckoned; the boy was a good Oxbridge candidate.

Maisie looked at Tom doubtfully, but the pride on his face reassured her. Seeing her glance Mr Prothero said gently, 'I'm afraid your son isn't destined to be a farmer, Mr Standing. I hope it isn't too much of a disappointment.'

'No. I've known for a long time that Peter wasn't interested in the farm. Oh, he helps whenever I ask him, but I know his heart's not in it. We'll not have to look to Peter when the time comes to hand it over.'

Their son was waiting for them in the corridor and seeing his earnest young face Maisie longed to throw her arms round him and hug him, but there were other boys around so instead she quickly kissed his cheek while his father said, 'Are you comin' home with us now, lad?'

'Not just yet, Dad. There's some clearing away to be done and you'll be wanting your cup of tea and one of Mrs Smith's buns.' He grinned at them.

'A cup of tea would be nice,' Maisie agreed. 'Mr Prothero was very kind, Peter. He spoke very highly of you.'

Peter blushed and Tom said quickly, 'We'll be leaving when we've had a cup of tea. How are you getting home?'

'Alan Martin's father'll drop me off. I shan't be too late, Dad.'

They saw him go off with his friends and then Maisie said, 'I'd like to call in to see our Bob, Tom. Have we time, do you think?'

'We'll make time, love. We'll not bother with the tea. You've enjoyed yourself tonight, haven't you? I told you the Head would have nothin' but good to say about our Peter.'

'I'm so proud of him, Tom. Where does he get it from, do you think? I was never clever, nor were you for that matter.'

'Well, we've not done badly, Maisie.'

'Oh Tom, I know we haven't! You've done wonders with that farm but it's been hard work with your hands, it hasn't taken a PhD and it's kept five of us and now we're actually makin' money.'

Bob's face registered the same sort of pride as Peter's parents when they told him about the headmaster's comments and Mary said stoutly, 'Peter's a good boy. I've allus said as much, haven't I, Bob? I just hope your Alice does as well at Lorivals.' Maisie changed the subject. 'We'll call to tell the others as we're so near. You can't blame us for being proud of him.'

'I doubt you'll find Gloria at home,' Mary sniffed. 'Goodness knows how that girl spends her time. She's always at the hairdresser's or shoppin' and she's learnin' to drive that little car Eric's bought her, flashin' her eyes at the drivin' instructor with skirts that short it's positively indecent.'

'Oh well, it's none of our business,' Tom said soothingly.

'What's Alice goin' to do when she leaves school?' Mary demanded. 'I asked her at Christmas but she didn't seem to know.'

'She'll make up her mind one of these days. In any case, she's a little while to go before she needs to make up her mind.'

'She didn't call to see us at Easter.'

'She spent Easter with a schoolfriend who lives in the south. We only saw her for a couple of days.'

'Hobnobbin' with girls whose parents have too much money and not enough to do isn't good for 'er,' Mary persisted. 'Look at you, Maisie. When do you ever see those girls you were so pally with at Lorivals?'

'I see Amelia and Nancy writes to me,' Maisie answered shortly.

'And that's all, so you can hardly call yourselves bosom friends.'

'They're all busy women,' Tom said calmly. 'Maisie and Amelia see each other at the court.'

'Has Alice said if she's friendly with the Garveston girls?' Mary asked.

'She doesn't room with them,' Maisie said. 'I never wanted them to think they had to look after Alice simply because I knew their mother.'

'How about a cup of tea then?' Bob enquired brightly, but immediately Tom said, 'Are you wantin' to see your Jimmy, Maisie? We haven't much time.'

'You'll not find him in,' Mary snapped. 'He shut up shop promptly at six o'clock and by half past he was off in that car of his dressed up to the nines.'

Tom grinned and unable to resist a wry jibe said, 'It was a blessin' you had that glass canopy put over the front of the shop, Mary. You can watch what goes on in some degree of comfort.'

'I don't pry on them,' Mary retorted, 'but I can't help seeing what they do when I'm clearing away the counters. I'll put the kettle on.'

'No, please, Mary, not on our account,' Maisie begged. 'Tom has work to do when we get home.'

Driving back to the farm Tom said sympathetically, 'You must be gaspin' for a cup of tea, love, but I knew you'd rather have it at home.'

'She always rubs me up the wrong way.'

'I know. She can't help it, it wouldn't be Mary without that sharp tongue of hers.'

As they drove into the farmyard they could hear the sound of the piano and Tom said, 'Lucy's practisin' her lesson. She seems to have taken to it all right.'

'Until somethin' else comes along to claim her attention,' Maisie added shrewdly.

The kitchen was tidy. A white linen cloth covered the table and on it rested four cups and saucers and a large brown teapot. Tom grinned. 'Looks as though they've been waitin' supper for us, love.'

At the sound of the front door, the door leading into the living room opened and Lucy's bright head appeared around it. She smiled and indicating the table said, 'I laid the table, Mummy, and I helped Mrs Murdock to wash the tea things and clear away.'

'Did you offer your piano teacher a cup of tea when you'd finished your lesson?'

'Yes, she had tea and scones and I buttered them just like I've seen you doing. I've got a new piece tonight, it's awfully hard.'

'You'll soon get into it, love. I'll make some tea for your dad and me, would you like a glass of milk?'

Tom sank into a chair in front of the Aga and Lucy went immediately to sit on the rug at his feet. She was a good child, had never been any trouble with her even temper and sunny smiles. Peter had always been on the shy side, but Lucy loved people and company and she tolerated Alice's ill-humour and peevish taunts with quiet calm.

Waiting for the kettle to boil Maisie's eyes fell on an envelope propped up against the clock on the mantelpiece and she exclaimed, 'Oh bother! I intended to post that on the way down to the school. It'll have to go tomorrow.'

Lucy jumped up and stood staring up at the envelope and Maisie said, 'It's to Alice, Lucy. I'm wantin' to know how her exams went.'

'I'll post it, Mummy,' Lucy said.

'Don't worry about it, I'll post it in town tomorrow.'

With all a child's unthinking candour Lucy said, 'I like it better when Alice isn't at home. She hardly ever talks to me and she doesn't like my toys about the bedroom.'

'Maybe she's teaching you to be tidy, love,' Tom said gently.

'She's anythin' but tidy herself,' Maisie put in sharply. 'Don't let Alice bully you, Lucy, tell me if she's nasty with you.'

'When is she coming home again?'

'At the end of July. For six weeks! I only hope the weather'll be good so that you're not under mi feet the whole time.'

'Maybe Alice'll go away again,' Lucy said hopefully.

Maisie didn't speak. She'd had words with Alice about her holiday in the south of England with Monica Darwin's family. It had become a ritual – Easter with the Darwins, Christmas with the Sharp family in Richmond and summer nothing but rows because she'd wanted to go off with Joanne Proctor, and Maisie'd said no, there was too much work on the farm.

She was glad that Alice had made new friends, thrilled that they invited her to their homes, but when she asked her daughter to invite them back Alice made excuses: it was too close to Lorivals, it wouldn't be a

231

change, there'd be nowhere different for them to go – and Maisie knew it was because she was ashamed of the farm, the way her father spoke, the entire set-up in her home.

In Alice's refusal to invite her friends back Maisie saw her own attitude. She'd never wanted to invite Amelia or Lois to spend a holiday in the shop across the park. She'd compared their little living room with Amelia's gracious country house and the grand hotels where Lois spent most of her holidays. She'd never once invited Barbara to her home, even when she'd lived just the other side of Greymont, but Nancy was a constant visitor. Nancy loved the informality of the cramped living room, its table littered with jigsaws and the appetising smells coming from the kitchen beyond.

Maisie had accused Alice of being ashamed of her home and her family, and Alice had burst into tears. 'You don't understand, Mummy! The others have servants and all sorts of things we haven't got. If they came here you'd be too busy to look after them – you'd be up to your ears with cooking and cleaning, bottling fruit and making chutneys. You'd be wanting us to clean the bedrooms and make ourselves useful and I'm never never asked to do anything like that when I go to them.'

So she'd given it up as a bad job, but she had insisted that Alice spend her summer holidays at the farm.

'There's the harvest to see to,' she'd scolded. 'Look at Peter, he hates farmwork but he helps out at such a time and you should do the same. Your father's tired out and so am I, it's the least you can do. At other times I don't mind what you get up to.'

She sensed in her heart that Alice had given her friends a glorified description of her home. She would have described a farmhouse looking like an Old English manor house surrounded by acres of well-tended farmland. Her father would be a gentleman farmer, her

232

mother a local JP with an army of servants, no doubt a sweet and simpering sister and a brother destined for university. Clever as he was, Peter had not lost his north-country accent and Lucy was a tomboy, made much of by all the farmhands.

After Lucy went back to the piano and Tom left to take his final look around, Maisie got out her mending basket and started to sew. She looked around her appreciatively. The kitchen was nice, warm and snug with its old flagged floor and bright rugs. Pots of geraniums stood on the windowsills whose width was indicative of the stout walls of the farmhouse. It was a pleasant kitchen with its shining copper pans and white walls. On the wall opposite she had hung the two water colours she'd bought at an antique fair over at Hambleton. She'd paid more for them than she'd intended but they were paintings of the farm as it was when it had been built, and of the fells surrounding it. She hadn't been able to resist them.

It was a good life. They hadn't started with much money but they'd worked hard and saved some. Everything they had was paid for and Peter was a son to be proud of. She knew Tom worried about the future of the farm when they were both too old to care for it, but she was pinning her hopes on Lucy. Her youngest daughter loved the fells and loved everything about the farm – the fields of grain and the animals. She enjoyed helping with the baking and the bottling, and perhaps one day there'd be somebody for Lucy like Tom, somebody kind and decent who liked the things she did and thought the way she thought.

Perhaps Alice would change. Perhaps one day she'd sort the wheat from the chaff but time went so quickly.

Maisie winced at the discordant sounds coming from the living room. She'd been the one to say Lucy should learn the piano, and as always the child had tried but, like she'd said, the piece was hard. She put her sewing

233

down on the kitchen table and went into the living room. Lucy sat at the piano, her small fingers struggling with the piece set in front of her, a frown of concentration on her brow. Maisie said, 'Leave it for now, love. Have your bath and get ready for bed, I'll bring some hot milk up to you.'

Dutifully Lucy closed the lid of the piano and placed the music in the piano stool, then with a bright smile she said, 'I'll be better tomorrow, my hands are tired.'

CHAPTER 23

Barbara stared at her friend Eileen Swenson in some surprise. It had been a busy morning, for she'd had over eighty people in the house for coffee and a light buffet meal in aid of the vicar's appeal for funds towards a new church roof. Most of them had gone, and those who were left were helping to clear away the remains of the repast which were being placed in cardboard boxes for a group of boy scouts to convey to the scoutmaster's Land Rover.

The occasion had gone very well. Barbara's home had been praised with some envy by most of those present, and the vicar had made a flattering speech thanking Mrs Walton for her kind hospitality and Mr Walton for his lavish gifts which they had duly raffled off.

Now Barbara stood in her kitchen staring defensively at Eileen who had just made a remark that had shaken her complacency. In Eileen's eyes she saw raw jealousy, and for the first time in years Barbara felt strangely vulnerable. 'I don't know what you mean, Eileen. How has my life changed?'

Eileen Swenson was wishing she'd kept quiet, but there were times when Barbara riled her, most of the time in fact since they'd moved away from the town. She was so sure of herself and her husband, so happy to be acting the part of Lady Bountiful. Eileen was jealous, she had to admit it, but she had spoken only the truth when she'd said, 'Nothing's the same for you these days, Barbara. Are you happier now than you were then?'

Now Barbara was asking her to explain herself.

'Well, you and Martin were always together – at the Golf Club, at functions in the town, that is, when you were here. You often went off together for weeks at a time to the most exotic places, but now Martin's always sailing his boat and you're into good works or riding your horse around the lanes.'

'Other people's lives change so why shouldn't ours?' Barbara said warily.

'Only that you enjoyed travelling with Martin, going to conferences with him, playing golf and meeting friends. When did you last go to the Club, for instance? People are grumbling that you're on the committee yet you hardly ever turn up, and Martin seems to go everywhere on his own.'

'There's no secret about it. None of the wives are going to the conferences these days and I don't think any of us are all that bothered. I'm not into sailing, Martin knew that when he bought his boats, and I've discovered I love riding. We spent an awful lot of money on this house and we both love it. I for one would rather stay at home than go off on some trip or other and Martin doesn't mind. He's happy with his boats.'

'I shouldn't have said anything, Barbara. It's none of my business.'

'Are other people talking about us?'

'Oh well, you know what people are like. They have to have somebody to talk about and you've never surrounded yourself with a lot of women friends.'

'No, that's true. It probably stems from the way I was brought up.'

'Your parents didn't like you to have friends?'

'When my friends were off on the fells I was shopping in the town with my mother. I hadn't to get my clothes soiled. I had to drink tea with her cronies in the cafés in town and remember that my father was a Town Councillor. It was even worse when he was the Mayor.'

Eileen laughed. 'But you had friends at boarding school, surely?'

'I roomed with four others and I suppose we were friends. You have met Mark Garveston — well, I shared a dormitory with his wife and three others.'

'I thought he was awfully dishy. Doesn't his wife care for racing? He always comes alone — will he be coming next year?'

'I expect so. I'll have to talk to Martin about it.'

'Mark's a charmer. If I had a husband like that I doubt if I'd let him go racing without me.'

'Oh, she's very much the lady of the manor. I doubt Amelia has much time for racing.'

At that moment one of the boy scouts carried the last cardboard box out of the kitchen and Barbara said feelingly, 'I'm glad all that's over. My two dailies are clearing up in the lounge so I'll tell them they can come in here now. Are you in a hurry to leave?'

'I mustn't be late. We're going to the theatre tonight with some friends but we're having a cold meal.'

'It seems ages since we went to the theatre.'

Eileen raised her eyebrows meaningfully. 'See what I mean, darling?'

After she'd watched her two dailies trundling their bicycles down the drive Barbara made herself walk round the house to check that not a thing was out of place, and that her beautiful home was restored to its original pristine perfection.

She settled down in front of the fire with a well-earned glass of sherry. The leaping flames had a hypnotic effect and she laid her head back against the cushions and closed her eyes. Old memories insinuated themselves into her thoughts at random — of the sun setting in a blaze of glory over Morecambe Bay, and the fells gently misted on an autumn morning, and three young girls wending their way to school along the leaf-covered paths in the park.

Barbara was not normally given to nostalgia, but for the first time in years she found an unexpected ache in her heart when recalling those three little girls. They'd often squabbled, because Maisie Jayson was provocative and given to jealousy, but she'd liked Nancy with her wide blue-grey eyes and hair like sun-kissed corn.

Even that long ago Barbara had wanted Martin Walton, and they'd teased her mercilessly about him. Maisie had wanted Tom Standing just as openly, but during that weekend when they'd all met up at Garveston Hall, for a reunion ten years after they'd left Lorivals, it had been Nancy who was the enigmatic one. While they'd talked about their comings and goings, their homes and their children, their holidays and their interests, Nancy had remained tantalisingly remote.

She had told them nothing about her life, her loves or her ambitions. She'd listened to them all with a serene expression which didn't quite hide the antagonism between her and Amelia, and Barbara had thought – it's because of Mark. Amelia is still seething inwardly over Mark's former feelings for Nancy. It had to be that, for what else could it have been?

Once she'd have been able to ask Nancy openly, but during that weekend there'd been something different about her old friend, something far removed from that open jolly little girl with whom she'd grown up.

Barbara was brought reluctantly back to the present by the sound of the door opening, and then Martin was there sitting across from her while he leafed through his mail. 'How was the buffet?' he asked with a smile. 'Did the caterers come up to scratch?'

'I think everybody enjoyed themselves. We made over four hundred pounds, and the vicar was delighted. Emma Gale won one of the raffles – I don't know who won the others.'

238

'I'm glad things went well.'

She watched him reading a letter, then as he replaced it in its envelope she said, 'Have you ever thought our life was changing, Martin, that somehow or other we're two different people?'

'What brought this on?'

'It was something Eileen Swenson said about our not doing the same things any more. We never go on holiday together these days, and we are a little cut off from the people we used to know.'

'Well, we're not living quite so near to them, are we?'

'No, that's true, but you never mention going abroad for holidays. We never seem to go anywhere these days.'

'We're older – I've got the boats, you've got your horse. Many people adopt new interests as they get older, it's inevitable.'

Martin was right of course. People did change, successful people more than most, but her parents hadn't. They still went on holiday to Scotland and Scarborough every year. Her father enjoyed his Council meetings, his bowls and his golf in that order, and Mrs Smythe thrived on her work as a JP and her bridge and coffee mornings with her friends; in the evenings they watched television and mulled over the day's activities together. Barbara couldn't visualise a time when she and Martin would be content to do the same.

Both her parents and Martin's had wanted success for their only children; they'd worked towards that goal and they'd not been disappointed – only now they constantly moaned that they were being neglected. Eileen Swenson's words echoed Mrs Smythe's when she unkindly informed Barbara that they'd outgrown all their old friends as well as their parents.

Martin talked about people changing when they got older, but they weren't old. Thirty-six wasn't old, for heaven's sake! She was still as slim as a reed and there wasn't a grey hair in her head. If anything, Martin was the stuffy one in his well-cut suits and he'd taken to wearing spectacles for close work, but he was still good-looking and prosperous.

Perhaps it was seeing them like this that made people envious. Eileen was envious. Her husband had developed a paunch and rumour had it that he'd lost a lot of money quite recently. It was probably true – the suit she'd worn that morning was last year's and it hung badly, probably because Eileen had lost weight, due to worries about Bob's business, or some other reason.

Later Barbara stared at herself critically in the bathroom mirror, running a finger lightly over the fine lines that had developed under her eyes before smoothing on her night cream. It might not be a bad idea to spend a bit of money on her face. So many women began to look horsey when they started to ride and Betty Bernstein had said the new salon in Cheltenham was very good. Better still, she could go up to London for a few days.

Martin lay in bed, propped up against the pillows with his working papers spread out in front of him. He was wearing his glasses, his face was absorbed and for a moment Barbara's expression softened. With that look on his face she was reminded of the boy she'd loved in that little school across the park, the same dark clever face poring over his schoolbooks, a frown of concentration between his eyes, occasionally tapping his chin with his pen.

She went to sit beside him on the edge of the bed. 'I thought I might go up to London for a few days. Would you mind, darling?'

'I can't get away at the moment to go with you. Why do you want to go just now?'

'I don't want you to come with me, I just feel like a change. It's not as though I go with you to the conferences now, and it's ages since we went on holiday.

240

'I'd like to go to the theatre and see the shops – I'm only thinking in terms of around three or four days.'

'Go by all means if you want to, Barbara. The syndicate have a flat in the West End and I could get it for you for a few days. Would you like that?'

'I don't want the flat, it will be nicer in some hotel. I'd get awfully bored in a flat by myself.'

'Do you want me to book in for you?'

'Would you, darling?'

'Why not go when I'm in Southampton? It would be a change from being here on your own.'

'No, I'd like to go sooner, next week if that's possible. Your conference isn't until the end of the month.'

'Leave it with me. I'll get my secretary to book you in somewhere in the morning. Any special place you fancy?'

'Not too large, but exclusive if you know what I mean.'

It had been so easy. A few years ago, Martin would have sulked about her wanting to go to London on her own, but now he accepted it as normal. She climbed into bed and picked up her novel.

'You'll be going up by train, of course?' he said.

'Yes, it's better than all the hassle of taking the car.'

With any luck she'd see Mark some time when Martin was at his conference, but the time in London would be exclusively her own to shop and go to shows. It wouldn't be Martin's cup of tea, or Mark's either for that matter.

She'd go to a first-class salon and have her hair styled and her face done, then she'd get some new clothes. Eileen would be pea-green with envy but she shouldn't have been so spiteful. After all, friends who were friends shouldn't be envious. If the boot had happened to be on the other foot she'd have rejoiced at Eileen and Bob's good fortune.

CHAPTER 24

Martin looked across the table at his wife with some degree of pride. You had to hand it to Barbara, she always looked the part, whether it was lazing on a beach or attending a grand ball. Tonight it was simply a dinner party at the Golf Club and she was wearing the gown she'd bought in London. He knew he'd have a ghastly shock if he dared to ask the price, but he'd given her the go-ahead even if it had largely been dictated by conscience.

He was aware of the admiration of the men and the envy of the women as Barbara moved amongst them, supremely confident and well aware of the furore she was creating.

Barbara had played her part in helping Martin to be the professional he'd become. She'd known how to entertain, to talk to his superiors as well as his under-lings, and she'd always been the gracious hostess, the charming companion. She'd smiled and cajoled, given her opinion when it was asked for, yet known when to keep silent, and he flattered himself that he'd known all those years ago in Greymont that she was what he wanted, for himself and his career.

He remembered standing on the hearthrug in her father's little study after their wedding when Mr Smythe had said feelingly, 'Well, lad, you've got her now and she'll need some livin' up to. She's got that expensive school behind her and then there's her mother. I'm just warnin' you what to expect.'

His own father had bristled indignantly at that. 'Martin's no slouch,' he'd retorted sharply. 'Barbara's damned lucky to have got him.'

Mr Smythe had merely chuckled, and Martin knew at that moment that he had to prove to everybody that he was worthy of Barbara's beauty and her Lorivals background. He'd never liked her mother; he regarded Mrs Smythe as too pushy by half, and he was wary of her father. He'd always been glad that they'd managed to make a life for themselves away from Greymont.

He sat back surveying the scene. In another week he'd be in Southampton with his boats and Sandra.

Sandra was comfortable to be with. She laughed a lot and she was entirely predictable, unlike Barbara. Sandra was always available when he was in Southampton and he often wondered if there were any young men around when he wasn't there. He never asked and she never told him. She knew when he'd be there and she was always waiting. He took her out to meals in quiet country inns and she loved the boats. He bought her little gifts – perfume and chocolates – and she was blushingly grateful. He would have been willing to leave it like that if Sandra hadn't fallen in love with him.

She was pretty and he enjoyed her company. With Sandra he found the carefree young courtship he'd never known with Barbara, but it wasn't really a courtship since he'd had no thoughts on where they were going.

He had been happy to drift until that afternoon in the Solent when the rain had swept down on them in torrents and they'd been buffeted about like a cockleshell in the strong wind. She'd been seasick and miserable, and he'd hotted soup up for them while they lay at anchor, and wrapped her in a thick fleecy robe he'd found in the locker. The rain had gone on and on. They'd sat in the tiny cabin listening to it beating relentlessly above them, heard the rigging screeching in the gale and she'd been afraid. She'd clung to him in tears and one thing had led to another, and before he knew it they were in his bunk and he was making love

243

to her more sensually than he'd ever made love to his wife.

He was fond of Sandra but he wasn't in love with her. If she'd come along and told him she'd met someone else he'd have felt a vague regret but he'd have been ready to wish her well. It never entered his head that Sandra loved him to the exclusion of everything and everybody else.

She knew he was married; she'd asked him outright and he'd answered her truthfully. He found himself telling her about Barbara and she'd asked to see a photograph. After handing it back to him she said, 'She looks like you. I mean, she's just the sort of wife I'd expect you to have.'

He asked her what she meant by that and she laughed a little sadly, saying, 'You know, beautiful and stylish. Are you in love with her?'

He stared at her. Of course he was in love with Barbara, he'd never fallen out of love with her, but looking into Sandra's suddenly solemn brown eyes he faced a question he hadn't asked himself for a long time.

Oh, but it would be good to get back, to feel the salt spray on his lips and the Solent wind in his hair. Barbara had never really liked sailing. The same old crowd would be there and he knew that among them affairs had started and ended and he'd no doubt they thought he was in the middle of one. None of them cared, none of them except Sam Barber. Sam had been instrumental in introducing Sandra into Martin Walton's life and yet now he had the distinct impression that Sam disapproved. He'd been sure of it when the old man had said dryly, 'I'm all talk, Martin. I don't practise what I preach. I'm sorry I got you involved but she's the one who'll get hurt.'

He saw little of Sam at the conferences. The other man avoided him when it was possible but made a fuss

244

of Sandra whenever he found her waiting for Martin. It was the only way Sam could ease his conscience.

Tonight Martin was so immersed in his thoughts that Eileen Swenson had to speak to him twice before he acknowledged her presence.

'Martin, you were miles away!' she laughed.

'I'm sorry, Eileen. Have you seen Barbara? She's around somewhere.'

'We've been chatting. I've been admiring the dress she bought in London.' He smiled. 'I hear you'll be leaving us again soon,' she went on. 'Another conference?'

'I'm afraid so.'

'Doesn't Barbara mind not going with you?'

'I'm sure she doesn't. Conferences have always bored her.'

'Even so, I'd want to go with my husband, but perhaps he isn't as safe as you, Martin.'

'You make me sound incredibly dull.'

'I don't mean to. I envy Barbara an awful lot – her home, her lifestyle and her husband. Don't tell her I said so.'

Sam was sitting in the residents' lounge when Martin arrived at the hotel in Southampton on the Saturday morning. He raised his hand in greeting and Martin walked across to him. 'Are we the first to arrive?' he asked.

'I got here early. I've left the little woman with her sister in Bournemouth and came on from there. I think one or two of them are upstairs, unpacking.'

Martin smiled. 'See you at dinner, then.'

Sam nodded. He watched Martin walk across the room towards the lifts and a certain anger stirred in him. Sam Barber was not a happy man, and yet it had all started innocently enough even if it had been born out of spite, spite brought on by that first conference he'd attended years before in the company of his wife.

They'd gone with such pride – pride at his promotion, pride at being asked to represent his firm – and Nellie'd bought new clothes and had an expensive hair-do, only to spend that long week in Harrogate being snubbed by a bevy of young executives with their dolly wives.

Sam knew exactly what they had thought of him – a rather common little man with a doubtful sense of humour – and Nellie, pleasant buxom Nellie, had looked like everybody's mother in her predictable clothes.

In the evenings they'd sat alone in the residents' lounge, and during the day when the women went on trips around the Dales Nellie sat by herself on the coach. Oh, it wasn't that the others were intentionally unkind, they were simply indifferent. When they'd arrived home Nellie had stated adamantly that it was the last conference she was ever going to.

After that it became Sam's mission in life to see what the young fellers were made of, and it was easy at the conferences where wives didn't attend.

He'd moved up a few leagues since then. The men were older, richer, more established and yet it amused him to see they were just like all the others when they'd had a few drinks and were confronted by a group of pretty girls.

Right from the first he'd thought Martin Walton might be different. He was a cultured stuffed shirt, too bloody pompous by half and he regarded Sam as he might have regarded a bothersome gnat. Sam had said as much to Sandra Stubbs when he saw the way the wind was blowing, but she'd defended him like a young tigress with her one cub. Martin was wonderful, he was kind, generous, he was marvellous – and Sam knew it was too late. Sandra was in love with the man and they were probably having one hell of an affair.

He warned Sandra – after all, she was about the same age as his daughter Jenny – and she'd listened to him with a calm smile on her face and he knew his words of wisdom had gone in one ear and come out the other.

'Think, lass!' he said urgently. 'Martin Walton's married, he's been married a long time and he's not going to leave his wife for you. He'll do nothing to cause a single ripple on that placid life of his.'

'I know,' she answered him. 'I just want to be with him as long as it's possible. One day he'll ditch me, of course he will, but please, Sam, don't spoil it for me yet.'

What more could he do? He'd warned her, but there was no use warning him – Walton wouldn't take kindly to his interference and he'd be quick to tell him it was none of his business. All the same, Sam was finding no joy in the prospect of the week ahead of them.

CHAPTER 25

Nancy's spirits soared as they drove from Haifa to Jerusalem on a golden morning when the white city nestling between its hills and valleys seemed too brilliant, too unreal in the white-gold of the afternoon sunlight. She was glad to be returning to Israel. Ethiopia had been a sad colourless land, a desert crying out for rain, a people hammered by despair.

In recent weeks she had sensed a restraint between herself and Noel. He was still charming and teasing, but there was no passion between them, and more and more she began to ask herself if he was keeping faith with some other woman in his life.

She spent the long evenings playing cribbage with Alec or arguing with the two younger men. Harry flirted with her, showing her quite plainly that he was not averse to their friendship ripening, but she kept him at arm's length. He was fun and he was brash, he was audacious and he made her laugh. Laughter was to be prized in that long hot summer when they all sensed the trouble seething under a surface normality.

As long as she lived she believed she would remember that afternoon when the sun blazed down and Jerusalem seemed to sleep like a taut aware cat on the torpid pavements.

Heat hung over Israel. The level fields lay baked and parched, gasping for air, the rivers moved glassily, as if stupefied, and the teeming streets sprawled helplessly beneath the sun, waiting for the hot noon to pass.

It was a heat, indeed, such as the oldest inhabitants could not remember. It rested like a pall on the close-packed hovels of the poor, and in the thronged holy places awe had given place to weariness; scarcely a dog moved.

Sitting beneath the canopy of their hotel balcony they were all aware that the noontide quiet of Jerusalem had an uneasy undercurrent. The stillness seemed to vibrate, the very heat seemed to quiver with a premonition of impending events, a threat of catastrophe to come.

Down in the Arab quarter hatred and anger began to coil into an ugly evil form against the Jews – those aliens who had spread over the land, and in the noon-tide heat men began to whisper together.

Nancy sat on the arm of Alec's chair watching him filling in the crossword in yesterday's paper. She sensed the tension: Noel had said earlier on that there was trouble brewing – he could smell it, even when the streets were empty and life in the hotel seemed normal.

It erupted suddenly in the early afternoon with Arab youths running down the street emitting blood-curdling yells, and as she ran to the edge of the balcony Nancy could see that they were armed with guns and knives.

'This is it,' Noel said quickly. 'We're here to write about it, to take photographs and to keep safe. Stay together if that is possible, but if not we'll meet back here as soon as we can.'

They followed the running feet through the narrow streets and into the broader avenues of Jerusalem, and it was here where the shooting and knifing began, irrespective of age or sex, until the Israeli soldiers came with their superior weapons and their discipline.

For a while the four of them hugged the shelter of a wall, and then they followed Noel as he set off across the square, with Alec bringing up the rear. Nancy had almost reached the other side when she heard a sudden cry and looking back saw Alec staggering behind her, his hands clutching at his abdomen; then he was writhing helplessly on the ground.

249

Without a second's thought she ran back to him, staring in horror at the blood that was spreading across his shirt, at his pale face and the life that was slowly ebbing from it. Then she heard the howling as a crowd of youths bore down on her and felt her arm taken in an iron grip as Noel's eyes blazed into hers.

'You little fool! For God's sake run for your life!'

She felt him dragging her to her feet, then he was running towards the edge of the square while she ran gasping beside him. When she lost a shoe he ordered her to take off the other one and slipping and sliding she was dragged along until she thought the pain in her feet and in her arm would kill her.

They turned to face the onrushing mob, and then once more the soldiers were there and the Arabs were halted in their tracks. A burst of gunfire echoed round the square and she watched a line of young boys sink lifeless on to the burning tarmac.

She stood with Noel watching the soldiers remove the dead, while their comrades crept stealthily towards the narrow streets that edged the square. They removed Alec's body from where it lay and she said haltingly, 'Where will they take him?'

Noel didn't answer, and looking up at his face she realized that it was filled with anguish – anguish and something else, a deep and abiding anger.

The long noon passed. The heat did not really lessen, but as the afternoon lengthened, the sun was not quite so fiery. People began to rouse themselves. They stood at the doors of their houses; they strolled into the streets; they looked about them.

The two cameramen and Nancy sat on the hotel balcony waiting for Noel. There was no conversation. They were numb from the events of the afternoon. Nancy's feet still throbbed painfully even after bathing them in salted water, and her arm was bruised from Noel's cruel grip.

250

It was dusk when Noel returned. He had discovered that Alec's body had been taken to the hospital mortuary but it was his opinion that the trials of the day were by no means over. He did not look at Nancy once as he told them of his findings, and even as he spoke the day blazed abruptly into action as another army of youths ran down the street urged on by agitators brandishing torches as the hot dusk fell, shouting, 'On to the Jews! Plunder! Rape! Burn! Down with the Jews, down with the infidels!'

Peaceful knots and groups of men gathered together in the streets suddenly became mobs, shouting, bellowing, snatching torches, grabbing up weapons, rushing down the streets in hysterical torrents, and suddenly roofs flared up into flames.

Her three colleagues gathered their things together and made to leave the hotel, but when Nancy started to go with them Noel addressed her for the first time.

'You will stay here,' he commanded. 'There is no place for you in tonight's events.'

'But I must go, Noel. I have to go!' she cried.

'No, Nancy, you have to obey my orders. You will stay here until we return. I shall have enough to worry about without having to keep an eye on you.'

She recoiled against the determination in his eyes but she obeyed him, watching helplessly as the little group ran down the street after the yelling mob, unsure what she would remember most about this terrible day – Alec's death, the screaming mob of young Arab boys barely out of the schoolroom facing the indomitable unrelenting strength of the Israeli soldiers, or the anger she had seen in Noel's eyes.

From the distance came the wailing sound of women keening, occasional gunshots and then silence, a silence all the more terrible after the clamour of what had gone before. An old man came to sit on the steps of the hotel staring vacantly in front of him while a young girl dragged at his clothing urging him to go with her. Wearily Nancy went to sit on her balcony where she could look out across the city. The smell of smoke was in her nostrils, the sound of silence clutching at her heart.

At four o'clock in the morning the city was quiet. The oppressive heat of the day had given way to a sticky humidity and a tranquil crescent moon shone in a deep blue sky.

Nancy stayed on her balcony, unable to sleep. She'd heard the others come in only an hour before but hurt pride kept her in her seat. Their doors closed quietly, there had been no conversation, and for a while she waited, hoping desperately that Noel might come into her room to relate something of the night's events as he often had before, but he didn't.

She was still smarting from his blazing eyes and the lash of his anger. She had disobeyed the rules they lived by and now she could only speculate on what he would do with her.

The long night crept on and she was relieved at last to see the dawn slowly breaking in the east, throwing into sharp relief the towers and domes, the minarets and rooftops of the sprawling city.

She showered and dressed. The others would probably sleep late although Noel never seemed to need much sleep. However traumatic the night before, he was always ready and waiting for the events of the following morning. She made her way to the dining room of the hotel where a weary waiter was already setting the breakfast tables. He smiled and wished her good morning, and to pass the time she sauntered out on to the terrace where street vendors were already arranging their wares as though the day before hadn't happened. Yesterday she'd seen them scattered in all directions, their faces filled with terror, their stalls left in rubble, but today miraculously those stalls were mended and life was going to go on as usual irrespective of those who were no more.

There was something entirely pitiless about it. Indeed, Noel had always said there was something pitiless about the East; the people there expected to suffer and in between their suffering, life had to go on.

The waiter came to tell her she could have breakfast if she wished it, so she went to sit alone in the empty room. She wasn't hungry, asking only for fruit juice and coffee whereupon he shook his head gently saying, 'There is good food, lady. Today is another day.'

'I know, Yusef, but I'm not hungry. I never eat much breakfast.'

'You are sad for your friend, him very nice man, good man.'

She felt the treacherous tears rise to her eyes and she looked down at her coffee quickly, feeling that if he said much more she would burst into tears.

Sensing her misery, Yusef said no more but went about his work allowing Nancy to drink her coffee in peace. It seemed incredible that Alec had gone from them, that never again would she watch his concentration over his crossword puzzle, or listen to his arguments with Noel, always good-natured, always ending with laughter. She had lost a dear good friend, and her entire future was in jeopardy.

She had almost finished her meagre breakfast when she heard Noel's voice in the passage outside, then her heart began to race until it felt like a physical pain within her breast. He came directly to her table, sitting opposite her with a murmured good morning, calmly asking for coffee and nothing more, so that Yusef shrugged his shoulders at this typical British sang-froid.

For a while they sat in silence, then when their eyes met he said quietly, 'I have to go to the hospital this morning. Alec's funeral will be later today.'

'Today!' Nancy echoed, dumbfounded.

253

'Yes, of course. This is a hot country and Alec always said if anything happened to him there was to be no thought of shipping him home.'

'Not even to be with his wife?'

'Rosalind was cremated so it doesn't really arise. I'll be back before lunch when I've made all the necessary arrangements.'

She nodded helplessly. She made no effort to accompany him, largely because she didn't think he was in the mood for her company and she couldn't face another rebuff. She hadn't expected him to behave cheerfully – he had lost a dear friend as well as a colleague – but it was his remoteness which troubled her most; this was a side of him she didn't know.

Noel had left the hotel by the time the other two surfaced, and even Harry Colman seemed strangely silent with all his usual bumptiousness forgotten. Phil was the one most affected by Alec's death. They had been together in a great many troubled corners of the world, and with Clive returned to England and having little in common with Harry, he seemed to have retreated behind a wall of reserve. Nancy understood his feelings and sympathised with them.

He set off alone after breakfast to walk into the city and her eyes followed him sorrowfully until Harry said, 'He's taking it badly. I'd thought we were all alike – thick-skinned and accustomed to this sort of thing.'

'I can't think you're as thick-skinned as all that,' she said softly.

He grinned. 'I'm like Templeton. One develops a hide like a rhino, shockproof.'

'You think Noel's like that?'

'Well, he has to be, doesn't he? You've been well and truly ticked off. He couldn't have been any more forthright if it had been one of us, and you're still smarting from it.'

'I know. He's right, though – but for the intervention of those soldiers we could all have died.'

'How long have you been nuts about him?'

She jumped to her feet in sudden anger saying sharply, 'Why don't you mind your own business! I'm not nuts about him, I'm here to work.'

She did not miss the sardonic sparkle in his eyes nor the disbelieving expression on his face as she turned away. She saw Phil returning along the street carrying a sheaf of newspapers and she hurried to meet him followed by Harry's amused chuckle.

'I'm not interested in them,' Phil told her quietly. 'I just wanted some fresh air. I don't suppose Noel's back yet?'

Noel returned later in the morning to say the funeral would take place at the English cemetery in the late afternoon; standing with the three men in the church-yard overshadowed by giant cypresses it all seemed a far cry from the rain-drenched churchyard in Greymont with its weather-beaten square tower and dark ancient yews. Alec had been well respected and well liked by many, but looking round the groups standing at the graveside Nancy's eyes were inevitably drawn to Noel standing somehow aloof, his face pale, his expression sombre. She watched Phil surreptitiously wipe away a stray tear, but although her throat ached she couldn't cry.

Noel had saved her life by putting his own in acute danger; it could have been three funerals the crowd were watching instead of one. She recognized now that his rules for survival were not harsh, only necessary, and again she found herself asking what he would do with her. Any feelings he had ever had for her would count as nothing, she knew that, and she dreaded the evening before them when he was sure to make his thoughts known.

255

As they drove back through the city Harry said feelingly, 'You can't believe anything really happened, can you? Just look at the way everybody's going about their business as if all that mayhem yesterday happened somewhere else to other people.'

'It's always like this on the streets,' Noel answered. 'There'll be questions asked in high places you can be sure, but for the people themselves it's business as usual – until the next time.'

'There'll be a next time, of course,' Harry said bitterly.

'You can depend on it,' Noel replied. 'It's there bubbling under the surface just waiting to erupt. That reminds me, Nancy, we're invited to dine with Abraham and Leah tomorrow evening.'

'Did they have much trouble in their neck of the woods?' Phil asked.

'No, it was quiet, but of course they heard the commotion from the city. The unrest could flare up again anywhere. Nowhere is safe.'

Nancy wished he would talk to her about Alec's death but he did not mention it. Instead, their life picked up its familiar pattern but she no longer felt safe. Death seemed close – and they were all vulnerable.

They drove out to Abraham's house in the late afternoon when it was cool, through a world of orange and olive groves, where giant date palms reared their graceful heads and the jingle of goat bells filled the air.

The restraint was with them still. Gone it seemed was their old camaraderie and rather than rack her brains for something to talk about she decided to remain silent. Noel too felt no need for conversation, but when his friends came out into their garden to greet them, he showed a sudden affability.

Nancy was glad of the normality, of Leah's involvement with their evening meal and the new dress she was wearing, while Abraham and Noel sauntered towards the perimeter of the garden and stood gazing out across the orange groves where men and women were working.

'How normal everything seems,' Nancy said softly.

'Yes. They will soon finish for the day – they go to their homes at sundown.'

'Have you ever lived in the city?'

'Abraham lived there when his first wife was alive, but when we married he bought this house and we came out here to live. We seldom visit the city now.'

'How can people do this to each other! I met Noel's Arab friends and they were good kind people, too; it's hard to think that those same people are doing these terrible things.'

'They are like Abraham and me, caught up in all the wrongs that are happening in this land. The innocent suffer as well as the people who have created those wrongs.'

'I have so much to learn. Sometimes I feel so ignorant about what is going on here and yet I am expected to write about it intelligently for those at home. How can we ever make them understand?'

'You can only write about what you see and what you believe to be true. How can you be expected to understand all the complexities when we who live here refuse to understand?'

Leah was smiling at her gently, recognizing the puzzlement in her face, then with a gesture of appeal she said, 'Abraham and I would very much like you to stay with us for a while. These last few days have been terrible for you. We knew Alec and liked him. His death was a great shock to us, and we feel you need time to come to terms with it.'

'But I have work to do, it wouldn't be possible for me to stay here!'

'Abraham has already suggested it to Noel, who seems to think it is an excellent idea.'

Nancy was quite sure at that moment that it had been Noel who had sugested it to Abraham. Noel didn't want her as part of his team any more: this was his subtle way of getting rid of her. As if sensing her disquiet Leah said gently, 'It will only be for a very short while, Nancy, just to give you some time. It would please us very much.'

'I shall need to speak to Noel.'

'But of course. I think you will find him in favour of it.'

They spoke of it over dinner that evening and immediately Noel said, 'I would like you to stay here for a day or two, Nancy. The city is quiet now and it will give you an opportunity to see the beauty of the countryside instead of the busy city streets.'

'If you think it's a good idea, Noel, then of course I would like to stay. When will you expect me to return?' she answered him curtly.

'I will come for you when I consider your holiday should end,' he replied, with a smile.

How impotent he made her feel, and yet there was logic in his argument. She did need to relax, for ever since Alec's death she'd felt like a trapped animal, tense and desperate. Now they were offering a few days of peace in this beautiful place, and whatever Noel's motives she had no reason to disagree with them.

Later that evening he drove off alone to the city after a brief handshake and a cool smile, and that night she cried herself to sleep.

CHAPTER 26

In the days that followed, Nancy rediscovered the Holy Land of her childhood dreams, the land of vineyards and rolling fertile hills. Her new friends were anxious to show her all that was good and beautiful in Israel while they studiously avoided the fences and concentration camp images.

The fences had been erected by the Israeli authorities to prevent Palestinian protesters from throwing stones at Israeli vehicles and troops, but Nancy was well aware of the refugee camps on the outskirts of Bethlehem and Hebron, and she was also aware of the underpaid Arab labour in Israeli factories.

She learned nothing of this from Abraham or Leah; she knew of it from Noel and she was very careful not to speak of such matters to her hosts.

With Leah she spent long hours in the gardens. While the other woman read to Benjamin, Nancy wrote her column for the paper. For the first time in months she also felt able to write home, long letters that would please Aunt Susan since they gave no hint of unrest and spoke only of pleasant things.

She had hoped that Noel might drive out one evening to eat dinner with them, but Abraham informed her that he was visiting the Gaza Strip in a time of relative serenity because normally the area was virtually sealed off to the outside world owing to internal strikes and perpetual unrest. This short spell of tranquillity was something Noel felt he had to utilise.

I ought to be with him, Nancy thought angrily. I'm an apology for a war correspondent if I can't be trusted to meet danger!

259

Abraham smiled gently at her frown, knowing quite well what had put it there. 'You would prefer to be visiting Gaza instead of spending the time with us?' he asked softly.

'Oh, please don't think that, Abraham! I've loved it here, I'm seeing a land I believed in, not that other Israel that is so terrible, but I'm not doing my job, and I'm desperately afraid Noel doesn't think I'm up to it.'

'Have you not thought that there might be another reason why he doesn't take you to Gaza?'

'No. What could there be?'

'Mightn't he wish to protect you?'

'If he wished to protect me, why did he ever want me to be part of his team? No, I can't think it's that, Abraham.'

'You don't think he is very fond of you?'

'He might wish to protect me if he loved me, but men like Noel Templeton don't fall in love. He's always made that very plain right from our first meeting.'

'You think it is easy to be so sure?'

'I think it is easy for Noel.'

'Perhaps you are right – if you know him as you say you do.'

She moved away from Abraham along the garden path and he stared after her. If she'd troubled to look back she would have seen the sudden compassion in his eyes. The British were a strange people. He had known and liked Noel Templeton for a great many years and yet he was quite unable to penetrate the man's reserve on anything other than his job. Noel could talk for hours on that subject, but on his feelings for this girl the shutters would come down and Abraham knew he would learn nothing.

Now Nancy went to sit on the terrace and look out to where the sun was setting like a great red globe in the western sky, turning the white city into a conglomeration of glowing pink and rose, hiding its heartbreak behind a screen of enchantment.

She seldom thought about the past; she had conditioned herself like Scarlett O'Hara into consigning it to another day, but there were times when she dreamed about it, so that the day which followed found her strangely vulnerable and sad. Now on this evening filled with the glory of the setting sun she was remembering Lois Brampton and that terrible night when she ended her life. Vividly the scene came back to her, the lights streaming out into the darkness from the open door of that old house in Hammersmith surrounded by rain-darkened streets. She could hear the sirens of the police cars and see Lois' white-shrouded body carried out to the waiting ambulance.

Lois, who had been part of her days at Lorivals with her laughing eyes and sharp whimsical humour. Nancy had never known until it was too late that Lois had been in love with Desmond Atherton, obsessed by him to the point of insanity, and Lois had died in the knowledge that Desmond had been in love with Nancy.

She had blamed herself for Lois' suicide and it was that, as well as Desmond's marriage, that had sent her to the other side of the world in an effort to forget. Then she had told herself that there would be no more loving, but she had met Noel and it had all begun again, the ecstasy, the heart-searching – and the despair . . .

How different they had been, those five girls who had shared that dormitory overlooking the gardens at Lorivals. Maisie and Barbara had been her first friends but they too were very different in temperament. Dear honest predictable Maisie, who had loved only Tom and found happiness with him in that farm way up on the fell, and Barbara, who had seen her future with Martin, secure in his ambition and the good life that would follow.

Then there was Amelia. She had adored Amelia with her remote patrician beauty but after that first reunion at Garveston Hall, held ten years after they had left school, in spite of Amelia's pride in her home and her children, Nancy had seen the flaws in her old friend's lifestyle. Mark was a fickle, resentful husband and there were undercurrents of hostility behind the serenity. Nancy had come away full of doubts about Amelia's happiness.

She turned away reluctantly to go back to the house. There would be talk over the dining table about tomorrow's festivities, for it was Benjamin's fifth birthday and a big party was planned. Occasionally Abraham's eyes would meet hers and she read in them a strange puzzlement.

He is wondering, like I am, why Noel doesn't come for me, she thought miserably.

There was great activity in the house from an early hour and Nancy watched the erection of a massive marquee in the centre of one of the lawns. A great many guests had been invited with their children, and the men sang as they worked, some Hebrew chant as old as time. Her eyes swept across the beautiful gardens towards the tall wrought-iron gates and then for the first time a certain disquiet entered her heart. Three boys stood looking through the bars, watching in silence, but she could guess the angry thoughts they shared. They were Arab boys from poor homes, urchins who had probably never celebrated a birthday, let alone one such as this in surroundings as perfect as the celestial homes they visualised from the pages of the Koran.

Minutes later Leah emerged from the house to inspect the progress of the marquee and to order her servants about their business. On seeing the youths at the gate, however, she returned to the house and menservants came out to shoo the boys away. They went grudgingly, belligerently, while Leah stared after them pensively from the steps.

Thoughtfully Nancy went down to breakfast and meeting Leah crossing the hall she said, 'Will you let me help, Leah?'

'There is no need, Nancy. The servants will do everything, but I would like you to come into the city with me. I promised Benjamin we would go to choose his present, he is so looking forward to it.'

'You think it is safe to go there?'

'Oh, but yes. Those boys out there are little more than children, they will give us no trouble. We will go this morning before it gets too hot. I have told Abraham we will get back very quickly.'

She hurried off in full enjoyment of her tasks in the garden while Nancy went into the breakfast room and helped herself to coffee. Noel had an instinct about trouble, he sensed it just as she was sensing it now. She had learned to share his intuition, mistrusting those moments when he had said it was all too quiet, like this morning that was too perfect; she had learned to beware of perfection – it was an illusion and too quickly gone.

Benjamin was excited at his promised trip into the city but she could tell that his father didn't share his enthusiasm.

'Why does he have to go today? Isn't the party excitement enough for one day?' he argued.

'I promised, Abraham, and today is his birthday,' Leah prevaricated.

She hurried away to prepare the boy for his trip into town and meeting Nancy's eyes Abraham said, 'I saw those boys standing at the gate. Today of all days we should be content to stay in our home. Sometimes we push our luck, and it is unwise.'

'We won't linger in the city, Abraham. I promise to hurry them back.'

263

'That will please me, my dear. Many times I tell Leah this is not America, she is not free to live her life as she once did and in spite of our troubles she tells me I fuss too much.'

Nancy quickly discovered that Leah was disposed to dawdle in the shops and when Nancy remonstrated with her she said, 'Oh, there's still heaps of time, Nancy. Why don't we have coffee somewhere? It's so long since I looked at the shops and had coffee in a civilised hotel.'

'I promised Abraham I'd encourage you to get back quickly.'

'Abraham fusses too much, and you've developed Noel's thirst for danger where none exists,' she replied sharply.

Leah had her way. They went for coffee at the King David Hotel and Benjamin sat with a large ice-cream sundae. It seemed to Nancy that Leah discovered that every woman enjoying her coffee in the lounge was her dearest friend. By the time they finally reached the street to pick up their car the sun shone high in the heavens and the heat had turned the city streets into a veritable furnace.

Benjamin's presents were piled into the back and he sat between them playing with a mechanical car. Leah was in a high good humour, and seeing Nancy's anxiety she leaned over and gently patted her hand.

'Don't worry, Nancy. I've enjoyed myself so much and look how quiet the streets are. Besides, it's siesta time and if there's going to be trouble anywhere it will be when the day has cooled.'

'Trouble doesn't wait for the sun to go down. If I've learned nothing else I've discovered that,' Nancy replied.

'I bought you a lovely present, but I won't give it to you if you persist in spoiling my day,' Leah said coyly.

'You shouldn't buy me presents. Spending this holiday with you has been a wonderful present in itself.'

'I felt like buying you something. I'm so very happy today. I do hope the servants have done everything I asked them to do. This is going to be the best birthday ever, darling,' she said gaily, hugging the child sitting next to her.

They were out of the city by this time and climbing the hill towards Abraham's house in the distance. Then suddenly they came from nowhere – groups of men and boys – shouting abuse, brandishing sticks, moving in towards the car, barring their way. In no time they had the doors opened and their driver was pulled out into the road while a man clambered into the driving seat and pulled on the hand-brake.

The other doors were wrenched open and brown hands were reaching in for them, clawing at their clothes. Benjamin was screaming in fear. It soon became evident to Nancy that Leah was the one they were interested in as they pushed and pulled her out on to the road, and in that moment Nancy leapt into the front seat. Everything Noel had ever told her came back to her: don't look back, never go back, go on as though your life depended on it, and the logic was there staring her in the face. If she'd stayed to help Leah it would have done no good. There were too many of them – they would have overpowered both of them and taken the child.

She drove like a mad thing towards Abraham's house while Benjamin's hysterical cries rang in her ears. In the distance she could hear Leah's screams and the demented shouts of the men, the thud of flying stones against the car, and then a group of men headed by Abraham were running down the hill towards her and she put her foot down hard on the accelerator. As soon as she reached them she leapt from the car dragging the boy after her, then six of them took possession of it and headed back down the hill. They were all armed with guns or revolvers and for a few moments she stood on the road where they had left her, then with her arm around the boy's shoulder she drew him towards the house.

Terrified servants stood weeping in the gardens, and she could see that a few of the guests had already arrived, dressed in their finery, still holding the gifts they had brought for Benjamin. They fussed round the tearful child, plying him with their presents, but his thoughts were all for Leah. From the distance they heard the sound of shots as the Arabs were driven backward, then a man standing at the gate reported that the car was being brought back to the house and the Arabs were scattering in all directions.

The rest of the afternoon and evening passed like a lantern show in Nancy's mind. They carried Leah into the house. Her body was battered and broken by the stones, her beautiful face bruised and swollen, and Abraham followed stern and silent while the visitors fell back so that the solemn party could walk between them.

There was no party on that soft tropical night filled with the scent of jasmine and orange blossom. One by one and sadly the visitors left for their homes and Nancy waited beside Benjamin's bed until he went to sleep, helped by the sedative prescribed by the local physician. Leah was still unconscious, moaning painfully in her stupor, and when Nancy at last joined Abraham in the garden he said gently, 'She sleeps at last, the house is quiet.'

Nancy didn't speak, and after a few moments he went on, 'I felt it this morning, the danger, the resentment, but I did not want to alarm anyone on this day of all days. Why were you so long?'

'Time went so quickly – it always does when women are enjoying themselves in the shops. Leah is going to be all right, isn't she, Abraham?'

266

He shrugged his shoulders in what appeared to be an entirely Eastern fashion, a strangely fatalistic shrug as if he had already consigned his wife to the workings of fate.

'You were brave today, Nancy,' he said. 'You saved my son's life.'

'For the first time I understood what Noel has been trying to teach me ever since I came here. He trained me to follow these rules: don't look back, don't wait, go on.'

'If you had stayed they would only have killed my son and you would not have been able to help Leah. They could have killed you, also.'

'I didn't feel very brave, Abraham.'

'No, I can understand that. I would like to send Benjamin away where he will be safe. We killed many of those young men today, unfortunately. They will seek their revenge and my son is a likely target.'

'But where would you send him? Surely not away from Israel – he would miss you so terribly.'

'Better to miss us than be murdered. I have a brother in Cairo who would be glad to have him. His children are grown up and living their own lives.'

'Would Benjamin be safe in Egypt? It is an Arab country.'

'Not entirely. It is true the Arabs have been in Egypt seven hundred years but not all Egyptians are Arabs. You are English – if Germany had won the last war would you in seven hundred years be happy to call yourself German?'

'I hadn't thought about it like that.'

'The Egyptians and the Arabs have largely integrated in that time, and it is a civilised country. I believe my son would be safe there.'

'It is strange that your brother has settled in Egypt. Why doesn't he want to live here in Israel?'

'He has a good business over there. He has never shown any desire to live here although he has visited us many times.'

'I wish Noel would come back. I feel I'm living in limbo, not knowing what is to become of me.'

'You are welcome to stay here as long as you like.'

'Thank you, Abraham, but that is not why I am here. I feel like a parcel Noel has left in the lost property office, something he can forget about indefinitely.'

He shook his head gently. 'You are pessimistic about your future, Nancy, and I think perhaps you are failing to understand the character of the man with whom you are in love.'

She stared at him sharply and he met her gaze with bland calm. 'I have known you were in love with him since the first day he brought you here.'

'Then you will know how hopeless everything is.'

'Perhaps not.'

'Oh yes, Abraham. Noel has never filled my foolish heart with false hope. I just wish he would come back to Jerusalem and that I had work to do.'

CHAPTER 27

Rarely had Amelia seen her mother so out of countenance. There was a half-smile on her sister Celia's face as she met her eyes across the table at the Dower House of Drummond, while Lady Urquart sat at the head of the table with a frown of annoyance on her face.

For the first time one of her labradors had been beaten at the local dog show and she was unused to such a result. Amelia was quick to sympathize.

'Honestly, Mummy, you mustn't mind so much,' she said gently. 'Honey's very young – next year she'll do better.'

'I've entered dogs as young as Honey before. I think the judges had a grudge – they probably resent me having won so many times over the years!'

'Maybe it's time you let somebody else have a chance,' Celia said calmly. 'You can't grumble, you've had a good run for your money.'

'I've always won fairly because I had the best dog,' her mother retorted. 'Of course, men just can't stand to be behind a woman in anything. That dog of Joe Pearson's had nothing on Honey.'

Amelia gave Celia a warning glance but uncontrite her sister continued, 'Thank heavens I've never been into competitions with either dogs or horses. You win some and you lose some, that's what I think.'

'That must be the sort of reasoning you've applied to your husband, Celia, a belief that he's going to go on ad infinitum putting up with your absences. If a woman isn't the companion she's meant to be, most men soon find somebody else who is.'

'That's unfair, Mummy, you know how I was fixed.'

'Dorinda's been dead almost four years and where are you? Still in Cornwall in that big house all on your own with Desmond living in London, only seeing you on the rare occasions you're expected to attend a function together.'

'I love Cornwall, Mother, and Desmond can come whenever he has the time.'

'He doesn't have the time, and I can't think what you see in that house with the sea crashing on the rocks and the foghorn sounding day and night.'

'You know it isn't like that. We don't have storms all through the year. Desmond says he likes it down there, but if he does, why doesn't he come more often?'

'Perhaps there's a very good reason.'

'What do you mean?'

'Another woman perhaps.'

'I'd know immediately if there was someone – he wouldn't be able to hide it.'

'He could easily hide it from somebody he seldom sees.'

'Really, Mother, I find all this terribly unkind. You're annoyed because your dog lost at the show and you're taking it out on me. Don't you think I've had quite enough anguish in my life without your making it worse!'

'It has nothing whatsoever to do with my dog losing, I've been meaning to bring this up for a long time. It worried your father and it's worried me. I've never had any illusions about Mark – I expect he goes his own way regardless of whether Amelia's there or not – but Desmond deserves something better. He's always worked very hard for his country, he did his best with Dorinda and it seems to me he's derived very little in return.'

Amelia looked down at her plate, expressionless. Her mother didn't like Mark, and Mark had been delighted when she'd suggested spending a few days with her mother and sister. He'd waved her off with relief because she hadn't asked him to accompany her and she knew he'd enjoy every moment of her absence with his peculiar choice of friends.

At the moment Lady Urquart was concentrating on her elder daughter. 'I wish you'd see sense,' she said firmly. 'Of course it's very nice to have you here with me, but what was to stop you going to Desmond in London, or at least have him come up here for the weekend?'

'He happens to be in Paris, Mother.'

'And do you know with whom he is in Paris?'

'I know that he's with Teddy Rowlands, and I also know that they've gone on government business.'

'And we all know what Teddy Rowlands is like. Isn't he on his third wife – and God knows how many mistresses in between?'

'Teddy Rowlands is merely a colleague, not a personal friend. Desmond goes where the department sends him – he is seldom allowed to choose his companions.'

'I know it has nothing to do with me but I come from a generation of people who stayed together regardless of their differences. I can't come to terms with the way married couples are behaving these days.'

'Desmond and I have stayed together, Mother.'

'If spending nine months of the year apart is staying together then it's beyond me and as for you, Amelia, I know that you and Mark have separate interests but it's all a very long way from being the ideal situation.'

Amelia was not disposed to argue with her mother so the rest of the meal continued in silence. They drank their coffee in the drawing room and Celia leafed through a pile of *Field* magazines while Lady Urquart sat rigidly upright staring into the fire.

There had never been a time when Amelia had answered her mother back. She'd adored her father,

271

stood a little in awe of her brothers, and admired her worldly, sophisticated sister.

It was Celia who had poured scorn on the fact that she was being educated by a governess. She'd said it was archaic and it was time Amelia entered the twentieth century. Consequently Lorivals was selected and Amelia remembered vividly that September afternoon when she stood in the company of four other girls who would be her room-mates for the next eight years.

She could see it now, that little dormitory overlooking the playing-fields and the mist-shrouded fells. Five narrow beds covered by pretty floral bedspreads to match the curtains at the windows, five white wardrobes and five chairs which had been none too comfortable – nothing to encourage them from spending too much time up there. Four pairs of eyes had looked at her curiously before introductions were performed and Lois had apologised profusely for her luggage which littered the room. Amelia remembered that much-travelled luggage, expensive suitcases bearing labels of places she'd only dreamed about.

Barbara Smythe was pushy and precociously sophisticated. Amelia recognized many of her own feelings of inferiority and insecurity in Maisie Jayson's early struggles, but whereas Maisie let everybody know she was suffering, Amelia remained silent so that people believed she was haughty and stuck-up. If she spoke to people she was patronizing, if she didn't she was snobbish: either way she couldn't win.

As the months passed she discovered she had an affinity with Nancy Graham. Nancy made no immediate effort to cultivate her, accepting her as she accepted the others, being open and friendly but letting Amelia make the running, and Nancy was the friend she'd missed most when her schooldays were over.

Amelia had been the one to insist on a reunion in ten years' time, and she'd gone to a great deal of trouble to arrange it. Her motives had been dubious ones. She didn't really care whether she saw Barbara and Maisie again, but she'd wanted to see Nancy, if only to confront her with some degree of hostility about her affair with Desmond.

Strangely she'd never blamed Desmond. In some odd, elusive way she blamed Nancy for everything. She'd known Desmond was married, and married to Amelia's sister Celia, so how could she have done such a terrible thing? And yet when Amelia had accused Nancy openly on that Sunday morning at Garveston Hall, she'd wished she hadn't spoken.

There had been so much pain in Nancy's eyes. She hadn't been ashamed or contrite, she hadn't told Amelia it was none of her business – which she'd every right to do – she'd hidden instead behind a cloak of reserve that Amelia recognized. It was the same sort of reserve she'd sheltered behind herself when Phillip was killed.

'You're very quiet, Amelia.' Her mother's voice came sharply across the room and she looked up to find Lady Urquart staring at her curiously.

'I'm sorry, Mummy, I was thinking about someone I haven't seen for years.'

'What do you suppose Mark is doing while you're spending this time with me?' her mother asked pointedly.

'There's plenty to do at the Hall, he's kept pretty busy,' she answered loyally.

Her mother sniffed audibly. 'I thought he had an estate manager.'

'He does.'

'Then surely he does most of the work?'

'He consults Mark about everything, they work together.'

'You mean they work when Mark isn't otherwise occupied.'

'You should come to see us, Mummy. Everything at

Garveston is quite beautiful, the house and the grounds. It is lovely, isn't it, Celia?'

'Yes, it's heavenly.'

'It cost a great deal of money to bring about that transformation,' her mother went on relentlessly.

'It also takes quite a lot of work to keep it in that condition,' Amelia retorted.

Realizing that both her daughters were ranged against her on the issue of their married lives, Lady Urquart rose to her feet, stating she was going to her room where she had letters to write. She swept out without a further glance at either of them.

Celia smiled. 'It's that damned dog show,' she said casually. 'If Honey had won she'd have been in high good humour and we'd have heard nothing but how well she'd done against fierce competition.'

When Amelia remained silent Celia went on, 'She's got to you, hasn't she? Is it because of what she said about Mark?'

'Mark and I are happy enough. I always knew he didn't like the things I liked, but we're together when we need to be together and we shall stay together.'

'Like Desmond and me. Together yet not together.'

'No, Celia, not like you and Desmond at all. Can you honestly tell me how often in the space of a year you're really together?'

'If you mean do we ever make love the answer is no. Desmond hasn't made love to me for years and now I don't think I want him to. We respect each other, we're good friends. I respect him as a man and he likes me as a woman – does that answer your question?'

'Would you blame him if he found somebody else, like you blamed him about Nancy Graham?'

'I hated him about her, largely because Dorinda was still alive. There was I stuck with an invalid child in Cornwall while he was in London sleeping with that girl, and he was in love with her, that's what hurt most.

It would never be the same now. He might have a dozen women in his life but I know he's not in love with any of them. He's got Nancy out of his system and he's not unhappy with our arrangement. It's none of Mother's business.'

'Have you thought of inviting him here?'

'Not really. I might consider it. We're dining up at Drummond tomorrow evening. I suppose that means another tirade if Georgina was really serious about letting that interior decorator loose on the place.'

'Mummy always thought Drummond was perfect as it was, and we both know how much she hates change.'

'Well, I thought there was a very frigid atmosphere when we were up there. You never notice things like that, Amelia, which probably makes you a nicer person than me. This place could do with a bob or two spending on it, or hadn't you noticed that either?'

'For heaven's sake don't say anything to Mother about it.'

Celia grinned. 'It's little things like that, dear sister, that alleviate the boredom in the country.'

'What sort of thing alleviates the boredom in Corn-wall then?'

Celia threw back her head and laughed delightedly. 'I never thought my little sister devious enough to ask that sort of question!'

Amelia's brother Charles, the present Lord Urquart, was graciously exerting his not inconsiderable charm to put his guests at ease. They sat at the long polished table in the dining room at Drummond, the Urquart stately home. The table was decked out in old lace, priceless glass and silver while three massive candelabra equipped with tall candles shed their light across the bowl of deep red roses in the centre.

He had chosen his guests carefully. Canon Barlass was sitting next to his mother, the Dowager Lady

Urquart, and the two were happily discussing their respective gardens, and the current Member of Parliament was sitting next to Celia; he hoped the chap would keep his sister entertained. He'd been none too sure about that arrangement when earlier in the evening Celia had complained, 'I can't think why people always assume I'll have a lot in common with some man from government circles. It's always so nice to get away from people who talk like Desmond and think like Desmond.'

Then there was Amelia. He was deucedly fond of his little sister but she always gave the impression of being in a world of her own, aloof and not very approachable. He'd decided after a chat with his wife Georgina to place her next to Peter Charnley.

Peter was a charming fellow, well travelled, worldly and the youngest son of the Marquis of Clavering. He was also very good-looking – it would do Amelia good to compare him with that cad Mark Garveston. Another guest was General Sir Algernon Fforbes-Grey and his wife Elisa. Algy could be decidedly amusing if he chose to forget the army for one night; opposite them was another politician, Sir Donald Jarvis and his wife Morag, who was undoubtedly the biggest flirt north of London.

Georgina disliked the woman intensely but admitted that she could be guaranteed to liven up the proceedings if they appeared to be flagging. Sir Donald was usually interested in three things, his stomach, his whisky and politics – in that order – and his wife was already flashing her eyes at her next-door neighbour, author Damien Marriot. Lord Urquart smiled to himself.

Surely Georgina couldn't seriously be thinking of changing this beautiful room, Amelia thought. She remembered it at Christmas-time when logs burnt in the huge stone fireplace and a giant Christmas tree sparkled across one corner. Once or twice she'd seen her mother's eyes rove round the room and knew her thoughts must have matched her own.

She wondered how long her mother had owned the gown she was wearing. It was grey, adorned with dark wine-coloured bugle beads, and she had little doubt that it had been fashionable and expensive when first purchased, but now it appeared old-fashioned, although she had to admit her mother commanded attention whatever she wore.

The two politicians were talking shop, Celia was chatting to Sir Algernon and his wife Elisa was eyeing young Lady Jarvis with a certain amount of alarm.

Her brother smiled encouragingly at Amelia from his seat at the top of the table, and then she became aware that her neighbour was addressing her.

'You probably don't remember me, Amelia,' he said with an engaging smile. 'I came to Drummond for a few weeks' holiday when you were only a little girl. I was at school with your youngest brother – he invited me to stay because my family lived in India.'

She gave him her full attention, and in doing so remembered the two boys racing their horses across the parkland while she watched wistfully from the seat in the nursery window. She smiled, and his heart gave a sudden lurch while he wondered if she had any idea how that sudden swift smile could illuminate the classic perfection of her face.

'I do remember you! I used to wish I could ride in the park with you.'

'Why didn't you?'

'I had a governess who was afraid to let me out of her sight. She was Austrian, and I was terribly afraid of disobeying her.'

He was remembering that pretty shy little girl, peering through the banister rails from the realms above, or sitting with her governess in the rose garden poring over some book or other yet watching her brother and his friend longingly whenever she thought her teacher wasn't looking.

'The last time I was a guest here you were at boarding school,' he said, hoping that he might learn a little about her since those early days. 'Were you happy there?'

'Oh yes, very happy.'

He felt bemused by her. The gentle timbre of her voice fascinated him, as did her cool smile. Peter Charnley was an archaeologist and most of his life had been spent in remote parts of the world investigating ancient civilizations. The one woman he had loved had married his best friend, largely because she couldn't face the sort of life he expected her to live. Marion had been amusing and beautiful. She had loved life, while so much of his career was concerned with death. She loved the shops and the cocktail bars of London, the theatres and long weekends in country houses, in fact most of the things he could easily live without. He had watched her pass out of his life with regret and because it had all been so long ago he had almost forgotten the urgent pangs of desire – until this moment.

He found himself wanting to know more about Amelia. He noticed the wedding ring and diamond engagement ring on her third finger, but who had this gentle desirable woman married? He longed to question her but wasn't quite sure how to do so without stirring the reserve he sensed in her. Miserably he racked his brains for the right approach.

She was speaking to Sir Donald Jarvis who was sitting next to her, but Peter imagined that conversation would be brief.

Amelia's mother addressed him graciously from the top of the table. 'And where are you now, Peter? Some remote part of our planet, I feel sure.'

'I'm returning to Central Asia, Lady Urquart, when I leave England again and like you say, it is very remote. I have to get accustomed to civilization and I'm not finding it very easy.'

'So this is just a brief holiday,' she said.

'A month, and already I've used up half of it.'

'I always thought you would join the navy, like my brother,' Amelia said.

'I'm afraid not. I'm more interested in the past than the present, or the future I'm afraid.'

'But you're enjoying your leave?'

'Oh yes, I like meeting up with old friends. Are you living near Drummond, Amelia?'

'No. My home is in north Lancashire.'

'With your husband and family?'

'Yes. I have twin girls, both at my old school which is quite near to where we live.'

'And your husband?'

'I married Sir Mark Garveston. We live at Garveston Hall.'

Suddenly he remembered the pictures of the plane crash that had killed Phillip Garveston in a newspaper he'd received weeks after the event. Seeing the puzzlement in his eyes Amelia said gently, 'I was engaged to Mark's brother but he was killed in a plane crash. A while later I married Mark.'

'I see. He isn't here with you?'

'No.'

She offered no explanation for Mark's absence and Charnley realized that he would learn nothing more of her marriage from Amelia. The talk around the table was the usual chitchat in country houses – of horses and dogs, gardens and hunting. He had little to contribute so he sat back to listen.

The ladies disappeared after dinner leaving the men with their port and brandy and Morag Jarvis said quickly, 'I believe you're having Drummond done up, Georgina. I'd like the name of your interior decorator, as we need to do something about our place.'

Georgina's mother-in-law frowned ominously. 'Modern décor is quite out of place in a house as old as this one,' she said firmly.

'Oh, I do agree,' murmured Lady Fforbes-Grey. 'I've always loved this house – nothing should be done to it.'

'With all its faded charm,' Celia put in maliciously.

'It's never really felt like my house,' Georgina said plaintively. 'You made a great many changes to Garveston Hall, Amelia, so you must understand how I feel about Drummond.'

'Changes to Garveston were necessary,' Lady Urquart said sharply. 'The house was in danger of disintegration until we stepped in to rescue it. Nobody can ever say that about Drummond.'

'The house is lovely and it will continue to be lovely,' Georgina said firmly. 'When you see it after the transformation I'm sure you'll agree.'

'What do you bet against the sparks flying before the end of the evening?' Celia muttered to Amelia as they entered the drawing room. 'Our dear sister-in-law has made up her mind and nothing is going to change it. Besides, mother was never houseproud. As long as the stables and kennels were comfortable, it didn't matter about the house.'

Amelia went to sit on the window seat so that she could gaze out across the parkland. Nostalgia filled her soul. She could see her father in his battered old trilby and carpet slippers walking across the grass followed by old Bolger his faithful bull terrier, see too the horses in the far paddock and the chestnut trees weighted down with blossom in the spring. How she had loved it, the calm meandering river and the ruined castle standing high on the windswept hill. She could remember her mother with her shapeless felt hat pulled down over her hair, her faded tweed skirt and stout mud-caked brogues hurrying across the grass waving her latest First Prize certificate joyfully in her hands, and then herself, waiting wistfully at the edge of the drive for Celia to arrive with her husband and two children.

Her face was sad as she remembered Dorinda sitting in an ungainly huddle in her invalid chair, her eyes empty, her mouth loose, a travesty of the beautiful child she'd been only a few months before.

Life could be so cruel. Why did everything have to change, why did people have to change? If time and people remained constant then surely the world would be a better place to live in. Her reverie was interrupted when Peter Charnley sat down on the window seat beside her.

'I was watching you from across the room, Amelia,' he said gently. 'Your thoughts were many miles away.'

She smiled. 'I was thinking about my childhood here and all the things that have happened to us. I was remembering Daddy – when I come here I can't believe that he's dead.'

'You were very fond of your father?'

'Oh yes. He used to look at me as though he couldn't really believe in me. I was his baby when the others were almost grown up.'

'What do you find to do up there in north Lancashire?'

'I'm a JP, I sit on several committees and of course I have a large house to run. Admittedly I have a great deal of help and very good and loyal servants, but I keep myself occupied.'

'And your husband, what does he do?'

'He hunts and has interests in racing stables. Cars and horses are his life. He also has the estate to run.'

'Are you turning out with the hunt tomorrow?'

'No, I dislike hunting. I shall probably watch them start out then I intend to walk as far as the castle. It's years since I was up there.'

'Would you mind if I came along?'

'You're not hunting?'

'No. If you'd rather walk alone please say so.'

'I'd like to have your company, Peter. I simply thought everybody else would be hunting.'

'We'll meet at breakfast, then. I've promised to make up a bridge four this evening.'

She watched him walk across the room, a tall slim man, his dark hair peppered with grey. Distinguished, Amelia thought, but she also thought he was a man surrounded by a singular loneliness.

CHAPTER 28

Amelia stood in the stableyard watching her mother mount her horse and thinking that in spite of her seventy-three years she looked quite splendid in her black hunting habit, with its distinctive white stock at her throat. She rode side-saddle, disdaining the modern fashion as being masculine and undignified.

Her sister strolled across the yard slim and elegant in her jodhpurs, her dark hair tied in a knot under her riding hat. Amelia thought how young she looked; it was almost as if the tragedy of Dorinda had caused hardly a ripple in her life, yet she knew that was untrue.

'You should be riding,' Celia said. 'What are you going to do with yourself?'

'I'm going to walk up to the castle.'

'Alone?'

'No, Peter Charnley is coming with me.'

'He's getting to be quite a buddy of yours, Amelia.' When Amelia didn't speak she went on, 'He was very friendly with Marion Hay years ago. I knew her well, we were at school together. He proposed to her, but she said she couldn't live in a tent in some godforsaken place for most of her married life watching Peter dig for buried treasure or old bones.'

'What did she do then?'

'She married a friend of his, politician, God help her.'

'She couldn't have cared enough for him.'

'Obviously not, but he must have got the message since he's never asked anybody else to marry him.'

'I think Mother's waiting for you, Celia.'

'Wouldn't you just think she'd join the twentieth

century and ride like everybody else does? Nobody rides side-saddle these days.'

'People respect her for being the way she is,' Amelia objected. 'Mummy's an institution – the people around here expect her to stay the same.'

'Peter Charnley's hardly likely to be bowled over by that ancient trenchcoat and your headscarf, my dear. Why didn't you set your stall out?'

Amelia merely smiled. She was used to her sister's innuendoes and Celia turned away, muttering, 'Here's your Peter now, Amelia, so make the most of him.'

She favoured Peter with a friendly smile before joining her mother and Amelia and Peter stood watching the riders walking their mounts across the grass towards the gates.

The hunt was meeting at the Old Boar's Head in the village. Peter indicated that they would drive there and leave his car at the inn before walking up to the castle.

There was the usual air of excitement, the gaggle of animated children, pink-coated men and more soberly attired women, while the hounds gathered round the huntsman, their tongues lolling, emitting high-pitched yelps in their anxiety to be off. Crowds of people had turned out to watch the spectacle and as usual there was a group of protesters howling their defiance and objections.

Peter smiled down at her. 'I notice most of them are wearing leather jackets, which indicates something,' he said calmly.

'People protest about everything these days. I wonder how many of them keep poultry that have been savaged by foxes?'

'Do you want to stay and listen to all this racket, or would you rather walk up to where we can watch them from the hillside?'

'I'd prefer to walk, Peter.'

The path was steep leading up to the castle and gave little scope for conversation. From halfway up the hill they looked down on the gathering outside the inn, and then after a while Peter said, 'It looks as though they're ready to move out.'

Led by the huntsman surrounded by his hounds, the procession of men, women and children moved off along the lane, then they were racing across the fields with the baying of the hounds echoing on the breeze that blew Amelia's headscarf skittishly across the grass. Peter retrieved it from where it clung to a cluster of rocks, and after handing it back to her she slotted it around her neck with a rueful smile.

The old medieval castle had been an enchanted place to her as a child. She had peopled it with fairytale princesses and knights in armour, hobgoblins and old women sitting over their spinning wheels. Today she saw it as it was – just an old ruin – and yet there was still a charm about its thick stout walls commanding breathtaking views of the countryside.

Peter was reluctant to intrude upon her reverie, content to delight in her tranquil beauty while he sat on a low stone wall watching her poking and prying into old and hidden corners of the ruin. When at last she joined him she said, 'Whenever I came up here as a child I was afraid to look in those doorways, but today you were here with me and I discovered a new courage.'

'What did you expect to find?'

'All sorts of terrible things when I was a child. Today, nothing at all.'

'But you're wondering what sort of people lived here, what sort of a life they had?'

'They were always people of my imagination – I expect reality was very different. You're an archaeologist – do you never find yourself mingling fact with fantasy?'

'Sometimes, and then there I am digging for fact and finding it equally absorbing.'

285

Amelia had never felt comfortable with men, largely because she'd been a solitary child thrust into a world given over exclusively to women. Cushioned by her reserve she'd always believed she had little to contribute in a man's world, but now here was this man drawing her out, listening to her views and respecting them.

When Mark talked it was always about cars and horses. A car to Amelia was a vehicle that got her from one place to the next, while horses were creatures she loved, to pet and to ride, not creatures to be pitted in speed and strength against others, for prize money.

For the first time in her life a man sat beside her listening to her words as if they meant something. Phillip had listened to her because her ideas were all for Garveston, Mark hardly ever listened to her, but here was Peter Charnley with his serious expression, his dark eyes filled with admiration and under his regard she came suddenly alive and warm.

People around Garveston admired her, for she was the lady of the manor and the old feudal system was very much alive in an environment where for centuries the great country house had towered over homely cottages and country pursuits. Amelia was accustomed to that sort of admiration even when she recognized its hollowness. A figurehead wasn't really a creature of flesh and blood at all. She'd gone about her life doing the correct thing automatically; now in the short space of an afternoon the old values were receding and the reserve she'd sheltered behind for most of her life was crumbling in the light of this man's desire.

In the glow of the setting sun they walked down the hillside later hand in hand, her brown hair blowing in the wind, her face rosy with a glow that came from inside and was not entirely a result of the wind that whistled through the cracks in the ancient stone walls. They walked in silence; it seemed that there was nothing else to say that hadn't already been said.

The inn yard was quiet by the time they reached the car, and he opened the passenger door so that she could enter. Amelia sat back in her seat suddenly bemused. It was almost over, this strange afternoon when she had dared to be herself, when she had shown to a man who was almost a stranger that shy imaginative woman who had cared too much for convention, even when it meant forgetting that she was a vibrant beautiful woman desperately in need of passionate love.

He took her hand as soon as he'd stopped the car outside the Dower House and she made no effort to draw away.

'Amelia,' he said gently. 'I have to see you again, there's so little time.'

'I know.'

'Why didn't we meet years ago?'

'We did.'

'Not like that, when you were a child and I was a bumptious schoolboy, I mean when you were ready for love and marriage. Where were you when I told myself I'd never fall in love again?'

She didn't answer and after a few moments he said, 'I'm in love with you, Amelia, and I can't believe it's happened. Last night when I saw you entering the room with your mother and sister it was like looking at the other half of me. I'm so useless with words and there's so much I want to say.'

'It's better left unsaid, Peter. I am married with two children whom I love very much. I couldn't do anything to hurt them.'

'I notice you don't say hurt my husband.'

'Husbands get over it, children seldom do.'

For a long moment he remained silent staring across the park, so thoughtful and sad she longed to put her arms round him and hold him close, but the moment was shattered by Celia's voice calling to them from the path, 'Hello, you two! Did you enjoy your walk?'

With a tremendous effort he turned away while Amelia let herself out of his car. She was glad that Celia seemed content to chatter on although it seemed to Amelia that the atmosphere was so charged with emotion even her sister must have been aware of it.

'How I need a bath,' Celia said lightly. 'The trouble with a long dry spell is the dust it creates. I'm going to make a luscious gin and tonic – do you care to join us, Peter?'

'No thank you, Celia, I'd better get back. Enjoy your ride?'

'Oh, it was all right. I never hunt in Cornwall, so I can't think why I decided to ride today. To please Mother, I expect.'

'Is Mummy home?' Amelia asked.

'She came on ahead. I was chatting to the Howells – they want us to drive over this evening, Amelia. I told them we'd nothing else on.'

'How about Mother?'

'She's going up to Drummond to play bridge. I suppose you'll be there, Peter?'

He smiled, then bidding them goodbye he drove off towards Drummond. Amelia followed her sister into the house with the sound of the car diminishing in the distance. She felt a strange and unreasonable anger that Celia had come along at that moment when it seemed her entire life was about to change. Now the moment had gone and she would never know how it would have resolved itself. She felt that she too had suddenly lost somebody she had known forever, a hope of joy irretrievably gone.

Celia was busy at the wine cabinet making herself the promised drink, enquiring whether Amelia would like one.

'I think I'd prefer sherry,' Amelia said.

'So you enjoyed your afternoon with Peter Charnley. He's rather nice, isn't he? What did you talk about?'

'A great many things. The interesting places he's seen, history, archaeology.'

'How terribly boring. Didn't he tell you something about himself, why he's never married?'

'No.'

'Wasn't he the least bit interested in your marriage?'

'He was interested in my life. I'm sure he didn't find it half as interesting as his own.'

'Marion Hay told me he was more interested in his job than her, a little bit like Desmond.'

'I don't think I will go over to the Howells' if you don't mind, Celia. I have a slight headache and I feel like a night in front of the fire. I really don't know them very well. You don't mind, do you?'

'Well no. You please yourself, of course. Mother's been on to me again about telephoning Desmond, she wants him to come up for the weekend.'

'I thought he was in Paris.'

'He'll be back. I really don't want her to start interfering in our lives. Desmond will simply withdraw into his shell and I'll bear the brunt of it. If I invite him she'll probably ask you to invite Mark.'

'I doubt it. My mother and Mark rarely exchange a polite word.'

'She's expecting us to stay on for a while.'

'Has she said so?'

'It's an impression I've formed. She's forever going on about things we can do together.'

'Then I'm going to have to make an excuse. I have commitments at home.'

'What sort of commitments?'

'The sort Mummy has here.'

Celia shrugged her shoulders. 'Oh well, I'm going upstairs to take a bath and get some of the dust out of my hair and skin. You'll be in the house on your own, as Mother's given the girls the night off to attend some hop in the village hall. What will you do?'

'Curl up with a book, probably go to bed early.'

Several hours later Amelia was enjoying the solitude. The house was so quiet. A single lamp vied with the leaping firelight and she sat curled up in a deep armchair gazing into the flames. Her mother's Burmese cat purred on the hearthrug and outside in the park she could hear the wind sighing plaintively through the branches of the beech leaves . . .

The shrill ringing of the telephone startled her and as she went to answer it she hoped fervently that it wasn't Mark or Desmond. It was Peter, his voice uncertain yet strangely urgent.

'I know you're alone down there, Amelia. Your mother's here playing bridge and your sister's out. I heard Lady Urquart telling them you'd decided not to go tonight. Look – I have to see you. Please don't say no.'

'Peter, I'm not sure. What good would it do?'

'Amelia, please! I have to talk to you, try to understand.'

'I understand only too well, Peter.'

'I'll be there in ten minutes. I *have* to see you.'

She should have been firmer, have feigned a headache, anything that would have kept him at arm's length, but she knew that in all honesty she wanted to see him as much as he wanted to see her.

There was danger in this meeting, danger to her heart and her ordered, peaceful world. Smug in the narrow environment of Garveston she was not cut out to find love outside her safe unemotional marriage. She had been quick to castigate Nancy over her involvement with Desmond, now it seemed as if her entire world was crumbling in the desire she felt for Peter Charnley.

She was white-faced and trembling when she met him at the door and immediately he took her in his arms and held her against him. She made no effort to draw away, instead she clung to him desperately, the

290

reserve that had sheltered her from every hurtful human emotion, cushioned her against death and every betrayal of her childhood dreams, suddenly forgotten.

This was not the Amelia who strolled serenely through life but a strange violent Amelia, demanding and primitive, her passion the culmination of all that the old Amelia had tried to hide.

They made love on the rug in front of the fire, deep sensual love that left them both drained, and after it was over the tears came, desperate torturing tears at the enormity of what she had done while Peter held her close, comforting her and whispering endearments against her hair that lay damp against her face.

At last when she was calm he whispered, 'Come away with me, my love. I have two more weeks before I need to go back, can't we spend them together?'

She didn't answer and he went on, his voice urgent, his whole being begging her to agree until suddenly they heard the sound of a car outside the window and jumping to her feet Amelia ran out of the room.

Gathering his scattered wits, by the time Lady Urquart entered the room Peter was sitting calmly in front of the fire with the daily newspaper opened on his knee. He rose to meet her and surprised she said, 'I didn't realize you were here, Peter. I thought you were playing bridge with the other four.'

'I wasn't in the mood for bridge, Lady Urquart. I thought I'd keep your daughters company and I found Amelia was alone.'

'Where is Amelia?'

'She was here a moment ago. She heard your car so she's probably in the kitchen making coffee.'

'It's been a long day. They suggested another rubber but I was feeling tired so I decided to come home. Were you at the meet today?'

'Yes. It was a good turnout.'

'Excellent. Don't you ride?'

'Yes, anything from a camel to an elephant, but I'm not a hunting man.'

'My husband wasn't either, but he always turned out to please me. Amelia takes after her father, she's fond of horses but never took to the hunt.'

Amelia sat at her dressing table repairing the ravages to her face. She was very pale, still trembling and she didn't know how she was going to face her mother. She crept downstairs and went directly into the kitchen to make coffee. It would give her a little longer to compose herself.

When she carried the tray into the drawing room Peter sat chatting to her mother in the most normal manner. She purposely didn't look at him but busied herself pouring coffee, wishing desperately that her hands would stop trembling otherwise her mother was sure to notice. Lady Urquart, however, was well launched into her favourite subject, the showing of labradors and their desirability as gun dogs.

She passed round the coffee and sat in the darkest corner of the room. How could Peter talk to her mother in such a casual way when she knew her voice would betray her if she was spoken to? Quite deliberately he kept the conversation on an even keel, and gradually she became calmer until, meeting his eyes across the room, she smiled.

At length her mother said, 'I don't propose to wait up for Celia, she's bound to be late. You look tired, Amelia. I wouldn't wait up either, if I were you.'

Taking the hint Peter said evenly, 'I'll be getting back to the house. I'll probably get roped in for a rubber if they're missing a four.'

'How long are you staying here?' Lady Urquart asked.

'I shall be leaving quite soon. I'm going back to my dig in two weeks' time, and I have quite a lot to do before then.'

'You'll be going home, I imagine. Let me see, where is it you live now?'

'In Sussex.'

'Of course, I remember it well – one of those lovely old manor houses peculiar to that area. You should get married, Peter. A man shouldn't live on his own.'

'I'm abroad most of the time, Lady Urquart. My life wouldn't suit a lot of women.'

'I always thought you were well rid of Marion Hay. She was always what I call a flibbertigibbet.'

Peter offered no reply, and shaking hands with the two women he made his way to the front door followed by Amelia. When they reached it he took her hand and gently kissed her.

'May I see you in the morning? We still have to talk.'

'Please let me think, Peter. Telephone me.'

He squeezed her hand and she watched while he walked to his car, waiting at the door until he was out of sight.

She was glad that her mother went to bed immediately, leaving her to remove the coffee cups.

'It's time those girls arrived home,' her mother said sharply. 'When do you suppose these village hops finish?'

'I've no idea.'

'They have them up north, though?'

'Well of course, and the servants go to them, but I never know what time they come home.'

'I make it my business to keep an eye on the girls. They're too young to be roaming the countryside at all hours. I was sorry when Mrs Parkins left me, I know she was old but she made three of the young ones. She was far more reliable and not wanting to be off at the drop of a hat.'

'The young ones will be old one day, Mummy.'

'I know, but will they be as good as the old ones even then? I doubt it.'

Amelia was in bed when she heard her sister enter the house. Sleep was a long way away. Her mind was still in turmoil after the events of the evening; she couldn't believe that she, Lady Garveston of Garveston Hall, had forgotten her husband, her children, and every convention she had nourished for one blinding experience of passionate love.

She heard Celia humming to herself as she passed her bedroom door, then after a few minutes there was a soft tap on her door and Celia poked her head round it.

'Ah, you're still awake,' she said softly. 'I'm not in the least bit tired, can we chat for a bit?'

Amelia sat up in bed hugging her knees and Celia took the chair nearby.

'You should have come to the Howells' – it was quite a lively party with lots of the hunt members there. They're having a barbecue next Wednesday, you're invited to that one.'

'I doubt if I shall be here.' Now why had she said that? She'd spoken without thinking about her plans and Celia was staring at her in some surprise.

'I understood Mother to say you were staying two weeks at least, and I've arranged to come for the same period. Where are you going?'

'Well, home of course. If I said I was coming for two weeks I didn't know what I was talking about. I ought to get back.'

'Why, for heaven's sake? The girls are at school, Mark goes his own way and nobody's indispensable, no matter what committee they're on. There's always somebody waiting to jump into their shoes.'

Amelia bit her lip nervously. She knew her sister was capable of going on and on about it simply because she never handled her mother well on her own.

'Really, Amelia,' Celia continued, 'Mother'll be annoyed if you go home so soon and so will I. I put myself out considerably to be here at the same time as you.' When she remained silent Celia concluded, 'Why not sleep on it? Tomorrow you'll change your mind, or better still, telephone Mark and invite him down.'

'I doubt if he'd come, he had quite a few things lined up.'

'Then there's no need for you to go rushing home,' her sister snapped before taking herself off to bed.

Amelia lay awake listening to the clock striking in the hall. The sound of its Westminster chimes echoed clearly in the stillness and in desperation she went to stand at the window. From there she could see Drummond in the distance. The house was in darkness apart from one window and she wondered irritably if this was Peter's room and if he too was lying sleepless through the night. In sheer desperation she started to bring her clothes out of the wardrobe, folding them and placing them in a neat pile on one of the chairs. Somewhere in the night a dog barked noisily and she stood with her hand pressed tight against her palpitating breast.

She would leave first thing in the morning. Her mother had a meeting at the village hall at nine, and when she came home she would find her gone. Of course she would probably telephone her at Garveston to register her displeasure, but by then it would be too late.

Peter had nothing to lose, while she had everything to lose. Amelia's world was not one to be jettisoned in the cause of love. Logic was taking over from the insanity of the last few hours, and with that logic came the will to cut and run.

She'd always been the pliable one, the one who conformed, the one who obeyed the rules; now she was risking her mother's anger, her sister's annoyance and Peter's misery in order to do what she believed was right. Early in the morning she would finish packing so that she could leave the moment her mother had left the house.

Her case was almost full the following morning when Celia entered her room unexpectedly. She stared at the suitcase with evident dismay, demanding sharply, 'What on earth are you doing?'

'I'm going home.'

'When?'

'Right now. I know Mummy will be furious but she'll just have to accept it.'

'You're surely not going because she's been getting at you? She gets at me all the time. She's lost Dad and Drummond, she's come second at the dog show, she has to lash out at somebody and here we are, sitting ducks.'

'It's not that.'

'What then? Really, Amelia, Charles has all sorts of things planned for our visit, so you'll be putting Mother and me out as well as Charles and Georgina. Don't you see they're going to think you're behaving very foolishly?'

'I need to see Mark and the girls.'

'Rubbish. I'd like to bet that Mark is taking advantage of your absence to indulge in one of his more nefarious pursuits and the girls are at school. It's Peter Charnley, isn't it?'

Amelia sat down on the edge of her chair sobbing wretchedly into her handkerchief and, suddenly concerned, Celia knelt beside her. 'What has happened to bring all this on? It *is* Peter, isn't it?'

Amelia nodded miserably.

'Well, for goodness sake, he hasn't raped you, has he? It's either that or you're in love with him.'

The tears flowed faster and then in a choked voice Amelia said, 'He's in love with me, Celia. He wants me to spend the last two weeks of his leave with him.'

'Well, why don't you?'

'I can't. He wants to talk about the future and you know what that would mean, leaving Mark and the girls. I can't do it, Celia, much as I love him.'

'So you love him too?' Amelia nodded. 'Poor you. He's so nice, I've always liked him.'

'I can't make him see that I have everything to lose.'

'You can't lose Mark's love because he doesn't know what love is about. Mark's a selfish animal – his idea of love is picking a woman up when he feels like it and conveniently dropping her when she's served her purpose. It suits him to be married to you, Amelia. You make no demands on him and you're a good meal ticket.'

'That's not fair! He idolizes the girls.'

'Possibly, but it's you who pays the bills while Mark's money is his own to spend how he likes.'

'None of this has anything to do with money.'

'I know, but it hasn't much to do with honour either.'

'I won't put myself in the wrong by being the one to walk out.'

'Then you'll never know what real love is all about. You'll go home to Mark and be the dutiful wife and mother, you'll play your part and pretend you have the perfect home and the perfect marriage and for the rest of your life you'll feel cheated.'

'You don't understand, Celia.'

'Oh, I understand only too well. Desmond and I might not be the ideal couple these days but there was a time when our life together was good. You can't say the same for yourself. Live a little before it's too late, darling.'

'You're persuading me to do something you hated Desmond for.'

'I know. Life's illogical, isn't it? Anyway you'll have to decided pretty soon, for if I'm not mistaken that was Peter's car pulling up at the door.'

Amelia jumped to her feet, her face flaming with colour, tense and ready to run if Celia hadn't kept a firm grip on her wrist.

'Come down and face it out,' she hissed. 'At least have the courage to do that.'

A maid ushered Peter into the hall, and for a moment he stared in consternation at the suitcase sitting at Amelia's feet.

She stared back at him miserably and Celia said briskly, 'I'll leave you two together. Amelia says she's going home, Peter. It's up to you to change her mind.'

He sat beside her on the settle, his hands gripping hers, his face earnest yet demanding, and Amelia's protests became pitifully shallow, her excuses childlike and immature.

Wearily she said at last, 'Don't you realize that you're asking me to prejudice my entire life for just two weeks of happiness with you?'

'It may not be just for two weeks. We can talk about the rest of our lives during that time.'

For a long moment she was silent, then lifting her eyes to his she said quietly, 'We have no long-term future together, Peter. All we have is two weeks. There can never be any act on my part that would shatter the lives of my children.'

In later years when she looked back on that morning it seemed to Amelia that others had conspired to make her time with Peter both memorable and easy. Peter informed her that he had spoken to her brother about his love for her and like Celia both Charles and Georgina encouraged him to persuade her to go with him.

Georgina had said, 'Amelia's never been really alive. She drifted from being a schoolgirl into becoming a wife, and a wife to the wrong man. It's doubtful if Phillip Garveston would have been right for her either, but Mark certainly never was.'

Her car was left in one of the garages at the house, out of sight of her mother, and by mid-morning she and Peter were driving south to Sussex.

She fell in love with his house on sight. It wasn't nearly as grand as Garveston Hall, simply an old manor house. Virginia creeper scrambled over the warm stone, it had diamond-leaded panes and tall chimneys and the gardens swept down to the clifftop. The sound of the sea breaking on the rocks could be heard inside its walls.

Amelia thought this was the happiest time of her entire life. She had known happiness when the twins were born, even when she had sensed Mark's disappointment that one of them wasn't a boy. She had been happy at Drummond rambling with her father in the parkland or helping him to tie up his roses, but this was happiness of a different kind. This was a complete emotional security and joy. They spent the long days roaming across the downs and sat before the fire in the late evening listening to the sea.

At night she lay in his arms, warm and complete after love, and neither of them spoke about the future or what would happen when the two joyous weeks came to an end.

Peter never once questioned her emphatic statement that this was all they would ever have. At the end of their time together they would go their separate ways and only time would resolve the rest of their lives.

She was grateful to him that he never pressurized her into changing her mind; he knew it was made up. On their last evening she telephoned Celia at her mother's house to say they were driving back to Drummond in the morning, and added anxiously, 'If I see Mother what shall I tell her?'

'Mother won't be here, she's gone to some function at Shrewsbury for a couple of days. Mark has been here, incidentally. He called on the way back from some race meeting or other.'

'Whatever did you tell him?' Amelia's heart raced in dismay.

'That you were visiting friends in the south for a few days. Mother wasn't here, thank goodness! We told her you'd gone home because you had urgent commitments. Isn't it amazing how things always go wrong whenever you try to deceive someone? Whoever would have thought Mark would show up!'

'Didn't he expect to stay?'

'Apparently not, but be prepared to answer some questions. I suppose there's no hope for you and Peter?'

'No, Celia. Peter knows that. I have to think of the girls – Mark too, for that matter. I think Peter understands, the upheaval would be simply too great.' As she laid down the receiver she turned to see Peter staring at her across the room. She knew he had heard every word and yet he made no attempt to change her mind.

He drove her back to Drummond on a morning of dull leaden skies and spasmodic rain. It was a day in keeping with the despair in their hearts and stealing a look at his face she saw that it was grave and heavy with pain.

They drove past the Dower House and direct to the garage where her car was waiting, and although there hadn't been a moment during the journey when she hadn't wanted his arms around her, she mechanically went about transferring her luggage to it, taking her suitcase from his hands without once looking at his face.

Unable to bear it a moment longer Peter said quietly, 'This is all there is, isn't it, Amelia? A polite goodbye and thanks for the memory?'

She looked at him then and the tears welled up into her eyes and ran slowly down her cheeks.

'Please don't make it hard for me. You know I love you, I just can't leave my children to be with you. Right from the very beginning I told you what the ending would be, now you must try to forget me as I must try to forget you.'

'Will it be easy, do you think?' There was vague sarcasm in his voice but she knew it was caused by the anguish in his heart. He was not a man to take refuge in ironic cynicism.

'You know it won't, but I have to pick up the pieces of my life. It will be the hardest thing I've ever had to do.'

He made no effort to embrace her and she was glad. Instead he stood in the driving rain until her car disappeared into the trees which edged the parkland.

Amelia was glad of the drive home and the misty miserable day that needed all her concentration. The Pennine hills loomed dark and dismal on the horizon and for the first time she started to think about Garveston and how it would greet her. Would Mark be home, she wondered, or would he be out pursuing one of his favourite activities? Would he even remember that she was coming home today?

For the first time she drove through the parkland without once staring round her with her usual appreciation. Leaving her car on the drive she let herself into the house and immediately encountered a parlourmaid crossing the hall. The girl smiled at her shyly and Amelia said quickly, 'I'd like some tea, Mabel please, but nothing to eat. I'll dine later.'

When Mabel brought in the tea tray Amelia looked up at her, asking quietly, 'Is Sir Mark out on the estate?'

'We haven't seen him since breakfast, milady. He told Mr 'Arris he wouldn't be in until late. Mr 'Arris says there's a mountain o' mail waitin' for you in the mornin' room, milady.'

'Yes, I expected that. I'll deal with some of it this evening.'

Amelia ate alone in the lofty dining room, aware that occasionally the butler looked at her sympathetically, but she didn't allow her composure to slip for a moment, and when she had finished her meal she said evenly, 'I'll have coffee in my study, Harris. Perhaps later I'll go through my mail.'

'Very well, milady,' he answered, before he summoned a maid to clear the table.

301

Mabel had been right. A mountain of mail covered the top of her desk and as she leafed idly through the envelopes she recognized that most of them were connected with her charities. Coffee was served to her and she started to answer the letters, sitting under the light of a standard lamp. After a while she turned to look out of the window and was surprised to find it almost dark. Mabel came in to draw the curtains and add coal to the fire, enquiring if Amelia required anything else.

'No thank you, Mabel. Goodnight,' she replied.

She looked at the marble clock on the mantelpiece – it was well after eleven. Mark's cavalier treatment was making her angry, even though it was no different from the treatment he'd meted out to her over the years. It was Peter who had made her dissatisfied, Peter who had shown her that loving a woman meant showing her consideration and kindness.

She heard the striking of the clock in the hall and went to the window, pulling back the heavy drapes. The park lay in darkness, there was no moonlight and mist still swirled across the grass. She was about to turn away when she saw the headlights of a car in the distance so she allowed the drapes to fall into place then returned to her chair and picked up her pen.

She did not have long to wait. Dimly she heard the closing of the front door, then his steps crossing the hall. The door was unceremoniously flung open and raising her eyes she saw Mark looking at her with undisguised anger. She knew at once that he had been drinking more heavily than usual.

'So,' he said sarcastically, 'my lady wife has condescended to come home.'

She didn't answer. There was good reason for his anger but she considered it prudent to wait.

'Well?' he demanded. 'Do I get an explanation or not?'

'An explanation?'

302

'Why weren't you at Drummond? That was where you were supposed to be, wasn't it?'

Only for a moment was she disconcerted, then some inner strength seemed to possess her and she realized it was his anger. If he'd come to her distraught and appealing she would have been ashamed; as it was, his anger, a change from his usual indifference, brought an answering retort to her lips.

'I was at Drummond for a week. You never wrote or telephoned – if I wished to spend a few days elsewhere why should you suddenly be concerned?'

'I'm not concerned about where you were, only who you were with!'

'I was with a friend.'

'You have no friends you would suddenly leave Drummond to be with.'

'How do you know who my friends are? In actual fact, Mark, you don't really know very much about me.'

'So I've realized in these last few days.'

'Why are you so angry? In all the years of our marriage you've done exactly as you pleased, gone where you wanted, and there have been other women. I don't know who they are, I don't want to know, but I never supposed for a moment that you lived like a monk.'

'And if there were women I gave you no reason to think that they were important. None of them affected our marriage.'

'That made it right, did it? For years people have gossiped about us. I've lived with the knowledge that your friends sniggered about me behind my back, amused that I seemed oblivious to your philandering, but I wasn't oblivious, it was unimportant to me. On the one weekend when I invited my friends here you tried to get Barbara Walton into your bed and now you have the colossal nerve to demand an explanation

303

for my movements over the last two weeks. I'm not going to tell you anything, Mark. I'm here and I'm here to stay, let that suffice.'

'In other words, forget it, Mark, it's none of your business,' he said sharply.

'How many times have I asked you to go with me to Drummond and you've always made some excuse or other? You don't like my mother, you have very little in common with any of my family, then suddenly you arrive there out of the blue and you're angry because I am not sitting there hoping you'd come.'

'Don't put the onus on me, Amelia. You were supposed to be there – it surely isn't too much to enquire where you were and with whom?'

For a moment her face softened and she held out her hand in a conciliatory gesture. 'Please, Mark, it's over and I'm unhappy that it's over. We have a marriage, such as it is, we've never pretended it was a love story but we have two children we both adore. Can't we remember that and forget the rest?'

'I seem to have very little choice in the matter,' he said bitterly, then after giving her a long straight stare he left her alone.

All the tears had been shed on that last night in Peter's arms; now she could only feel a deep and abiding sadness. Her heart felt like lead. The future stretched before her like a dark and shadowy waste. Her children would grow up and one day they would leave her, alone with Mark in a loveless marriage, living their separate lives behind a façade of unity.

She wondered dismally how many other women surrendered the rest of their lives at thirty-five but that was what she had done. Unthinkingly she bundled the letters lying on her desk together and placed them in the drawer. There would be time enough to answer them another day; it seemed at that moment that all she had was time.

Mechanically she walked across to the fireplace. The fire was dying now but she poked the embers into place, then after reassuring herself it was safe she went to the sideboard and poured herself a small glass of brandy.

She did not normally drink, and as the sharp liquid ran down her throat she shivered delicately, making a grimace of repugnance, then when she began to feel the sudden glow the brandy aroused in her she poured a far larger measure into her glass, followed by another. It was the first time, though not the last, that Amelia Garveston was to resort to the comfort of alcohol.

CHAPTER 29

Maisie stood at the farm window staring out across the fields. Peter had gone off willingly enough to help his father as soon as breakfast was over, happy in the knowledge that it was only for a short time because after the summer holidays he would be going up to Cambridge. Now she could see Lucy and her school-friend Penny running for dear life across the field, blonde curls flying in the wind, calling excitedly to each other as they ran.

What a lot she had to be thankful for. Peter had done so well in his last year at the grammar school, Lucy got good reports from the small private school they were sending her to in Greymont, the summer had begun well, promising them a more than usually ample harvest – so why was she so hurt and angry? As usual it was Alice.

Alice was off soon to spend the four weeks of half-term with Joanne Proctor's family in St Tropez. The trouble had started when she was home to pack and looking through her things. Her clothes were unsuitable, old-fashioned and cheap, she'd stormed. Maisie had gone into Greymont and bought material which she'd been busy making into skirts and dresses; now, it seemed, they were not to her liking, either.

Alice was lying on her bed in a fit of the sulks. Peter had called her an ungrateful spoiled brat and even Tom had said that if they had any more trouble with her, he would telephone Joanne's mother to say the holiday was off.

Maisie wanted her to go, for weeks of Alice sulking about the house would drive her mad. After they'd eaten lunch Alice had disappeared as usual to her room while Lucy dutifully dried the dishes, confiding to her mother, 'I wish she was going today. It's always nicer when she's away.'

'You shouldn't say that,' Maisie chided her. 'She's your sister, I'd like you to be good friends.'

'She doesn't want to be friends with me,' Lucy said firmly. 'She thinks I'm a nuisance because I play in the living room when she only wants to read.'

'You'll want to read more when you're older. Try to get along together, that's a good girl.'

The door behind her opened quietly and Maisie turned to see Alice standing there, her face petulant, her cheeks tear-stained.

For a few minutes they stared at each other then Maisie said gently, 'You worry me, Alice. I wish you got along with Peter and Lucy better than you do.'

'Peter thinks he knows everything just because he's going to Cambridge. One thing's for sure, I shan't be asking *him* to escort me to the school dance when I leave. I'd rather go on my own than take him.'

'It's some time off, you don't need to think about it yet.'

'The others are already talking about who they're taking and what they're going to wear. Mother, I do want my dress to be something special, not something home-made.'

'We'll see, nearer the time.'

'Joanne has a brother I could take and there's another boy Monica knows but she might want to take him herself.'

'You'd do better to look to your lessons and think about the dance nearer the time,' Maisie warned her. 'We never gave it a thought until after our examinations.'

'It must have been dead stuffy in your time, Mother. I suppose Lady Garveston took Sir Mark.'

'As a matter of fact she didn't, she took his older brother.'

Alice showed more interest. 'Why didn't she marry his brother, then?'

'He was killed in a flying accident when they were engaged. She married Sir Mark some time later.'

'If she was in love with his brother she couldn't have been in love with Sir Mark, could she?'

'She didn't marry him immediately, only after a decent interval.'

'Who took Sir Mark to the dance?'

'Nancy Graham.'

'Didn't he want to marry her?'

'They were friends for a time then it all fizzled out. Your father and I stuck together. I suppose that sounds very ordinary to you.'

'Heavens, yes. I shan't be making my mind up at eighteen. I want to meet lots of boys. I want to see the world and do lots of exciting things before I get married, and I definitely *don't* want to spend the rest of my life on a farm!'

'Don't lose sight of the fact that the farm is paying for your education, all your clothes and your holidays with your friends. Your dad and I have worked hard all our married life on this farm and he's worried about what's going to happen to it one day. It's evident Peter won't want it.'

'Neither shall I. I'm not going to marry a farmer.'

'There's plenty of time for you to change your mind.'

'I shan't. Let Lucy have the farm, she's happy on it, I'm not.'

She flounced off and Maisie followed thoughtfully. Alice was helping herself to milk out of the fridge when Maisie said, 'What are your plans for today?'

'I thought I'd call in to see Granny and Grandad this afternoon.'

Maisie knew that Alice was only going because they gave her money. Mr Jayson had always spoiled his grandchildren. Peter called to do errands for them and odd jobs around the garden, Lucy went because she loved them, but Alice only visited them for money, and was quick to make an exit. When Maisie remonstrated with her she said airily, 'Granny's so deaf, Mother, she doesn't hear what I'm telling her, and Grandad goes to sleep in his chair. They're glad I don't stay long. I might call and see Uncle Jimmy, he's fun,' she added.

'Now don't go believing everything he tells you. He's always had a big opinion of himself.'

Alice laughed. She was on the same wavelength as her Uncle Jimmy. She encouraged him to talk about his women friends, something he wasn't reluctant to do, then there would be Gloria with her pathetic attempts at housekeeping which sent Alice off into howls of laughter as soon as she'd closed their door. While Maisie stood watching her thoughtfully Alice said airily, 'I'm off now, Mum. I'm not calling to see Aunt Mary, she doesn't like me and I don't like her.'

The following morning Maisie drove Alice to the station to catch the London train. Alice was in high good humour. She had a new suitcase her father had bought her, a purse filled with holiday money given by her grandparents, her parents and Uncle Jimmy, and in her suitcase were new cotton dresses, shorts and blouses. She wasn't so bothered now that the dresses were home-made – she had enough funds to buy more when they reached their destination.

Maisie eyed her pink excited face with some trepidation. She had betrayed an unusually sunny temperament on her last breakfast at the farm, been sweeter to her brother and sister than at any time during the few days she'd spent at home, and Tom had looked upon her with great affection.

She could twist Tom round her little finger, make him feel Maisie was too hard on her; in fact, the only time they ever had words was about Alice.

They were early for the train. Alice had been following her about all morning urging her to hurry and now they had over half an hour to kill so Maisie suggested a cup of tea in the station café.

'I'd like to get something to read on the train,' Alice said, jumping to her feet, so Maisie handed over a fistful of change and Alice skipped out of the café to go to the newsagents on the platform. When she returned she had a new magazine in her hands and a newspaper which she handed to her mother saying, 'I thought you'd like to read this, Mum. There's a picture of Nancy Graham on the front page.'

Maisie stared down at Nancy's face looking back at her. Underneath was a report of an attack made upon her and an Israeli woman on a road leading from Jerusalem. Alice grinned at her. 'She never settled for mediocrity, did she, Mum?' she said lightly.

Her words were too grown-up. Was that how girls talked these days, Maisie wondered, then looking back she remembered she'd always been the odd one out, the country bumpkin. While the others moved on she'd been happy to stay with Tom on the farm in a calm familiar world.

To change the subject she said, 'Who do you suppose the Garveston girls will be taking to the dance?'

'They're a year ahead of me anyway but it's bound to be somebody very uppish.'

'I hope you are friends with them now, Alice.'

'They're not my sort. Pippa's not so bad but I can't stand Berenice. I don't have to be friends with them, I have my own friends.'

'All the same it would have been nice, in view of the fact that I was at school with their mother,' Maisie said quietly.

'That was then, Mother, this is now. Don't go pushing me into a friendship with them, it's not what any of us want.'

How grown-up her daughter seemed these days. She was younger than Peter but nobody would have believed it. Peter was still a boy, caring and immature in spite of his cleverness, but not Alice. She was naturally streetwise, and the cloistered seclusion of Lorivals had done nothing to erase this; it was something that had been born in her.

A fellow traveller helped Alice with her luggage and then she turned to embrace her mother.

'You'll write as soon as you get there, love?' Maisie asked. 'We'll be anxious to know if you're enjoying yourself.'

'I'll write, Mum, but please don't expect a lot of postcards. They run away with so much money.'

Maisie smiled, then Alice turned and followed her luggage into the compartment. She stood at the window until the train gathered speed, then Maisie turned away to go to her car. There would be peace in the house now, no more quarrels between her children, no more insinuations from Tom that Alice just needed a bit more understanding. It was terrible that she was feeling such relief that Alice had gone.

Tom was in the farmyard when she arrived home and immediately he said, 'Alice get away on time, then?' She nodded. 'If you're making tea, love, I'll be in in a jiffy,' he said.

She made the tea and was sitting reading the newspaper when he came into the kitchen. She held it out to him after he'd poured his tea and he sat staring down at the report of the mayhem in the Middle East.

Maisie made it her duty to read Noel Templeton's column and Nancy's, and she watched avidly whenever they appeared on television news reels – not because she understood the situation, but because Nancy was

311

her friend. She wondered idly if there was something going on between her and Noel Templeton, whom she considered to be decidedly dishy with his good looks and sardonic eyes.

Tom said the world was in a mess. The news from the Middle East, Africa and Sri Lanka was grave and something would have to be done about it. Maisie thought Nancy should come home and leave the reporting to men, while Tom thought she was a brick to stay on and see things through.

Maisie was glad that all the troubles were occurring in countries she'd only read about; she didn't see why it was Britain's affair but Tom told her she was being very short-sighted since everything that went on anywhere was Britain's affair.

Maisie didn't agree with him. 'Why do we have to talk about war when we have peace?' she argued, and Tom was quick to tell her that the sort of peace we had in the world was an uneasy one, like a slumbering volcano which was unpredictable enough to erupt at any moment.

How peaceful everything was in the kitchen. She was aware of Tom sitting at the table calmly drinking his tea, reading Nancy's column with great interest. The clock ticked steadily on the wall, and the canary sang in his cage near the window. Geraniums bloomed on the windowsill and yet her thoughts moved constantly from the harmonious atmosphere of her kitchen to Alice speeding on her way to London.

CHAPTER 30

Nancy felt she had been a prisoner in Abraham's house for too long. Whenever she passed Leah's room she heard the mournful sounds of her delirium as she lay in the coma from which they prayed she would return.

Every day she went in to see her, only to be confronted by the nurse sadly shaking her head. Nancy spent her days with young Benjamin, trying to comfort him in the absence of his stepmother.

At first Benjamin had been inconsolable, but as the days passed he began to forget those harrowing moments out there on the way back from Jerusalem, when Leah had borne the brunt of the Arabs' anger. He recognized Nancy as the woman who had saved his life, and the life of Leah, also.

There were no more trips into the city, no more wandering over the verdant hills; now she must sit with Benjamin in the gardens while she read to him or helped him with his lessons and waited for news from Noel that he remembered her existence.

In the evenings she kept Abraham company, talking to him about his future in Israel.

'Will you be happy to stay on here when Leah is well again?' she asked and Abraham only answered after several minutes of thoughtful silence.

'You have to understand, Nancy, that this is our land. We came to it with so much joy, so much gratitude after years of humiliation and tragedy. It is ours by our industry and our patience that has made the desert bloom. All we asked was to be allowed to live in peace in this land that God gave us but it was not to be; we were viciously attacked and we had to defend ourselves.

313

One day there must be a reckoning, but that time is a long way off. In the meantime, we must do what we can.'

'So you do intend to remain here?' she persisted.

He shrugged his shoulders with that familiar, fatalistic gesture. 'I am concerned about Benjamin,' he confided to her. 'He should not grow up with the sort of memories I did – he should know peace and security in his early years, not the trauma of sudden death and separation.'

'But if you send him away, that would be separation, surely?'

'I know, but he would not be with strangers, he would be with people who love him.'

'Your brother in Egypt?'

'Yes. I have thought very carefully about it since that dreadful afternoon. I have no guarantee that Leah will ever fully recover, much as I pray for it, and now my brother is urging me to send Benjamin to them for a while, at least until he is a little older and more able to understand.'

'But wouldn't that be terrible for him? He has already lost Leah for the moment; to lose you and his familiar surroundings would be even worse.'

'My brother's family would adore him, make much of him – and the young heal very quickly. Their memories are short. My brother has a summer villa in Alexandria, and I could easily visit him there.'

'Have you spoken about it to Benjamin?'

'Not yet. There are problems, as I could not take him myself and I am reluctant to entrust him to a servant.'

Nancy was silent and after a little while Abraham said, 'Perhaps when Noel comes he and I can talk about it.'

'I'm beginning to think he'll never return, Abraham,' Nancy said ruefully. 'He seems to have dumped me like an unwanted parcel and conveniently forgotten about me.'

'He will come, Nancy. I hope for the day when he recognizes his love for you as something he can no longer run away from.'

Three days later Noel returned and Nancy stood in the gardens with a fast-beating heart watching his battered, dust-encrusted car climbing the hill towards the gates. She didn't go to him but waited in the gardens until a servant came to tell her that Mr Templeton had arrived and her presence was required on the terrace. Noel had already spent over an hour alone with Abraham, and that had added to her resentment.

Both men rose as she walked across the terrace, then Noel was smiling down into her eyes and the familiar charm of his smile robbed her heart of its anger before he gripped her hands.

He pulled a chair forward so that she could sit facing them, and deliberately keeping his voice light he said, 'I've been hearing about your excitement, Nancy. Abraham has told me how brave you were – I'm very proud of you.'

She said nothing; she was waiting to hear if he had any plans for her immediate future. She did not have long to wait, and that too was like Noel. She was accustomed to the quickness of his mind, the urgency of his plans.

'Abraham tells me that he wishes to send Benjamin away to Egypt. Would you be willing to take him?'

She stared at him dumbfounded, and Abraham rose to his feet. 'I'll leave you two to talk. I can see this has come as something of a shock to Nancy.'

He left them together and immediately Nancy said angrily, 'But why me? I didn't come here to act as a nursemaid to a small boy. I am a journalist. How dare you discuss my future with Abraham without consulting me first? Escorting a child out of Israel is surely not my reason for being here.'

315

'No,' he said evenly, 'but I can make it one of the reasons, Nancy. Think what a story it will make. The fracas when you saved his life and your subsequent journey to Egypt to ensure that his life remains safe. I will arrange for you to stay at the Mena House Hotel in Egypt until you hear from me. It will be a golden opportunity for you to see something of the country and you will have helped Abraham more than you know.'

'I didn't join your team to see Egypt, I came to be a part of what goes on here. What do I report on there – Nile cruises and trips around the pyramids?'

She hated the tight ache in her throat and the treacherous tears that threatened to fill her eyes. She turned her head impatiently, wishing with all her heart that she could remove that logical calmness from his expression, the gentleness covering implacable steel from his voice. Angrily she moved away to seek a quiet place where she could give vent to her hurt pride.

Why had he brought her here? He would have done better to leave her in that small-town environment where she hadn't been unhappy writing about golden weddings and charitable fêtes; instead he'd raised her hopes, made her feel that she had the makings of a first-class journalist. But she'd loved him – she had never had the singleness of purpose he'd expected of her.

She gazed down the long dusty road and the distant city through a haze of tears, then heard a small sound in the bushes behind her and saw Benjamin cowering against the wall, his face bleak and tear-stained.

'Benjamin!' she cried, startled. 'What are you doing here? I didn't know you were in the garden.'

His bottom lip trembled ominously and gathering himself into a ball he started to sob. She went to sit beside him, attempting to hold him, but he backed instantly away from her.

'Tell me what's the matter,' she coaxed him. 'Why are you being such a cry baby?'

Again she tried to draw him into her embrace and again he struggled, then in a muffled voice he said, 'I don't like you any more.'

'But why? What have I done, my precious?'

For a moment he was silent, then sulkily he said, 'You don't want to take me to Egypt. I was listening in the garden.'

'Oh, Benjamin, if things were different I would love to take you to Egypt but that isn't why I'm here. Your father has servants who could take you.'

'No he hasn't. I thought you were my friend.'

With a stifled sob he wrenched himself from her reaching hands and ran quickly across the gardens. She stared after him with pain-filled eyes, then Abraham was there gazing down at her sadly.

'I'm sorry Benjamin heard your refusal, Nancy. I hadn't realized he was in the garden. Don't worry, children soon forget.'

'I don't want to hurt any of you, Abraham, but please try to see my point of view. If I go with your son to Alexandria I'm sure that will be the end of me as a journalist. I'll never see Noel again.'

'I can assure you you will. My servants are not equipped for escorting Benjamin into the city, let alone a strange country. The child loves you, he will go happily with you, and Leah and I will be content. You will take a great weight off our minds at a time when we need it most.'

At that moment she knew that Noel had won. She would go to Egypt with Benjamin, she would stay at the Mena House Hotel until Noel remembered her existence, and then no doubt the next step would be home to England.

'When do you want us to leave?' she asked resignedly.

He smiled, taking both her hands in his. 'I'll see

317

about a passage on the next boat sailing from Haifa, either to Port Said or Alexandria. You will be a tourist travelling with your nephew. I'll see about getting the appropriate papers so that you can travel in the next day or so, and I will make sure that you are met when you arrive at your destination.'

'Does that mean I am not to use my own passport?'

'No. As Nancy Graham you are too well-known and already the Intifada will know all about your part in the stoning of Leah and the death of those young Arabs. It is quite likely they will expect me to try to get my son out of the country, and that is why I am not suggesting that you go by plane. Anonymity is easier by boat.'

'You are expecting us to be followed, then?'

'Yes. You will both be dressed in Arab clothing. You will be an Egyptian lady returning home with your nephew. You know enough Arabic to indulge in small-talk and to answer questions.' He smiled. 'Think of it, Nancy, think of the headlines: "How I smuggled a small Jewish boy out of Israel dressed as an Arab, how I saved his life". In England you'll be more famous than the rest of your team.'

Nancy scowled. 'I'm not looking for that sort of fame. What happens if I'm discovered?'

'Once you are on the ship you'll be relatively safe. Before then I'll do my best to see that you have every protection.'

Thirty-six hours later she found herself being robed in Arab dress, wearing a yashmak over her face, her eyes adorned with kohl although she could tell that Abraham was troubled over their blueness.

'Try to keep them shadowed as much as you can,' he advised, 'but if anybody remarks about their colour explain that your mother was a European.'

'Tell them she was English,' Noel agreed. 'That will account for your ease in speaking the language. Ben-

318

jamin looks the part, you shouldn't have any trouble with him.'

'How are we to get out of the house?' she asked curiously.

'You will leave in the morning in the van that delivers provisions. It will take you into the warehouse yard where you will board another van which is leaving for Haifa. The journey won't be too comfortable, but there is no alternative.'

'Won't they be watching the house all the time?'

'All the time, but they have no reason to suspect a van carrying groceries. No doubt they'll report it but there's nothing else for it.' Noel looked down at her and laughed suddenly. 'You look like the very devil in that outfit, Nancy, so full of Eastern promise that you'll be more in danger from amorous Arabs than dangerous ones.'

Noel made no effort to embrace her but instead said gently, 'Take care, and wait until I contact you. Enjoy Egypt.'

She sat with Benjamin on the floor of the provision van and felt every bone in her body aching with each jolt in the road, each swerve round every corner, although Benjamin seemed not to mind. His father had embraced them both with tears in his eyes as they climbed into the van, but Leah was still unconscious and Nancy could only guess at her sadness if she ever came out of her coma to find Benjamin gone.

The journey was uneventful. She could tell they had entered the city by the sounds of street vendors and traffic, by the slowness of the vehicle and by the stifling heat as the sun climbed higher into the brassy blue sky.

At last she was being assisted to climb down into the warehouse yard, and then strong hands were pulling her into another van while they lifted Benjamin up beside her. Some semblance of comfort was offered by the mattresses laid on the floor of the vehicle, and then once more they were off on their journey, slowly and haltingly until they left the city gates and were at last speeding along the road from Jerusalem to Haifa.

It was cooler as they climbed up the slopes of Mount Carmel, and with the petrol fumes came rare wafts of mimosa. She knew that below them was the port and the Mediterranean and once Benjamin asked plaintively, 'Will my father be coming to Egypt soon?'

'Yes, darling, just as soon as Leah is well enough to travel,' she answered tenderly.

He seemed content with her answer and she was glad to see his eyes close in sleep. The long curling lashes lay on his cheek in fringed crescents and he looked so beautiful and so innocent that tears filled her eyes. He was only a child, and yet he had lost his mother and now his stepmother was dangerously ill. He was leaving all those he loved to take up a life with strangers in a strange country, and he was doing it bravely while she did nothing but fill her heart with resentment. Perhaps children didn't feel so deeply or perhaps they were more philosophical about things. Maybe only maturity brought this sadness and feeling of despair.

At last they were on the quayside mingling with the crowds. Benjamin's hand clung tightly to her own as she endeavoured to pull the veil more closely over her face. Israeli soldiers strutted in pairs, but she noticed a group of Arabs standing motionless near the warehouse wall, their eyes scanning the crowds. If those men were assassins they would not care that the quayside crawled with Israeli soldiers and innocent people. They were fanatics, ready to die for Islam.

How slowly the queue moved as the hot sun beat down unrelentingly on their heads. From somewhere behind them a baby was screeching and scrawny pariah dogs ran about, their eyes searching hopefully for food.

She could see the gangway now but her elation was momentary. The Arabs moved in a stealthy group towards it as people mounted, while at the same time the Israeli soldiers marched forward and stood in a straight line observing the queue moving sluggishly in front of them.

Nancy held on to her veil, sickeningly aware that her eyes would betray her to the Arabs who were carefully scrutinising every person who walked up the gangway. She encouraged Benjamin by asking if he was hungry and telling him that very soon they would be on the ship where there would be food waiting for them.

There was no escaping the watchfulness of the Arabs who stood on either side of the crowd. Her hand was on the rail when she heard her name called softly, sibilantly: '*Miss Graham*,' then, shaken into rigidity, she opened her eyes wide and found herself gazing into the dark haughty face of Girgis Boutrous.

She could feel the crowd around her, aware of their stares and the sudden alertness of the soldiers and in sheer desperation she said, 'Please, Mr Boutrous. He's only a child.'

For what seemed an eternity their eyes were locked, his cold and filled with bitter resentment, hers in silent prayer, then disdainfully he turned away muttering in Arabic, 'Come, I was mistaken.'

She couldn't believe it – there would be no scene, no shooting, they were free to go! Holding Benjamin's hand tightly she started to mount the gangway. Memories of her conversation with Girgis Boutrous in the garden of his uncle's house near Jericho came back to her. Had there been something in that conversation that had prompted him to be merciful? She couldn't remember. Or did she fear his uncle's anger more than he feared the Intifada? Or could it simply be that he would justify his moment of weakness and humanity by more atrocities in Jerusalem or elsewhere . . .

They sat on the lower deck with other women similarly attired. She was just an Arab matron travelling

321

with an Arab child, and beside her an elderly woman made a fuss of Benjamin and spoke to him rapidly. Nancy was inordinately relieved when he responded in faultless Arabic which necessitated few comments from her.

They were served soup and some sort of sweet confection which she disliked but which Benjamin ate with relish. Her companion seemed surprised when she put aside the sweetmeat until Nancy motioned to her stomach and indicated that the ship might roll and she was not eating.

After a while Benjamin curled up on the seat and closed his eyes. The woman beside him laid his head on her lap and cradled him gently, while Nancy went to stand at the ship's rail to see the lights of Haifa disappear in the distance. Noel had informed her that they would be met by Benjamin's relatives in Alexandria and she supposed that after that she would have to make her own way to Cairo. She had deliberately asked no questions about any of Noel's arrangements: that was to be his punishment for making her go. She presumed she would simply take the Cairo train still wearing the garb of an Arab woman. At least Noel would never be able to say she had created difficulties.

The long night stretched ahead of her, and from the deck above she could hear the sound of music and people laughing and dancing. As the night cooled, she was glad of the rugs provided by the crew until her companion declined one. Seeing Nancy's surprised look she indicated that they would be dirty and she rubbed her skin savagely to show that they were probably infested with insects. From a large raffia bag lying at her feet she produced two patterned blankets and gratefully they snuggled together beneath them until dawn.

The passengers for Port Said left the ship in the early morning, and it was here that Nancy and Benjamin lost their new friend, who departed with waving hands to be met on the quayside by a crowd of smiling relatives.

'Who will meet us?' Benjamin asked plaintively.

'I don't know, darling. Will you recognize your uncle?'

'I think so.'

'Have you been to Egypt before?'

'Oh yes, once, a long time ago.'

She smiled down at the boy. Months, weeks even seemed a long time to a child. 'Did you like Egypt?' she asked quietly.

'Oh yes, I think so.'

She realized then that he had been too young to remember much about it. In the distance between Port Said and Alexandria she occupied his mind by telling him all she had ever read about the country. She told him about the pyramids and the sphinx, the treasures of Tutankhamen and the magnificent temples and tombs near Luxor, and for the first time in days her spirits soared when she realized that all these wonders would soon be within her grasp.

They had little time to explore Alexandria because immediately on their arrival they were captured by smiling relatives and friends of Abraham's, all drooling and cooing over the boy, whisking them away in an opulent limousine so that all she could see of the city was the curve of the exquisite sickle-shaped bay edged with white buildings and graceful white minarets.

The golden glowing light filled her senses. Soon they were driving along streets edged by delightful old gardens full of heavily scented oriental flowering trees planted before beautiful villas.

The limousine swept up the curved drive of a house set high on the hillside and when she alighted from it Nancy gasped with delight at the port of Alexandria spread out before her in all its shimmering whiteness.

She soon learned that this was the family's summer home and her eyes lit up with joy at the room she was ushered into, with its pale pink bathroom and flower-filled balcony. Her joy knew no bounds when she found her trunk containing all her European clothes lying on the carpet, until she realized suddenly that everything she owned was there – a sure indication that she would not be returning to Israel. She was shattered and angry. How subtly Noel had engineered her departure. What excuses would he next bring forward for sending her off to England – and out of his life forever?

She was invited to spend long weeks in Alexandria and in the short time she was there she fell in love with the city which even in ancient times had been more Greek than Egyptian. She explained to her hosts that her hotel accommodation was waiting for her in Cairo where she expected to hear what was going to happen to her next.

'You are not going back to Israel then?' David, Abraham's brother, asked.

'I don't know where I'm going, but hopefully Mr Templeton will not keep me waiting too long to find out.'

They escorted her in a body to the station and waited until the Cairo train started its journey. She would have been happy to have been left in peace to enjoy the passing scenery of the Delta with its forest of gracefully waving palms, mud villages, their roofs covered by palm fronds, and the life that strolled and loitered along the river's banks, but instead of the peace she had hoped for she shared a compartment with an Arab schoolboy who insisted on mentioning the name of everything they passed in slow but very loud English.

He was at a boarding school where his father paid a great deal of money for his keep and tuition. Of his English and his school he was enormously proud.

'My father very rich man – oh! yeas, he pay hundreds of pounds for my brother and me; I learn the football and the cricket. Oh! yeas, it is very good school.'

324

When Nancy remarked on the singular ugliness of the buffalo cows they encountered the boy asked in a surprised voice, 'You have no cows in England?'

'No buffalo cows,' she answered him. From that moment he proceeded to mention the name of every object they passed on the journey. 'That bird, that horse, that donkey, that Arab woman, that Arab man.'

After a very brief silence he asked, 'What you do in England?'

'I am a journalist.'

'You write about Egypt, about Nile?'

'Perhaps.'

'Then send it if you please, I read very much, I will buy your book. Oh yeas, my father he very rich man.'

She longed for the hour of his departure and yet to tell him to stop would have been unkind. He saw her interest in a long train of camels crossing the horizon, and in the fellahin in their blue galabeahs picking cotton in the fields, and immediately asked, 'Have you no camels in England?'

She had to confess that they had not.

'And no cotton?' he persisted.

'No, no cotton.'

'Or palm trees?'

He sat back in his seat to contemplate his vision of a country without such necessities for living, thus giving Nancy a moment to reflect on the glorious colours of the setting son, as beautiful as a carved opal of oriental magnificence.

'You write a book about the sunset also?' he asked.

'I doubt if I could ever do justice to such a spectacle,' she answered gently.

She felt at that moment that she could cheerfully strangle this modern Egyptian schoolboy who was doing his best to be kind, but how she wanted to watch the patient fellahin as they wandered staff in hand along the river's bank, and the graceful carriage of the women

325

as they carried the tall water pots on their heads. She permitted herself a small smile at the stupefied face of the boy sitting beside her. He was hard at work trying to discover what England really had to commend her. No oranges, no millet, no saints' tombs, no minarets and, worst of all, no sugar cane for boys to eat coming home from school.

At that moment an older boy in similar garb poked his head through the door to tell him they had almost arrived at their destination so that he shook hands with Nancy rather hurriedly, a fact which upset his English considerably.

'Goodbye tomorrow,' he said urgently. 'I hope you will always be very happy and always be very good.'

CHAPTER 31

Barbara had spent her morning helping out at the riding school. Lucy Belbin was missing two of her helpers and she was hoping to prepare several of her most promising pupils for a gymkhana event later in the week. She'd asked Barbara as a last resort, largely because she always had other things to do and she'd been amazed when she accepted.

She'd helped Lucy to groom the ponies, and she'd chatted quite happily to the mothers of the children when they came to collect them before lunch.

Barbara was glad of the diversion. She'd seen Martin off to his conference and she'd had lunch just one day with Mark who was on his way to Cornwall to pick up Amelia.

He'd looked as glum as she felt. 'Celia uses Amelia all the time,' he complained. 'Whenever she's in a miserable mood Amelia has to go down there to cheer her up. I wouldn't care but the child's been dead for years now, and it was like living with death in the time she was alive.'

'Doesn't Amelia's sister have a husband to cheer her up?'

'Don't mention him. He's tied up at the Foreign Office and he's probably fed up with the gloom and doom anyway. The trouble with Amelia's family is that they can't accept there ever being anything wrong with any of them. They talk about Dorinda as if she was the perfect child and we all know she was anything but that.'

'I should be very honoured that you've stopped by to see me.'

'I wanted to see you, love. I'm sorry it can't be for longer.'

He'd gone off with a cheerful wave of his hand and she'd wondered savagely why Amelia couldn't simply have taken the train home to Lancaster. After he'd gone she felt strangely alone. She considered asking her mother down for a few days then thought better of it. Mrs Smythe wouldn't want to go home when Martin returned. Instead she'd stay on, Martin would be polite and distant, her mother domineering and curious, and after she'd gone Martin would state quite categorically that that was the last he wanted to see of his mother-in-law for some considerable time. That in turn meant she'd have to make excuses again when her father telephoned to see when she was visiting.

Lucy came out of the yard to thank her for her help and Barbara said hopefully, 'Will you want me again tomorrow? I've all the time in the world with Martin away.'

'I've never heard you say that before, you're usually far too occupied.'

'Well, there's nothing more to do at the house, I'm off golf and Martin won't be home until next Sunday. Don't be afraid to ask, Lucy, I've enjoyed helping out.'

'He's looking well, isn't he?' Lucy said, indicating Jupiter who was pawing the ground, eager to be off.

'Oh yes, the boy looks after him very well and so do I. He has a lovely temperament.'

'Yes he has, a little nervous perhaps. How do you cope in traffic?'

'Well, there isn't much around here unless it's farm carts and wagons. I never have any trouble.'

'That's good. I'll telephone you then, probably first thing in the morning.'

They cantered down the lane and Barbara's spirits revived. New leaf was sprouting in the hedgerows and the sun slanted through the branches of the horse chestnuts overhead. Men were working in the fields and over the whole scene lay such an atmosphere of peace she was unprepared for the sudden shattering of that peace by the throbbing of engines as two youths riding high-powered motor cycles screeched round the bend and headed towards them.

Jupiter shied, and before she was aware of it the horse had jumped the fence and was galloping madly across the field, while the bikes spun into the banking scattering their riders.

Terrified, she clung to the mane, agonisingly aware of the horse's speed and the ground flying beneath his feet. She dimly heard men's voices shouting in the background and then Jupiter was rearing in the air and she was falling. In that split second before she hit the ground she thought, This is it, I'm going to die, then mercifully she was lying on something soft and squelchy and a sea of faces was ringed round her; they were staring at her with smiles on their faces!

Two of them leaned forward and helped her up, then she felt the sticky manure clinging to her clothing, in her hair and on her face, and she retched sickeningly.

'Yer not 'urt are ye, luv?' one of the men asked, then he was chuckling. 'My, but it were a good job ye fell into that manure. No tellin' what'd 'ave happened if it 'adn't bin there.'

She felt faint and one of the men pushed her down on to a small cart standing nearby, then she saw Jupiter calmly munching grass at the side of the barn.

'Young devils,' one of the men said. 'Roaring round the country as if they were on a race track, no consideration for nobody they 'aven't. They've gone, so they can't 'ave bin 'urt. 'Ow are ye feelin', luv?'

Barbara was winded but she knew there were no bones broken. Her hands hurt where she'd clung to the reins before she lost them, but it was the sight of her filthy riding breeches and hacking jacket that worried her most.

329

'Now ye'll get right on 'is back and ride 'im or you'll lose yer nerve,' one of the men said. 'You 'aven't all that far to go, 'ave ye?'

'No, my house is over there.'

'Well, I'll 'elp ye on to his back and you get straight into a hot bath as soon as ye get 'ome. It could 'ave bin a whole lot worse, and them clothes'll clean.'

In spite of the logic of his words she felt miserably inadequate as they helped her into the saddle. Her head was throbbing painfully as she rode at a walking pace the few miles to her home. The boy who looked after Jupiter grinned at her appearance, but curtly she told him to take care of the horse before she limped inside.

Her bones ached and by this time much of the manure had dried and clung in clumps to her clothing. She let herself in by the conservatory and went into the cloakroom. Her eyes opened wide at the sight of her stained face and matted hair, and her stomach churned at the stench. She stripped, leaving her clothes in a heap on the floor. She'd never want to wear them again. She'd have to buy more, but at that particular moment she didn't want to ride again, ever.

She was relieved that Martin was away. She was glad he didn't have to see her like this, and he'd only smirk that he hadn't wanted her to take up riding anyway. She poured scented crystals into her bath and lay in it for a long time until she felt the aches slowly lessening, then she got out of the bath and rubbed herself dry.

The clothes lay where she had left them and fastidiously she picked them up, holding them away from her, wrinkling her nose at the smell. Tomorrow she'd ask the boy to burn them.

She dressed in slacks and a woollen jumper before going into the kitchen where one of her daily women was polishing the silver. She looked up with a smile. 'I didn't 'ear ye come in, Mrs Walton. 'Ave you had lunch?'

'No, Gertrude, I'm not hungry. Some boys on motor bikes frightened the horse so that he bolted and threw me off.'

'Lordy, Mrs Walton, are you 'urt?'

'No, I fell in some manure fortunately or unfortunately. I have a headache and I shan't want to wear the clothes again. I've left them out by the side door so would you mind asking Arthur to have them burnt?'

'No doubt they'd clean, Mrs Walton.'

'They smell so horrible, I'd be aware of it even if they were cleaned.'

'It's a shame to have them burnt.'

'If you know anybody who would like them, they're welcome to them.'

'Well, thanks, Mrs Walton. Mi niece 'elps out at the stables. I think they might just fit 'er and she'd be that thrilled.'

'I'd like a cup of tea, but nothing to eat.'

'Right you are. You go and rest yourself. I'll bring your tea when it's ready.'

Barbara had to admit that she'd been lucky – she could quite easily have died in the horse's mad rush across the fields and fences. There were bruises on both wrists but the worst of her sufferings was her splitting headache which was getting worse rather than better.

Martin occasionally suffered from migraine and she knew he had some excellent tablets which the doctor had prescribed, but he probably had them with him. She lay on the couch with her eyes closed, but the headache refused to go away. Instead, it seemed to intensify and, unable to bear the pain, she went upstairs and looked in the bathroom and the drawers in both the bedroom and the dressing room, but the tablets were not there.

By now her eyes were refusing to focus, and clinging on to the banister rail she went downstairs and into the kitchen. She took some aspirins but they had little

331

effect. Later, she dragged herself into Martin's study in the hope that there might be some of his tablets in the drawer of his desk.

The study was scrupulously tidy. The bookshelves were neat, the top of the desk furnished with a clean white blotter on which his paperknife lay, symmetrically placed. It was a subdued clinical room, entirely masculine, furnished in good taste with a deep olive-green carpet and cream leather upholstery, solid elm furniture and Martin's large functional desk with its twin telephones and neatly stacked stationery box.

She opened the middle drawer of his desk and to her relief a half-filled bottle of tablets stared up at her.

It could be a little early to take some other drug after the aspirins, so she laid her head on the blotter and closed her eyes, wishing that Martin was coming home, wishing she wasn't so alone. Her head throbbed mercilessly while her fingers clutched the bottle.

She had no idea how long she remained there, semi-conscious, but suddenly she was aware that the pain was receding: the aspirins were working, after all. She sat quietly, not daring to move, and now the pain in her head was just a dull ache and her eyes focused on the contours of the room and the leaves tossing gently against the window.

It was bearable now and Martin had once warned her that his tablets were very strong and must not be taken for a normal headache. She opened the top lefthand drawer to put them back, then curiosity got the better of her. The drawer was tidy, filled with folders containing correspondence, innumerable pencils and pens, rubber bands and staples, then she opened the drawers beneath it. Files were neatly docketed, along with reference books and road maps, then in the bottom drawer were balls of string and a tape recorder.

She turned her attention to the other side and here she suffered a setback, for the top drawer was locked.

332

She searched for a key but realized that Martin must have it with him. Then she remembered the box of spare keys in the dressing room and she made her way back there.

The small leather box was filled with keys so she took it back with her, trying first one and then the other until she was rewarded by a sudden click which told her she'd found the right one.

Again the drawer was filled with folders but then she began to realize that these had nothing to do with his work. They were filled with letters about his boat, bills from restaurants around Southampton, meals at the yacht club – and some photographs.

For several minutes she stared at them blankly, then her heart started to race. She knew some of the faces in those photographs, but the women she didn't know, standing around in groups, laughing, calling to each other, Martin happy and laughing wearing a yachting cap and reefer jacket, his arm round a girl who was looking up at him adoringly.

Barbara sat back, stunned, then after a few minutes she rummaged in the drawer again and brought out other photographs of Martin and the same girl, taken near the car, outside some inn, on the downs, but mostly with the boats, sometimes the yacht, sometimes the speedboat, but always with the same girl.

Barbara studied her face. She was pretty, but not the sort of girl she'd ever have thought Martin would be interested in. She wasn't exactly a fashion-plate as her skirt was too short, her shoes cheap and fashionable and her hair a mess. All the same, her face was alive and piquant and there was no disguising how she felt about Martin.

She studied her husband's face. When he looked at the girl there was no yearning in his face like there was in hers, he was simply happy. He found her amusing and companionable. He liked her.

With shaking fingers Barbara replaced the photographs in their folders and locked the drawer, then sat back in Martin's chair, trembling with anger. How dared he go off on his own to Southampton half a dozen times a year to be with this girl? How dared he tell her wives were no longer welcome? Of course they weren't, not when there was a string of dollies waiting for the men at the other end!

If he'd walked through the door at that moment she could cheerfully have killed him. It was only later when she knelt on the rug in front of the fire with the tears streaming down her face that she faced the truth. Martin had lied to her, he'd cheated her over this girl, but hadn't she done the same thing?

She knew Martin too well. He wouldn't put his marriage, his job, his entire life in jeopardy for any little light of love he'd happened to meet on his travels. Martin wasn't the sort of man to think all was well lost in the cause of love; he wouldn't leave her any more than Mark would leave Amelia.

In the days that followed Barbara planned her strategy. At first she couldn't wait for him to get home so that she could confront him with her suspicions, but as the days passed she found herself feeling reluctant to admit that she'd been prying into his desk.

Instead she telephoned Joan Forbes, inviting her casually to have lunch with her in Cheltenham. They chatted amicably about things in general, then Joan went on about her children until Barbara said anxiously, 'Don't you get fed up when the men are away in Southampton? I know I do. Besides, some of my friends are saying my life seems to be changing because Martin and I are apart so often. Conferences used to be a bore, but there's nothing to say we couldn't go. We could visit the shops and there are some very interesting places in the area. What do you think?'

'We'd have to pay for ourselves. The syndicate wouldn't pay for us if wives are taboo.'

'I'm quite prepared to pay for myself, and Martin would foot the bill anyway. What do you do when Justin's away?'

'Oh, the usual things. In summer I play tennis and a little golf. It's not so bad when the children are home on holiday but I must confess I get a bit lonely when I'm on my own.'

'Well, of course you do, and so do I. We wouldn't be in the way if we went with them, and it might make them realize that we do have some claim on their time and attention.'

'I shall mention it to Justin when he comes home.'

'Do that, Joan, and I'll do the same with Martin. Don't be put off, I know I won't be.'

She was over the first hurdle. She had to see this girl for herself: she felt sure that even if she went to the conference with him, Martin would make some excuse to see her, and she'd keep her eyes and ears open.

When Martin arrived home bronzed and happy on the Sunday afternoon, Barbara was waiting for him. She'd cooked his favourite food and she'd set the table with candlelight falling on polished glass and silver so that when he saw it he raised his eyebrows in surprise.

'Is it something special?' he asked cautiously. 'Something I should have remembered?'

'Of course it's something special, darling. You're home and I've missed you. Did you have a good conference?'

'Oh yes, excellent. What did you do with yourself?'

'I helped Lucy at the stables and I wrote to people I haven't seen for ages. Mother phoned, she thinks we should drive up to see them soon. I said we would.'

'I don't know when, you know how busy I am.'

'I told her so, but Dad's got some new clubs he wants you to look at and we could drive on from there and

335

spend a few days with your parents in the Lakes. Oh, and I telephoned Joan Forbes so we met one day and had lunch together.'

'That's nice.'

She'd known Martin would be mellow. He'd have enjoyed his time in Southampton with the girl who made him feel ten feet tall, and he'd be in the mood to listen to her. By the time they'd eaten their exquisitely cooked meal and he'd drunk several glasses of wine followed by some of his favourite brandy she thought she might never have a better opportunity to tell him she was going to Southampton the next time he went there.

If she hadn't been inwardly warned, the look on his face would have been comical. 'But none of the wives go, Barbara. I told you that when Southampton was first mooted.'

'I know you did, darling, and I'm not asking the syndicate to pay my expenses. I can pay for myself.'

'I couldn't allow you to do that, but you'd feel awfully out of place, on your own.'

'I don't intend to be on my own. Joan will be there.'

'I honestly don't think it's a good idea, Barbara. I don't suppose Justin will, either.'

'If Joan and I make the effort, it might make the syndicate think twice about banning all wives.'

'I doubt it.'

'Well, we're going, and besides, I want to take a look at those two boats of yours. I've had a lot of time to think about things while I've been here on my own and I've come to the conclusion that I've been selfish. Marian Trainer lost her husband because she didn't like the things he liked and because he was away a lot and she never went with him. I don't want to lose you, Martin. It would be the end of my world if I did.'

She made herself sip her wine normally although she knew his eyes were on her, then after a few moments he said quietly, 'How have you been selfish, Barbara?'

336

'I've been selfish about your boats. I knew you enjoy sailing, and I could have made a little more effort.'

'You either like it or you don't.'

'I could enjoy sailing in the Lake District and your father would be delighted. It would mean they'd see more of us.'

He decided not to take her up on the subject of the boats, but she knew she had disconcerted him by his heightened colour and the awareness in his eyes when they met her bland expression.

Joan Forbes telephoned her the following day to say Justin hadn't taken to the idea but she'd convinced him it was the right thing to do. Barbara was left wondering if Justin too had a woman friend in Southampton but she'd leave Joan to fight her own battles; it was sufficient that she'd got her as an ally.

Life took up its familiar pattern and nothing more was said until Martin announced casually at the beginning of June, 'I'm off to Southampton in two weeks' time. I don't suppose you've given any more thought to going with me – it's hardly your cup of tea, Barbara.'

'But of course I've given it some thought. Joan is going with Justin and I am going with you. When the other men see us it might conceivably nudge their memory that they too have wives.'

He wasn't pleased but offered no further comment. Now there was only Mark to appease.

He telephoned her several days later, his voice tantalisingly sexy. 'Have you given much thought to where you want to go for those few days we're let off the leash?' he enquired confidently.

'I'm sorry, Mark, I'm going to Southampton with Martin this time. I couldn't get out of it.'

For a few moments there was silence and even across the miles she sensed his displeasure, before he said lightly, 'I thought a wife was persona non grata on these occasions.'

'Not at this one. Apparently they've relented.'

'And you want to go?'

'Don't you do things with Amelia that you have to do, regardless of whether you enjoy them or not?'

He laughed. 'All the time, love, all the time. Oh well, if we can't meet I suppose we can't. I'll be in touch.'

His voice was offhand but Barbara had always known which line she would take when the chips were down. She'd reached a crossroad in her life and only Martin was real. She wanted him back, exclusively her own, not somebody she was going to share with another woman at regular intervals throughout the year. Her affair with Mark she deemed as transient as a butterfly. It had been exciting, passionate and provocative but to rely on Mark was like building a house with sand.

CHAPTER 32

Barbara had not missed the surprised and knowing glances of Martin's and Justin's colleagues as she and Joan took their place in the dining room of the Southampton hotel. She also noticed that after their meal the men left surreptitiously, one by one, no doubt to keep a longstanding appointment with the girls.

Martin and Justin talked business while she and Joan discussed where they would go the following day. On the drive down Martin had been quiet and she knew he was worried. He'd probably promised to meet the girl in the evening but now it wouldn't be possible, and Barbara sat outwardly serene and unconcerned, yet inwardly enjoying his discomfort.

'What do you usually do in the evenings?' she asked innocently.

'Talk shop most of the time,' Justin put in quietly. 'What would you girls like to do?'

'We don't really mind, do we, Joan? What has happened to the others – they appear to have beaten a hasty retreat.'

'Oh, they'll probably be in the public bar. There's more going on in there than here.'

'Well, we don't mind if you prefer to go in there.'

'Oh, you wouldn't like it, the cocktail bar is much nicer,' Justin insisted, and Martin remained silent, playing with the stem of his glass.

She was accustomed to Martin's silences – there had been a great many of them recently – but when his eyes met hers across the table he smiled, and her eyes lit up with a sudden warmth.

Martin couldn't understand Barbara these days. She

was sweeter, not so abrasive as she'd been in recent years, and they'd talked more and argued less. He couldn't understand her sudden interest in his boats nor her desire to have them taken up to the Lakes, but not for a single moment did he think she knew about Sandra – how could she?

Those photographs had been locked in his desk and she never went into his study anyway. She wasn't one to pry into his desk, for as long as he was making money she'd never been unduly concerned about how he made it.

He'd destroyed the photographs recently, anyway. True, they'd been safely hidden away, but he shuddered to think what would have happened had Barbara come across them. She had a temper and there would have been such a scene he wouldn't have been allowed to forget it in a hurry.

Sandra would be in the public bar with her friends now, waiting for him to join her. The other men would tell her that his wife was with him and she'd go away after a while, probably rather hurt and miserably aware of the others' sympathy.

He loved Barbara, of course he did, but in the public bar there would be laughter and the carefree camaraderie of men and women who met so seldom there had not been time to become bored with each other. Sandra was a nice girl, not one to demand the earth and touchingly grateful for his small gifts and the time she spent in his company.

He wished he could make an excuse to see her for just a few minutes to explain, but he knew it wasn't possible. She'd asked him never to telephone her at the shop, as private calls were frowned upon, and on the one occasion he'd telephoned her at home a man had answered and informed him tersely that Sandra was out. He'd have a word with Sam; Sam would tell her he'd been asking about her. The man was a rough

diamond but he possessed a rugged kindness underneath his brash exterior. He wished he'd had the
foresight to write to Sandra but right until the last
moment he'd thought Barbara would cry off, then in
the week leading up to the conference he'd been too
busy. He had to admit that cowardice lay at the bottom
of it – that, and the knowledge that Sandra would
undoubtedly be miserable and hurt.

The Waltons retired soon after ten and Martin said
feelingly, 'I'm sure you're bored out of your skin by all
this, Barbara. It's not much fun for you and Joan.'

'On the contrary, darling, it's a very nice change.
Still, I've been to rather better hotels for your past
conferences – have you considered a different venue?
I'm sure you're fed up with this hotel by now and in
future wherever it is Joan and I intend to be with you.'

At that moment Martin made up his mind that the
next conference would not be held in Southampton;
they'd find somewhere else.

Sandra Stubbs had never felt so wretched in her entire
life. She sat with her friends in the public bar and
watched as one by one the men joined them, but there
was no Martin. Instead Sam said, 'Martin's got his wife
in tow, love, along with Justin's wife. I reckon you two
girls'll be keeping each other company tonight.'

Enid Watson had not been Justin's girl, just one of
many he'd been friendly with during his time in Southampton, whereas Martin had always singled Sandra out.
She didn't know Enid very well, but she wished she
could treat Martin's absence with the same cheerfulness.

Sam sensed her misery and sat beside her. 'Gettin'
quite fond of him, were you, love?' he asked gently.

She didn't answer, but her eyes filled with tears and
patting her hand he said, 'He's not the chap for you,
duck. You liked him because he's different and you
were thrilled with his boats and his car. You're a pretty

girl and there'll be somebody else for you, somebody a lot better than Martin Walton.'

She managed a wobbly smile. 'I've seen her photograph, but what is she really like?' she asked curiously.

'Well now, Barbara's smart and good-looking, but not a bit prettier than you. I reckon she feels he's been let off the leash long enough and she's here to keep her eye on him.'

'She doesn't know about me, does she?' Sandra asked sharply.

'Of course not, but she's probably a bit fed up with being left on her own while he's down here. I reckon Justin's wife and herself decided enough was enough – wouldn't you have felt the same in her place?'

'I expect so.'

'Well now, just have a drink with me and forget about Martin. You'll soon find somebody else and you know, love, if you're honest with yourself, you and Martin didn't have a future together.'

She understood the logic of his words but the misery was still there. She'd been so looking forward to seeing him again. There'd never been anybody like Martin, and at that moment she didn't think there ever would be. She felt humiliated by the sympathy of her friends and Sam's kindness. He was making himself attentive in an effort to cheer her up, but he was no substitute for Martin and in all probability he would rather be propping the bar up chatting to the barman than entertaining her.

She still felt curious about Martin's wife. Perhaps one day if she hung around the hotel there would be a chance that she might see her.

Two days later Barbara sat in the lounge waiting for Martin to join her. They were sitting late in the Conference Hall and Joan had a sick headache and decided she didn't want to dine. Barbara passed the time reading the evening paper and was surprised when a man

342

approached her with a bright smile saying, 'Good evening, Mrs Walton. All alone then?'

She smiled faintly, recognising him now as one of the men at the conference, a rather common little fellow, not the usual type she'd become accustomed to over the years.

Sam was well aware of her thoughts but, undeterred, he took the seat next to hers. 'I got browned off listening to the same old arguments. They'll be no nearer a solution even if they are sitting late,' he said comfortably. 'Enjoying yourself then, Mrs Walton? You're not finding it dull?'

'Not at all. I can usually amuse myself.'

'The name's Sam Barber, by the way. I'm from Barnsley.'

Barbara smiled. 'Won't you be missed in there, Mr Barber?'

'Shouldn't think so. They're used to my slipping off when I get fed up. I'll hear all about it from one or another of them. I expect this'll be the last time we'll be meeting here in Southampton,' he volunteered.

'Why do you say that?'

'Well, now that you ladies have decided to tag along it'll be London or Edinburgh, perhaps Torquay. My wife might just like that.'

'Do you think wives have no place at a conference, Mr Barber?' Barbara asked with a slight smile on her face.

'Nay, I've not said that, have I? My wife's only been with me to one and that was at Harrogate. She went off on coach tours during the day and she liked the shops. She's a bit of a home bird really, considers the kids too much as well as her mother. You don't have a family, Mrs Walton?'

'No.'

'Them's two bonnie boats Martin has in the harbour here. Are you fond of sailin' yourself?'

'I think I could be, but not here. Martin's parents live in the Lake District and it makes more sense to keep the boats there. In any case, what does he want with two of them?'

Sam permitted himself a small smile – here was a lady accustomed to getting her own way. My, but she was a smasher, beautiful, sophisticated, all the things little Sandra wasn't, but he had no doubt which one would be the most comfortable to be with. Sandra'd been good for Martin. She'd made him laugh, knocked some of that pomposity out of him, made him appreciate things this lady'd left behind her a long time ago.

He looked up to see Martin leaving the Conference Hall in the company of a group of the others, shuffling their papers, still arguing, and turning to Barbara he said, 'Here he is, Mrs Walton. Will you be going straight in to dinner or will you join me for a drink?'

'No, thank you, Mr Barber. I seldom drink before my evening meal but please don't let that stop you.'

'Well, I like my drinks in the public bar after dinner. It's a bit too stuffy in here and there's considerably more life in there. Why don't you and Martin join us later?'

Their eyes met and in his she read a certain malicious amusement: he was well aware that she knew about Martin's lady friend. Then Martin was with them and Sam grinned. 'Well, Martin – are you any nearer a solution after all this time?'

'I'm afraid not, it was the usual waste of time. Too many arguments, not enough resolutions.'

'That's what I thought. Will you and your good wife be joining us in the public bar for a last drink?'

'I doubt it. I have a little work to do tonight and I'm afraid all this has been very boring for Barbara.'

'Then perhaps Mrs Walton would like to join me while you get on with your work.'

Barbara did not miss the fleeting look of alarm on Martin's face, nor the glee on Sam's.

'Thank you, Mr Barber,' she said easily. 'I've promised myself an early night and I have packing to

344

do. We're leaving in the morning. What time *are* we leaving?' she asked Martin on their way upstairs.

'Well, actually, I want to go down to Langstone in the morning. I've been having thoughts about the boats. Perhaps I'll put a few feelers out about selling the power boat.'

'Won't you mind?'

'I'll keep the yacht.'

'Here in Southampton?'

'No, I'll probably have it taken to the Lakes.'

She permitted herself a small smile. She had won the first hurdle.

Later that evening as she packed her suitcase Martin made an excuse to go down to the Conference Hall where he said he had left some papers. Barbara knew quite well he was hoping to see Sandra and when he returned she said casually, 'Do you want me to drive down to Langstone with you? I do have a little last-minute shopping to do.'

'You carry on with your shopping, dear. I'll drop you in the town.'

He was unusually thoughtful as he drove her into Southampton the following morning, dropping her close to the shops. She waited until his car had disappeared down the road before turning down a side street and entering a garage with an array of parked cars on the forecourt.

She chose to hire a modest inconspicuous grey Ford Escort and the young man who handed over the keys watched her drive away before turning to another young man busily engaged in polishing a new vehicle.

'She looked more like a Ferrari than an Escort, Matt,' he said cheerfully.

'She's up at the Headlands with a conference group – her husband drives a new Jaguar.'

'What do you reckon she's doin' with that Escort, then?'

Matt shrugged his shoulders. 'He's probably golfing.'

345

Unaware of their interest Barbara drove through the town until she hit the Portsmouth Road and the signposts for Southsea. She was unfamiliar with Langstone but after making several enquiries soon found herself driving towards the harbour where she could now plainly see the stretch of water and its flotilla of boats. She pulled the car into the side of the road and waited. She had driven quickly and it was possible Martin had not yet arrived. Ten minutes passed, and then through her mirror she saw the long dark green Jaguar coming slowly down the lane. She turned her head away until it had passed, then slowly she followed in its wake.

He drove into a parking lot near one of the boathouses, and she stood on the harbour wall watching while he walked towards the slipway. With him was a woman tripping lightly by his side. They were chatting amicably together and she saw him take her arm to help her down a flight of stone steps.

Anger filled Barbara's being. She wanted to run after them, screaming abuse, raking her long crimson nails across the girl's pretty insipid face. She watched as a small power boat left the harbour wall and made for the yachts anchored out at sea. She had little doubt at all about how they intended to spend the rest of their morning, and felt physically sick at the pictures her thoughts conjured up.

Later that afternoon, Barbara and Martin drove home to Cheltenham in a summer storm, which exactly matched her mood.

Long grey fingers of rain raked from leaden skies, and the fleeting bright glimpses of a watery sun came and went almost unnoticed. The pattering of rain on the roof of the car, the hypnotic effect of the wipers, the steady throb of the engine held her in a trancelike state, and beside her Martin remained silent, concentrating on the road ahead.

346

His thoughts were anything but serene. Sandra had clung to him, tears streaming down her face, begging him to see her again, it didn't matter where, but some time in the future. She was desolate when he told her that he was selling one boat and taking the other away. She knew it was the end of the road.

They had made love in the narrow bunk, and later she'd sat huddled in his towelling robe while he'd searched through the drawers for things he wanted to take away. He'd been very aware of her tear-stained face, her shaking hands as she cupped them round the mug of coffee he'd made for her.

He'd become very fond of her, she was a nice girl, but this was where it had to end. There were Barbara and her parents, his parents, and their friends. There was too much at stake and it wasn't as though he hadn't spelt it out for her that first day. All the same, he knew in the years to come he'd think of her a great deal. Apart from his wife she was the only woman he'd ever cared for. Other chaps he knew had women all over the place and he'd always felt rather sorry for them and superior, but now he understood them better. With a bevy of women it was easier not to get too attached to one.

He stole a look at Barbara sitting next to him. She'd been quiet all over lunch and she'd hardly spoken on the journey. She'd probably been bored out of her skin but she couldn't say he hadn't warned her. He'd telephone Justin and Joan when they got home to invite them over to dinner one day next week. Barbara would like that.

It was late when they reached Cheltenham. He'd suggested calling in somewhere for a meal but she said she wasn't hungry so he drove on, faintly puzzled by her manner.

He dropped her at the front door, then after taking in the luggage he went to put the car away.

347

There was a pile of mail in the hall and casually he leafed through it, picking out envelopes which looked important, calling to Barbara who was in the kitchen, 'There's a letter here from your parents. I recognized your mother's writing.'

She came back into the hall and he held out the envelope to her.

Plaintive as usual, her mother said her arthritis hadn't been too good lately and she had to go into hospital for a suspected kidney stone. She hoped Barbara would manage to stay with them. Her mother's letters always meandered from one subject to the next – her friends, her activities and her ailments – and Barbara laid it down on the hall table and walked slowly into the lounge.

Martin stared after her, a puzzled frown on his brow, then picking up his mail he followed her.

She had turned on the gas fire, and stood on the hearth-rug looking down at it, her face unusually pensive.

'Not bad news from your mother, I hope,' he said quietly.

'She's not well. She wants me to go up and stay for a while.'

'Well, why don't you? I can get along quite well, and I can always eat at the club.'

'What a pity your Southampton girlfriend doesn't live nearer. She'd give you all the solace you'd need in my absence.'

He stared at her dumbstruck, and she was looking at him with narrowed eyes, eyes that were always greener when she was in a temper. He made no effort to defend himself, instead he waited, unsure of what was coming next.

'I followed you this morning, Martin. I saw you with that girl, I saw you go to your boat. I can only guess what you were doing there.'

'I can see that you've condemned me without asking any questions,' he said quietly.

348

'I guessed there was somebody. All those conferences without wives, always in the same city, and then I saw the others disappearing into the public bar night after night and I guessed what they were up to, what *you'd* been up to.'

An expression of distaste passed across his face and Barbara longed to scream at him, 'All right it sounds crude, but it's not half as crude as the reality!' Instead she went over to the cocktail cabinet and poured herself a large whisky.

Then turning to face him again she said, 'Are you in love with her?'

'Well, of course not.'

She smiled mockingly. 'Of course you don't need to be in love with her, do you, as long as she was there to be made love to. Is there any chance you'd have asked me for a divorce if it had gone on any longer?'

'I don't want a divorce. I don't suppose I'll ever see her again.'

'You've made that plain to her, have you, or have you only just decided?'

'She knows this morning was our last meeting.'

'Did you meet her at the hotel?'

'Yes. Sam got us all together in the bar one evening. It started out very innocently. I took her out for a few meals – I bought her a few presents – I never wanted it to go beyond that.'

'Who is she?'

'Her name is Sandra Stubbs. She works in one of the city shops, she's a nice girl.'

'Is that something I should be thankful for, when so many men go off with trollops?'

'It wasn't planned, it was simply something we drifted into, something that is over. Please believe that, Barbara.'

She shrugged her shoulders. 'As I feel at the moment I don't want to be with you, Martin. I don't trust you

349

any more. I'm going north to stay with my parents and I don't know when I'm coming back, if at all.'

She saw the sudden spasm of fear cross his face and he came quickly to take her in his arms. She held back, silently punishing him, relishing the desperate fear in his eyes.

'Barbara, you can't leave me! We've been together a long time, and there's never really been anybody but you. I swear nothing like this will ever happen again.'

'I'd like to believe you, Martin.'

'Barbara, I mean it! I liked her, I never loved her. There was never a single moment when I thought she could take your place.'

'I need some time to think. I want to go home. Perhaps surrounded by familiar sights and sounds I can forgive you, I don't know.'

'Give me a few days and I'll come with you.'

'I don't want you to come with me. I'm not ready to forgive you yet and I don't want anybody asking questions when I can't bear to be near you.'

'But without you I'll be worried to death. I'll be thinking all sorts of terrible things – that you're never coming back, that it's over between us.'

'That's too bad, Martin. How do you think I felt when I saw you with that girl? Don't you think you deserve to suffer? Surely you don't think I can just brush it on one side as if it never happened!'

He had the grace to look contrite. He reached out to draw her close but she moved away. '*No.*'

'Will you telephone me when you get to your parents' house?'

'I'll telephone you some time, when I've had time to think. I'll get off early in the morning, I won't bother to let them know I'm coming.'

He watched her go with a feeling of utter desolation. Nothing that had happened between Sandra and himself had been worth this.

350

CHAPTER 33

It was several years since Barbara had spent longer than a couple of days in Greymont, but her mother was having treatment for her kidney stone and she seemed to have aged a great deal in recent months.

Martin had loaded her luggage into the boot of her car, and she'd offered him a cool cheek for his kiss. She had deliberately not looked at him, for she knew what she would have seen – that miserable little-boy face, and dark eyes pleading for her forgiveness.

He pressed a twenty-pound note into her hand, saying, 'Get your mother some flowers, Barbara, and let me know if there's anything else she would like.'

'You're not usually so solicitous about my mother,' she'd commented cynically.

'Well, she is an invalid. I hope I've always been a dutiful son-in-law.'

That was when she did look at him, disconcerting him utterly by saying calmly, 'You were a dutiful husband too, Martin, even when you were having it off with that little shop-girl.'

Without another word she slid into the driving seat of her car while he stepped back to watch her drive away. Through her mirror she could see that he stood outside the house until she reached the end of the drive, but not once did she pause to wave to him.

She called in the town for the flowers and later when she handed them to her mother saying they were from Martin, Mrs Smythe said cuttingly, 'Flowers are all very well, and it's kind of Martin to think of me, but he could have driven up for a few days. After all, it's not much to ask.'

351

'A couple of hours and he could be here,' her father agreed caustically. 'Is he coming up at the weekend?'

'I don't think you've ever liked Martin, Dad,' she replied without answering his question.

'I like him well enough when I see him.'

In spite of his irritation with Martin, her father was glad to have her with them on her own. She pandered to her mother's whims and fancies, walked with him across the golf course and in the evenings after her mother had gone to bed she played chess with him like she had often done as a child.

She relieved her father of the shopping, took her mother to the hospital for check-ups and welcomed Mrs Smythe's visitors with charm and hospitality.

As the days passed it seemed to Barbara that she had never been away from Greymont. She had just driven her father to one of his Council meetings and after parking her car saw Maisie Standing rushing across the square holding the hand of a young girl. She waited until Maisie reached her, thinking she seemed particularly harassed with her coat flying in the wind and a silk headscarf covering her hair.

Maisie smiled breathlessly. 'I heard you were up here lookin' after your mother. How is she?'

'Much better, thank you.'

'You'll soon be goin' back, then?'

'One of these days. Is this your youngest child?'

'Yes, our Lucy. I'm late for her dental appointment and I'm at the court this afternoon. I'm a Magistrate now, you know.'

'Yes, my mother told me.'

'Is Martin with you?'

'No. He was too busy. How is Tom, and your other children?'

'Tom's very fit and the farm's doin' well. Our Peter's got a place at Cambridge and our Alice is at Lorivals.'

'Glutton for punishment, are you?'

Maisie grinned. 'If you're ever up on the fell you're very welcome to visit.'

'Thank you, it will depend how long I'm here for. Do you ever see Amelia?'

'I see her at the court, but of course we don't get much time for chatting there.'

'And Amelia was never one for small-talk, was she?'

'Well, no. I'll mention to her that I've seen you in the town. Please tell your mother I'm glad she's feeling better.'

Barbara watched her dragging Lucy across the town hall square. The girl was pretty, and obviously reluctant to keep her dental appointment, but somehow or other Maisie never changed. Barbara thought she'd look exactly the same when she was seventy.

She finished her shopping then went into the post office, relieved to see that there was an empty telephone booth, hoping against hope that it would be Mark who answered and not his agent.

His voice was curt. 'Mark Garveston speaking,' and as curtly she replied, 'Mark, this is Barbara. I have to see you, it's very important. I'm in Greymont.'

'Barbara,' he echoed with wary surprise, and she thought angrily, Gracious me, surely he doesn't think I've come here to break up his happy home! They'd always said they would keep their longstanding affair quite separate from their marriages and homes, so surely he wasn't thinking she was out to break that promise?

'Is Martin up here with you?' he asked cautiously.

'No. I'm here alone to look after my mother. When can we meet?'

'Well, I'm not sure. I should go over to Ripon this afternoon and I'm tied up in the morning.'

'Would you like me to put it in writing?'

'Now you're being sarcastic.'

'It's imperative that I see you, Mark. I'll leave it up

to you to say when and where but I'd like it to be as soon as possible.'

'Very well, I'll skip Ripon. How about this afternoon?'

'Where?'

'On the fell where we met once before. You can leave your car in that clearing at the bottom and I'll wait for you near the Cross.'

'Very well, Mark. I'll be there around two.'

How cold and terse it all was, as much on her part as his. It seemed incredible that all that passion and loving had come to this, a casual meeting on the hillside that would finally end it.

She'd seldom walked on the fells as a child, she had always been a townie at heart and she found herself hating the sharp wind that tore at her hair and her skirt.

Mark was waiting for her near the Pilgrims' Cross and at that moment the years slipped away and it seemed like that first moment when she'd walked towards him across the short springing grass and into his life. Now he didn't attempt to take her in his arms, but fell into step beside her leading his horse. They walked towards the summit from where she could look down on the tall chimneys of Lorivals and for a moment her face was reflective. It was then that Mark placed both his hands on her shoulders and looked anxiously into her eyes.

'Now what is all this, Barbara? What has happened?'

Swiftly she told him about finding the photographs of the girl and all that had transpired in Southampton, and with her telling came all her anger, her sense of betrayal, until Mark amazed her by throwing back his head and laughing loud and long.

Angrily she pulled herself away from him, her green eyes glinting dangerously. 'I'm glad you can find it so amusing,' she said icily.

354

Composing his merriment he said evenly, 'Come on, Barbara. You've cheated on Martin for years and now because he's played you at your own game you're affronted. What a bloody little hypocrite you are.'

She stared at him, stupefied, too angry to find words, then her expression changed and she was angry with him for being right.

Tears of resentment filled her eyes as she turned away. She went to stand where the ground fell away and giant crags crowned the summit of the hill. Mark stayed where he was, reluctant to follow her until she was in the mood to think straight.

Crossly, she wiped the tears from her eyes. She felt suddenly alone and vulnerable. The cold sharp wind stirred the bracken, filling her nostrils with its pungent scent, and overhead two gulls sailed effortlessly on the wind. She was acutely aware of Mark's horse champing the grass and her lover's impassive stance as he leaned against the crag watching her with narrowed eyes.

She turned and walked back to him. He wasn't yet sure why she'd needed to see him so urgently but not, he hoped, to reassure herself that he would be there to pick up the pieces.

He had to know however, and he posed the question lightly even when her answer was important to him.

'You haven't left him, I hope. A man's allowed one mistake, surely?'

'I told him I was coming home to think about it. I haven't seen him or spoken to him for weeks. I told him to leave me alone until I've sorted it all out in my mind.'

'And he's done as you asked?'

'Yes.'

'And have you sorted it out in your mind?'

'I wasn't going to forgive him immediately. I wanted to make him stew before I forgave him.'

'I take it it's over between this woman and himself?'

355

'Yes. There will be no more conferences in Southampton, no more conferences where I can't go with him.'

'What was she like, your rival?'

'Younger than me. Pretty, but not the sort of woman Martin would want to be married to. She worked in some shop or other in Southampton, hardly the type to run his home and entertain his guests.'

'So you really didn't have anything to worry about?'

'Well, of course I did! I couldn't let it go on, Mark.'

'Are you going to tell me how I come into all this?'

'I had to tell you that it's over between us. There will be no more meetings. As far as we're concerned it's over.'

Relief flooded his being, relief tinged with regret. Barbara wanted no commitment from him; he should have known that she was not the woman to make demands simply because her own world had crumbled. And yet he'd miss her, that vitally passionate woman who hid beneath the cool efficient Barbara.

And Martin, he'd always thought old Martin was a one-woman man, a little dull perhaps, a little bit stodgy, but oh so honourable. He pulled himself together when he realized that she was staring at him, waiting for his answer.

He'd told her years before that they were both alike – selfish and greedy, obsessed with the excitement of the moment, so sure that they could have their cake and eat it. Now her secure beautiful world had been shaken, and like a lost child she'd run home to lick her wounds and make Martin suffer.

'I'm going to miss you like the very devil, Barbara,' he said feelingly. 'Won't Martin think it rather funny that I don't come down for the Gold Cup any more?'

'Oh you'll come back, not next year perhaps but the year after when I've got you out of my system.'

'Is that all the time it will take?'

'You'll be over me long before that. I have no

illusions about you, Mark. You're probably already thinking about my replacement.'

He reached out then and pulled her into the circle of his arms, standing with his chin on her hair. For the first time there was kindness in his embrace, kindness without passion, and she knew she was going to miss him too, his humour and his audacity. Dear serious Martin would never give her the sheer excitement she'd experienced at being with Mark, but Martin was reality, Mark was thistledown.

As if he read her thoughts Mark said lightly, 'Don't make him suffer too long, my dear. Don't risk sending him back to her.'

That night she telephoned Martin after her parents had gone to bed. His voice was cautious, unsure, waiting for her to tell him what she had decided to do.

'Martin, I've decided to come home. Being apart like this is solving nothing.'

'When are you coming home?'

'On Friday. I've promised to take Mother to see some friends tomorrow. We've both had some time to think things over. Do you want me to come home?'

'You know very well I do.'

'And we'll never talk about it, simply get on with our lives?'

'If that's what you want, Barbara. Have you told your mother?'

'My mother is the last person I would tell. She'd never let us forget it, never. I'll be home around four in the afternoon, Martin, so I'll see you at dinner.'

'Yes, of course. I love you, Barbara,' he said after a few minutes' silence, then there was another silence waiting for her answer.

'Thank you, Martin. I want to believe you. I love you too.'

She replaced the receiver on its hook, then with a small smile on her face she walked slowly up the stairs.

357

CHAPTER 34

The clamour of Cairo had been left behind and Nancy stood at last on her balcony at the Mena House Hotel looking out at the majesty of the pyramids on the edge of the vast Sahara. The cool desert breeze fanned her cheek, and because they were floodlit, the pyramids dominated the hotel and its gardens, their perfect shapes standing out in sharp contrast to the midnight blue of the jewelled sky.

She had hoped there would be mail waiting for her at the hotel but there was none, apart from a sum of money sent by Noel and deposited for her in the hotel safe. The sum was generous in the extreme, sufficient for her to see as much of Egypt as she wanted.

From somewhere in the hotel she could hear dance music, and from the gardens below there came occasional laughter and the aroma of cigar smoke. Tomorrow she would get her first glimpse of the other guests enjoying the hospitality of the hotel and she realized with something like shock that apart from her colleagues she had had very little conversation with other Europeans for many months.

It seemed the following morning that she was the only person eating alone. At the surrounding tables families chatted together, lovers held hands and at the next table, an American lady dining with a young man smiled at her in a friendly way.

It was Nancy's idea that she would explore the area around the pyramids and for this purpose she had donned her faded blue trousers and cotton shirt. Her attire was functional and businesslike but she began to doubt her choice when she saw some of the elegant

358

sun-dresses worn by some of the women. She was very gratified a few moments later when the American lady said, 'I've been thinking how sensible you are to wear what you're wearing. I got terribly burnt the first day I was here in a dress.'

'Thank you so much,' Nancy said smiling. 'I was just beginning to doubt my choice.'

'My name's Judith Palmer, I'm from Florida and this is my son Justin.'

Nancy encountered them again later in the morning when she strolled towards the base of the sphinx and spotted Mrs Palmer sitting on a large boulder fanning herself. She smiled and Mrs Palmer said amiably, 'I've done enough sightseeing for one morning, it's far too hot. You'd think living in Florida I'd be used to the heat.'

Nancy sat down beside her. 'Your son isn't with you?' she remarked.

'No. He wants to take a horse and ride round the pyramids. Did you go inside them?'

'Inside the second pyramid but I wouldn't advise you to go in if you're at all claustrophobic. I had to walk on all fours for some of the time up a quite narrow passage, and really when you get to the end of it there's only a chamber containing two sarcophagi which were apparently never occupied.'

'Believe me, I don't intend to go inside any one of them. I had enough sightseeing at Luxor to last me a lifetime.'

'But it was very worthwhile, surely?'

'Gracious me yes. It's an experience I'll never forget. Are you travelling alone?'

'Yes. I've been in Israel for the last few months, before that I was in Ethiopia, and where I go from here is anybody's guess.'

'Also on your own?'

'Oh no, there was a team of us. I'm a journalist.'

359

'I see. Ah, here comes Justin now.'

He arrived riding a presentable-looking horse and after greeting Nancy he said boyishly, 'I say, I don't suppose you'd like to come with me? It would be nice to have company.'

'Where did you get your horse?' she asked.

'Take this one, I'll get myself another. You'll be OK while we're gone, Mother?'

'Well, of course I shall – just so long as you don't try to get me on one of those things, or worse still, a camel.'

Together they rode their horses round the base of the Great Pyramid while below them spread the teeming city of Cairo and beyond lay the vast dunes of the Libyan Desert and the broad placid river. From the plateau the medieval city had a fairytale appearance with its array of delicate minarets and domes but Nancy knew that it was the golden glowing light that embellished Cairo's disorder, ignoring its squalor, turning it into a city of enchantment.

'I'm glad I'm staying out here at Heliopolis,' she said. 'Cairo isn't really Egypt. Egypt is the river and the desert – Cairo is just an Arab city.'

He agreed and by the time they rejoined his mother she felt as if she'd known him many years instead of just one morning. He was eager to talk, interested in her and what she'd done, and extremely frank about himself. He'd come to Egypt with his mother because his father had died last year and she didn't want to travel alone, but largely he'd come to forget an unrequited love. Nancy understood that feeling only too well.

In the afternoon they went together to the museum and had an ecstatic time looking at the wonders brought from Tutankhamen's tomb, and by the time they were back on the terrace drinking tea, Justin was looking at Nancy with something rather more intense than friendship.

He was ready to fall in love on the rebound but she was not. He was too young, too eager and when he held her hand and stammered out his sudden yearning for her she smiled gently. 'Don't look for love, Justin. One day it will come again when you're least expecting it. I know it did for me.'

'You're in love with somebody else!' he exclaimed, and she smiled at the 'somebody else' from a man she hadn't known a few days before.

'Yes.'

'Then where is he? Why isn't he here with you?'

'He has work to do.'

'Is he in love with you?'

'I very much doubt it.'

'Then why waste your time on him! You're so beautiful, how can he know you and not love you?'

'And you, Justin, are very young.'

'I'm twenty-five, I don't call that very young. I'd thought to be married this year.'

She was looking away from him, at the early evening mist swirling gently among the palm fronds, drifting towards the great white shapes of the pyramids, and he thought he had never seen anything more beautiful in his life than the haunting curve of her cheek and the pale moonlight illuminating her hair. With all the optimism of youth he believed he could make this beautiful woman love him, but when their eyes met she merely smiled and rising to her feet said, 'I should dress for dinner. Your mother will wonder what has become of you.'

'Oh, she'll be glad to be rid of me, I tire her out. There's a dance here tomorrow evening, will you go with me?'

'Justin, I have nothing to wear for a dance. I haven't danced for ages, and I left all my suitable clothes at home in England. I never needed a ballgown in Israel and anything here will be a very dressed-up affair.'

361

'I don't care what you wear. If you came dressed like that you'd be the most beautiful woman in the ballroom.'

'You know that's not true, you'd hate me to come like this!'

'Can't you get something in the shops tomorrow? You should dance, you should make the most of your time here, please say you'll come.'

His young boy's face was so appealing she hadn't the heart to turn him down. 'If I find something suitable to wear I'll come to the dance with you, Justin, but I'm not hopeful. I know nothing about the shops in Cairo.'

Justin's mother, however, was more than knowledgeable. She advised Nancy to try the shops within the hotels and by the time the evening was over, Nancy believed there was nothing she could say or do to avoid accompanying Justin to the dance in the hotel ballroom. Indeed, Mrs Palmer insisted on going with her to the Cairo Hilton where she was bullied into buying the most beautifully embroidered kaftan. It was a rich peacock blue, embroidered with tiny silver beads and gold thread, and by the time the shop assistant and Mrs Palmer had rhapsodised over it Nancy couldn't do anything else but buy it.

Later in her room she took it out of its box and held it against her. It emphasized the beauty of her eyes but it had been a foolish purchase. The cost was astronomical, and when after tomorrow evening could she ever be expected to wear such a thing? She was in half a mind to take it back, but Justin's mother had already enthused about it to her son, and his delight was too obvious.

'Dine with us tonight,' he urged her. 'Mother's not in the least interested in the dance but she's happy for us to go.'

At that moment two young girls went tripping down the terrace steps in front of them; like two young colts they ran towards the pool, all long slim legs and swinging strands of straight hair, and Nancy said gently, 'The hotel is full of girls like that – why aren't you with one of them?'

'They all remind me of Julie.'

'Is that such a bad thing?'

'They'd only bore me after you. They talk about nothing but enjoying themselves.'

'Isn't that what they're here for?'

'Yes, but they're not interested in culture or history. They should be when they come to Egypt.'

'Justin, how old do you think I am?'

Taken aback a little he said hesitantly, 'I don't know, does it matter?'

'I think it matters a great deal.'

'I don't agree, but I'd guess you were about twenty-eight, no more.'

'And that is the nicest compliment I have ever had paid to me,' she smiled. 'I'm thirty-seven – a lifetime older than you. When I was a young girl I thought I was in love but it was only a voyage of discovery; when I did fall in love I knew the difference. I doubt if love and I are compatible, my love stories are always doomed to failure.'

'This one wouldn't be, Nancy. This one would only bring you happiness.'

'Justin, I'm over ten years older than you. For some people it might work, but I don't think it would for me. In any case, I love somebody else. I don't believe I can forget him as quickly as you appear to have forgotten your Julie.'

His young good-looking face became sulky and she squeezed his hand. 'I've bought my dress, I've promised to go with you to the dance, can't we just enjoy this evening without the complication of love?'

Suddenly he grinned at her. 'You'll come, then?'

'I certainly will.'

363

He drew her into the closeness of his embrace but she avoided his lips, then he let her go and with a gay wave of his hand he ran up the steps towards the hotel.

It was some time before dinner but this was the time of day Nancy loved, when a pale crescent moon shone high in the heavens, when the mist had cleared and the stars seemed so close she felt she could touch them. It was still balmy in the hotel gardens and soon people would be coming in droves from the city to watch the performance of the son et lumière at the pyramids.

They stood illuminated in gentle light, three gigantic perfect structures surrounded by lesser ones, the tombs of the Pharaohs' minions, and then the giant body of the sphinx with its lion's body and human head. The silence of the surrounding desert was profound where Nancy stood out of earshot of the music from the hotel behind her, and she felt the cool wind on her cheeks stirring the folds of her kaftan, bringing with it the faint scent of mimosa and jasmine.

In the distance she heard the rumbling of the first coachload of sightseers and regretfully turned away to walk back to the hotel. Along the path a solitary man walked towards her; he was wearing evening dress, and at first sight she thought it was Justin until he stood for a moment in the light from one of the tall lamps set in the hotel's garden and she gasped with amazement. It was Noel.

He smiled and came forward to meet her, and for a long moment they stood staring into each other's eyes before he reached forward and brought her into the circle of his arms. He bent his head and kissed the top of her hair, then holding her at arm's length he looked down at her and she saw his mouth twitch with momentary amusement.

'I haven't seen you looking so beautiful since that party in Hong Kong all those years ago. You didn't know I was coming so I can't think all this glamour is on my account.'

'Why didn't you let me know you were coming?'

'I thought I'd surprise you. I came equipped as you see. It seemed appropriate to do justice to a first-class hotel. I'm glad you bought that kaftan, Nancy, you look very beautiful.'

'There's a dance at the hotel tonight, I was invited.'

His expression didn't change – if anything, it became more debonair. 'Then please don't let me stop you. Perhaps we can eat dinner together then you can go to your dance and I'll retire. I seem to spend my life travelling these days.'

Nancy clenched her hands in anger. He'd asked no questions about who had invited her to the dance, oh but he was maddening, he obviously didn't care. They fell into step and looking up at his face she could only see that it was serene and untroubled.

As they entered the foyer Justin came forward to meet her and introductions were performed. Justin appeared disconcerted although Noel greeted him charmingly and throughout dinner devoted his attention to Mrs Palmer, who appeared to find him irresistible.

Immediately after dinner he excused himself on the grounds of feeling weary. Mrs Palmer settled down in the hotel lounge to read her book and Nancy went with Justin into the ballroom.

She danced dutifully, she chatted when he chatted but they both knew the dance was not a success. An American couple came to sit with them and after a few minutes their daughter Melanie arrived. She was eighteen and pretty, anxious to dance, nor did she lack for partners, but she was also anxious to dance with Justin and Nancy gave them every encouragement.

Justin was sulky but she knew he would recover. The young American girl would make a fuss of him whenever they met and by the end of the holiday he would begin to realize he'd been too anxious to fall in love with a woman who was too old for him, and too much involved with somebody else.

While he danced with Melanie Nancy excused herself on the grounds that she wanted some air but she hadn't been outside for long before Noel joined her. She was surprised to see that he was still wearing evening dress.

'I thought you were retiring for the night,' she said in some surprise.

'I went out to the pyramids instead. They're really something, aren't they? Unfortunately this is the night they give the history of them in German so I didn't understand all of it. French would have been better. What happened to your partner?'

'He's dancing with an American girl we met.'

'I see. Would you care to dance?'

Without a word she walked back to the ballroom and he followed. She turned and he took her in his arms. It had been a long long time since she had danced with Noel; the last occasion had been under the stars on Victoria Peak in far-off Hong Kong, and as if he too was remembering it he said, 'It's been a long time since we danced together, Nancy. Life has been too real.'

'When do you have to go back?' she asked.

He smiled. 'Not a very encouraging question considering that I've only just arrived,' he said evenly.

'I'm sorry but I know you hate being anywhere except where you're needed.'

'You don't think I'm needed here?'

'There's no unrest here, no bullets flying or stone throwing.'

'I've given myself fourteen days to absorb the peace and the quiet. Have you any suggestions on what we can do with them?'

'I'm sure you have your own ideas about how you want to spend the time.'

'What can I do with a girl who's so prickly?'

366

The music drew to a close and taking hold of her hand Noel said, 'We can't talk here with Justin hunting round for you like an abandoned spaniel and that pretty little thing looking forlorn because she hasn't got his undivided attention. I suggest we go into the gardens and observe the firmament.'

The gardens were crowded with others who had the same idea, so Noel led her to a tiny wicker gate that let them out of the gardens and into the desert. The lights of Cairo blazed in the distance, but out in the desert there was only the stillness and the glory of the night sky.

Noel spoke softly. 'I wonder how many other people have stood together in this same spot looking across the desert to the pyramids. All those crumbling centuries. Did Antony stand here with Cleopatra, I wonder? Did he drown in the beauty of those dark Egyptian eyes, did the great Caesar ride out with his legions over that plain and did they too stand in awe at the sight of those pyramids? I never felt it in Israel like I feel it here, the weight of the years, the eternal recurrence of all things. Do you feel it too, Nancy?'

'Yes, ever since I arrived here. All the mystery of this civilization that was already old when there was no Rome on the seven hills. Did those stern Egyptian gods ever grow gentle, and those beautiful remote faces on the temple walls, did they ever smile?'

'You know, Nancy, there are some places where the gods suggest laughter and revelry. The Olympian gods, sunkissed and dimpled who bestowed their gift of eternal youth on the landscape as an inheritance forever, those laughing lands where happiness plays on the mountain tops and sunshine kisses the high hills. You've never been to Italy have you, Nancy, or Greece, where the gods sported with their infidelities and human frailties. One day I will take you to Italy. Italy steals you from yourself, you live with Italy in your heart,

367

talking her, thinking her, dreaming her, as you live under the dominance of the lover who is your world. Here in Egypt I can only feel the omnipotence of Time, Egypt's overpowering grandeur.'

She was staring at him wide-eyed, unable to believe that she had just heard him say that one day he would take her to Italy. His arm was around her shoulders and she could see the moonlight shining on his face, illuminating the passion of enthusiasm on it, and she was loving his way with words, the way he could make her feel and see things as never before.

He looked down at her and in a voice suddenly gentle he said, 'So – what *are* we going to do with our fourteen days, Nancy?'

'I don't know. I am waiting for you to tell me.'

For a few moments he was thoughtful, staring out across the desert, then he said softly, 'We could go to Luxor. We could see the temples and the tombs, follow the tourists in their search for culture, and then we could go on to Aswan, sail the river in the morning sunshine, walk in the gardens in the cool of the evening, discover that part of ourselves which we seem to have lost lately.'

'And afterwards?'

'We'll talk about the afterwards later, Nancy. We have fourteen days, time to discover Egypt and get married.'

She stared at him in disbelief and his face grew suddenly anxious. 'You do want to marry me, don't you, Nancy?'

'You never wanted to marry me. You never wanted to commit yourself to anybody. It was your mission in life to be a free agent, something no woman was ever going to change. What has happened to change your mind?'

'The knowledge that I love you. I didn't want to love you, I was happy simply liking you, thinking that you were a great girl, a good pal, but I found out that I wasn't really the master of my own fate at all. I fell in love with you.'

'I thought you hated me, or at least I thought you believed me to be an encumbrance you were anxious to get rid of.'

'I was angry that afternoon when you ran back to Alec. I was angry because I was desperately afraid. Have you never seen a mother shake an erring child because for a brief moment he has run away, and then when he returns her relief is so great she shakes him. That afternoon when you disobeyed all I had tried to teach you I was more frightened than I had ever been in my life. I knew then that if they had killed you my own life wouldn't have been worth anything.'

'Oh Noel, why didn't you tell me? You would have spared me so much misery!'

'Then there was something my father said before he died, something that made me sit back and take stock of myself.'

'What did your father say?'

'I won't tell you now, Nancy, I'll tell you later. Are you going to marry me?'

'Yes. Oh yes please, Noel! I was getting used to the idea that I'd never marry anybody.'

From the balcony of the hotel Justin Palmer looked out morosely across the gardens to the desert beyond where a man and a woman were wrapped in each other's arms, oblivious to the music and the magic of the night. Disconsolately he turned and walked back into the ballroom, and almost immediately Melanie seized him by the hand and dragged him on to the floor.

'Were you in love with her?' she asked anxiously.

He was too quick to deny it. 'Well, of course not,' he said sharply. 'I only met her a couple of days ago.'

Relieved, he was aware of the sudden joy that filled her face, and his heart grew suddenly light. After all, the world was full of girls and this one was very pretty . . .

369

CHAPTER 35

Fourteen days was not long enough to discover Egypt but fourteen days was all they had.

For ten long days they had followed slavishly the guides and listened to their teachings until Nancy thought her head would explode as she tried to remember the names of gods and Pharaohs. Egypt had eaten into her soul until she knew that as long as she lived she would remember the magnificent tombs and the majestic temples, the golden sun shining on sandstone reliefs, the statues of the Pharaohs striding out into eternity from every temple wall.

In her ears she could hear the rumble of chariot wheels, see the purple plumes on the heads of snow-white horses, and some Pharaoh, it didn't much matter which one, standing omnipotent in his golden chariot, the blue enamelled war crown on his head, his uniform fashioned like the wings of a bird, forever staring out over the heads of those who came to wonder and admire, and Nancy whispered to Noel, 'I wonder if they ever fell in love, if they ever felt joy and sadness, the pain of rejection. They seem too proud for human emotions.'

Noel took her hand and held it fast. 'Oh they were human all right,' he assured her. 'So human that they were afraid to appear less than godlike in case their subjects came to believe that they were just like them.'

'It must have been very easy to love in this land,' she murmured.

'Why do you say that?'

'The river is so blue, the light so golden, and at night the stars closer than anywhere else on earth. I'm so glad we married in Egypt, loving you in Egypt has been the most magical thing in my life.'

He smiled down at her gently. They had left the tourist sites behind and were now enjoying the last few days of their honeymoon on the Island of Elephantine near the first cataract. It was an enchanting place, alive with flowers and their perfume, where brilliantly plumaged birds flitted through the branches of exotic trees.

It was their last day in Aswan and they sat on the balcony of their hotel looking out across the river. Giant boulders shone like ebony in the swiftly flowing river and from the dovecotes a thousand white doves flew up into the sky. It was the hour of sunset when the sky glowed with iridescent tints of orange and purple, rose and tragic crimson. There was no navigation beyond this point and the boulders seemed to Nancy like giant prehistoric beasts sunning themselves in the glowing warmth that lit up the landscape.

'How beautiful it is,' she said to Noel, 'I could spend the rest of my life watching the life on that great river, the endless unforgettable sunsets and golden glowing mornings. Shall we ever come back do you think?'

He smiled but made no answer, and after a while she said plaintively, 'Do you miss the danger, Noel? This wouldn't be enough for you, the peace and silence of the desert, the endless searching after old things.'

'One day we will come back, Nancy, but how can we say when? Will you be happy to go back to Israel where terrible things happened to you?'

'I have to go back, I have to prove to myself that I can face up to things like that and overcome them. I have to prove to you that you didn't make a mistake when you offered me a job.'

'I know I didn't make a mistake.'

'You can say that now, but you must have wondered.'

'About your ability to be a good journalist, never, about whether you would ever develop that hard core

371

which is necessary if you wish to survive in our particular field of journalism, yes, I wondered about that.'

'And now?'

'Keep that wide eyed belief in the intrinsic goodness of human nature. It will let you down again and again but you are a better person for believing in it and I am a better person for loving you and having you near me.'

Almost shyly she reached down into her handbag and drew out a sheaf of papers which she handed across the table to Noel.

He stared at them curiously, asking, 'What is this?'

'My story about how I brought Benjamin from Israel to Egypt. Is it any good do you think?'

He read it carefully, and when at last he laid it aside his eyes were shining. 'It's damned good, Nancy, and it's something you did on your own, without me or the others. When did you write it?'

'Whenever there was a spare moment. I started it in Cairo but then you came and there wasn't much time to do anything except keep pace with you.'

'There surely wasn't much time in Luxor, I was exhausted after climbing in and out of tombs and roaming round temples.'

'I managed a little, but most of it was written here. I found this beautiful place conducive to helping the story along.'

'You realise they're going to go to town on our marriage, don't you; this story will merely add to the excitement.'

'I can imagine how they'll lap it up in the local rag at home, Aunt Susan's going to bask in her reflected glory for weeks.'

He grinned. 'They might conceivably unveil a plaque in your honour within the hallowed halls of Lorivals.'

They laughed together, happy and light-hearted, and in the days which followed she drew upon his words to give her the necessary courage to face the dangers they were returning to.

The plane dipped and righted itself, and in that brief moment she had been able to look down on the domes and minarets of Jerusalem and the familiar white city filled her with a strange and inexplicable excitement.

Noel informed her that his car was waiting for them in the parking lot and suddenly she was conscious of the heat of the sun and the torpid midday intermission before the seething life of the city took up its familiar pattern.

It was as though she had never been away. The cameramen greeted them joyfully, showering them with good wishes, and as Harry fell into step beside her he said with a grin, 'I was dropped on, Nancy, I'd seriously thought you were for me.'

She laughed. 'I'm too old for you, Harry, find yourself a younger woman.'

'You've spoiled me for other women,' he said half seriously.

'Noel and I go back a long way,' she replied.

'So you're happy?'

'Ecstatically.'

On that first evening they drove out to see Abraham and he received them with joy. He took Nancy's hands and held them while he looked down at her with a gentle smile on his lips.

'Thank you for caring for my son, Nancy, he is happy with my brother in Alexandria. I hope that before long I shall be able to visit them.'

'How is Leah?'

'She recovers slowly. My poor beautiful Leah who is not yet able to understand what happened to her.'

'Can I see her?'

'If she continues to improve she will be allowed visitors, but not just yet I think. Sight of you might bring it all back to her too quickly, too harshly.'

'I understand.'

She left Abraham and Noel together while she wandered through the garden. It was here in the arbour she had read to Benjamin, watching the tears drying on his cheeks, seeing the dimpled smiles come and go on his face as she recounted stories from her own childhood.

It was here on the velvet lawns that guests had gathered to celebrate his birthday party, and it was there on the winding dusty road within sight of the house that the mob had faced them with hatred in their eyes, and missiles in their hands.

At that moment a strange and unexpected nostalgia filled her heart. She had not known Noel when she wandered over the hills of her childhood, and fate had ordained that they should meet in an alien land at the other side of the world; why then should she suddenly remember those dark clouded Pennine hills that could be unpredictable, made suddenly beautiful by shafts of sunlight?

Noel stood for a long moment watching her staring pensively at the city shining in the distance, then he went to take her hand.

'What were you thinking about?' he asked her gently. 'That moment on the road?'

'I was thinking about home. I was thinking that you must have wandered across the fells above the town when you were a boy, before I knew you. We must have been so close and yet I never saw you there.'

'I know. Strange that we had to meet so far away from familiar things.'

'But we had to meet didn't we, Noel? It would have been so terrible if we'd missed each other.'

'I think tomorrow we should drive out to see Hadassah and Ali. Abraham has been telling me that Girgis Boutrous was wounded in a fracas in the city several days ago, he doesn't know how badly but they have taken him to his uncle's house.'

'Then it can't have been badly or they would have taken him into the hospital.'

'He may not have wished to go into a Jewish hospital, I don't know, but for the sake of his uncle I feel we should find out what has happened.'

She didn't answer; she was thinking of that moment when she had stood at the bottom of the gangplank with Benjamin's hand held tightly in her own, staring into Girgis' proud angry eyes before suddenly he turned away.

Why had he suddenly spared her? She couldn't think it was because of the close proximity of the Israeli soldiers; Girgis would have been contemptuous of personal danger, he would have gloried in it, and yet he had spared her life and the life of the boy. At least she should be allowed to thank him for that.

They drove out to Jericho in the cool of the early morning and Nancy sat back in silence, revelling in the beauty of the familiar scenery which brought back all the early visions she had cherished of the land of her scriptures.

Their hosts greeted them graciously and Noel was quick to ask if Girgis had been badly wounded.

'Fortunately it was only a flesh wound,' Ali said evenly. 'He lost a lot of blood but it could have been a lot worse.'

'I heard some of his friends were killed,' Noel said.

'That is so, three of them. One is the only son of friends of ours, a boy born to them late in life and now he is dead. A pointless death since it will bring about no change in the way many of our people exist.'

'And in Girgis' heart there will be deeper anger, more desperate need for revenge?' Noel added.

'We fear so, and the next time it could be Girgis lying dead somewhere out there in the wilderness.'

Nancy stared at them in horror but she was thinking of that handsome young Arab striding out proudly in

375

his white robes, his dark eyes flashing in his smooth brown face, his teeth even and white behind red Eastern lips that smiled without mirth and curled with insolent arrogance.

She surprised herself by asking, 'Shall I be able to see Girgis do you think? I wish to thank him for sparing my life and Benjamin's.'

Neither Ali nor Hadassah showed surprise which made her think they might have known something of the incident, and later she found herself sitting opposite Girgis at the dinner table.

He and Noel had greeted each other stiffly, but Nancy had held out her hand saying, 'I wish to thank you for helping us in Haifa, Girgis, I was so desperately afraid at that moment when you turned away.'

'The boy did not concern me, it was your life I saved,' he answered stiffly.

'Whatever hatred you feel for the Jews should not be levelled at a child, Girgis.'

'Children grow up but we will not speak of it if you please. If you stay here a hundred years you will never understand.'

While the talk became general he stared at her through narrowed eyes. She seemed more beautiful to him now than she had before; there was a radiance about her, a new serenity which he thought savagely had a lot to do with Noel Templeton.

Nancy was busy familiarising herself with eating with her fingers which she quickly discovered was not nearly so disagreeable as she had imagined, for the meat, of whatsoever kind it might be, was cut up into small pieces and piled lightly on the top of watercress and parsley.

It was Girgis who showed Nancy how to help herself to a piece of grilled meat, which was deliciously savoury, from the centre dish, with the assistance of a piece of bread. When she had successfully carried the morsel from the centre of the table to her own crust she had to dip it in one of the four small dishes of appetizing sauces which were placed in front of her, and looking up she encountered Noel's look of amusement at Girgis' attentive behaviour.

She could hear the murmur of their voices, see Noel's dark head bent to hear Ali's words, words which he apparently did not mean Girgis to hear. Fortunately the table was large and Hadassah was telling her about her last visit to her brother's home in Damascus.

After they had eaten coffee was served to them in tiny gold cups, sweet Turkish coffee that was not really to her palate but which she accepted in case to refuse it would have offended.

She walked out on to the terrace where she could look out across the gardens to the distant hills. Behind her she could hear the hum of Ali and Noel's voices and suddenly Girgis was by her side staring out in silence. She was strangely aware of him beside her, a tormenting dangerous presence, mercurial and menacing. She would have been amazed at the passions inflaming his proud unyielding heart.

He wanted this woman of the West as he had never wanted anything in his entire life. Through narrowed eyes he studied her face under its halo of fine pale hair; the curve of her cheek was like a sunkissed peach, her lips were wistful and sensitive but it was her eyes he loved the most, eyes as azure blue as the summer skies above the hills of Moab. She would never be his, this white-skinned daughter of the rains that swept across her native land so that the women blossomed like the flowers of the spring under the hedgerows, but if he could not have her, she should not be here to do Templeton's bidding.

'Why don't you go home to England where there is peace? Why do you stay here to be near a man who allows you to face danger, who sends you to Egypt with a Jewish child?' he asked angrily.

'Girgis, you don't understand. It is my job to be here. Noel has never led me to believe that it would be easy, and now I must stay because I love him and because he is my husband.'

She would never know that her words were like the twisting of a knife in his heart; instead he inclined his head a mere fraction of an inch before he strode away from her.

Nancy had no means of knowing that her words had filled Girgis' fierce heart with such a desire for vengeance that he could not contain himself. He went immediately to his room and stood there with clenched fists beseeching Allah to deliver Noel Templeton into his hands.

He did not show himself again all afternoon but he stood with an angry heart listening to their voices drifting up to him from the terraces below, then he watched with burning eyes until Noel's car was out of sight.

'How strange he is,' Nancy said. 'Why didn't he come to say goodbye?'

'He's fallen in love with you,' Noel said lightly. 'Didn't you guess?'

'Oh Noel, of course Girgis isn't in love with me, – why, we hardly know each other.'

'Everything happens quickly in the East, my darling, love, hate death. Haven't you accepted that yet?'

'Death yes, I'm not so sure about the other two.'

'You will be before you shake the sand off your shoes forever.'

She did not realise it at the time; it was only later that she realised how strangely prophetic his words had been.

CHAPTER 36

Amelia stood on the dais waiting for her daughter to come forward to collect her silver cup. There was a smile of deep satisfaction on her face. Tondelao had jumped effortlessly, both horse and rider a perfect unit, and she smiled fondly at Pippa's rosy excited face as she came up to her. Standing beside her Mark smiled down at his daughter murmuring, 'Well done, love,' before bestowing his attention on Alison Steadwell who came forward for the second prize.

It could have been Amelia's mother he watched as Amelia congratulated Alison warmly, saying, 'Better luck next time, my dear,' then with a generous gesture that won the approval of all the onlookers she placed her bouquet of roses in Alison's arms saying, 'Do give these to your mother, Alison. I know she hasn't been well for some time now.'

Alison stared down at the flowers in amazement, Amelia and Pippa smiled, Mark looked on with cynical detachment before they all moved out of the stands. It was a little later when Mark followed Alison out of one of the tents and watched as she looked down at the flowers before depositing them in one of the trash bins. She looked up and saw him there, and when he grinned the warm red colour flooded her cheeks.

'I know exactly how you feel,' he said. 'I used to feel like that every time my brother came home with the History prize and I had nothing. It's a rotten feeling, isn't it?'

'I shouldn't mind so much. After all, Pippa's horse jumped better than mine.'

'And cost twice as much, I can assure you.'

She looked back at the flowers and went to retrieve them. 'It was kind of Lady Garveston to give them to me, my mother will love them.'

'Do you have anywhere to jump Gypsy besides that old field up at the farm?' Mark asked her.

'No, but it's not too bad.'

'You have my full permission to use our paddock. Pippa goes to Switzerland next week, so she'll not be using it for some time.'

'Won't Lady Garveston mind?'

'I've told you you can use it, Alison. You don't need her permission.'

Standing with her husband at the back of the tent Maisie had heard every word of Mark's conversation with Alison. She had never credited him with so much sensitivity and as he left the tent she said to Tom, 'What a nice thing for him to have done. Alison can't expect to win every year.'

'She'll probably never win again, love. A rider's only as good as her horse and Garveston can afford the best.'

'Amelia can, you mean,' Maisie said feelingly.

They moved out to join the throng of people walking towards the exit gate and it was then that she saw Alice, chatting vivaciously to a young man standing nonchalantly beside an open sports car. She was looking a great deal older than her seventeen years.

Alice had said agricultural shows were a bore, but she didn't look very bored now. She turned and when she saw them waved her hand gaily, then after a few words with the young man she hurried across to them.

'A few young people are going to a hop over at Carlton and they want me to go with them,' she said with a confident smile on her face.

'Which young people?' her father asked.

'There's about half a dozen of us. Timothy Barnett has invited me,' she explained.

'Who else is going?' Maisie asked.

'Berenice Garveston for one and some of her friends.'

'I always thought you didn't like Berenice Garveston,' Maisie said pointedly.

'I like her better now.'

'Is her sister going?'

'I shouldn't think so. They're not alike, they have different friends now and Berenice isn't into horses.'

Maisie looked at Tom. 'What do you think?' she asked him. 'Do you know anything about this boy?'

Alice was quick to say, 'He's very nice, Mother. It's a sort of farewell party for Berenice, as she and Pippa are off to Switzerland next week.'

'I don't want you to be late home, you're only seventeen after all.'

'The hop finishes about twelve and I'll get Timothy to bring me straight home. Lady Garveston's given permission for Berenice to go.'

'She's twelve months older than you are Alice, but if you promise to come straight home after the dance you can go.'

Alice sped off, and they watched her climb into the boy's car, then a few minutes later they saw Berenice climb into her new open sports car with a young man and Tom remarked dourly, 'Alice'll be asking us for a car next. She's runnin' with the wrong crowd, Maisie.'

'It'll sort itself out. The Garveston girls will be away next week and Alice'll soon be back at Lorivals, with her exams to worry about.'

She turned as Amelia and her entourage swept through the field. Amelia favoured them with her swift elusive smile and Maisie said quickly, 'Pippa rode well. You must be very proud of her.'

'Well yes, we are. I'm so glad we got the show brought forward a few weeks so that she could compete. I've been trying to get them to do that for quite some time. Have you seen my husband and Berenice?'

'Sir Mark left a few minutes ago and your daughter has gone off to a dance over at Carlton. My daughter

Alice went with them.'

For a moment Amelia stood staring at her, then smiling she said, 'Oh well, they know how to look after themselves these days. I just wish she'd mentioned it first, that's all.'

Amelia found Mark in conversation with Deirdre Forsythe. She favoured Deirdre with a small smile and in some confusion the other woman said, 'I was just telling Sir Mark how very much John and I have enjoyed the show, Lady Garveston. You must be very proud of your daughter.'

'Yes of course,' Amelia replied, then handing Pippa's cup to Mark she said, 'Berenice has gone off to a dance and Pippa's taking care of her horse. I think we're ready to leave now, Mark.'

She moved off after a brief farewell smile, and Mark murmured swiftly, 'I'll ring you, Deirdre, probably early next week.'

Deirdre reminded Mark of Barbara. They had the same colouring, the same air of sophistication but Deirdre was still climbing whereas Barbara had undoubtedly arrived. She was not as demanding as Barbara had been, however, and she was undeniably flattered by his attentions.

It was no use having any regrets about Barbara. She and Martin had come to terms with their marriage and were probably happier now than they had ever been. Martin no longer went on conferences without his wife and they were back to exotic holidays and foreign travel. Martin had sold his power boat and his yacht was safely anchored in the Lake District at the bottom of his parents' garden.

Mark had given them a miss for the Gold Cup following his meeting with Barbara on the fell but the year afterwards he'd decided to wangle an invitation. After all, it was more likely Martin might smell a rat by his absence than by his presence.

He enjoyed Cheltenham, and the hospitality Martin and his wife dished out was superb. There was nothing complicated about his stay with them; they were visibly happy together, and he had Deirdre to come back to.

Next week both his daughters were off to their finishing school in the Bernese Oberland and he was going to miss Pippa like the very devil. Berenice had wangled her Mercedes Coupé out of them, and when he'd said it was too expensive she'd tossed her pretty head saying it was no more costly than Pippa's mare and livery.

Amelia was the puzzling one; ever since that time she'd spent at her mother's she was a changed woman, although she'd never said another word about that time and he'd be damned if he'd raise it again. Life had taken up its normal pattern and he'd seen to it that much as he disliked the Dowager Lady Urquart, he'd accompany Amelia the next time she decided to visit Drummond. Thank God there were not too many of those occasions.

He often thought that Celia gave him some odd looks, as if she knew something he didn't, but he'd got nothing out of Desmond. The latter seemed completely immune to his wife's comings and goings so was hardly likely to concern himself with Amelia's foibles.

Amelia now had this bee in her bonnet about another reunion with her old schoolfriends. Personally he thought it was nonsense. Tom and Maisie Standing were too busy at the farm to think much of it, Martin and Barbara would probably make some excuse and Nancy Graham was overseas and hardly likely to come home for such a trivial occasion.

He'd tried talking her out of it, but Amelia had merely looked at him blankly, and he knew none of his views had registered. She'd have her way: it would take her friends' excuses to make her realize the reunion wasn't on.

383

CHAPTER 37

Nancy left the doctor's surgery with mixed feelings. Did she really want a baby at thirty-eight and how would Noel feel about it? They'd never talked about having children. By the time this child was twenty-one she'd be pushing sixty and Noel would be sixty-three; at the same time a small, sneaking feeling of elation crept into her heart, excluding all the doubts and misgivings.

She would tell him tonight after dinner, sitting on their balcony under the midnight-blue sky ablaze with stars, listening to the sounds of the city, feeling the fresh breeze on their faces after the heat of the day.

Trouble had flared in the night on the outskirts of the city and Noel had set out soon after midnight with the others. She had feigned a headache because she knew she must go to the surgery in the morning, and Noel had accepted her excuses readily.

At the end of the week Abraham was taking Leah to Alexandria but she was a very different Leah from the woman Nancy had met on her arrival. She was forgetful, lethargic, and there were still deep bruises on her body from the rocks the Arabs had hurled at her. The marks left by the stitches still showed on the tender skin of her face and throat and there were times when Nancy wondered if the ready smiles would ever come back to illuminate her face.

Ali and Hadassah hardly ever saw Girgis. He seemed to have cut them off without compunction, and yet Noel said he was heavily involved in every uprising within the city and outside it. She looked forward to the mail from home, bitty letters from Maisie filled with news of her husband, her children and the farm in that order, and from her Aunt Susan because Aunt Susan wrote about Amelia and Barbara as well as others she had known in Greymont. Maisie was only concerned with her own family; unmarried Aunt Susan was a respected institution in Greymont, an authority on life and people.

Noel was forever saying they must go home to see to his father's house but somehow or other the opportunity never seemed to arrive, or if it did he ignored it.

She knew something was wrong as soon as she entered the hotel. Abdullah normally greeted her with toothy smiles and much bowing; today he sidled behind the screens into the servants' quarters beyond. Even the little serving girl who followed Abdullah about carrying a heavy tray piled high with cutlery and crockery turned away and busied herself at the other side of the room.

Nancy began to feel the first pangs of disquiet. She hurried upstairs to their room but it stared back at her impersonal and strangely empty. She ran down into the courtyard behind the hotel but Noel's car was not there, and catching sight of Abdullah crossing the foyer she ran back down the stairs to speak to him.

He turned as she called his name, his eyes met hers, then shifted, and she knew something had happened, something he was afraid to tell her.

'Did Mr Templeton return while I was out?' she asked him.

'I not see him,' he replied, his entire manner betraying the fact that he was anxious to turn away.

'Something is wrong, Abdullah,' she said anxiously. 'Please tell me what it is.'

He shrugged his shoulders, but his eyes refused to meet hers.

'Abdullah,' she cried sternly, 'answer me! Has something happened that I should know about?'

385

He raised his eyes to hers sorrowfully. 'There was shootings on the road to Jericho, people were hurt, that is all I know, lady.'

'Was my husband hurt?'

Again he shrugged. 'I not know who hurt. He will come soon, lady, you wait.'

She turned on her heel and ran out into the street. It was crowded with people going about their business. On her unheeding ears fell the beautiful and familiar words which caused the Arabs close by to turn their eyes towards Mecca while those who were not of their faith passed by idly with little interest.

Helplessly she gazed around her. The morning was full of sounds. The sun shone out of a colourless sky causing the buildings to shimmer with heat; the air she breathed was filled with the scent of the spices set out on the city pavements. She could do nothing but wait and disconsolately she went back to her bedroom where she could watch from the balcony for his car to come along the crowded street, see his tall slender figure and the friendly wave of his hand when he saw her waiting there.

Time passed slowly. Again and again she consulted her watch, unable to believe that only minutes had passed. Nothing could have happened; it was all too normal, too uncaring, and yet whenever people gathered to whisper she read disaster in their whisperings, every glance turned in her direction an admission of something terrible.

Noon brought quiet to the teeming streets; men sat outside their shops asleep under awnings, street cries became silent, but to Nancy it was the uneasy quiet that heralded a new sinister happening.

She heard the sound of the car's engine long before it came into view, a sound that shattered the quiet of the dozing city, then, she saw it approaching slowly, avoiding the carts and those sleeping under them, and

Nancy jumped to her feet and ran desperately down to the street outside. Harry was the only person in the car, and as soon as he saw her he brought it to a stop and opened the door.

Anxiety stared out of her eyes, and taking her arm he said hoarsely, 'Get into the car, Nancy. I'll tell you what has happened when we get out of the city.'

'It's Noel isn't it, is he hurt?'

For a moment he gave his entire concentration to the winding street, then when he had reassured himself that they could proceed easily he said, 'There was trouble on the road to Jericho. We arrived when they were shooting at each other, then suddenly one of them turned to shoot at us.'

'I want to know about Noel. Is he hurt?'

'We don't know how badly. He's been taken to hospital and I'm taking you there now. Phil is with him.'

She sat in silence, her hands clenched against her knees as she prayed silently for Noel's life. Phil met them in the hospital corridor and he smiled reassuringly.

'Try not to worry, love,' he said to her gently. 'He's tough, we got him here as quickly as we could.'

'Do you know how badly he's injured?'

'Not yet, they'll tell us as soon as they can.'

Tea was served to them, and a young nurse said gently, 'Try not to worry, Mrs Templeton, your husband is in good hands.'

'Why did they suddenly shoot at you?' Nancy asked. 'They have no quarrel with foreign journalists.'

'It was young Boutrous, the man was a madman. There he was with a gang of them shooting at Israeli soldiers, then he saw us and turned his weapon on Noel. The soldiers retaliated – I hope they killed him.'

'Don't you know?'

'No, and we didn't stay to find out. Noel was bleeding like a stuck pig, we had to get him into hospital right away. Sorry, Nancy, blood always looks worse than it is.'

'Was Noel conscious?'

'Not when we got him here but he wasn't dead either. He'll be all right, Nancy, I've seen him in worse scrapes than this.'

Her hands were trembling as she held the hot tea to her lips. The cup chattered against her teeth and then she was staring at a group of white-clothed orderlies pushing Noel's stretcher along the corridor. He looked so pale and delicate against the white pillow. One lock of dark hair fell across his forehead, and as she bent down to push it aside she became instantly aware of his cold damp skin against her hand.

The young doctor walking beside the trolley smiled at her cheerfully. 'He had a narrow escape, half an inch from his heart it was. My, but his guardian angel was with him this morning.'

His accent was faintly Irish and as relief flooded her being she smiled across at him. 'Thank you,' she breathed, 'thank you so much.'

'Why don't you go back to your hotel for a little while,' a young nurse advised her. 'Mr Templeton will not be conscious until later this afternoon and you look desperately tired. No doubt it was the shock, but when did you last eat?'

Nancy had to confess that it was breakfast early that morning and the nurse said firmly, 'Then you should go back. Eat something, and later, when it is cool, you may return here to see your husband. By that time he will be looking forward to your visit.'

The two cameramen added their persuasions and she could do nothing but agree. She felt strangely calm as she walked between the two men along the corridors of the hospital and as they reached the head of the stairs she could see Ali and Hadassah talking seriously to two doctors only feet away from her.

Hadassah looked up and immediately tears filled her eyes and she looked quickly away so that Nancy went forward anxiously only to find that Hadassah shrank away from her.

Ali spoke quietly. 'We are ashamed, Nancy. Girgis was our nephew, it is a terrible thing that he has done. We do not expect you to forgive any of us.'

'But you had nothing to do with it. Noel will not blame you and neither do I.'

'Then that is very generous, but Noel was our friend, we gave him our hospitality, he was not expecting treachery.'

'Please, Hadassah, you must not feel that any of this is your fault. Noel is going to be all right; the bullet narrowly missed his heart but now he is sleeping and I have been assured that he will be well. It was Girgis who did this terrible thing, not you.'

'Girgis is dead,' Hadassah said. She stated the fact baldly, and Nancy could only stare at her because any words she might have said would have been inadequate.

Ali went on to explain. 'One of his own men shot him – they believed he had endangered their lives and their cause by firing on a group of journalists.'

'But why did he do it – he knew they would not be armed?'

'He hated Noel,' Hadassah said bitterly. 'He hated him from the first moment they met. It was a strange illogical hatred that festered deeper after he met you.'

Nancy felt the hot blood suffusing her face and Hadassah went on relentlessly, 'Girgis was a man of sudden sweeping passions, he could not think or reason like an Englishman, you were his goddess. He was content to worship you from afar but he could not bear to think that you belonged to Noel. He hated Noel because he was English, because he was fairer skinned, and he loathed him because Noel didn't care that he

389

hated him. Then you came like a breath of English spring into the unwatered desert and the hatred that had lain dormant since the first day they met became a living breathing nightmare in his untamed heart.'

Nancy stared at her helplessly, then after a few minutes she said quietly, 'How pitiless it all is. The East gets down so remorselessly to the bedrock of cruelty and of passions. In England we have forgotten elemental things.'

Ali said calmly, 'We go now to look upon Girgis for the last time. We go with shame in our hearts and a prayer for forgiveness on our lips.' Hadassah smiled, the saddest smile Nancy had ever seen, while Ali afforded her the graceful Arab salute of touching his heart, his lips and his head.

A few minutes later they stood by Girgis' dead body and in a flat unemotional voice Ali said, 'And the goat shall bear upon him all their iniquities into a land not inhabited.'

CHAPTER 38

Nancy sat across from Noel in the airport lounge waiting for her flight to be called. Her hands were held in his, and his eyes were tender as they rested on her. He looked fit and well and he was happy. She had been unsure how he would receive the news of her pregnancy but she need not have worried. He was delighted.

'But we'll be so old,' she'd said doubtfully, and he'd thrown back his head and laughed.

'We'll not be the old dodderers you're thinking about, darling, we'll be wise and charming. You'll still be beautiful and he'll adore you.'

'He?'

'He or she, what does it matter?'

'I needn't have gone home yet, it's such a long time off.'

'There's the house to see to, and I'll wangle leave as soon as I can so that we can take another short holiday together. What do you say to Scotland?'

'Anywhere.'

'I've written to Mrs Harris. She'll be expecting you and she'll see to it that the house is sparkling.'

The announcement of her flight came over the intercom and Noel gathered her hand luggage together before taking her arm in his. His conversation was light because he hated goodbyes and there had been so many of them since that first one in distant Hong Kong. He held her in his arms, his chin resting lightly on her hair. She could feel his heart beating steadily against her, and sternly she commanded herself not to cry.

'I'll be up with the onlookers until the plane leaves,' he reassured her, 'but don't look back. My father always said it was bad luck to look back.'

'My father too,' she said with a smile.

For several minutes she clung to him then with a smile which belied the tears in her eyes she turned away, both loving and hating the unborn child that was tearing them apart.

She could not see the terraces from her side of the plane yet she knew he would be waiting until the aircraft became a distant speck in the burning sky. It seemed incredible that in just over five hours she would be stepping down on to her native soil. Noel had said that he would come home soon but she had no guarantee that he would be able to keep his promise.

That morning, as they left the hotel in Jerusalem to which they had returned for a few weeks after a blissful honeymoon, he had handed her some mail, saying, 'These are for you, darling. Read them on the plane, as they might help to relieve the boredom of the flight.'

She had stared down at the envelopes, recognizing her aunt's neat precise writing and Maisie's scrawl which was often difficult to read. Her preoccupation with the third envelope caused Noel to raise his eyebrows and enquire lightly, 'You hadn't expected that one?'

'No, but I recognize the handwriting.'

'Well, I recognized your Aunt Susan's. I'm very much looking forward to meeting that redoubtable lady.'

'I don't see why,' she said crossly. 'She wasn't exactly complimentary about our wedding. She said I should have married a nice man who worked on a proper job with reasonable hours and a pension at the end of it!'

'And so you should,' he grinned. 'Nobody in their right senses would want to marry a war correspondent who gets himself shot at every now and again.'

'I'll read them on the plane,' she said, stuffing the letters in her handbag. 'I suppose Aunt Susan's dined out on our marriage, and Amelia will be writing to wish us happiness.'

Now with the plane winging high above the clouds she opened Aunt Susan's letter first, and as usual it was filled with news of Greymont. Amelia's letter, however, had nothing to do with her marriage; instead it was an invitation to spend a weekend at Garveston in early September. Nancy could see that it had been readdressed from the paper's London office. Several excuses came readily into mind – Noel's leave and a holiday together in Scotland, as well as the beginning of work on the book she had resolved to write – but no doubt she'd be pressured into accepting by Aunt Susan who still ascribed to the old feudal system as being right and proper.

Maisie's letter was full of her children – Peter who was proving every bit as clever as they had hoped, and Lucy who had won a scholarship to the local grammar school. Little was said about Alice and Nancy soon realized that Alice was the fly in the ointment; she'd be hearing all about the girl in due course, no doubt.

How strange it was to be going back to a small provincial town where the local paper was concerned only with weddings and funerals, church fêtes and Rotarian dinners, where people who had never lived anywhere else thought it was important to have presided over Council meetings, run charity committees or captained the local cricket team.

There was something indescribably comforting in looking back at half-forgotten memories. And much later, as Nancy's train carried her steadily northward from London, she revelled in the sight of winding country lanes and hedgerows, tall church spires and banks of blue lupins. She was very tired but was glad she'd decided to go straight to Euston in the hope of catching a train for Kendal instead of spending the night in London. It would be dark when she arrived, but there would be taxis waiting and another hour would find her at home.

Home from now on would be Noel's father's house, and she couldn't wait to see it again, remembering her first brief visit there years before.

It was after midnight when she arrived at the gate of the house Noel's father had retired to in the rambling village of Applethwaite. She had listened to the taxi driver indulging himself by telling her about the many changes she would find in Greymont, but Applethwaite he assured her never changed. He cheerfully trundled her trunk through the gate and up the garden path while she coped with the rest of her luggage. She stared with some surprise at the glow from the large window on the right of the door. She had thought the house would stare back at her, dark and impersonal, but when she was only halfway up the path the door opened and a voice said cheerfully, 'I thought I heard the gate. Come in, love, I've put a match to the fire and there's a meal waiting for you.'

She stared at the small cheerful woman in her flowered apron and smiling the woman said, 'I'm Mrs Harris, love. I was old Mr Templeton's daily for more years than I like to remember. I live just down the road there in the village and I was givin' miself a bit longer to see if you came in on the train from London.'

'Where do you want this trunk, love?' the taxi driver asked her.

'You can leave it in the hall, please. I'll see to it in the morning.'

'Well, if you're sure. I'll say goodnight then.'

She paid him what she owed him then followed Mrs Harris inside. She'd been dreading coming home to an empty house, but now her heart felt warm at the sound of north-country voices and the homely chink of crockery coming from the kitchen as Mrs Harris bustled about.

She looked round the living room appreciatively. There were flowers in a large bowl on a table near the window and the fire blazed cheerfully. It was early August but she was glad of the warmth after the heat she'd lived with over recent years. Mrs Harris called cheerfully, 'I've laid the table in the dining room, love. Just leave everything where it is and I'll help to carry your things upstairs when you've eaten.'

'Shouldn't you be thinking of getting off home, Mrs Harris?'

'I've only a cockstride to go, love. You'll know these parts. Mr Noel said in his letter that you came from Greymont.'

'Yes, that's right. I still have an aunt here, Miss Lester. She doesn't know yet that I'm coming home, so I shall surprise her.'

'You'll do that all right. There's food in the fridge for tomorrow as I've done quite a lot o' shoppin'. Mr Noel left some money for me when his father died in case I had to spend money on the house. I've never stopped lookin' after it and keepin' it nice.'

She was appreciative of the hot meal Mrs Harris put in front of her. The house sparkled from her efforts and although Noel had told Nancy to make any changes she thought necessary she could only think that the house was lovely as it was. After she had eaten, with the help of Mrs Harris she carried her luggage upstairs and when she stood on the landing the woman said, 'I've put the central heatin' on in the bedroom and you're in Mr Noel's room for the time bein'. I expect you'll be wantin' to make a few changes. It's a nice 'ouse, but Mr Templeton always said it needed a woman's touch.'

The bedroom was large and impersonal. There was a photograph of Noel on top of a chest of drawers – a very much younger Noel from his university days – and on one wall a long photograph of the boys at his

395

school. Nancy had little difficulty in locating her husband near the end of the second row.

There were only tennis rackets in the wardrobe and nothing in any of the drawers so she was able to unpack quickly and put her things away. Mrs Harris was in the hall when she went back downstairs and she could well imagine this small sparrow of a woman keeping Mr Templeton informed and up to date about the goings-on in the village when she said, 'I'll be off now, Mrs Templeton. My 'usband'll be lookin' out for me I'm sure. I've washed the dishes and stoked up the fire. The vicar'll most likely be in in the mornin', likes to keep 'is eye on things, he does. He'll be shovin' you into 'elpin' with all sorts o' things connected with the church if ye don't watch 'im. Will you be wantin' me again? I used to come in three days a week when Mr Templeton was alive. Still, women look after things better, so ye might not be needin' me quite so often. Perhaps you'd like to think about it a bit, ye can allus let me know. I only lives at the first cottage just along the main street there.'

'I'd like you to come here as usual, Mrs Harris. I'm hoping to continue with some sort of work after I've settled down. I'm not sure when I'll see my husband again, but I can't just do nothing while I wait for him to come home.'

'No, of course you can't. Well, I'll see ye next Monday mornin' then I'll get my 'usband to see to your trunk. Mr Templeton was a nice gentleman to work for, he'd 'ave bin so glad to know Mr Noel was married. He used to say it was a long road to travel on your own, the boy should be married with a nice wife and children.'

'I met him once. I came here one day in the summer and I was talking to his cat when he came out into the garden.'

'That'd be Matilda. She died and he was that cut

396

up about it but she was a good age. He had a kitten but Domino's livin' next door at the moment. They likes their creature comforts do cats and he wouldn't stop 'ere on his own. I has a little cat miself, runs our lives for us she does.'

'Perhaps Domino will come home now.'

'Maybe he will, love. Independent they are, they only do what they want to do, but they can be very lovin' when they 'ave a mind to be.'

The sitting room looked charming. Mrs Harris had drawn the long chintz curtains at the window and the firelight fell on polished walnut and the bowl filled with yellow roses and copper leaves. For a long moment Nancy sat in an armchair staring into the flames while memories crowded in on her. After a while she lay back in her chair, her eyes closed and, lulled by the warmth of the room and the quiet, she fell asleep. She didn't know how long she'd dozed but she was roused by a loud plaintive cry from the garden and hurriedly she rose to her feet and went to the door.

A large marmalade-coloured cat stared at her from the doorstep, huge amber eyes unsure at the sight of a stranger, and for a moment it hesitated, then in an encouraging voice she said, 'Hello, Domino. Have you come home?'

He hesitated for a further moment, then lifting his tail high he sauntered through the open door, and she followed, watching him sniff the fire appreciatively before he settled on the rug and started to wash his face.

She desperately wanted him to stay. He was somebody to talk to, and he seemed contented enough sitting on the rug, occasionally staring at her with wide unblinking eyes, then making up his mind suddenly he rose to his feet and leapt on her knee.

Delighted, she stroked his thick soft fur, and with a sigh he settled down in a ball on her knee, then started to purr. They had both come home.

CHAPTER 39

It was market day in Greymont and the roads into town were busy. Miss Susan Lester chafed at the delay as she drove in the direction of the Magistrates' court because this morning she'd particularly wanted to be early before they all split up to go to their separate courts.

On duty today were Mrs Nellie Smythe and Lady Amelia Garveston. Mrs Maisie Standing should also be in evidence but she wasn't too sure about Maisie. Young Lucy had the chicken-pox and she'd asked permission to absent herself on one or two occasions lately. At last she reached the court, just in time to see Nellie Smythe's husband driving out having deposited his wife several minutes ago. He favoured Susan with a bright smile and lowering her window she addressed a young policeman standing just within the gates.

'Young man,' she said sharply. 'I don't want to waste any time, so can you direct me to a good parking place?'

The young man smiled and pointed to a row of cars halfway across the yard. 'It's a full court this morning, ma'am,' he said. 'You'll no doubt find a space there.'

'There's too much traffic in this town,' Miss Lester admonished him, 'and some people don't care how they park.'

'No, ma'am,' he said feelingly. 'Some of 'em don't park, they abandon 'em.'

Satisfied that they'd struck the right note, she hurried to park where he'd indicated while the Magistrate sitting fuming behind her had to drive to the far corner of the yard.

She hurried into the court and made for the Magistrates' room where those who had already arrived were drinking cups of tea and chatting. Nellie Smythe was well launched into her favourite topic – her daughter's house and garden, which she hadn't visited for at least a year – and waiting for the first lull in the conversation Susan said casually, 'I had a very nice surprise last night. My niece is home from Israel.'

A sudden silence descended on the crowded room. Miss Lester was talking about Nancy Templeton and she was something of a celebrity in the small town of Greymont. For a local girl to be one of Noel Templeton's team was noteworthy in itself – to be Noel Templeton's wife was fame indeed.

'Didn't you know she was coming home?' Mrs Smythe enquired sharply. 'Is she staying with you?'

'No, she's over at Applethwaite. She telephoned me this morning.'

'Is her husband with her?' another person enquired.

'No, she's on her own, living in his father's house. I'll be driving over there this afternoon as soon as I can get away from here.'

She was gratified to see that everybody in the room was giving her their full attention. Nellie Smythe's eyes were snapping with curiosity but just then the door opened and Lady Garveston entered and Miss Lester walked immediately across the room to join her.

'I've just been telling everyone that Nancy is home. She telephoned me this morning.'

Not a flicker of curiosity or amazement altered the smiling composure of Amelia Garveston's beautiful face. 'Oh, that is wonderful news. I wonder if she received my letter, I do hope so.'

Not to be outdone Mrs Smythe said quickly, 'I was speaking to my daughter on the telephone last night and she said she'd heard from you some little while back.'

Amelia smiled. 'Yes, I've written to them all, simply to put them in the picture and in the hope that they will all keep that weekend free.'

She moved away and at that moment Maisie arrived, her red hair tousled, her face flushed from hurrying, but as soon as she saw Miss Lester she almost ran across the room, a wide excited smile on her face.

'Oh Miss Lester, isn't it marvellous! I can't wait to see her.'

'You mean she's spoken to you too?' Miss Lester said, slightly put out.

'She phoned me. It's wonderful. I ran out into the fields to tell Tom, in all that mud and only wearin' my bedroom slippers, I was so excited. I've asked her to come to see me really soon but she's settling in first.'

Miss Lester smiled. Maisie Standing was a good genuine soul. When she said she was pleased she really meant it, while nobody ever really knew how Amelia felt. These days she was worse than ever: Nellie Smythe had hit the nail on the head when she said she sometimes looked like a sleepwalker.

It was early afternoon before Susan Lester was able to drive out to Applethwaite and she found Nancy in her garden tying up the hollyhocks. A large ginger cat was chasing a fly across the flowerbeds, and the vicar next door was clipping his hedge, smiling affably as she left her car to walk up the path.

Nancy came forward immediately and kissed her cheek. They had never been a demonstrative family but looking at her niece critically Susan remarked after a few minutes, 'That tan doesn't cover the fact that you're very tired. You've been doing too much, I suppose.'

'No, Aunt Susan, simply travelling. Yesterday morning I was in Israel, last night I was home.'

'And you're thinner.'

'Perhaps heat does that to you.'

'I've seen Lady Garveston. I told her you were home and she said she'd written to you all about some weekend do in September.'

'Yes, I read her letter on the plane.'

'You'll be going, of course?'

'I don't know. Noel might be home, the weekend is several weeks away and really, Aunt Susan, it's twenty years now since we all left Lorivals. We have very little in common now, surely you must see that?'

'I only see that it will be impolite to refuse, and why should you? Amelia was your very dear friend once. I remember how much you admired her.'

'People change. I've changed and Amelia's changed, too. Why does she want to keep up this charade of four jolly girls nattering over the teacups about things that might have happened to us in the last ten years? The men aren't the least bit interested.'

'Well, I think it's a lovely idea. It's a time to revive old friendships.'

'True friendships shouldn't need reviving, though. I didn't have to revive my friendship with Maisie, it was there just waiting to be enjoyed as if we'd never been apart. I listen to her troubles and she listens to mine.'

'The aristocracy are different. They probably don't talk about their troubles. You can't think about Maisie Standing and Amelia Garveston in the same terms.'

'I know. We'll come away believing Amelia lives in the perfect world with her perfect husband and her perfect daughters, and we'll no doubt listen to Barbara's glowing account of her clever husband's achievements and her beautiful home. Maisie will clam up because she can't compete with either of them.'

'And what about *your* clever husband? You'll have plenty to talk about so why not indulge yourself a little?'

Nancy smiled and decided to change the subject. 'I don't suppose you've had lunch, Aunt Susan.'

'No, but don't worry if it isn't convenient.'

'It is very convenient. I've left a buffet meal out for us in the dining room. Come and have a look at the house, I think you'll like it.'

'Is that the vicar's cat running about your garden?'

'No, Aunt Susan, it's my cat. His name is Domino.'

'I never did like cats, haughty superior creatures they are.'

Domino had sauntered over to walk into the house with them, and was engaged in winding himself round Aunt Susan's feet.

'He likes you,' Nancy said with a little laugh. 'He's trying to ingratiate himself with you, he knows you don't like him.'

'Well he won't manage it.'

'Poor Domino,' Nancy said, picking him up and cradling him in her arms. 'I would have thought you and Domino had a lot in common. He doesn't suffer fools gladly either, he's cautious about whom he trusts and he's quite fastidious about his person.'

Aunt Susan merely sniffed before asking, 'When are you going to write to Amelia?'

'I'll answer her formal invitation which apparently is coming later. Noel said he would try to get home if there was a chance. If he does, we hope to take a holiday together.'

'You could take him to Garveston with you; the other husbands will be there.'

Nancy didn't respond. She was wishing Aunt Susan would stop going on about the invitation but she knew it was a forlorn hope. Like a dog with a bone she wouldn't let it drop until she was reassured that her niece at least would not let Amelia down.

It was mid-morning the next day before she climbed the fell to Maisie's farm. She sniffed the warm bracken-scented air appreciatively, and stood for a while looking down on the spreading town of Greymont and the long silver line of the sea. Haze hung over the Lakeland

402

hills, but up on the fells the years dropped away and she was a girl again, running with Maisie across the short springing turf.

Maisie was waiting for her in the doorway, a smile on her pretty face, coming forward immediately to fling her arms round her.

'Let me look at you,' she cried. 'My, but it's ages since I've seen you. How thin you are!'

'Not you too, Maisie. I've heard all that from Aunt Susan.'

'You'll stay for lunch, won't you? We've got to fatten you up and a farmer's wife's the one to do it. Tom's out in the fields and Peter's with him. Lucy's gone for her music lesson but Alice is at home.'

The kitchen looked clean and inviting. Huge fruit loaves were spread out under clean cotton teacloths but Nancy could smell the aroma of cinnamon and fruit mixture and Maisie said laughing, 'They're always hungry when they come in from the fields. I'll pack a box of cakes and jams when you go home, Nancy. Tom'll take you back. I don't suppose you've got a car yet.'

'No, I must think about that within the next few days.'

Maisie busied herself making coffee while Nancy sat at the kitchen table listening to her old friend going on about Peter's accomplishments and Lucy's good school reports. When the coffee was made and poured out Maisie indicated a folded letter on the table.

'I don't know what to do about that,' she said feelingly. 'We're only invited for the Sunday evening because Amelia knows how busy we are. Work on the farm doesn't stop for weekends at Garveston Hall. Will you be going?'

'It's too early to say.'

'Why does she want to keep it up? Why does she have to fool herself that it means anything any more?'

403

'Quite obviously it means something to Amelia.'

'How can it? I see her at the courtroom but she never asks any questions about Tom or the kids. I want to know about my friends, I want to know about your life in Israel and about Noel, it's normal to want to know about people but Amelia always keeps her distance. I could never ask questions about her sister, her mother or her daughters, I'd feel I was out of order.'

Nancy smiled. 'Are you really very interested in her sister or her mother?'

'No, but it would be polite, wouldn't it?'

'You think so, but Amelia might not see it that way.'

'All the same there's something not quite normal about that reserve of hers, and it's getting worse — people are noticing.'

'Noticing what?'

'That she's become so absent-minded. She quite often forgets she's due in court and has to be sent for. I always make a note of my court days to be sure I don't forget. And when people are talking to her she looks as if she's listening but she's not, her thoughts are miles away.'

'Perhaps she isn't well.'

'I don't know. Alice is up in her room, by the way. She's going off to spend a few days with a friend in Essex tomorrow. I'll tell her you're here.'

'Don't bother, Maisie. I'd much rather talk to you and no doubt she's busy.'

'Oh, but she'll want to meet you,' Maisie protested before jumping to her feet and hurrying out of the room.

She found Alice lying face downward on her bed looking at a magazine. The room was untidy and angrily Maisie snapped, 'I thought I told you to clean your bedroom! It looks worse than a pigsty. There's no time to read magazines, you have your packing to do.'

Alice didn't answer her but went on reading, and in a temper Maisie grasped the magazine and dragged it away from her, only to be rewarded by Alice's baleful look and the tossing of her red head.

'It's my holiday,' she stormed, 'and I don't even get to do what I want. I told you I'd tidy the room, I will too when I'm ready.'

'You'll do it now, young lady, and then you'll come downstairs and say hello to Mrs Templeton.'

'Has she come, then?'

'Mrs Templeton is my oldest friend, and I'll ask you to be polite and mind your manners. Those years at Lorivals have taught you nothin', not even how you're goin' to earn your living.'

'I suppose you're going to tell her that my examination results were bad, then I'll have to listen to you saying how marvellous Peter and Lucy are.'

'Hurry up and tidy this room, then I want you downstairs, and I want you in a better frame of mind than you are at the moment.'

As she ran downstairs she could hear Alice dragging furniture, throwing things in the wardrobe, but she entered the kitchen with a smile on her lips saying, 'Alice is tidying her room, she'll be down in a few minutes. More coffee, love?'

'Do you ever see Barbara?' Nancy asked.

'I've seen her in the town once or twice. They're still living in Cheltenham but in a bigger house, her mother says. I wonder if she'll go to the reunion.'

Just then the door opened and Alice came into the room. Nancy thought she was pretty with her pale fine skin and bright red hair, but there was a sulky look on her face and her eyes met Nancy's warily as her mother performed the introduction.

'You were only a child the last time I saw you,' Nancy said gently. 'You won't remember me.'

Alice didn't answer.

'How did you like Lorivals?' Nancy tried.

'It was all right. I had some nice friends there.'

405

'I'm sure you did.'

'I'm going to stay with one of them tomorrow.'

'How nice. Have you left Lorivals now?'

'Yes, I left in July.'

'And have you decided what to do with your life?'

'No, not yet. I'm still thinking about it.'

'She's just like I was,' Maisie said defensively. 'I was never any good with exams and Alice wasn't either. It's a pity there isn't a farmer waitin' round the corner for Alice just like there was for me.'

'I wouldn't want to marry a farmer even if there was one,' Alice retorted spitefully. 'I'm hoping for something better than a farmer.'

Nancy felt uncomfortable sitting between mother and daughter. Alice's face was mutinous and Maisie was glaring at her with heightened colour in her cheeks and anger in her eyes.

'It's a farmer who's paid your school fees and fed and clothed you, young Alice, and don't you ever forget it!' she snapped.

The girl tossed her head and after jumping to her feet went to stare through the kitchen window. Maisie bit her lip, momentarily ashamed of her anger, and Nancy looked at her sympathetically before changing the subject. 'I hope you'll come to see me during the next few days, Maisie. I've settled in at Applethwaite very well but I need to do something about one or two of the rooms. The vicar's trying to persuade me to have a dog.'

'What sort of a dog?'

'A golden retriever. Apparently, he knows somebody in the village who breeds them.'

'That'll be Mrs Williams. Lovely dogs they are, nice temperaments.'

'Yes, the vicar already has one. There's only one snag, I have a cat.'

'You needn't worry about that. After a few days they'll get along fine, particularly if the cat's installed first. We have both dogs and cats here at the farm and they rub along all right.'

They heard the door close as Alice went out into the yard. Meeting Maisie's eyes Nancy was aware of the strain in them.

'She's always been a problem,' Maisie said. 'She got two A-levels, but they weren't good grades and neither of them will do much for her future. She wanted to go abroad like her friend to work at one of the embassies but her friend was good at languages, and Alice isn't.'

'She's evidently little interest in farming.'

'No, none. She goes off to see these friends of hers and they're all well off so she comes back home dissatisfied, hating it here, finding fault with the way I do things, the way we talk, with just about everything.'

'What is going to happen, then?'

'She's pretty, she's got her heart set on a modelling course but that means more expense again and Alice has had so much already. Tom is totally against it.'

'Locally?'

'Heavens no. She's heard about one in London, some friend of Joanne's is on it and she's been told she can stay with the family if her father will allow her to go. She must be a very different girl outside the house from the one we see here.'

'And if she isn't allowed to go, what is left?'

'That's just it. Nothing.'

Maisie's face was reflective. Nancy had hit upon a point; Alice away in London doing what she wanted to do was preferable to Alice at home with her head in a magazine and deep resentment in her heart. She'd talk to Tom again. Perhaps he'd listen to her this time, especially if she got Nancy to back her up.

When he came back for lunch, Tom greeted her affectionately, and Nancy was delighted to see Peter looking so tall and grown-up. Lucy was a jolly little girl, but looking across the table at Alice's sulky face, and the way she pushed her food around her plate, Nancy felt sorry for her friend. You could never really be sure how your children were going to turn out. Maisie had been lucky with two of them but it must be very worrying to have one like Alice.

Nancy had decided to keep the news of her pregnancy quiet for the time being. It was early days yet, and having a first baby at thirty-eight wasn't quite the same as having it in one's teens or twenties.

That afternoon as she walked back down the fell, refusing Tom's offer of a lift, Alice caught up with her. This was a different smiling Alice, anxious to talk and ask questions.

'They didn't believe me at school when I said Nancy Graham was a friend of my mother's,' she confided.

'Why didn't they believe you?' Nancy asked curiously.

'They thought I was showing off.'

'And were you?'

'I suppose so. When I went there I thought they were all snobs, and some of them were.'

'How did you get on with the Garveston girls?'

'I used to like Pippa best but now I prefer her sister. Pippa's mad keen on horses but Berenice likes the things I like. She has a new car – all that crowd have cars. I don't, and I don't suppose I ever will.'

'What sort of things do you like to do, Alice?'

'You know, discos and parties. They didn't ask me to the last one because Mother always insists I'm home so early. I'll make up for it when I get to Essex, though.'

'Yes, I'm sure you will,' Nancy said dryly.

Alice bade her farewell at the bottom of the fell and Nancy walked on alone. She was wishing she liked Alice as much as she liked the other two, and hoped fervently that she'd have better luck with hers.

Martin Walton was meticulous about his mail. For eighteen years Barbara had sat across from him at the

408

breakfast table watching him carefully sort his mail into the important, the casual and the frivolous. Her own mail consisted of agendas for the meetings of her different committees, invitations to fashion shows and do-good efforts. Her mother seldom wrote unless it was to complain about something; normally she preferred to talk over the telephone.

'Hello, what have we here?' Martin said, and Barbara looked up.

He had extracted a long slender envelope bearing a crest she recognized immediately, and when their eyes met Martin said, 'I suppose this must be an official invitation.'

He opened the envelope, briefly scanned the single formal card and passed it across the table, then calmly went on opening the rest of his mail. Barbara read the invitation and put it down on her plate. For a few moments she stared across the table then she said briskly, 'Well, do we go?'

'Do you want to go?'

'Of course.'

'Only a few weeks ago you wanted to get out of it. What's changed your mind?'

'I've had a chance to think it over. I'm not bothered about seeing Maisie and her husband, or Amelia either for that matter, but Mark's always good company and then there's Nancy. It might be very interesting to meet Nancy Templeton if it's only to find out if fame has changed her.'

'I suppose I could manage a weekend off. We could stop by in Manchester on our way back as there are one or two business associates I could do with meeting there.'

'I suppose she's still friendly with Maisie Standing. I was in half a mind to drive over to see her the last time I was home but I didn't want her to think I was hobnobbing on the strength of her marriage to Noel Templeton. I don't really have to cultivate anybody.'

Martin wasn't listening. He was accustomed to his wife's chatter about this and that over the breakfast table, and he had long since developed an immunity to it. He might not have been quite so complacent if he could have known the trend of Barbara's thoughts.

It was a long time since her affair with Mark had ended. By now there was probably someone else. She knew Mark too well – there had to be another woman to flatter his ego, pander to his passions. Amelia would never be enough for Mark.

This weekend could be interesting. She could put up with Maisie's talk about her chutneys and fruit-bottling, live with Tom's wish to inveigle Mark into long discussions on estate management or the breeding of beef cattle, then of course there would be Maisie and Amelia discussing their children, that was inevitable. All the same, if she kept her eyes and ears open, she might learn something about Mark's latest extra-marital activities.

She wondered how marriage would have changed Nancy. Nancy had been a dark horse, she'd never disclosed exactly what had happened with Lois Brampton, and there'd been a subtle something between her and Amelia. Barbara would be able to find out if that was still there.

Her mother said Nancy had changed very little. She had some unusual clothes, and a super tan; she was also hoping her husband might be home quite soon. If Noel Templeton was with Nancy at Garveston things could take a turn for the better; at least the weekend would be more interesting.

She watched Martin leave for Birmingham, offering him her cheek for his perfunctory kiss, then she went into the kitchen where her daily woman was busy seeing to the breakfast things.

'I shall be out most of the day, Gertrude,' she said amiably. 'There's lamb and salad in the fridge, so just help yourself to something for your lunch.'

The entire day stretched in front of her. She'd telephone Molly Rigby and tell her something had cropped up and she wouldn't be able to go to her coffee morning. There had been some quite lovely clothes in the window of the new dress shop in Cheltenham and it would be reasonably quiet this morning. She'd try those new Italian shoes in Nino's and she'd book a hair and facial appointment for the day before they drove north. She supposed they'd have to call to see her mother if only for an hour or so, as Mrs Smythe would be very interested in their weekend at Garveston Hall.

She settled down to answer Amelia's invitation. She could imagine Mark opening the envelope, wishing she could be there to see the expression on his face, one that might tell her if he was looking forward to seeing her again.

Life with Martin was comfortable. They were at ease with each other, liking the same things, even sailing whenever he got the time to visit his parents in Cumbria. Martin enjoyed the pressures of his business life, his trips abroad, his conferences and executive meetings. She had learned to accept the boredom of being left alone in hotel lounges and strange cities while he attended to his duties, and she felt sure he had long ago forgotten Sandra Stubbs' existence even if she had not. They both had their golf, she had her horse riding, her committees and her coffee mornings. Life was very full, even when there were times when she asked herself if it was full enough. Mark had been such fun.

CHAPTER 40

Mark galloped his horse across the parkland in the early morning breathing a heartfelt thanks that the weekend promised to be fine. The hills of Cumbria were shrouded in mist which was a good sign, and the early sun felt warm. Entertaining guests when the rain lashed against the windows and the trees tossed in the park was the very devil. They got fed up reading the papers, some of them played bridge, some of them didn't, sometimes they argued, and he'd known certain of his guests not speak to each other for weeks after they'd left Garveston Hall. It wasn't a pattern likely to affect the guests who were arriving today, however: they went for years without speaking!

The longer he lived with Amelia the less he understood her. He couldn't fathom what prompted her to insist on meeting her old schoolfriends every ten years when she had the opportunity to be with them as often as she pleased. Nancy Templeton was back in the area, Maisie lived on the farm just across the fell and Barbara could visit whenever she came north to see her parents.

Amelia treated this weekend like a ritual. She'd been the one to propose it all those years ago so she must be the one to bring it to life. It had nothing to do with warmth or caring, it merely emphasized her remoteness and Amelia could be so bloody remote; these days she was getting worse. She was a lot like her mother – he'd always thought her mother hard going – but Amelia could be warm with her children, he had no complaints on that score. The girls adored her, or at least Pippa did. Berenice was going to be a lot like her father; nobody would ever know what she was really thinking.

Why had Amelia wanted to pack them both off to Switzerland? Lorivals had cost the earth and he didn't see that finishing school would add any more lustre. All Pippa's hopes and dreams were centred around horses and Berenice would most likely run through a string of would-be husbands until she sorted out the one she wanted. Amelia had never been like that — she'd only ever wanted Garveston.

Nancy Templeton had been back in the area almost a month and he'd seen her with that aunt of hers at one or two functions in the town. She was as lovely as ever with that haunting elusive beauty he'd treasured so lightly. She'd greeted him charmingly but there'd been no fluttering of her pulse, no excitement in her blue eyes; as far as Nancy was concerned he was a dead duck and he knew it.

He'd be seeing Barbara again but Barbara was something else. Barbara had a different kind of beauty, a more obvious kind, and she and Martin had settled down. He doubted if Martin would ever stray again and a complacently bored Barbara might be tempted.

He was getting very tired of Deirdre Forsythe. She was too available, too pushy. She telephoned him at his office on the estate with all sorts of excuses to see him or ask his advice about something, and she was forever hinting that she and her husband would like to be invited to the Hall, to which end she was trying to cultivate Amelia. His wife had so far proved intractable, which made him feel she knew about Deirdre and himself.

He brought his horse to a halt on the rise of the hill where he could see the placid river meandering gently through the meadowlands beyond the park. Willows dipped their feathery branches into the water and at that moment the sun came out in all its full glory, lighting up the mellow stone house, illuminating the length of the terrace with its great stone urns filled with geraniums.

A fierce sense of pride filled him. *Mine*, he thought savagely – all mine – even though it was thanks to Amelia that the place was now a thing of beauty instead of the crumbling spectacle his father had bequeathed to him. She'd failed him in other ways, though. She'd not given him the son he'd wanted, the heir to Garveston. One day this house and everything else would go to his cousin, and after him to his sons. Much as he loved his daughters they would not inherit Garveston and Amelia had made it plain that she had no intention of having another child.

Who could blame him for his infidelities, when his wife remained so resolutely remote? Something had happened during that week she'd vanished from her mother's house but he'd never been able to find out what. Amelia refused to discuss it and her sister feigned ignorance. He only knew that Amelia hadn't been the same since she returned – and another thing worried him: his wife was tippling his brandy.

He'd referred to it over dinner one evening, lifting the bottle so that the light fell on it. Looking her straight in the eyes he'd announced, 'I'm going to have a talk to Harris. I want to know who is drinking my brandy.'

'Harris will think you are accusing him,' she'd said without batting an eyelid.

'I could well be doing that.'

'Harris is a good servant, he was with my family for years. I'd really prefer that you didn't speak to him, Mark.'

'So I just sit back and watch my brandy disappear, do I?'

'I know for a fact that Harris doesn't drink.'

'In that case he won't mind if I bring the subject up and ask him to find out who does.'

'I don't want you to mention it to him at all. Hide your brandy if it's so precious.'

414

'Why should I hide it in my own house!'

'Then let me speak to him. You allow your friends and our guests to help themselves freely, so perhaps you should keep an eye on it from now on.'

So he'd kept an eye on it and had been satisfied that nobody had touched it, but one afternoon when he knew Amelia was out he went into her sitting room and had found several bottles of brandy hidden in the cupboard, as well as an array of glasses. Amelia rarely entertained guests in her sitting room and invariably if she did they drank tea or coffee. He was coming to the conclusion that it was Amelia herself who had developed a taste for the hard stuff.

Mark's face was morose as he returned his horse to the stables and strolled back to the house. Amelia had finished breakfast and was sitting reading her mail. As always she looked delicately elegant in a pale grey skirt and sweater, and as he took his seat opposite her he reflected on the different patterns of their lifestyle. Her mail was more extensive than his and he knew that it consisted of letters from the many societies of which she was patron while his was mainly circulars on farm produce and correspondence to do with his interests in several racing stables.

'What time are our guests arriving?' he asked casually.

'In time for afternoon tea. I thought we'd have it on the terrace as the day is so nice.'

'Good idea.'

'The Standings are not coming until tomorrow evening. Maisie said Tom was busy on the farm and they have Lucy to consider although I did think the child might have stayed with one of her friends for the night.'

'I doubt if this sort of thing is popular with Tom or his wife.'

'Perhaps not, but I can't not invite them. They may not want to come but they'd be awfully offended if I didn't include them.'

'I expect you're right. So, there's afternoon tea and there's dinner, then do we show the usual family videos, play bridge or simply gossip?'

'I've accepted invitations to go into Kendal. This weekend coincides with a concert by the Hallé Orchestra in aid of one of my charities. I couldn't change anything so I simply said we'd all attend.'

'All!'

'Why, yes. The concert will be well worthwhile and I'd like to think my guests will enjoy good music. Oh, I know it's not your kind of a musical evening but just for once you can put up with it, surely?'

'So I take it there'll be five of us? We can go in one car.'

'I've invited Major Garfield to dinner and the concert afterwards. I thought if I did that he could escort Nancy as she will be the one without a partner.'

Mark grinned. 'I can assure you, Amelia, that Johnny Garfield will hate every moment of that concert. His taste leads to girlie shows and risqué revues. Poor chap, when he took on the job as our estate manager he never visualised a night of boredom.'

Amelia ignored this last remark. She recognized Mark's mood as being one of cynical detachment. He regarded the weekend as a bore, a meeting of old schoolfriends who no longer had anything in common, and it had largely been his attitude that had forced her to go on with it.

She recognized in her innermost heart that she was probably the one who had changed the most but she would have defied anybody to see it. Externally she was still the same serenely remote, gracious aristocrat she'd always been, but inside were bottled up worlds of resentment and frustration.

She despised herself for those midnight sessions in her sitting room when the house was quiet, sessions where she could sit quietly in her chair in front of the fire

416

drinking her brandy and watching the cinders turn into ashes. She was aware that Mark knew about her drinking, but he said nothing, so far apart were their worlds.

The house looked beautiful. Every vase was filled with flowers and on the grand piano stood a bowl containing orchids brought in that morning from the conservatory. None of her guests would have anything remotely to compare with Garveston.

She was brought out of her reverie by Mark asking, 'Have we anything planned for Sunday, or do we just sit and chatter and wait for Monday morning?'

'I've invited Major Garfield to join us again, and Colonel Stuart and his wife. The Desboroughs and the Fields are coming – can you think of anybody else?'

'I could have thought of a few people if you'd consulted me first.'

'I'm sorry, Mark, I must have forgotten that I hadn't mentioned it. I thought we'd have drinks and a buffet supper. Who would you like to ask?'

'How about the Forsythes? She's been angling for an invite for years and you rather like him don't you?'

'Oh yes, I like *him* well enough.'

Mark grinned. 'Well, she's a pretty little thing, pretty enough to set Mrs Walton back on her heels.'

'I doubt if anything or anybody could do that to Barbara; it's possible the boot could be on the other foot.'

'But interesting, don't you think?'

'Possibly.'

'Will you telephone them or shall I?'

'You, I think, Mark. Mrs Forsythe knows you far better than she knows me.'

He looked at her sharply but her expression was bland. He had not been sure if there was underlying sarcasm in her voice.

Barbara and Martin had sat through lunch with Barbara's parents and they were ready to leave. Mrs

417

Smythe thought she had never seen her daughter looking quite so elegant; her dress was new and evidently expensive, but then if Martin didn't mind who else was there to mind?

Barbara carried her thirty-eight years well. There wasn't a streak of grey in her dark hair, and as always it was expertly cut and styled. She remonstrated with her on the height of her navy- and wine-coloured shoes that exactly matched the soft leather handbag she carried, and she told herself happily that neither Maisie Standing nor Nancy Templeton could hold a candle to Barbara when it came to dress – and that went for Lady Garveston, too.

Barbara was well aware of the thoughts passing through her mother's mind. She'd always been a spoilt brat. Ever since she could remember her mother had poked and prodded her into being a cut above the rest, but she'd never loved her for it, not like she'd loved her father who was happier with the daughter who tramped over the links with him in a shabby old mac and headscarf.

'I wonder what Nancy'll be wearing,' her mother was saying for the umpteenth time. 'She had on a very exotic dinner gown at the Magistrates' dinner – it was obviously bought overseas. I hope you've got something nice for the evening, Barbara.'

'I suppose there's no sign of her husband coming home?' Barbara said.

'I shouldn't think so. I don't know why she ever bothered to get married, and I imagine her aunt's thinking on similar lines.'

Nancy stood in the hall of her aunt's house while Aunt Susan and Sarah appraised her. She was wearing a plain French navy skirt and cream silk blouse, its collar edged with the same navy as the skirt. It was simple but undeniably elegant, and her figure had as yet lost none of its youthful slenderness.

418

'Hmmm,' Aunt Susan said at length. 'You look very nice, dear. I'm not sure that a skirt and blouse are quite the thing, mind. Nellie Smythe said Barbara was wearing an afternoon dress.'

'You look right bonnie, love. Take no notice of what Mrs Smythe's girl's wearin',' Sarah said stoutly.

Nancy smiled. 'I have a jacket to this skirt, Aunt Susan. It's in the car, and I've packed a couple of evening frocks and an afternoon dress. I'm not sure just how we shall be occupying ourselves this weekend.'

'Did Maisie Standing say what she'd got?'

'A new dress for tomorrow evening. I haven't seen it, as she hadn't time to show it to me.'

'Oh well, I suppose you'll do. They'll all be asking questions about your husband and when he's likely to be home, so just tell them what you want them to know.'

'There's nothing I can tell them, Aunt Susan. I wish it was otherwise.'

'Well, you'd best get off then. You'll probably be the last to arrive and it's not right to keep them waiting tea for you.'

All the same Nancy didn't drive fast, and as she passed at last through the gates of Garveston Hall she reflected that the house looked as beautiful as ever. A white Mercedes was parked outside and she guessed this belonged to Martin – the last time it had been a long, hungry-looking Jaguar. She slung her jacket round her shoulders, picked up her case and after locking the car proceeded to walk towards the terrace. She had gone only a little way when she saw Mark raise his hand in greeting, then he was hurrying along the path to meet her and for a split second she was a teenager again, watching Mark run towards her across the sunlit park.

Martin rose to greet her and politely kissed her cheek, then Amelia was there holding her cheek against hers, and Barbara extended a slim brown hand adorned with long crimson nails and a cluster of expensive rings.

She was aware of Barbara's close scrutiny as she accepted sandwiches and scones, and after she had settled back in her chair she turned to say, 'You look well, Barbara. I often hear about you from Aunt Susan.'

'I'm sure you do. Mother bores everybody to death about us, it's the only thing she has to talk about. You've worn well, Nancy. I thought you'd be dried up like an old prune after all that sunshine but I always did envy you that fine English complexion.'

'We're ten years older than the last time we met, remember.'

'Don't I know it!'

Amelia was chatting to Martin about the gardens, suggesting that they walked a little way along the terrace to admire the display of geraniums. This gave Barbara the opportunity to hiss, 'Amelia's looking older – I suppose it's inevitable.'

'Well, of course.'

Martin was greeting Major Garfield, a boyish tubby man wearing an immaculate moustache and a broad smile. He introduced him to the two women and immediately the Major said, 'I've been looking forward to meeting you, Mrs Templeton. I've followed your husband's adventures for years, and yours too when you were overseas.'

Nancy smiled. 'Thank you, you're very kind.'

'I suppose you don't know when he'll be joining you at home?'

'I have no idea.'

'What rotten luck,' Mark said feelingly. 'And you a new bride, more or less.'

'I fear I've been a very brief new bride.'

'What's it like being married to a celebrity?' Barbara asked curiously.

'My life's no different from when I was plain Nancy Graham working on the *Gazette*, except that now I'm struggling to write a book and I have anxieties I never had before.'

Sitting on the terrace wall Mark faced the two women who had once meant something to him. Nancy, his first love, and Barbara, his illicit one. Nancy had changed the least. Barbara on the other hand seemed to him more exotic than ever. She had worn well, but it was a cultivated beauty that owed much of its perfection to beauty parlours and expensive clothes, but was none the less potent for all that.

He watched Martin stroll with Amelia along the terrace. Martin didn't alter, he never put on weight and still wore that prosperous air. Mark couldn't for the life of him see why the man didn't unbend a bit. Why did he always have to look as if he'd just emerged from a business meeting? The world wouldn't come to an end if he wore something a bit more casual!

Johnny Garfield was obviously much taken with Nancy. He hung on her words, at times his eyes were fairly popping out of his head, and Barbara looked none too pleased at being ignored.

'Care to take a look at the gardens, Barbara?' Mark called out tactfully, and in one easy movement she rose from her chair and walked towards him.

'Thank God you asked,' she said sharply. 'In another moment he'd have eaten her – I thought we'd be mopping up the bits.'

'Jealous?' he asked smiling.

'Of course not, he isn't my type.'

'Who is your type these days, Barbara?'

'I'm too busy getting on with my life to have discovered who is and who isn't my type. Like I said, I'm devoting my life to Martin.'

'I know what you said, but that was a couple of years ago, time to have changed your mind.'

'I haven't changed my mind, Mark.'

'And has Martin stayed on the straight and narrow?'

'I know everywhere he goes and who he goes with. When I can go with him, I do.'

'And isn't it all a little bit boring?'

'The older I get the less boring it becomes. I wanted everything when I was young – I was brought up to want everything. My mother spent hours telling me I was beautiful, that I deserved the best. I can see now where I got it from, she's expected it from my father all their married life.'

'I never thought to hear you talk about your wants in quite that way.'

'I know. And how about you, what have you been filling your life with since that morning out there on the fell?'

'I've been busy looking after the house and the farms, the horses and seeing that my wife and children were comfortable.'

'I don't know anything about your children, Mark, but Amelia would be comfortable whether you were here or not. If she wasn't she could persuade herself into thinking that she was.'

'You know Amelia pretty well, don't you?'

'I studied her for years. I thought it might be nice to be like her but now I'm not so sure.'

'Has Amelia told you what she's planned for the weekend?'

'She said something about a concert in Kendal. That should be a change, although Martin doesn't like the highbrow stuff. He's happier with musical comedy, something like *The Sound of Music* would have suited him better.'

'Me too. It's all arranged, however, so we'll just have to grin and bear it for one evening.'

'I'll like it so long as it's tuneful. I take it the Standings are coming tomorrow?'

'Yes, and we've invited a few other people for drinks and a buffet supper.'

'I'm glad Amelia wasn't depending on her old school-friends entirely for entertainment.'

Amelia took a seat next to Nancy on the terrace and said immediately, 'You knew of course that Dorinda had died?'

Nancy stared at her, momentarily at a loss. By mentioning Dorinda she'd brought their old antagonism into focus. Amelia had been disdainful of her affair with Desmond, now here she was talking about his dead daughter as if it was something Nancy ought to grieve over.

'Yes, I heard it from Maisie.'

'Poor Dorinda, she was such a sweet little thing. It was all so sad and dreadful for my sister. Celia still can't tear herself away from that house in Cornwall where they were all so happy.'

Anger rose into Nancy's throat. Who did Amelia think she was fooling? Desmond had never been happy in Cornwall – the house had been a shrine to his ailing daughter and her distraught mother. What did she expect Nancy to say?

She was glad of Major Garfield's interruption to ask what time they were expected at the concert in Kendal that evening.

'We're dining early,' Amelia said. 'Perhaps you'll drive Nancy and we can travel with Martin. There are parking spaces reserved for us at the rear of the hall, and seats kept for us inside.'

'I'm not much of a classical music wallah,' he protested.

'Neither is Mark but this is one of my favourite charities and it would be terrible if I didn't attend. You like music, don't you, Nancy? I remember how much you enjoyed the concerts in London.'

Nancy bit her lip. Amelia had only known about those concerts in London from Desmond – she'd learned nothing from her. What was the matter with Amelia! Why was she insisting on dragging the past into the present, particularly now when she knew Nancy was married to Noel? In the next breath Amelia said, 'Did you know Noel in London, Nancy?'

'Yes. Desmond introduced me to him. There's nothing Noel doesn't know about my past life.'

'How fortunate. I think husbands should be best friends, but alas, not all of us can be so frank about the things that happen to us.'

It was not like Amelia to be vindictive, but as Nancy stared at her face, suddenly pensive as she stared out across the park, she realized that Amelia in this instance was not being vindictive. She was merely voicing her innermost thoughts, and Nancy wondered what terrible secret she wished she could talk about if there was anyone there to listen.

'Will you excuse us, Major Garfield?' Amelia said, abruptly changing the subject. 'I've just remembered that I haven't shown Nancy her room and no doubt she'd like to freshen up before dinner.'

Nancy picked up her case and jacket and followed Amelia along the terrace and into the house. They did not speak again as they walked across the hall and up the shallow curving staircase. The house looked as charming as Nancy remembered and guessing her thoughts Amelia said, 'I love this house. It was worth every penny Daddy spent on it.'

Nancy didn't respond and Amelia went on, 'Mark wants me to do something with the bell-tower. He thinks it would make a suitable dovecote and I agree with him, but I'm so tired of workmen knocking masonry about, and these last few years have been so peaceful. Have you settled in Applethwaite, Nancy?'

'Yes, I love it. It's a very nice old manor house that would quite easily fit into a quarter of this one.'

'Will Noel be happy in it, though?'

424

'I'm sure he will, as it belonged to his father.'

'Will he be in it long enough to be sure?'

'I can only hope so.'

'You see a lot of Maisie Standing, don't you?'

'No, not a lot, but we were good friends before Lorivals and we've maintained that friendship.'

'It's nice to have friends like that.'

'We all have the same opportunities for friendship, but some of us make more of them, that's all.'

'I have little time to gossip over the teacups, what with my magisterial duties and goodness knows how many committees to think about. Perhaps I should make more time.'

Nancy didn't speak, but instead began to unpack her small case and, a little flustered, Amelia went to the window saying, 'The view is particularly nice from this window, I think, but then all the views across the park are lovely.'

Nancy joined her at the window. She noted that Amelia's face was faintly pink and felt pleased that her words had had the power to ruffle if only for a moment that impenetrable composure. She agreed that the view was lovely, and Amelia said, 'Dinner's at six-thirty to enable us to get to Kendal in good time for the concert. You don't mind if Major Garfield drives you, do you, Nancy?'

'No, of course not.'

'Take as long as you like.'

Nancy took a long leisurely bath then decided on the dress she would wear. It was one she had bought in a sudden burst of enthusiasm since arriving back in England – a simply cut wild silk dress in blue and mauve. With it she wore a single fire opal pendant and the long drop earrings she had bought in Cairo. Her reflection in the mirror was one that satisfied her, and with her toilet complete, she went to sit at the window with its view of the distant mountains and gently sloping gardens.

425

After a brief knock on the door Barbara's dark head appeared round it and seeing Nancy was alone she quietly closed the door and came into the room.

'You look very nice. Is that new?' was her opening remark.

'Fairly new.'

'I must say you haven't changed much, I can't get over it.'

'So you keep saying. I do think it's a good idea to go to this concert, I find I have less and less to talk about to people I see so seldom.'

'Oh I agree, and having extra visitors in tomorrow is a good idea too. I wonder who they are?'

'The Garvestons must know a great many people in the area.'

'I suppose so, but I wonder if they're her friends or his? Tell me about your husband, Nancy. Are you very much in love with him?'

'Very much.'

'For how long?'

'Too long, I'm afraid.'

'You're not the type to console yourself with anybody else, are you? If my husband left me alone for weeks let alone years I'd soon be looking around, but then we never were alike, were we?'

'No, we never were.'

'There we were the five of us all thrust together like peas in a pod and all of us so terribly different – that's what makes these reunions so farcical. Oh, I admit we did have a certain friendship, we visited each other's homes and met our respective parents, but I always knew that when school was over we'd go our separate ways.'

Nancy didn't speak, but her face was strangely pensive as she stared across the park and after a few moments Barbara said, 'You never did tell me what really happened with Lois, why she did that terrible

426

thing. My God, she must have been in a state to take her own life!'

'Yes, it was tragic.'

'I suppose it was some man or other?'

'Lois would never say. I saw less and less of her even though we were living in the same house. It was as much a shock to me as it was to everybody else.'

'She never seemed the type to do something so stupid.'

'I suppose none of us really know what life is going to do to us.'

'Do you ever hear from her father?'

'I had a very nice letter from David when I married. He said if he was ever in the north he'd look us up.'

'What do you think about Amelia?'

'I'm not sure what you mean.'

'She's changed. Oh, it's still there, that maddening superiority, but underneath she's edgy. When you look at her her eyes move away and she was never caustic with Mark before. Once or twice before you arrived she really let the acid show through.'

'Perhaps she's tired. She's been staying with her sister, I gather, and I expect they've been rehashing the death of Dorinda all over again.'

'Well, that was a blessing not a disaster.'

'We think so, perhaps they didn't.'

'What's her sister doing staying on in Cornwall when her husband's in London? Everything's not too rosy in that garden.'

'I like your dress, Barbara, did you buy it in Cheltenham?'

'Do you really like it? I bought it at a new shop that's recently opened. It was wildly expensive, so were the shoes, but I always think one has to keep one's end up here, even when Amelia never shines in that sense.'

'She always looks extremely elegant.'

'I suppose so, but all her clothes look the same, don't they? Beige and grey – colours she can wear when she's

427

a hundred. It will be interesting to see if she's changed her colour scheme along with her personality.'

Nancy stared back at her. She hadn't really noticed anything terribly unusual about Amelia, unless it was her insistence on talking about Desmond.

Barbara was looking in the long mirror, twisting and twirling so that the black beaded gown swirled above her ankles. She wore no jewelry around her neck and the deeply cut neckline showed off her golden tan to great advantage. She wore heavy gold bracelets around her wrist and long gold earrings in her ears, and she was frowning. 'Really, I don't look my best in black. I'm too dark and far too tanned. Black is your colour, Nancy, but I couldn't resist this gown. Martin would die if I told him how much it cost – he'd cut my dress allowance for sure.'

Nancy laughed. Barbara hadn't changed from the girl who had railed against school uniform throughout their time at Lorivals, longing for the day when she could wear high heels and designer clothes.

'I suppose it *is* a dressed-up affair?' she wondered aloud on their way down. 'Whenever I invite guests I always warn them of what is in store, and that way they know exactly what sort of clothes to pack.'

They were the last to arrive downstairs where Mark was dispensing sherry aided by Johnny Garfield. The men wore dinner jackets and Amelia to their surprise was wearing mauve. The dress was very plain and Nancy wasn't entirely sure that the colour did much for her pale complexion and dark cloudy hair, but she complimented their gowns and explained that she had chosen hers very soon after Dorinda died and worn it so seldom she thought she would bring it out tonight.

Nancy was conscious of Barbara's slight prod but merely smiled her understanding.

Mark and Barbara chatted about their experiences in Cheltenham over the race week, Martin, Johnny

Garfield and Nancy talked about the Middle East and the current situation there, while Amelia occasionally joined in their conversation although for the most part she sat in silence.

She had declined the sherry before dinner, and now sat with her one glass of wine, idly twisting the stem, and yet she appeared nervous, gulping her wine instead of sipping it, but refusing a second glass.

Across the table Nancy's eyes met Barbara's and she looked away quickly so that Amelia would not see the look that passed between them.

The party received special attention in the concert hall where they had been awarded prominent seats, and as they followed Amelia down the centre aisle they were all aware of the lull in the conversation followed by the speculation no doubt as to who Her Ladyship had included in her party.

The orchestra performed beautifully. Major Garfield after the first half hour slept, Martin fidgeted, Mark sat back obviously thinking of other things but the three ladies enjoyed the concert and applauded enthusiastically. They returned to the Hall for more drinks then Amelia said she was sorry to break up the party but she had to be up very early in the morning and there was a great deal to be seen to. 'Please don't think you have to follow suit. Stay up as long as you like,' she added with a gracious smile.

Martin was the next to leave, saying he'd had a busy week and was rather tired, then Nancy decided to retire also. Johnny Garfield made good his escape and then only Barbara and Mark were left, sitting in front of the drawing-room fire, their glasses full, pleasantly drowsy.

'Doesn't this remind you of the last time you were here?' Mark asked quietly.

'I suppose it does, except that it's not going to end the same way,' Barbara said.

'Not even if I said I wouldn't mind? You can still make my pulses race, Barbara. I couldn't take my eyes off you at dinner tonight – perhaps you noticed.'

'Are you telling me I've worn better than Nancy?'

He threw back his head and laughed. 'No. Her beauty surprised me. I remember Nancy as a nice jolly girl who was fun to be with, a frank open sort of girl not given to the usual bitchiness of most women. Tonight, perhaps for the first time, I saw that haunting beauty that Noel Templeton obviously saw.'

'Why aren't you chatting Nancy up then instead of me?' she asked petulantly.

'Because that ice-cool beauty is reserved for her husband.'

'So is mine.'

'Ah, but yours can be changed. Boredom can change you, banality can change you.'

He reached out and pulled her towards him and for a moment she allowed his arm to hold her, his cheek dangerously close to hers, then with a little laugh she struggled free and looking down on his cynical laughing face she said lightly, 'See you in the morning, Mark. Sleep well!'

Without a backward glance she left him, closing the door quietly behind her. He heard the sound of her light footsteps crossing the hall, then throughout the house there was silence.

For a long time he sat looking into the fire. His thoughts were entirely on the past, with Barbara who had matched his passion with her own, and Nancy who had loved him in the days before she discovered real love with its pain and uncertainty, and lastly on Amelia who had come to him fresh from the trauma of his brother's death, not because she loved him but because she loved Garveston.

There was a time when Amelia had been happy with Garveston but now neither the house nor the things in it could make her happy, and he sighed heavily for something that had been irretrievably lost across the years.

He rose to his feet and switched off the lamps, then after satisfying himself that the dying embers were safe he walked out of the room. One single lamp burned in the hall but as he glanced towards the corridor he saw that a light shone under Amelia's sitting-room door. For a moment he hesitated, then turned and walked towards it.

Slowly he opened the door. One lamp burned but firelight played across the walls. Amelia was sitting in a chair drawn up to the fire, wearing a quilted dressing gown, her hair falling loosely around her face, and as he opened the door her eyes met his and the rich red colour suddenly flooded her face. He went towards her and gently removed the empty glass from her hand. She didn't speak as he quietly laid it on the small table near her chair, then he took the bottle of brandy and replaced it in the open cupboard. She didn't move, and returning to her chair he said softly, 'Give me your hand, Amelia.'

Like a child she complied, and he held her close against him as they made their way to the door. He switched off the lamp and closed the door behind them, then they walked slowly across the hall. She was unsteady, and he hoped desperately that they could reach her room before one of their guests decided they needed something from the library.

Amelia would sleep it off. She invariably arrived at the breakfast table serene and unruffled although he recognised the signs well, the absent-minded playing with her letter opener, the fixed glazed expression, the disinclination to talk. Would the others notice it also, and what explanation would they put on it?

He breathed a sigh of relief when she was safely installed in her room. He lifted her up and carried her

431

over to her bed, then he laid her down and pulled the covers over her. By the time he left she was already asleep. He doubted if she would remember anything of the night's events, but she was getting careless.

He'd seen the servants glancing at her covertly, noticed the pain on Pippa's face and the sharp anger on the face of Berenice. He'd explained to them both that their mother wasn't well but Berenice was a sophisticated little minx. She hadn't believed him and he'd found her one day emptying a full bottle of his best brandy down the sink.

Amelia didn't drink his brandy any more; she smuggled in her own.

He now found himself praying that the weekend would pass without incident. There was one more night to be got through and then the guests would be leaving: it couldn't come soon enough.

CHAPTER 41

The day passed pleasantly enough. Martin and Mark played golf, while Barbara and Nancy walked along the river's banks as far as the weir just below the grounds of Lorivals.

As they sat looking down at the water within earshot of the girls singing in the chapel, Barbara said, 'You can almost see us can't you, Nancy – five very earnest young faces with stars in our eyes, listening to Clarkson going on and on about the clamour of the world and how we should walk calmly in our paths.'

'I know,' Nancy said softly, and she quoted, ' "Spare them from bitterness and from the sharp passions of unguarded moments. May they not forget that poverty and riches are of the spirit; though the world know them not may their thoughts and actions be such as shall keep them friendly with themselves." '

'She meant every word of it,' Barbara said reflectively. 'So – was it like that for you, Nancy?'

'Not entirely. None of us really knew what life would throw at us. I wonder which one of us has remained most faithful to Miss Clarkson's teachings?'

'Amelia, I should think,' Barbara answered without hesitation. When Nancy remained silent, staring thoughtfully into the water, she said, 'Don't you agree?'

'I'm not sure.'

'She's the one who is into charitable efforts. Amelia's a great do-gooder, she's a good wife and mother even if her marriage isn't all it's cracked up to be, she'd never stray and she's always been a very dutiful daughter. Oh yes, I'd say it's definitely Amelia.'

'Maisie's the contented one. She wanted Tom Standing for as long as I can remember and their marriage works. Maisie never hankered after the fleshpots, she never wanted to dig up her roots and move away, not like the rest of us.'

'Speak for yourself! I married Martin, didn't I, and *I* always wanted *him*.'

'Have you always been content with Martin, though? Hasn't there ever been a time when you've wanted more?'

'You're too perceptive, Nancy. I thought you were the cagey one – look at those years in London and Hong Kong. Life didn't stand still for you – and yet the last time we were together we learned absolutely nothing. I've often wondered why Amelia was so distant with you, particularly on that last morning.'

'Something happened to me in London that I want to forget. It is no longer important, perhaps it never was, but now I'm married to Noel and I love him very much. I've learned to take each day as it comes and not to ask for the moon. Nothing is important to me except Noel's safety. I so desperately want him to come home.'

They sat in silence, each busy with her own thoughts, and then they heard the organ from the chapel and Barbara smiled. 'There it goes, we always ended morning service with that hymn.' And across the meadowland came the old familiar strains of 'Jerusalem' and they began to sing along with the girlish voices in the chapel.

Maisie and Tom arrived shortly after six o'clock and Maisie immediately sought Nancy out, her face anxious. 'Do I look all right?' she blurted out. 'I wasn't sure about this frock but Tom says he likes it.'

Nancy smiled approvingly even though she was doubtful about the frock. Maisie had always had an unfortunate liking for red, which didn't really do her own vivid hair justice, and her ruddy complexion wasn't helped by it. The gown was pretty and it fitted her well

434

but the colour was definitely unsuitable and Nancy thought she could have chosen something more flattering. She was careful not to upset her however, and merely said, 'The dress is lovely – is it new?'

'I've only worn it once for the Magistrates' dinner. When do I ever get to wear clothes like this? It would have been a waste of money to buy something new.'

'Barbara is over there talking to Major Garfield. She's looking very exotic, isn't she?'

Maisie followed Nancy's gaze and after a few minutes said, 'I'd never dare wear a dress like that. Look at that neckline *and* those earrings!'

Nancy smiled. Barbara had chosen to wear red also but on her it glowed, throwing her shining hair into sharp relief, flattering her tan rather than diminishing it. The long red and gold earrings gave her a strangely foreign air but seeing their eyes on her she merely raised her glass in greeting and Maisie said tartly, 'I suppose she's just the same.'

'Yes, the same old Barbara.'

'You look nice, Nancy. I love silk jersey and that blue suits you.'

'I bought a kaftan in Egypt, in fact I nearly brought it to wear here but I thought it would look too foreign in an English house.'

'You should have worn it – just to show Barbara that she can't have it all her own way.'

At that moment Barbara left Major Garfield and sauntered towards them. Eyeing Maisie with a half-smile she said, 'You're looking well, better since you lost a bit of weight.'

'Yes, I've lost half a stone.'

'Purposely?'

'Well yes, I have been trying. I had to if I wanted to get into this dress again.'

'How do you think Martin and I look? Have we changed much?'

'Martin hasn't changed at all, and you always look so fashionable. I could never look like you do in a thousand years.'

Not displeased Barbara warmed to her. 'How are the children and your brothers and their wives?'

'Very well, thank you. Our Peter's at the university and doing fine.'

'I'm glad. Are all your brothers married?'

'Jimmy's still a bachelor. He's too fond of a good time.'

'Well, why not? There's plenty of time for the other.'

'Have you seen Amelia? She's usually down long before this. It's almost seven and Mark's beginning to look a bit anxious. They've invited a few people in.'

At that moment Amelia came into the room greeting Tom with a serene smile and offering Maisie her cheek to kiss.

As always her gown was simple, emphasizing her tall slender figure and moulding her body into lissom grace. It was a creation of beige silk taffeta, its only adornment the three strands of perfectly matched pearls she was wearing and the large pearl studs in her ears.

As she moved away Barbara whispered, 'I would never have worn pearls with beige but those are obviously real and on her they look so right. Do you remember how we used to question her choice of colour, then on the night she'd make us all feel like country bumpkins in our pretty-pretty frocks!'

Major Garfield was heading across the room towards Nancy and Barbara said, 'Noel should be here to look after his interests! I'd say he's fallen heavily for you, my dear.'

The other guests began to arrive and Mark said cheerfully, 'It's a good idea to mingle. I expect you'll know most of them, Nancy, you too, Barbara. John Desborough sat on the Council with your father and the Fields are pillars of the town. The Forsythes haven't

been here all that long but he sits on the Bench.
I expect they're all very anxious to meet you, Nancy.'

'Why me? I'm not important.'

'But you *are* Mrs Noel Templeton,' he remarked with
a little smile.

'Why did Amelia have to ask so many people?' Maisie
complained in a whisper. 'None of them are my sort.
I thought it was to be a reunion just for us.'

At that moment Mrs Desborough said, 'You're Mrs
Standing, aren't you? I am so glad to meet you. I
bought some of your preserves at the summer show and
they were simply delicious. I am hoping you can give
me one or two recipes.'

After that Nancy thought she could conveniently
leave Maisie to chat to Mrs Desborough and so dutifully she mingled, answering questions about her life in
Israel, her anxieties about her husband and her hopes
for their future. Then, as she moved away from Colonel
Stuart and his pretty young wife whose thoughts had
obviously been straying while Nancy and her husband
talked of things she evidently wasn't in the least interested in, the Forsythes arrived.

From across the room Barbara, jolted out of her
complacency, found herself looking very closely at Deirdre Forsythe. She was undeniably beautiful with that
long lustrous hair and eyes that flashed provocatively
in her pretty dimpled face; Mark was obviously very
taken with her. Were they lovers?

Deirdre stood looking up at Mark, flattering him with
her eyes, smiling at his words. She was tall, slender and
young – all of ten years younger than herself – and her
gown was as revealing as it was expensive. Amelia was
greeting Mr Forsythe, but offering only a perfunctory
welcome to his wife, then she was introducing Mr
Forsythe to her weekend guests. Barbara smiled up at
him – two could play at that game.

Martin very soon found his own level amongst the other businessmen and this gave his wife an opportunity to say to Nancy, 'What do you think of the woman standing with Mark?'

'She's pretty.'

'And obviously Mark knows her pretty well. Amelia wasn't too gracious which is totally unlike her. Either it's because Mark is having an affair with her or for some other reason we don't know about.'

'I think I can tell you. She's a very pushy lady and Amelia has never responded to that sort.'

'I suppose that would account for it.'

Maisie joined them and Barbara said sharply, 'Isn't that the woman your brother was friendly with some little while back?'

'Not any more they're not.' Maisie was quick to deny it.

'Perhaps she's better fish to fry.'

'I suppose you mean Sir Mark? I have heard rumours.'

Casually Barbara sauntered across the room and in her sweetest tone said, 'You haven't introduced us, Mark.'

Dutifully Mark performed the introductions and was more than amused by the sight of the two beautiful women facing each other like exotic cats, hackles up and ready to spit at the first false move.

Deirdre was unprepared for Barbara; Barbara was her sort of woman, with the advantage of at least ten years' experience, a beautiful sophisticated person who had no need to look up at Mark Garveston in evident admiration. She could meet him on his own level and was not looking for something more. Shrewdly, Deirdre came to the conclusion that Barbara Walton knew Mark Garveston very well indeed, as was made evident by the proprietary assurance of her hand resting on his arm and the casual way she spoke to him.

438

From across the room Nancy and Maisie watched the performance and Maisie said, 'I can't stand Deirdre Forsythe, but what's Barbara trying to prove?'

'That's she's the fairest one of all, perhaps. One never knows with Barbara.'

'It's almost eleven o'clock. Our babysitter will be wantin' to get off home.'

'Do you want to leave, then?'

'I'll check if Tom's ready. Shall I see you soon?'

'I'll telephone you, Maisie.'

Major Garfield handed Nancy a glass of champagne saying, 'They're certainly pushing the boat out this evening. They'll be eating all this up for weeks!'

'Have you known Mark long, Johnny?' Nancy asked.

'Gracious yes, we were at school together. Of course in those days Mark was very much the younger son. He thought he might go into the army like me but fate decreed otherwise – his brother was killed and he married Amelia.'

'How did you come to be his estate manager?'

'He knew I was looking for a job when I left the army, he had a word with Amelia and offered me the post. We're learning the business together, and I must say he's more interested in the house and the land than I thought he would be.'

'Why do you say that, I wonder?'

'Well, his father did nothing. Phillip had great plans for it but no money, and it's thanks to Amelia and her parents that Garveston's the show place it is.'

'Yes, I know. I suppose it's been hard for Mark to accept this at times.'

'Gracious yes, you can't imagine how hard. I greatly admire Amelia, she's charming and I don't think for a moment she's ever rammed her money down his throat, but it's been there all the same. No woman'll ever marry me for my money but I'll sure as hell never marry a woman for hers.'

Nancy laughed, and he went on in a conspiratorial tone, 'I see Mrs Walton's dragged him away from Mrs Forsythe. Deirdre's not exactly my favourite lady in these parts – she's set her cap at one or two notable men in the area – but I'd suspect Mark is item number one.'

'Her husband seems rather nice.'

'He is, a very nice chap. A bit blind where his wife's concerned, though. It's time he put her in her place.'

Amelia was standing at the door, looking round hesitantly before quietly slipping out of the room.

The conversation went on, more food was eaten and the wine flowed, Barbara monopolised Mark much to Deirdre's mortification and Maisie and Tom had long since disappeared. Nancy looked round the room for Amelia but realised she hadn't seen her for some considerable time. Surely she hadn't retired leaving Mark to entertain her guests? Thinking that perhaps she was feeling unwell Nancy decided to go in search of her.

Lights from the crystal chandeliers flooded the hall and the curving staircase. The night was balmy and several of the guests were out on the terrace, she could see them in the lights that streamed out from the house, but she could not see Amelia.

She ran lightly upstairs and knocked quietly on Amelia's door. When there was no response she opened it but the room was empty and in total darkness.

Thoughtfully she walked downstairs and then she remembered that Amelia's sitting room was just down the corridor; as she approached it she could see the light shining under the door. She knocked, but there was no response so quietly she opened the door. Amelia stood at the window looking out into the night, nor did she turn when the door opened and Nancy could see the glass in her hand and the half-empty bottle on the table near the fire.

Amelia looked up and their eyes met. In a dull monotonous tone she said, 'You've discovered my secret, Nancy. I drink. Oh, not because I like it, I hate the taste of it, it burns my throat and it makes my eyes water, but after a little while the glow it brings is wonderful. It helps me to forget things I'm ashamed to remember, and it makes it so much easier to face the future.'

Nancy stared at her sorrowfully. Never in a thousand years had she expected to hear such an admission from this usually composed and reserved woman. Pity filled her heart. Tomorrow Amelia would hate herself for this revelation. Gently she reached out and touched her friend's arm. 'Come and sit near the fire for a few moments, and please, put the brandy down.'

'You needn't worry, Nancy, I'm not drunk. Not yet at any rate.'

'You have guests – they will be missing you, surely?'

'I don't think so. Mark will cope very well without me.'

'It's getting late. Some people will be leaving soon – don't you think you should at least wish them goodnight?'

For a long moment Amelia stared at her, then she said softly, 'Thank you for teaching me my manners, Nancy. I'm not usually so inconsiderate.'

With her head held high she walked back to her guests while Nancy watched her progress, uncertain and afraid. She need not have worried, though, for Amelia was the complete mistress of her actions – a little smile here, another there, a slight air of condescension in her attitude towards Deirdre Forsythe who was talking too much, a little breathless at the honour done to her, and when Amelia moved away her eyes flickered immediately to the window where Mark stood with Barbara.

How much more the onlooker sees, Nancy thought reflectively. Mark and Barbara, Mark and Deirdre, was

441

that why Amelia was drinking? Yet Barbara was too far away for most of the time, and Deirdre was surely only a passing fancy in Mark's life. Something else had happened, something that had cracked forever that ice-cool veneer behind which Amelia had always sheltered.

The other guests made their departure and now only Nancy and the Waltons were left. Barbara had made her point and was content to say wearily, 'Well, I'm for bed. It's been a lovely evening, Amelia, it was an inspiration to invite such interesting people.'

Amelia smiled mechanically. 'They would be flattered to know you thought them interesting. I simply invited them because they are friends of ours, isn't that so, Mark?'

'Oh yes, dear, all of them.'

'You're not staying up for anything are you, Martin?' Barbara asked. 'Don't forget you have associates to meet tomorrow in Manchester.'

Wishing the rest of them goodnight, Barbara and Martin mounted the staircase together, and almost immediately Amelia said, 'Well, I'll say goodnight too. We'll meet at breakfast and tomorrow, Mark, I might just have a look at the bell-tower. It will make an admirable dovecote.'

Then Nancy and Mark were alone and smiling across the room at her he said, 'Talk to me for a while, Nancy. We haven't really chatted at all, have we, and I'd like to know something about you, and about Noel too of course.'

She accepted the glass of wine he handed her and went to sit on the settee while Mark sat opposite. For a while they remained in silence and it was Mark who spoke first.

'What will you do when Noel comes home? Will he be content to stay in these parts?'

'I don't know. I can't put chains around him – he's been a free spirit too long and he loves his job.'

'Will he want you with him if he goes away again?'

'I rather think I'm in the vicinity for some time to come.'

'When did you decide you were in love with him – in Israel?'

'Long before that. In Hong Kong, actually, but please don't ask me when he decided he was in love with me. I think he fought against it for a very long time.'

'And before Noel? Who was there between me and Noel?'

'Somebody I don't want to talk about.'

'It was that painful?'

'Yes.'

'But not so painful that you didn't get over him?'

'No. Even if Noel hadn't asked me to marry him, I'd be grateful to him for that. He made me forget the past completely; he erased every tragic dismal memory.'

'But surely it wasn't all tragic and dismal?'

'He erased the good parts, too, Mark. I couldn't believe how easily and quickly I was made to forget something I thought would colour my entire life.'

'Are you quite sure you didn't marry him out of gratitude?'

She laughed. 'I'm quite sure. If Noel had never asked me to marry him I'd have gone on loving him, it was that inevitable.'

'I doubt if I'm given to undying emotions. I'd have been no use to you, Nancy, in the long term.'

'My father saw that long before I did. But you've been happy enough with Amelia, surely? She's very beautiful and you have two lovely daughters.'

'Some of it's been good. She set the house up but it's given me an incentive to work on it. It hasn't been easy, though. I've never been the provider and there are times when that sort of situation makes a man feel less than a man, but I can't honestly say she's dangled her money in front of me. Amelia's like her father, and

443

he was an aristocrat of the very finest order. I can't say the same about her mother.'

'You don't get along with the Dowager Lady Urquart?'

'On the surface yes, but underneath she despises me, and I find her overbearing and objectionable. When she comes here she talks to Amelia about the house as though I had nothing to do with it and that I resent. After she's gone I take it out on Amelia although one can never really tell whether she minds or not.'

'Perhaps she does mind, Mark. Perhaps she's unhappy about something.'

He stared at her sharply. 'You think she's unhappy?'

'I don't know. I just thought she seemed more remote than usual.'

For several minutes he was silent, staring morosely into the fire. He longed to take this sane intelligent woman into his confidence but he was reluctant to talk about his wife's failings. He owed Amelia a lot – loyalty more than anything.

Watching him Nancy thought, he knows about Amelia's drinking problem but he's reluctant to discuss it. She could understand this and in view of his reticence there was nothing she could say. Putting her glass down on the table between them she said softly, 'Goodnight, Mark. See you at breakfast.'

He rose to his feet and walked with her to the door. The hall was in darkness and when he went to put on the lights she stole a swift look at the sitting-room door. No light showed, and relieved she smiled at Mark and made her way across the hall. He waited until Nancy had reached the top of the stairs and was in her room before he switched off the lights in the room behind him, then quietly made his way to the sitting room.

Dying embers burned in the grate and there was a faint smell of cigarette smoke and brandy. He knew that Amelia had started smoking the odd cigarette

444

where before she had detested them and objected to her guests smoking. She never smoked in public, but he knew if he opened her desk he would find a packet of cigarettes in it.

A half-filled bottle of brandy stood on the small wine table near her chair and he guessed that this was where she had disappeared to earlier in the evening. He felt sure that Nancy knew something. She'd been waiting for his confidence but loyalty had stopped him. Now he was wishing he'd continued the conversation.

He closed the door and made his way upstairs. For a brief moment he paused outside his wife's room but there was no sound from inside, then he went into his own bedroom.

The house was as quiet as a grave when an hour or so later Amelia opened her bedroom door and crept down the stairs.

Her sitting room felt cold and she shivered, drawing her robe tighter around her. She poured herself a large glass of brandy then went to sit at her desk. She could feel the brandy warming her as it went down, and pulling her diary towards her she started to record the day's events, meticulously, as she had done since she started to keep a diary as a child, while all around her silence reigned on that cool September night.

CHAPTER 42

Barbara and Nancy stared at each other across the breakfast table. Barbara was the first to speak.

'This is the strangest weekend. They know we're leaving early this morning, but Mark's out on the estate somewhere and goodness knows where Amelia is. Martin's already taken our luggage out to the car – he has meetings in Manchester soon after eleven.'

'I'm not in any hurry to leave as I haven't very far to go.'

'Maisie had the right idea. An evening for drinks and supper would have suited us all better.'

Nancy didn't speak.

After a few minutes Barbara said irritably, 'Perhaps I'll go up to Amelia's room and tell her we'll be leaving soon.'

She had reached the door when they heard the sound of footsteps along the terrace and then Mark was entering the room, all smiles and geniality.

'Gracious, have you almost finished breakfast?' he said brightly. 'I had to go down to the office – I didn't realize I'd been gone so long. Where is my wife?'

'I was just going up to her room to tell her we are ready to leave,' Barbara answered shortly. 'Martin's taken the luggage to the car. It looks as if she's overslept.'

'I doubt it, she's a very light sleeper. I'll take a look round for her. It isn't like Amelia to be forgetful or neglectful.'

Barbara came back to her place at the table and Mark went off, feeling faintly irritated. What was Amelia playing at? She was getting careless.

Amelia's bedroom was empty; the covers thrown back on the bed, her nightgown draped carelessly across a chair. In the bathroom her shower cap was still wet. He went to the windows to stare out across the parkland but there was no sign of her and he knew she hadn't taken a horse out that morning. Surely she hadn't taken to drinking before breakfast? Anxiously he ran down the stairs and made his way to her sitting room.

The room was empty. An open newspaper lay across her desk, its front page crumpled and torn. He went to smooth it out, staring down at it curiously. Some chap he didn't know, a noted archaeologist, had been murdered in his tent in some godforsaken spot in Central Asia. It was hardly the sort of thing Amelia would be interested in. He scanned the back of the page. Some elderly politician had died, possibly a friend of her father's, again hardly the stuff to make her forget that her guests were leaving that morning. Where the devil was she? It was evident Barbara was rattled. She herself would never have treated her guests in such a cavalier fashion. She prided herself on being the perfect hostess and he had to hand it to her, she invariably was.

Mark returned to the breakfast room puzzled and apologetic but Barbara was not prepared to go along with his apologies.

'Really, Mark, we do have to go,' she said acidly. 'I explained to Amelia when we arrived that Martin had a business appointment later this morning.'

'I'm sorry, Barbara, of course you must go. I'll explain things to her when she arrives.'

Martin came into the room, looking from one to the other, at Mark's concerned face and his wife's obvious chagrin.

'Anything wrong?' he asked cheerfully.

'We don't know where Amelia is,' Barbara said. 'I've told Mark we shall have to leave.'

'Well, we can hang on for a little while yet. I can always telephone if we're going to be late.'

At that moment Nancy liked him more than she'd ever liked him before. She'd been thinking all weekend that there was a new maturity about him – he was less pompous than before, more inclined to listen to other people. Barbara was the one who hadn't changed.

They sat down and started to chat about any topic that came into their heads and the marble clock on the mantelpiece struck ten. Martin checked his watch uncomfortably and Barbara got up and walked to the window.

'There's not a sign of her in the park or the gardens,' she complained. 'Has she taken one of the horses out?'

'No,' Mark said briefly.

It was all so totally unlike the Amelia they knew, always punctilious, never the one to cause raised eyebrows over one of her actions. Barbara came back to the table and fixed Nancy with an accusing look.

'Did you see Amelia after we all went to bed last night?'

'No, why do you ask?'

'Oh, I just wondered if you'd had words about something. I thought last time we were here you'd had words.'

'Ten years ago?' Nancy said wryly.

'Oh well, things do crop up again, don't they?'

'Amelia doesn't invite guests to "have words" with them, Barbara. She'll have a perfectly good explanation when she gets here,' Mark said firmly.

'If you don't mind I think I will make that telephone call to Manchester,' Martin said. 'I'll call off the meeting – it wasn't all that important anyway.'

Nobody spoke, and he was gone only a few minutes before returning and saying, 'Well, that's that done with. Now what do you say about taking a look round for your wife?'

448

'Why don't we have some more coffee,' Mark suggested. 'She'll be awfully upset if we all go out looking for her, she'll feel such a fool. I'll ring for some fresh coffee.'

The maid who answered the bell looked at them curiously, and Nancy felt sure their anxieties would be duly reported when she returned to the kitchen. Hot coffee appeared within minutes and Mark made a thing about pouring it out. Anything at all was a relief from the tedious apprehension of waiting for Amelia.

'Wouldn't the servants know if she was out and about this morning?' Barbara asked.

'The morning newspaper was open in her study,' Mark said evenly, 'so I know she's been up and about. I don't intend to convey our anxieties to the servants at this stage.'

Warning bells were already beginning to ring in Nancy's head. She'd first been aware of them in Israel, and she'd known that some of Noel's instinct for danger had triggered them off.

She could feel it now, the tightening in her throat, the trembling hands which she clenched together, hoping nobody had noticed. Something somewhere was very wrong. The Amelia she'd known would never have done this and fearfully she said, 'Don't you think we ought to take a look round the park? Maybe she's had an accident somewhere.'

Mark stared at her. 'There are gardeners in the gardens and in the parkland, Nancy. Amelia couldn't have had an accident without one or another of them knowing about it.'

'But if they were busy they might not have noticed. I do think we should look for her instead of sitting here doing nothing.'

'Well, I'm going upstairs to check if we've packed everything,' Barbara said sharply. 'I'll be here when you get back but please don't be long, Martin.'

They walked briskly across the parkland, then they hugged the river's banks as far as the weir. Nancy felt partially relieved when there was no sign of her and Mark said cheerfully, 'By the time we get back she'll be there wondering what all the fuss is about.'

Nancy hoped so but still the doubts persisted. She could almost hear Noel saying softly, 'It's too damned quiet, something's brewing somewhere.'

The house looked so peaceful and normal in the morning sunlight. They all looked back at the turrets and towers of Garveston and Nancy suddenly exclaimed, 'I remember now – Amelia said she was going to look at the bell-tower. I wonder if she's up there?'

'Well, she wouldn't stay there for long,' Mark demurred. 'The place is practically a ruin. It was only an idea we had about restoring it.'

'We could make sure,' she persisted. 'We've looked everywhere else.'

They climbed the hill and made their way back to the house, then just as they reached the shrubbery they saw Barbara running through the gardens waving her arms madly above her head.

For a moment they stared at each other, then they hurried towards her and one look at her ashen face told them something was grievously wrong. Her words tumbled over one another until Martin got hold of her arm saying, 'Slow down, Barbara. What is wrong?'

She made a great effort to pull herself together, then catching hold of Mark's arm she cried urgently, 'It's Amelia, Mark, she's had an accident. You must hurry!'

'An accident, but where?'

She pointed wildly in the direction of the bell-tower. 'Over there, by the bell-tower! One of the workmen found her on the ground. She must have fallen from the tower!'

They ran through the gardens followed by the staring eyes of the gardeners who immediately downed tools

450

and followed in their wake. As they rounded the house the tower lay before them and on the path was the still form of Amelia.

Incredulously Nancy's first thoughts were that she'd slipped on the loose gravel and then she looked up at the tower casting its menacing shadow over the group around Amelia. Her neck was twisted strangely, her head turned away from them, her dark cloudy hair spread out on the path.

Mark knelt beside her and gently turned her to face him. They all gasped. A dark bruise coloured that side of her face they hadn't been able to see. Her eyes were wide open, staring at them, but she was unable to see them. Amelia Garveston was dead.

Martin was the practical one.

'Leave her for the time being, Mark. The police will have to be called. I'll go back to the house and telephone.'

Mark stared stupidly down at his dead wife while Nancy and Barbara watched, their faces pale and filled with horror. It seemed incredible to both of them that Amelia, serene ethereal Amelia, should have met her death in such a fashion but Nancy's thoughts were already on those few moments when she'd watched Amelia pouring brandy into her glass.

Had she come down in the middle of the night to drink more of it, then in a half-drunken state made her way to the bell-tower and . . . but then with some relief she discounted that theory, remembering that Mark had said the morning newspaper lay open on her desk.

A gardener appeared with a clean sheet of plastic from the greenhouse, touching his cap respectfully and saying, 'I'd cover Her Ladyship up if I was you, Sir Mark. It isn't right to leave her like that with all of us just starin' at 'er.'

451

Mark took the sheet and laid it over her, then the gardener said, 'I'll stay 'ere, sir. There'll be things you 'ave to see to at the house.'

'That's all right, Merton, the police will be here presently,' Mark said. 'If the police want to question you I'll send for you.'

It seemed only minutes before they heard sirens along the drive and then the ambulance was there followed by two police cars. They came along the path, walking quickly, two ambulance men carrying a stretcher followed by four policemen, and after a few moments Amelia's body was lifted on to the stretcher and carried to the ambulance.

One of the policemen said, 'The Inspector's on his way, sir. I suggest we go into the house.'

Mark was staring after his wife's body and gently Nancy took his arm. 'There's nothing more we can do out here. We should go inside as the officer suggested.'

They sat in the drawing room in silence. Two of the policemen stood at the windows waiting for the Inspector, while the other two sat at the back of the room. Mark stared down at the carpet, then in a bemused voice he said, 'The girls will have to be told. How am I going to tell them their mother is dead?'

Nobody answered, then Martin came back into the room. He went to sit beside Barbara and whispered, 'We'll be here for some time. There's to be no talk of going, Barbara.'

A young housemaid came into the room carrying a tray which she put down near Nancy. It was obvious that she had been crying as tears stained her cheeks, and when Nancy attempted to thank her for the tea she burst into sobs.

Nancy dispensed the tea, but Mark shook his head dismally until she urged him to drink it.

'You should have something, Mark. It may be a long time before you can have anything else.'

The Inspector arrived, offering condolences, taking Mark's hand in a firm grip and saying, 'This is a nasty business, sir, so we'll try to get the formalities over quickly and leave you in peace. There'll have to be an inquest of course, but then you'll know that.'

Mark nodded, and then there followed the questions about the weekend: the reason for the guests' presence there, the long years of their association and why they had decided on a reunion this particular weekend. Nancy wondered why the man had to go back over the years to find reasons, but obviously he knew his job, though once Martin said sharply, 'Is all this necessary, Inspector? We were all here on Lady Garveston's invitation. My wife and Mrs Templeton were old school-friends.'

'I must ask you to bear with me, sir. Everything has to be gone into in a case of sudden death. Now I have to ask you this, Sir Mark. Were you and your wife on the best of terms?'

'Well, of course we were. I was expecting to find her here this morning to say goodbye to our guests.'

'Was Lady Garveston still in the bedroom when you left this morning?'

'I assumed she was. My wife and I occupy separate rooms.'

Not a flicker of emotion showed on the Inspector's face, then he said, 'Would there be any reason for Lady Garveston to go out to the bell-tower in the middle of the night?'

'We know she didn't go there in the middle of the night,' Mark said testily. 'The morning newspaper was open on her desk so obviously she was in her study early this morning. The tests will surely show the time of death.'

'But why the bell-tower, sir?'

'We'd talked about having it restored to make a dovecote – we both fancied the idea. She said she'd

453

take a look at it today then she'd get an estimate for the work involved. I never thought she'd clamber up there herself, alone.'

'No sir, of course not. Had you and Lady Garveston had words about the bell-tower?'

'My wife and I hadn't quarrelled about anything, Inspector.'

'I have to ask these questions, sir.'

'All right, get on with it then.'

'You say your guests were leaving this morning?'

'Yes.'

'I had a meeting arranged in Manchester,' Martin explained. 'Obviously I have cancelled it.'

'Obviously, sir.'

'You were also leaving this morning, Mrs Templeton?'

'Yes.'

'You also had a reason for leaving early?'

'I was leaving because the weekend was over. I only live in Applethwaite.'

'I know where you live, Mrs Templeton,' he said, smiling at her in a manner which told her he knew considerably more about her than her address.

Mark accompanied him to the bedrooms, then to the bell-tower, and looking up at the crumbling steps the Inspector said, 'It's hard to imagine why Her Ladyship should climb up to the parapet alone. Perhaps we should go up there and take a look round.'

Cautiously they climbed the steps and the Inspector said at one stage, 'The rail is loose, Sir Mark. I'm surprised she went on when she saw the state of the steps and the loose handrail.'

Mark said nothing, and as they emerged into the light at the top of the tower and stood on the balcony with the bell behind them they were able to look down on the park and gardens below them. At one stage the Inspector touched one of the parapet stones and it fell

454

with a dismal clatter on to the path below. Turning he said thoughtfully, 'If she leaned against any of these she would see how unsafe they were.'

He started to walk around the tower until he came to a place where the stones were missing.

'I think it was from this spot that she fell, sir. She may have become dizzy for a moment, possibly put her hands on the stones to steady herself and when they gave way, pitched headlong on to the path below. Yes, I rather think that is what happened. We'll have a better idea after the postmortem, of course.'

By this time Mark was feeling nauseous. It was like a bad dream from which he prayed to wake up, but the Inspector was saying, 'We'll go down now, sir. There's nothing else to see up here. Take care on the steps.'

When they reached the path Mark said, stumbling over his words, 'I have to inform my daughters about their mother. This is going to be terrible for them.'

'At Lorivals aren't they, sir?'

'No, they're in Switzerland. They will want to come home immediately.'

'Perhaps Mrs Templeton will stay on until they get home, sir.'

'My wife's mother, or her sister, will come up immediately they know what has happened.'

'Oh well, that would be the best thing, sir,' he said heartily. 'Relatives are useful sometimes. There's no reason why your guests can't leave now; we know where we can get in touch with them. Mrs Walton's father is Councillor Smythe, I believe?'

'Yes.'

'And Mrs Templeton is Mrs Noel Templeton? That lady can be guaranteed to keep a cool head on her shoulders, she's used to trauma.'

Mark didn't speak. What did it matter that Barbara's father was Councillor Smythe or that Nancy was the

455

wife of a noted journalist! Amelia was dead. There'd be a postmortem; people would discover that his wife had been an alcoholic and there'd be more scandal surrounding her death than there had ever been during her entire life. There would be speculations about their marriage, his indiscretions, whether real or imaginary, would be made public and he'd get short shrift from her family. Filled with self-pity he returned to the house.

'The Inspector feels there's no reason for you to stay on,' he informed his guests. 'I'll be in touch with all of you during the next few days. Thank you for your help and support.'

Barbara and Martin were the first to leave and Nancy knew that their first call would be at Barbara's parents' house to inform them of what had happened. She stood on the steps with Mark watching their car drive through the gates then she turned and held out her hand.

Mark took it, and she was stunned by the lost little-boy expression on his face. Instinctively she cried, 'Are you sure you want to be alone just now, Mark? I can quite easily stay on for a while.'

'I'm all right, Nancy. It's been such a shock, that's all. The police will be here for some time, and then I have to let the girls know and Amelia's family. What do you think about it all?'

'I know that Amelia was drinking.'

He stared at her. 'How? How do you know?'

'I went to her sitting room last night. She told me she liked her brandy, she was drinking then but she wasn't drunk. She went back to her guests at my request.'

'It'll all come out now, I suppose.'

'Why did she start to drink? It wasn't like her.'

'Something triggered it off, I've never known what. She was all right until one week that she spent at her mother's. Something happened then but she wouldn't admit to anything. She'd never really got on with her mother although she strove to be like her in a great many ways. Celia was there, but it was something else. Her family close ranks, so I'll never get to know what it was.'

'Some man, perhaps?'

'Why do you say that? Has Amelia . . .' He was flabbergasted.

Nancy was quick to deny it. 'Amelia would never tell me, Mark. She would never tell anybody, but she wouldn't behave like either me or Barbara – or like any other woman I know – if another man entered her life. She'd fight it, she'd weigh her feelings for him against you and the girls, her family, her commitments, this house even, and she'd suffer, not the pangs of love, but the pangs of having failed, having been just like everybody else.'

'You knew her so well, Nancy. So you think it may have been a man?'

'Mark, I just don't know. Amelia will take that secret to the grave with her.'

For a long moment they stood looking into each other's eyes, then sadly she turned away and walked towards her car.

She hadn't wanted this weekend, she'd driven towards Garveston reluctantly and now she was driving home, devastated. It had been a weekend of golden sunshine and meetings between old friends, but it was a weekend she would never forget. As she drove the few miles between Garveston and Applethwaite she was remembering Amelia's dark head bent over her needlework, every stitch perfect, and then when she raised her head, the serene gentle smile, the soft, faintly sad voice. Amelia had moved through life like a graceful swan, cocooned in her gentility, cushioned by her pride against life's disasters. Amelia had never been able to acknowledge the frailties and desperation of lesser mortals.

How normal and peaceful the straggling sunlit street seemed, as it meandered up towards the stone tower of the old Saxon church. Dark shadows lay across the street, and in the pond the ducks swam lazily while old men snored or chatted under the ancient yew. What a far cry all this was from the trauma of sudden death.

As she reached the gates of her house the church clock struck three and the scene which met her weary eyes was one of serenity. Green lawns and flowerbeds, stone walls over which geraniums tumbled and Domino, sunning himself underneath the bird-table, lazy but hopeful.

By the time she'd parked her car he was waiting for her at the front door, unconcernedly washing his face, and the vicar called out, 'Now a dog would have been leaping all over you giving you a right royal welcome, Nancy. Cats don't want you to think they're interested.'

She picked Domino up and smiled. 'Undemonstrative people are quite often more genuine than the other kind,' she said gently.

He laughed. 'I'll persuade you to have that retriever yet. How did the weekend go?'

For a moment she hesitated. Tomorrow it would be in all the papers but right now she didn't want to talk about it. She merely said, 'I'll see you in the morning and tell you all about it then.'

He nodded, then as he was about to turn away he said, 'Oh look – you've got another visitor. Good job you didn't shut the gates.'

She turned to see an unfamiliar car entering the gate and then her heart lifted with sudden joy when she recognized Noel at the wheel. She dropped the cat who protested with a plaintive wail, then she was running across the lawn and Noel was climbing out of the car to take her in his arms.

CHAPTER 43

A week later Nancy and Noel stood in the crowded churchyard in Greymont at Amelia Garveston's funeral. With them were Barbara and Martin, Maisie and Tom, and the golden autumn sun shone down on the carpet of flowers that spread unbroken across the ancient gravestones as far as the stone walls surrounding the church.

It seemed that all Greymont had turned out to see Amelia laid to rest in the family vault and their eyes were drawn to Mark standing stern and motionless and singularly alone. His two daughters, pale and tearful, stood with their grandmother, an erect dark-clad figure, expressionless and tearless. Behind her were her two sons and their wives, her daughter Celia and her husband Desmond but it was the impassive figure of Lady Urquart that people were to remember most.

Mark had been prepared for the antagonism of his wife's family but strangely enough they had been supportive, warmer than he had ever known them. It was almost as if they knew something he didn't, but if that was the case he would never learn what it was. People like the Urquarts closed ranks. If there had been some guilty secret in his wife's life they would defend it as long as they lived.

He knew that around that crowded churchyard people were already speculating about his future. They'd been proud of Amelia, ever-respectful, always grateful for her presence among them; now the cynical ones were surmising how quickly he would replace her.

Across the gravestones Nancy's eyes met Desmond's but she felt nothing. Was this what it came to, then –

all that heart-searching misery forgotten as if it had never been? All she was aware of now was Noel's hand holding hers, his comforting presence beside her, reassuring, belonging.

Celia's eyes followed her husband's gaze but his thoughts were his own. She was beautiful, this woman he'd once loved, with a blonde frailty which obviously hid steely strengths not evident in her willowy slenderness and the haunting sadness of her face.

Then it was over and the funeral party were moving away. People were looking at the wreaths and Barbara was saying tearfully, 'I'll never forget this day, never. We must keep in touch, we have to. Once there were five of us, now there's just the three of us left.'

Maisie didn't speak and Nancy said gently, 'I'll always be very glad to see you, Barbara.'

Farewells were said and Barbara and Martin hurried to their car while Maisie murmured, 'I wonder if she really means it, or if it's just today that's making her talk like that.'

They shook hands with one another, then they parted. On their drive up to the farm Maisie said, 'What's Mark going to do without her?' and Tom answered dryly, 'I think you'll find Mark Garveston is a survivor, love. He'll bounce back.'

'Did you hear some of the talk around us, even at her funeral? I wouldn't put it past some people to say she did it deliberately. How can they say that about Amelia?'

'The inquest decided it was accidental death, so they should be very careful about spreading rumours.'

'But it's horrible for them even to think of suicide, especially about Amelia.'

'There'll soon be something else for them to gossip about.'

Maisie sat back morosely in her seat. Mark and Amelia hadn't exactly been her idea of a devoted

460

couple, but they'd got along, hadn't they? Now the girls would go back to Switzerland and Mark would be alone. Nancy Templeton was in her seventh heaven with Noel, but given a few weeks he'd be off again on his travels. Nancy had hinted that she might not be going with him, but she'd be desolate without him. Barbara was the one who'd led a charmed life. Plenty of money, no family to worry about – not like Alice – and Martin like the Rock of Gibraltar behind her. Immersed in her golf and her racing, her bridge parties and coffee mornings, Barbara had nothing to worry about, ever.

The Waltons were silent as they drove south to Cheltenham. Occasionally Barbara dabbed at her eyes and Martin kept his thoughts to himself. They had almost reached their destination when she said quietly, 'I meant it when I said we had to keep in touch, Martin. Amelia would have wanted that.'

'Yes, I'm sure she would,' he agreed kindly.

Barbara was unhappy today and her thoughts were sentimental about old friendships and the scenes of her childhood, but he knew that perhaps tomorrow or in a few days her thoughts could change and what was important today might be considered irrelevant then. Today her heart was plagued with anxieties, tomorrow was another day.

In the early evening Nancy and Noel walked on the fells above the village. Sadness and ecstasy had mingled in the days since that fateful morning at Garveston Hall and nobody better than Nancy knew that joy, like sorrow, could be transient.

They climbed up towards the old Pilgrims' Cross where they could look down on Garveston Hall and the chimneys and turrets of Lorivals. Nostalgia filled Nancy's heart as they stood together, oblivious to the wind and the gathering clouds.

461

Her thoughts were suddenly interrupted by the lash of rain against her face and they turned and half running, half stumbling, made their way laughingly to the shelter of the stone crags.

She had always known that the hills could be unpredictable, and she said softly, 'How very different it will be in Israel where no sudden storms erase the sunlight.'

'I know,' he answered her. 'The hot sun will be shining on the purple hills of Moab, the Mount of Olives will be green and lush with olive trees and on Mount Zion there will be pilgrims forever searching for their early faith. Neither of us really belongs there. This is our Eden, Nancy – the misted moors, the lonely hills and the unpredictable weather.'

At that moment the clouds broke and sunlight streamed down on to the waving moorland grass. It seemed to Nancy like the smile on the face of a stern countenance not given to too much smiling, and she was content to believe it was an omen that in the end all would be well.

Epilogue

Mark Garveston stood on the terrace watching the last of his wife's family drive through the gates. Earlier they had dined together, and he had surprised a look of cynical amusement on Desmond Atherton's face when Lady Urquart took Amelia's place at the head of the table. She appeared totally unconcerned, even when the rest of them were momentarily disconcerted.

He watched his two daughters tearfully pushing the food around their plates. The servants wore doleful expressions and he was glad when the meal was over and they could escape into the drawing room where Lady Urquart said fretfully, 'This place shrieks of Amelia. Surely she'd done quite enough without having to turn her attention to making a dovecote out of that old tower.'

Before he could think of a reply Celia said quickly, 'Actually, Mother, Amelia mentioned it to me in the spring. It would have been beautiful.'

'Maybe, but what made her go there at some unearthly hour and climb up to the balcony? Why didn't she wait until somebody could go with her?'

Nobody answered; it had all been gone into before, and after a few minutes Lady Urquart continued testily, 'I understood her so well when she was a child but she became secretive about a lot of things. The last time she came to stay with me she disappeared after a week saying she had things to do here and yet I'd made plans for her to spend another week with me.'

Across the room Mark's eyes met Celia's and she was the first to look away. Oh, quite definitely they knew something – they were too nice, too much on his side,

463

all except Lady Urquart who was as much in the dark as he was. At that moment Pippa ran out of the room sobbing wildly and Amelia's mother said, 'The girls are taking it very badly. It would do them good to return to Hereford with me for a few days. Staying here in this house will make matters worse.'

Berenice stared through the window, her face blotched with drying tears, and Mark said gently, 'Go after Pippa, dear. A walk across the park will do you both good.'

Then he turned to Lady Urquart and said, 'Another time perhaps. They are better here for the time being.'

Well, the family had gone now and only he and the girls were left. He'd not seen either of them since they'd disappeared in the direction of the stables after saying their farewells to their grandmother and the rest of them. They were immersed in their private grief and in his opinion were better left alone for the time being.

Slowly he walked back into the house. Amelia was everywhere. He could see her arranging her flowers, sitting with her needlepoint, amusing herself at the piano, soft brown hair caressing the curve of her cheek, wide pansy-brown eyes and a mouth that curved wistfully when she smiled. He could smell her perfume – light, flowery – hear her quick footsteps on the stairs and he cursed the resentment that had coloured their life together.

Lately he'd often been cross with her; she forgot things, her thoughts always seemed miles away, almost as if she lived in another world, among memories in which he had no part.

He felt suddenly tortured by all those long lonely nights she had spent in this house while he drank with his raggle-taggle friends. He'd paid her back for the rancour she aroused in him by his affairs with other women, particularly the one with Barbara Walton because Barbara had been Amelia's friend. Now for the very first time a feeling of shame arose in him. Could it all have been so very different if he'd accepted her largesse with gratitude instead of hostility?

In spite of the Coroner's verdict on her death people would be speculating, discussing their lifestyle, that they had rarely been seen together. Amelia's involvement with the community and local traditions had only bored him, and while no breath of scandal had ever touched her, he had flirted outrageously with every attractive woman in the vicinity. People were not to know that Amelia had been more amused by his antics than offended. Let them speculate. Amelia had had no reason to take her own life – she had just spent a delightful weekend entertaining old friends. She had a home she delighted in and children who adored her; it was nonsense to search for hidden reasons.

He went to her sitting room, staring round him at the room she had loved and upon which she had stamped her own individual personality. He'd poked fun at the water colours because they had been painted by a local artist she'd graciously allowed to set up his easel in the park. They were all views of the river, the old ruined abbey and the gardens, and now when he had finally taken the trouble to look at them closely he had to admit they were good. Why hadn't he examined them properly before so that he could have agreed with her for once? Why was everything too late?

A bowl of roses had been placed on a low table near her chair by one of the servants, but the top of her desk was tidy, her gold pen placed on top of her diary as if waiting for her to come into the room and start to write in it.

Curiously he picked the diary up, staring at the gold embossed letters on the cream leather surface, then idly he started to turn the pages. It never entered his head that he was intruding into his wife's private world. There was nothing written on the day of her death but the previous pages were filled with her engagements and her comments on their success or otherwise. He had always been amused at the size and weight of Amelia's five-year diary when he scribbled his own engagements in haphazard fashion in the one-year diary the racing stable sent him every December, but wherever she went her diary went with her and he sat at her desk flipping through the closely written pages until he came to several blank pages – fourteen of them.

He frowned. It was totally unlike Amelia to leave blank pages in her diary, and in the week before them she wrote enthusiastically about the scenes of her childhood, memories of her father and her meeting with various people, some of whom were unknown to him.

What had happened in those two weeks Amelia had felt unable to write about? Suddenly he was remembering her pale tortured face staring at him across this same room, telling him nothing, her eyes filled with a desperate remembered pain.

He sat staring in front of him. What had happened to Amelia on that visit to Hereford? Why the need for secrecy, what was her family hiding? He looked back at the diary, and one name sprang out at him – *Peter Charnley*. He didn't know any Peter Charnley but still the name persisted, then suddenly he remembered the newspaper lying on Amelia's desk on the morning he had come in here to look for her. He remembered that it was Peter Charnley who had been brutally murdered in some remote part of Central Asia and he knew from the photograph what he looked like: a man with a lean face and straight clear eyes, a remotely handsome face. He could imagine Amelia liking a man who looked like that, but could she have loved him?

He would never know. Amelia would never tell him, and the blank pages in her diary and that newspaper would tantalize him for the rest of his life.

466

He was suddenly startled by the shrilling of the telephone on the desk and lifting the receiver he was surprised to hear Deirdre Forsythe's voice saying gently, 'Mark, I've been thinking about you all day. Are you alone?'

'Yes, quite alone,' he answered calmly.

'You shouldn't be alone today of all days. John and I would like you to come over and spend the evening with us. Will you?'

'I'm sorry, Deirdre, but it isn't possible. For one thing I'd be very poor company and for another my daughters are here.'

'Oh, I see.'

'Thank you for your kind thought, though. You do understand?' he said.

'Yes, of course. But Mark, you will ring me when you're feeling a little more like company? Promise me, Mark.'

'Thank you again, Deirdre. Goodbye,' he answered her.

The door opened just as he replaced the receiver and Pippa came into the room. She saw the open diary in his hand and said quickly, 'Please, Daddy, do you really think you should be reading Mummy's diary? It isn't fair.'

'Your mother never had any secrets, love – at least, I don't think she did.'

'Daddy, it was an accident. The Coroner said so, so you're not to go on looking for reasons that don't exist.' She was looking at him earnestly with Amelia's eyes, reassuring him in case he was still doubtful about her mother's death.

'We've been to look at the tower, Daddy. It's old and crumbling and Mother should never have gone up there alone but she wouldn't be thinking about the danger, only about how it would look when it had been restored.'

He smiled. 'I'm sure you're right, love. Your mother was a great one for restoring things.' With a little sigh he closed the diary, holding it in his hands for a few minutes before replacing it in the drawer of her desk.

'Daddy, we've decided to go back to Switzerland the day after tomorrow. Neither of us can do anything here and we have to get on with our lives. You don't mind, do you?'

'No, I don't mind. It's better for you to go back.'

'And we don't want to come home for Christmas this year, as it will be so awful without Mummy. Why don't you come out to Switzerland? We can ski and we'll be together.'

'Now why didn't I think of that? I'll book in somewhere – you and Berenice can decide where it's going to be.'

Pippa was right. Life had to go on and he had Garveston. He owed it to Amelia to look after the place and time would resolve many things. One thing was sure, there would be no room for Deirdre Forsythe in his new life. He would not be looking for comfort from that quarter.

As the days passed people in the town stopped talking about Amelia. They gossiped instead about Nancy and Noel Templeton who were obviously very much in love and they speculated on how long it would be before he returned to the excitement of his life as a foreign correspondent.

Maisie said as much to Tom. 'I just can't see him staying on here indefinitely,' she said. 'He's goin' to be so bored living in that village when he's used to other things.'

'Has Nancy said if she's goin' back with him?' Tom asked curiously.

'Not a word, and whenever I've mentioned it she sort of changes the subject.'

'Oh well, I reckon we'll know soon enough.'

A few days later Maisie was more concerned with a letter she received from Alice who informed her that she had found a job with some hunting stables as a groom. They'd taken her on because she was a farmer's daughter and was used to horses.

Tom snorted in disbelief on reading that sentence. 'Used to horses, indeed!' he said shortly. 'She never went near them, and she'll be no great shakes as a groom.'

'Wait a minute, Tom, there's more,' Maisie said quickly. 'She's saving her salary to spend on that modelling course in London. Joanne's mother has no objection to her staying with them, and she says it's not going to cost you a penny. Oh Tom, what can we do about it? We can't allow her to stay there without contributing something to her keep and there's no certainty that she'll even make a model.'

'We're going to stop worrying about her for a start,' Tom said adamantly. 'We'll write to the Proctors and ask if there's any way we can help and no doubt they'll give us some information about these hunting stables. Stop worrying, love, the Proctors wouldn't have told her she could stay with them if there'd been anythin' dubious about this job. As for the modellin', that'll come later if it comes at all.'

Several days later Maisie discussed her problems with Nancy, who informed her that Noel was in London for a few days. Nancy agreed with Tom that for the time being they should give Alice free rein to do as she liked.

Reluctantly Maisie saw the sense in this, and meeting Nancy's amused eyes she said with a little laugh, 'I'm a right worrier, Nancy, but then I've always had to worry about Alice.'

'And Bob and Mary, and your two other brothers,' Nancy joked.

'I know. And now you're worryin' about Noel having to go back.'

Nancy nodded soberly. 'It's his life and I've accepted it.'

'Then I'm glad my husband's a country farmer and I know he'll be in for the next meal. Are you going back with him?'

'No, not this time.'

'Why ever not? I thought that was what you wanted, too?'

'I did once. I'm expecting a baby, Maisie, and even if I did want to go back Noel wouldn't hear of it.'

Maisie's face lit up with pure delight. 'Oh Nancy, I'm so pleased for you! I thought it'd never happen. I thought you were going to turn out to be one of those career women who never settle down to a home and children. What do you want most, a boy or a girl?'

'We don't mind. I told Aunt Susan this morning and she thinks it's quite ridiculous to be having a first baby at my age.'

'Oh well, she would, wouldn't she? I think it's wonderful and I'm so glad you're not going back. It'll be just like old times, won't it — you and me swopping stories together about all sorts of things.'

Nancy laughed. 'Just like old times,' she agreed. 'Old times without Barbara.'

'Gracious yes, I wonder what she'll have to say when she hears about your baby. You can bet your life her mother'll be on the telephone as soon as your Aunt Susan tells her.'

'You think Aunt Susan will be in a hurry to tell her, then?'

'Probably she's already done it.'

They were not to know but at that very moment Mrs Smythe was fuming inwardly that she was unable to speak to her daughter. 'She's never in,' she complained to her long-suffering husband. 'She's probably out playing golf or riding that horse of hers. *She* should have had a family. It would have found her more to do than spending all day out of her home.'

Barbara and Martin had just finished their evening meal when her mother telephoned again and after several minutes Barbara returned to the dining table wearing a thoughtful expression.

Martin made no comment. He rarely asked what her mother had to talk to her about, as Mrs Smythe's telephone calls were invariably to do with people he didn't know or had largely forgotten. Sometimes Barbara chatted on about her mother, but this evening for some reason she seemed strangely preoccupied, so much so that he was tempted to say, 'Your parents all right, then?'

'Oh yes.' Then after a brief silence she went on, 'She rang to tell me that Nancy Templeton was expecting her first baby. I'd have thought she wouldn't want to be bothered at her age.'

'Oh, I don't know,' Martin said.

'Well, would you want to be bothered? Can you imagine the disruption a baby would create in our lives?'

'I can imagine it. Have you missed not having children, Barbara?'

'Well, of course I haven't. We talked about it, and neither of us wanted them. What a strange question to ask now.'

'It's only that you seemed suddenly thoughtful, almost as if you minded, that you'd missed something. You haven't, then?'

'No, of course not. I like my life, I'm happy as we are. Children don't necessarily make a marriage, they can often destroy it.'

'As long as you're convinced, darling,' he said easily. 'What do you say we have a long weekend in Paris at the end of November? I have to go there on business. You could come with me and we could stay on for a few days.'

'That would be lovely, Martin. I'll ring Mother tomorrow and tell her when we shall be away. I just

471

know she'll be dying to visit if she hears any more news.'

He smiled. Barbara was blooming again. For weeks after Amelia's death she'd been sorrowful and would talk about nothing else; now at last the old Barbara was re-emerging. He hoped news of Nancy's baby wouldn't make her too thoughtful – after all, they were too old to start thinking about raising a family.

'Are you going to write to Nancy?' he asked her.

'Yes. I did say we'd keep in touch, didn't I? We're now back to the original three, so the next time we visit my parents I'll have to make an effort to see both Nancy and Maisie. I wouldn't like to be having a baby at her age with my husband thousands of miles away.'

'No, perhaps not.' Martin thought she was protesting too much.

'I wonder how Mark's coping without Amelia? No doubt he's being expertly comforted by that woman we met at Garveston.'

'Mrs Forsythe? I very much doubt it.'

She stared at him in some surprise. 'There was definitely something going on there, Martin. Of course she'll be in evidence.'

'I spoke to Mark recently on the telephone and he's off to Switzerland for Christmas. Then he's going out to Canada to talk about cattle. He and Tom Standing are interested in a new breed there.'

'Is he going alone?'

'Yes. This is a new Mark we're talking about, Barbara, a new circumspect Mark. There'll be no scandal surrounding him when the second Lady Garveston arrives on the scene.'

'The second Lady Garveston!'

'He'll marry again, Barbara. Some very suitable young woman with the right background. Mark will want an heir for Garveston. You can't surely think he was happy about the fact that one day everything

472

would go to his cousin simply because his children were girls. He'll not do anything in a hurry, but I do believe there's no future for Deirdre Forsythe in his life.'

She stared at him across the table. She'd always been so sure that she knew Martin too well, knew what he was thinking, how he would react; now more and more he was surprising her, intriguing her in an strangely exciting way. He stared into her eyes and smiled. Her answering smile was warmer than it had been for some considerable time. Maybe it wasn't too late to think about babies . . .

It was mid-October when Nancy stood at the gate watching Noel's car disappearing down the lane. She had always loved the autumn even when she recognized it was a season tinged with sadness and the glorious dying of the old year. The lane stretched before her like a golden ribbon and turning to go back to the house she saw that Domino was in his element, chasing after every errant leaf that crossed his path.

Noel had assured her that he was coming back soon, in time for the birth of the baby, and that he would be staying home from then on to write his memoirs. There was a queue of young men simply waiting to take his place to walk into danger and get shot at.

She believed him, but in the melting pot that was the Middle East anything could happen and Noel had been talking about several months. She knew too well what months could bring. He had put his hands on her shoulders and made her face him, his dark eyes searching hers. 'I've told you I'm coming home, darling,' he'd said earnestly, 'and I mean it. I shall be here in time for our baby and then I'm staying home for a very long time. Believe me.'

She believed him – she simply didn't trust fate. Later that afternoon she walked on the fell with Honey her golden retriever puppy, the last gift Noel had given her.

She watched the dog racing across the short harsh moorland grass in the late afternoon sunlight before she turned and made her way back to the house. Domino sat on the doorstep waiting for them and she looked with affection at the house which was home.

Her imagination strayed to future years when they would be a family living in this house and she offered up a silent prayer that her dreams might be realized. She ate her solitary meal on a tray in front of the fire and was about to put on the television when she heard the telephone ringing in the hall. She thought it was probably Aunt Susan with a string of instructions on how to take care of herself, but her heart lifted when she heard Noel's voice.

'I've arrived, darling,' he said. 'I'm ringing you from the airport. Take care of yourself, I'll see you soon.'

She returned to her chair near the fire. Domino stared into the flames with wide unblinking eyes while the retriever thumped his tail against the floor. It was a scene of quiet domesticity and in her heart she asked if it would be enough for Noel, if it could ever replace the heady moments of danger and excitement that had coloured his life. Only time would resolve her doubts, but his voice had been warm and tender, he had told her he loved her and was missing her. She could picture his face when he said it, his swift sweet smile that made a slave of her heart, and she told herself that Noel had never lied to her about anything. He would never lie to her about love, nor that one day soon he was coming home to stay.